NATURAL CAUSES

A Murder Mystery

By
Eugénie D. West

THE SAMOTHRACE PRESS

For S.I.R.

&

N.P.C.

About the Author

The author of 'Natural Causes,' Eugénie D. West, was a news reporter for a weekly newspaper for more than 15 years. All of the books in her 'Reporting is Murder!'© series, of which 'Natural Causes' is the seventh, are drawn from real cases the author encountered during her time on the news beat. However, the treatments given these cases in West's books are fictional, with details and outcomes that are not the same as the actual adjudications. West writes her novels under a *nom de plume* borrowed from a paternal great great grandmother.

'Natural Causes' features West's protagonist, sleuthing journalist Gracie Barufaldi, along with her on again off again boyfriend Jack and several other intriguing recurring characters. The ensemble players interact with each other and carry forward their own personal stories against the backdrop of puzzling murders and their eventual solutions. Like most of the books West writes, the featured murder isn't the only crime in the story, nor is the thread of Gracie and Jack's relationship the only sub plot. Like life, other misdemeanors, dramas and passions intervene, making for a richly woven tale that is satisfyingly blended and concluded.

West is inspired by people she has known and places she has been, but the characters in her books are fictional: amalgams of qualities, characteristics and traits from scores of acquaintances, strangers and other personalities. They are created to fit with and further the story. To read any more into them, or to attempt to identify real people in West's characters is foolhardy.

West holds a Ph.D. in English and enjoys history, languages, music, science and travel. Like Gracie, she lives in a rural part of the northeastern United States, is a bit of a techno-geek, and is an accomplished cook.

Visit West on her Amazon Author Page, and find her on Twitter, Facebook, Pinterest, Goodreads and on her blog, ThebooksofEugnieDWest.blogspot.com.

NATURAL CAUSES

Chapter One

Not quite awake yet, Gracie touched a button on the remote control and brought the large flat screen TV in her Oak Room to life. It was a few days after her return from her cousin Verena's in England, and while the jet lag had mostly gone, Gracie still thought she was groggier than usual in the mornings.

She settled on the sofa and sipped at her hot, strong morning coffee; her brain synapses started firing efficiently after a minute or so, and she focused on the morning 'news' program.

So much of what passed for news on these shows, she thought as she listened to a recounting of that morning's top trends on the internet, was a waste of time. If she wanted to know what the hot topics were on Google, Facebook, Yahoo and Twitter, for example, all she had to do was visit these sites on her laptop, iPad or smart phone, and find out: each posted statistics listing precisely that. Gracie didn't see how a cobbled together amalgam created by the morning news show was of any real value.

Pumpkin, Gracie's large orange and white tabby, strolled into the Oak Room and hopped delicately up on the dark brown leather sofa next to Gracie. She was light on her paws for such a big cat, but as her fur was on the long side, most of Pumpkin's bulk was 'floof.' She sat, and then began washing her face with concentration: Gracie had just fed Pumpkin her breakfast, consisting of a can of high quality chicken with gravy and vegetables. Clearly, it had met with the cat's approval. Her gooseberry green eyes were squeezed shut in pleasure as she methodically groomed herself.

Gracie gave Pumpkin a smile, and reached out to stroke the top of her head. "You're a good girl," she told the cat, who gave her a look as if to say, 'well, yes, what else is new?'

Gracie took a couple more sips of coffee and turned back to the television. Now they were talking about shopping discounts available through the television program's web site. She gave a 'tut' of disgust. Really: this was news? A glance at one of the several key-wound clocks that graced the room--a crystal regulator, a replica 16th century carriage clock, an art nouveau style clock and a large Grandfather clock in the corner--told Gracie that the local news would come on in under a minute. While these short news inserts were generally not too exciting, at least they contained genuine news items. And then, she decided, she would check out the BBC website for some actual, hard international news stories.

Gracie always listened to the local news, partly to be informed, but largely to see how other news outlets besides the newspaper she wrote for, the *Intelligencer*, were reporting on stories she was covering. This week, she had already filed her articles for her paper: the big news had come from the county Jail, where a major drug smuggling operation had been discovered inside its walls. Charges were being filed against three officers and a shift supervisor.

Gracie's friend Jean, who was a Corporal at the Jail, had been instrumental in uncovering the scheme, and had let Gracie in on her suspicions weeks before. Since the information she'd divulged had been off the record, Gracie of course hadn't written anything about the matter and had in fact left for her trip to England shortly after Jean's initial conversation with her.

However, the two friends had stayed in touch through texts and emails, and Jean had alerted Gracie when the Warden had called the four suspects into his office and fired them on the strength of the evidence that had been gathered against them.

Jean had recommended Gracie speak to the Assistant Warden to get comments and facts for her article. 'He's willing to talk to you on the record,' she had said. 'I told him I knew you and that you wanted to get the story, and get it right,' Jean had added. "And since the Warden is directly involved in the case, it's better if you talk to someone besides him," she explained.

Once she was back home, Gracie had called the Assistant Warden, and had spoken with him about the evidence that had been collected against the corrections officers, the same evidence that had meant that the county would file charges against them. Gracie's on line article had broken the story early Wednesday morning. Her article in the print edition wouldn't see the light of day until Friday, but that didn't matter much in the world of news: the *Intelligencer* had been the first with the story, and now others were picking it up. That was what mattered.

Now it was Thursday morning, and the local news station gave the drug bust a sixty second sound byte and a grainy clip of two of the four officers who were allegedly involved, walking out of the jail, holding their hands in front of their faces. They gave no information beyond what Gracie had given in her on line article.

Gracie smirked. She couldn't help but feel good about getting the story, and getting it first. Oh yes, and getting it right, of course: her paper's major competition, the Pittsfield *Gazetteer,* would probably have an article in its weekly edition today. And it would just as probably have several errors in it: the *Gazetteer* was not known for its correctness.

Gracie, on the other hand, had built up a reputation for accuracy and confidentiality; the *Intelligencer,* which covered all of Berkshire and the surrounding counties, was the paper everyone looked to for the facts. The *Gazetteer* focused mainly on Pittsfield, but the *Intelligencer* was nonetheless the paper most people read, even for news of the county seat.

A change in the newsreader's tone piqued Gracie's attention: 'This just in, State Senator Fred Jesperson has been taken to Pittsfield General Hospital,' said the attractive young woman anchoring the local news show. There was a pause. 'No further information is available at this time,' she said, her face expressing concern. Then her brow cleared: 'And now to the weather--Scott, I hear we can expect a lot of spring sunshine today!' she concluded in a cheery voice.

Gracie was frowning. Fred Jesperson was the husband of one of her friends in the Pittsfield Junior League, Maddie Jesperson. Maddie had been a member for years, and had been one of the first women to welcome Gracie when she'd joined 'Club,' as members called it, right after moving to the area from Boston. Gracie hardly knew Fred at all: she'd met him, of course, but it was his wife, Maddie, that Gracie knew well.

They'd formed a friendship initially over a discussion of the food served at one of the Club dinner-meetings, and Maddie had learned that in addition to being a 'foodie' and a gourmet cook, Gracie was also very interested in herbs. She grew several, not only culinary ones, but some of the more unusual herbs as well, such as wolfsbane and monkshood. Maddie also had an herb garden, and the two had shared cuttings, seeds and more as their friendship had developed over several years.

When Courtney Proulx had opened Planet Provisions, a small health food store, in Cheshire, both Gracie and Maddie had become loyal customers. There was no denying the vast array of items available at the large regional chain health food store on the south side of town, and both women also shopped there. But Courtney's shop focused on special orders and personal service. She carried a few things the bigger store did not, and also had a unique, if small, jewelry selection with unusual and lovely items that made great gifts. Both Maddie and Gracie had started popping in to Planet Provisions on a weekly basis.

Before long, Courtney had been sponsored for membership in Club by both Maddie and Gracie, and now the three were quite close.

Gracie reached for her iPhone and shot off a quick text to Courtney: 'Morning. Did you hear about Fred Jesperson?' She also texted Maddie, although she was certain the woman had other things to concern herself with besides answering texts: 'Maddie, just heard about Fred, hope all is okay. If I can help, just ask,' Gracie's text read. She knew Maddie would read the text eventually: with a married daughter, a son in college and two small grandchildren, Maddie had set her smart phone so it would flash until a received text had been read.

Courtney's reply came quickly: 'Just saw it on the news. What happened?' Courtney always thought Gracie was up on the latest information, and even called her 'Scoop' sometimes, as an earnest joke.

Gracie quickly texted back that she didn't know, but was planning on finding out and would keep Courtney apprised. Then she shut off the television, finished her coffee, and stood.

Pumpkin moved into the warm spot where Gracie had been sitting, and curled up for a nap.

"Well, no rest for the weary, as they say," Gracie murmured as she headed to her kitchen to wash her coffee cup and grab a quick breakfast. Then she'd dress and head into Pittsfield: maybe she'd swing by the Jespersons' house in the gracious residential section. If Maddie were home, perhaps Gracie could be of some assistance, or at least find out what was going on with Fred. If not, Gracie thought, well, she'd see what she could see at the Hospital, although it was likely that, now the story had been on television, the place would be swarming with reporters.

At any rate, Gracie wanted to have a few paragraphs to email in to the *Intelligencer* for the front page: her deadline for that was noon. If she hurried, she should be able to make it.

Chapter Two

A quick email to Gracie's editor, Dave Tiller, had brought an equally fast response and now, a scant hour after she'd seen the news clip on television, Gracie was in her Jeep headed for Pittsfield. Dave wanted her to get whatever information she could on the State Senator's hospitalization. Chiefly, he wanted her to find out what the issue was: Jesperson was in his early 60's but generally quite fit: an avid golfer, he kept a demanding schedule, and Gracie couldn't recall hearing of any health issues. His trip to the ER was a surprise.

Interest in Jesperson was natural in the Pittsfield area: not only was he a State Senator, Jesperson was a Pittsfield native, a descendant of early settlers emigrating from Scandinavia in the early 1800's. He had taught political science at the local community college at the start of his career. Then he'd been elected Mayor of Pittsfield, and had begun to form friendships and associations with area business leaders, developers, fellow politicians and other influential residents. Fred had won a second term, and done a lot for his home town in his twelve years as Mayor: a new downtown streetscape, grants to develop enterprise zones, community arts grants that helped revitalize a downtown playhouse and theatre, and lots of money for new construction and infrastructure improvements.

Then a group of Pittsfield lawyers, business leaders, and developers had put up huge amounts of cash, and had mounted a campaign to elect Fred to the State Senate.

The election, which had taken place during Gracie's first year in Western Massachusetts, had been a landslide for Jesperson, and he'd gone off to the State Capitol in Boson, a shining example of what the rural county of Berkshire could produce.

Naturally, the man's hospitalization, even if it were for something relatively minor, was news.

As Gracie approached the outskirts of the county seat, she detoured to the side street where Maddie and Fred lived. All was quiet at the gracious Georgian brick home. Maddie was probably at the hospital, Gracie reasoned, and drove on.

The hospital, just a couple of blocks from the town center of Pittsfield where the courthouse, the police station, the Jail, and most county offices were located, looked typically busy. But Gracie spied a news van in the main parking lot, and as she drove slowly around to the smaller lot generally used by employees, she noted the ancient more-rust-than-paint Chevy Suburban that belonged to the *Gazetteer's* editor, Gil Butcher: it was parked just behind the television news van.

Gracie tucked her Jeep in a corner of the smaller lot, and made her way to a back entrance little used by the public because it was marked 'Morgue.' The front entrance was, of course, where most people and where the television reporters and probably Butcher had entered. The official employees' entrance was a small unmarked door several yards to the right of the Morgue's double doors, and both entrances were along the rear wall of the hospital. Its ER was to one side, and its short stay clinic on the other side.

Gracie opened one of the Morgue's oversized doors, and walked in. She'd only gone a few steps when a figure stepped out of the Morgue itself, and greeted her cheerily.

"Good morning, Gracie," said the County Coroner, ME Tom Spears. Spears, who was the father of Gracie's friend Anne, had known Gracie for years and had developed a good working relationship with her. He'd even let her observe at a couple of routine autopsies, and had been impressed with the reporter's stamina as well as with her intelligent questions.

"Hi, Doc," Gracie said, just a little bit surprised.

"Trying to avoid all the hoopla upstairs?" Spears asked genially. He was in his usual Morgue attire of bile green scrubs, and he was smiling.

"Oh, you mean Senator Jesperson? Yes," Gracie admitted. She turned, and gestured to the wide doors through which she'd just come. "Well, it doesn't say, 'employees only,' does it?" she asked in self defense.

"No, it doesn't!" agreed the ME with a chuckle. "The word 'Morgue' generally keeps people out," he added, still smiling.

Gracie shrugged. "I just wanted to see what I could see without running into the TV crew or Mr. Butcher," she told the coroner honestly.

"No reason why you shouldn't," he agreed.

"Have you heard anything about the Senator's visit here?" Gracie asked obliquely.

Spears shook his head. "No: they generally forget I'm here until they need me," he admitted, but he was still smiling. "I just heard on the news that he'd been brought in. I imagine it's something minor, like kidney stones, you know, that sort of thing," he went on, "but if you find out, and have time, drop back on your way out and let me know, eh?" he asked.

Gracie nodded. "Sure."

"The elevator's there," Spears pointed, although he knew Gracie was aware of its location.

"And the stairs are here," Gracie put in with a grin. Three flights of stairs would bring her out to the main lobby. But two flights would bring her out to a short corridor that led to the rear of the ER: that was where she wanted to go.

Spears shot her an admiring grin of his own, shook his head, and went back inside the Morgue proper. Gracie opened the door to the stairwell, and tripped lightly up the stairs. Then she opened a door off the second floor landing and peeked out cautiously.

A jumble of noise assaulted Gracie's ears: electronic bleeps, controlled whooshing, the rattle of gurney wheels, the sound of rubber soles on linoleum and over all the faint sounds of conversation and the occasional whimper or moan.

Gracie shut the door silently behind her and walked slowly towards the main part of the ER, emerging into a brightly lit area in the center of which was the nurses' station. This was ringed by consultation rooms. White coated and scrub-garbed personnel of all descriptions walked briskly to and fro, occasionally stopping at the station to ask a question, make a note in a chart, or pick up a report.

In one room, a middle aged woman complaining of severe back pain was being helped into a wheel chair that would take her for an X-ray. In another, a young boy was trying to be brave while having his broken arm set in a cast. In a third, an elderly woman with shortness of breath was being evaluated.

Gracie walked on, anticipating that at any moment she would be asked her business in the ER, and then politely told to leave.

Just past a room in which a very pregnant woman was being readied for transport to Delivery, there was a closed door. Gracie walked up to it, and put one eye to the small vertical netted glass window set in the door: all she could see were a lot of doctors and nurses, an ER 'crash cart,' and blood: a lot of blood, everywhere it seemed, on the gloves and gowns of the medical staff bending over the gurney, and dripping onto the floor itself.

Amidst all that blood stood Gracie's friend Maddie, off to one side, leaning against a pale blue wall for support, and staring fixedly at the activity in the center of the small consult room.

Just as Gracie was debating whether she should go inside or not, a nurse appeared at her side.

"Excuse me," the nurse said, placing her hand on the door knob and effectively moving Gracie away from the window. "Who are you?" she asked bluntly.

"I'm her friend--Maddie Jesperson's friend," Gracie blurted.

"Oh." The nurse seemed disappointed, somehow. "Well, you can wait here," she pointed to a couple of grey plastic and aluminum chairs that flanked the doorway. "Family only inside," she said brusquely. Then she pulled a mask up over her face and entered the room quickly, shutting the door behind her.

In those brief seconds that the door was open, Gracie heard a single steady tone.

Chapter Three

"He's dead," Gracie told her editor a short while later. She'd retreated to the stairwell to make the short phone call to her paper.

"How do you know that?" Dave asked.

"I'm here," Gracie explained, and in a shaky voice went on to tell him what had transpired.

Rather than take one of the chairs the crusty nurse had indicated to her, Gracie had gone to the small waiting room on the other side of the central hub. From here, she had watched as a parade of people had exit the treatment room, and then finally Maddie had left, on the arm of a nursing assistant.

The assistant had been saying something about bringing Maddie to the Nurses' Lounge to wait for her daughter, and Gracie had presumed that Maddie had called her family. Part of Gracie had wanted to go to Maddie and stay with her friend until her family arrived. The other part of Gracie hadn't wanted to intrude: she and Maddie were friends, of course. But at a time like this, would her friendship be welcomed?

And yet another part of Gracie, the reporter part, had wanted to wait and see what would happen next.

The reporter had won out: Gracie had next seen the gurney with, she presumed, Fred Jesperson on it, being wheeled out of the treatment room and swiftly being taken to the elevator. It had been impossible to identify the person on the gurney, as it had been entirely covered in sheeting, and the head and torso encased in what looked like a plastic oxygen tent.

Clever, Gracie had thought: casual onlookers would assume it was a patient being taken to ICU perhaps, or surgery. But given Maddie's expression, the attitude of the nursing assistant with her, and most of all, that steady tone she'd heard from the treatment room, Gracie had deduced that Jesperson had died. True, she'd had no proof of this, and there had been no way to tell if the patient on that gurney had, in fact, been dead.

But once the elevator doors had closed on the gurney with the Senator on it, Gracie had surreptitiously crept back down the stairs to the sub-basement where the Morgue was located. Peeking out of the stairwell door, she'd seen the same gurney arrive, exit the elevator, and be greeted by Dr. Spears and his Diener, Heather Wilcox. They accepted the gurney into the Morgue, and then the transport staff departed on the elevator once again.

That had seemed pretty conclusive, if circumstantial, proof to Gracie: she'd seen Maddie in the treatment room after hearing that Fred had been brought to the hospital. She'd heard the steady tone of a 'flatlined' cardiac monitor when the nurse had opened the door. She'd seen a gurney leave the treatment room and be brought to the Morgue. And she'd seen Maddie, who had looked shattered, and who had apparently called her family to the hospital.

Once the transport people had left, Gracie had slipped into the Morgue.

'Doctor Spears?' she had called from just inside the doorway. Spears and Wilcox, gloved and gowned, had just been transferring the body to one of the autopsy tables. 'Looks like you'll know about Jesperson before I will,' Gracie had said quietly.

The coroner had turned and put out a staying hand. 'Don't come any farther, Gracie,' he'd admonished her. 'I can't tell you anything, yet, anyway.' The ME's voice had been muffled by the face mask he wore and his eyes had been stern behind his clear goggles.

'Can you confirm that that's Fred Jesperson?' Gracie had asked with a nod towards the prone figure on the table: it was still completely shrouded. 'I was upstairs in the ER, near his treatment room, and I saw--erm--what happened,' Gracie had said, truthfully but vaguely. She had seen what she'd seen, and could form logical conclusions. But for anything to be printed in the *Intelligencer*, it had to be fact, not inference.

Spears had sighed then, but still hadn't moved from the table, or motioned Gracie closer. 'Well, I'm sure his wife and family will be telling people soon, so it probably doesn't matter,' he'd said a moment later, thinking aloud. 'Yes, this is Senator Jesperson,' he'd confirmed then. 'But the autopsy--'

'I can't be here, I understand,' Gracie had put in quickly. 'But could you let me know the results, as soon as you have them?' Gracie had asked quickly.

Spears had nodded. 'Give me a call this evening,' he had told her gravely. 'I should know something by then.'

"Well, that's good enough for us to run a blurb on the front page tomorrow," came Dave Tiller's voice now, after Gracie had recounted what she'd observed. "And I'll get a bulletin out on line now. You don't have any idea of the cause?" he pursued.

"No. There was a lot of blood," Gracie added, thinking. Something was niggling at her brain, but she couldn't put her finger on what it was. "But I don't know whether they'd done some kind of emergency surgery or what," she finished uncertainly.

"How did you get in there, anyway?" Dave asked curiously. "They were keeping the media out, from what I heard," he told her.

Gracie grinned. "I just went in the back way," she said vaguely: no reason to give away all her secrets, even to her editor.

"Okay. And Gracie, there's something else we have to talk about," Dave said, sounding guarded.

"Oh? What?" Gracie asked, heading out of the stairwell and down the hall to the Morgue doors, to go back to her Jeep.

"The DA called here today, all pissed off about your article on the drug bust at the Jail."

Gracie started to snigger.

"He wanted to know who your source was," Dave said, his voice grim, "and how we knew about the charges, since they weren't filed until Wednesday morning and that's when the story went live on line."

"Hmmm...did you tell him?" Gracie asked. She'd protected her source's identity because he'd asked her to, but she had told Dave, who was her editor after all.

"Yes, I did. I told him you'd talked to the Assistant Warden, Henry Kavenaugh," Dave explained, "but I told Popovitch that Kavenaugh had spoken on the condition of anonymity, so I told him he had to keep it quiet," he finished.

"Good."

"Well--I don't know about that," Dave replied cryptically. "A few minutes later, Kavenaugh himself called me, and he's madder than hell about the article, too."

"He is? Why?" Gracie asked, surprised.

"He said he had talked to you off the record," Dave told her.

"Absolutely not," Gracie put in swiftly and firmly. She got into her Jeep. "He asked me to not use his name, and I didn't, and he said one detail about the way they discovered which officers were involved in the scheme was off the record, and I kept that detail out of the story," she added. "The rest was on record," she told him firmly.

"You're sure?"

"I'm sure."

"Well, that's not what he's saying," Dave responded tersely. "He said both he and Warden Jones had got a chewing out by the DA, and said Jones had threatened to fire him over this."

"Oh my god, that's horrible," Gracie exclaimed. "But Kavenaugh knew our discussion was for publication: I even told him what I was going to say in the article when we'd finished speaking, to be sure I had got everything right," she continued. "And I told him I wouldn't use his name, or mention the way the scheme had been uncovered: those had been his conditions."

"Could be he's saying that the conversation was off the record to save his own skin," Dave theorized. "But it still makes us look like we don't keep confidentiality," he noted.

"But that's crap," Gracie returned, angry. "No one will believe him. We're known for keeping confidences and getting things right: that's why I told him what I was going to write!" she said again. "Why else would I have said to him, 'okay here's what I'm going to write,' and then summarized the conversation?"

"And when you said that, what did Kavenaugh say?" Dave asked, still sounding upset.

"He said, 'that's fine,' and I thanked him for his time, and that was it," Gracie elaborated. "I didn't record the conversation, so I have no proof. It's my word against his." She paused.

Dave sighed. "I believe you, Gracie: you were just doing your job, and that *is* the job," he agreed. "Sometimes, people don't like what we write, or don't like that we break a story before they want us to. And then they'll try to say we got it wrong, or mis-spoke, or spoke out of turn."

Gracie, seething, said nothing. Wait until she told Jean about what Kavenaugh was saying, if her friend hadn't already heard. Suddenly, Gracie realized that

Kavenaugh might even try to get Jean in trouble, to deflect the heat from himself. Oh, god, she hoped that wouldn't happen!

"Well, anyway, just be aware, and be careful," Dave said solemnly.

"I always am," Gracie replied. "I'm glad I asked Dr. Spears to confirm the identity of the body, that it was Jesperson, I mean," she put in thoughtfully. "Maybe I'll double check with him, and be sure he knows we're going to print that," she suggested.

Dave sighed again. "Yes, maybe just be sure on that, Gracie: we don't want another case of someone saying they told you something in confidence that we end up publishing."

Spears looked quizzically at Gracie a few minutes later when she stuck her head in the Morgue again, and asked if it was okay for her to use him as a source when she wrote about the Senator's death.

"Of course, Gracie," he told her. "No offense to you, but I imagine the news will be out by tonight, anyway," he added mildly.

Gracie texted Dave that Spears had given his okay for them to use him as a source for the online blurb about Jesperson's demise. Then she got back in her Jeep and, still riled by Assistant Warden Kavenaugh's statements about her, drove back home.

Chapter Four

"Where'd your girlfriend get off publishing that story on the drug bust?" Berkshire County District Attorney Peter Paul Popovitch asked Jack angrily. The obese DA's florid face was almost puce colored as he glared at Jack from beneath beetling brows that were begging to be trimmed. "Her article went live the same time Phyllida brought the paperwork down to the Prothonotary's to be filed."

"I don't know," Jack answered truthfully. It was Thursday morning, and he'd been summoned a few moments before by the DA, who had bellowed for him from across their third floor suite at the County Courthouse in Pittsfield. "And, Peter, she's not my girlfriend," Jack added now, sounding quite grumpy himself.

"Whatever--" Popovitch waved a pudgy hand as though dismissing the need for accuracy. "I called that moron who runs the *Intelligencer*, and he said Barufaldi's source had been Kavenaugh, the Assistant Warden," Popovitch continued, referencing Gracie's editor, Dave Tiller.

"Oh. So what's the problem?" Jack asked mildly. He'd seen the online story on Wednesday, when it had been put up on the *Intelligencer*'s website as a 'breaking news bulletin.' Gracie hadn't mentioned anyone's name, just said 'county officials' were going to be filing charges after uncovering a drug smuggling operation at the Jail.

He had to admit, the timing had been close: Gracie's story had gone online within minutes of the charges having been filed. But he didn't see that as a problem: what she had said in the article had been true and correct, as far as he knew, and he'd admired her for uncovering the story, too.

"The problem is, Jack, that Kavenaugh says he talked to her, but that it was off the record."

Jack gave the DA a long look. "And you believe Kavenaugh?" he asked, sounding incredulous.

The DA snorted. "Of course I believe Kavenaugh, why shouldn't I? He's a sworn officer of the law, he's the Assistant Warden for cripes' sake! Why shouldn't I take his word over that jumped up note taker's?" Popovitch continued derisively. "You can't trust the press, Jack, I've always told you that," he went on, sanctimonious, "and this here's proof: that bitch wanted her big scoop so she ran her article with information she'd got in confidence. She shoulda waited until we called a press conference," he added with a self righteous pat to his chest.

Jack stared at him. Aha! So that was what was really going on: the DA had wanted to take all the credit for the drug bust, and bask in the resultant glory. But Gracie's story had precluded that. Jack was quite sure that Popovitch had reamed out Assistant Warden Kavenaugh, and that was probably why Kavenaugh had told the DA he'd thought the conversation had been off the record, to try to downplay his involvement. Coward.

"Gracie would never write something she'd been told off the record," Jack told the DA flatly. "I would stake my life on that." He paused. "And she's not into getting scoops for the sake of making a name for herself. She just wants to get the story and get it right." He took a breath. "And in this case, she probably wanted to get the story out there so people would know that the county is vigilant about keeping prisoners safe and the prison drug free."

"Gee, you're awfully quick to defend someone who's 'not your girlfriend'," sneered Popovitch.

Jack's jaw tightened but he said nothing.

"So you think Kavenaugh's lying," the DA said dubiously.

Jack nodded. "Either that, or he was mistaken about the conversation being off the record. Look, Peter: I haven't talked to Gracie. I don't know what was said."

The DA snorted again. "Well, why don't you do that little thing, Jack: why not call your girl--your 'friend'," he leered suggestively. "Find out why she ran with something that was confidential."

Jack didn't respond, but turned, and went back to his own office.

How could he do that, he wondered to himself as he shut his office door, and sat behind his desk. The radio on the shelf behind him was tuned to the usual country music station that Jack liked, but at that moment he found it irritating, and so switched it off.

He lit a cigarette and inhaled. Calling Gracie was not something he wanted to do in general at this particular time. And calling her to question her about a story she had written was really not something he'd relish doing, even at the best of times. He knew that Gracie kept confidential things confidential. He could also easily believe that Kavenaugh was lying about the conditions of his discussion with Gracie in order to save his own neck. Few people were as principled as Gracie was, and fewer still were as committed to accuracy.

Reluctantly, Jack punched Gracie's number on his Blackberry, wryly noting that she was still number one on his speed dial, even though they had broken up more than a year before.

"This is Gracie," she answered, sounding wary.

"Hi Gracie: Jack," he said. But he knew she had known who was calling: his name popped up on her iPhone's screen when the call connected.

"Hi."

Jack sighed. "I'm calling about your article on the drug bust at the Jail," he said mildly.

"Oh, not you too!" Gracie exploded, then went on to tell him about her conversation with her editor, and what Kavenaugh was saying.

Jack listened patiently. "So you're telling me the conversation was on record, and you even *told* Kavenaugh what you were going to write?" Jack asked, wanting to hear her confirm it: he was dedicated to accuracy, too.

"Yes. Absolutely! The only part of the conversation that was off the record was his identity, and the part about Jean and one of the inmates being the ones who had figured out what was going on, and them being willing to testify to that," Gracie explained again. "And when I said, 'here's what I'm going to write,' and told him, he said, 'okay that's fine.' I don't know how else I'm supposed to interpret 'okay that's fine' in that context other than his consent for me to publish what we'd talked about!" she continued angrily. "And I can't believe he'd lie about the conversation."

"Yeah, well, it seems that maybe he shouldn't have spoken to you until the charges were filed, and maybe not even then," Jack said cautiously. "It seems that Peter intended to hold a news conference about the whole thing and now--"

"Oh my god, that's it: it's Popovitch! I've stolen his thunder," Gracie exclaimed, her tone sour. "I get it now."

Jack continued calmly. "Apparently Peter is the one who got upset that your story had run almost concurrent to the charges being filed," Jack continued. As he spoke, he realized that his outline of the situation was exactly right. "He confronted Kavenaugh, who claimed that he'd thought he'd spoken to you off the record."

"But it wasn't!" Gracie insisted. "I didn't reveal anything I wasn't supposed to. I wrote what Kavenaugh told me, on the record, and if my story pissed off the DA because now he can't hold his big news conference and make himself out to be the great, grand uncoverer of corruption, well tough!" Gracie spluttered. "He shouldn't threaten Kavenaugh, and Kavenaugh should be honest about the fact that he spoke to me on the record: he shouldn't make it look like I did something wrong just to save his own skin!"

Jack could hear the anger and frustration in her voice, but knew he couldn't say anything to make her feel better. She was right, but she was caught, being made the scapegoat in the situation.

"Uhm--what did your editor say?" Jack asked after a few seconds of uncomfortable silence.

Gracie sighed. "He says he believes me, but he's not happy. He said it makes the paper look bad," she told Jack in a small voice. "I never wanted to do that. I've always tried to do my best, have my articles be a credit to the paper."

"And they are, Gracie," Jack put in. "And so are you."

She swallowed, and when she answered, her voice was strained. Jack wondered if she were upset enough about the situation to be in tears. He knew Gracie was pretty tough, but it was extremely unpleasant to have your ethics questioned, and he guessed she'd be quite hurt. He knew he would be.

"I don't feel that way," she said.

"You didn't make a mistake. You didn't make an error. You didn't do anything wrong: you did your job, you did everything correctly," Jack reassured her. "I'm certain people won't believe Kavenaugh, they'll realize he's just frightened because Popovitch got angry that you stole his thunder, as you put it, and took it out on him. People will believe you. And I'll tell Peter what you've told me."

"It won't make any difference," Gracie rejoined, despondent.

"Well, I'll tell him anyway," Jack reassured her.

They hung up, and Jack switched his radio back on, fiddling with the dial to find a station playing something he liked. His fingers stopped as a catchy intro came over the airwaves: it was a 60's station he rarely listened to, but something made him pause.

'Walk along the lake with someone new
Have yourself a summer fling or two
But remember I'm in love with you,
So save your heart for me,'

The lyrics were by Gary Lewis and the Playboys, from 1965, too long ago for Jack to remember, but the words grabbed him and he listened intently until the two minute ditty was over.

The song described exactly how he felt about Gracie: he loved her, and would always love her, no matter who else she—or he, for that matter—might date in the meantime.

The song didn't make him much happier, but he kept his radio tuned to that station for the rest of the day.

Gracie's next call was from Jean, in response to a text Gracie had sent earlier.

"I'm fine: I told Warden Jones exactly what had happened: that I and inmate Carruthers had noticed the suspect activity separately, and that we had confided in each other several weeks back. Then I explained that I'd told you about it back in April, but that the conversation had been off the record, and that you'd kept it that way."

"Of course!" Gracie put in, still defensive.

"Right. Then I told him that once I had brought our suspicions and evidence to him, and he'd contacted the DA who was preparing to file charges, I'd asked Kavenaugh if he would give you the official story, so you could write it up. I knew I couldn't be your source officially, since I am going to testify. And I didn't think the Warden should be the one to speak to you, either, since he was directly involved as well."

"And I called Kavenaugh, and he spoke to me, and Jean, he did tell me not to use his name, and I didn't. And he told me not to mention the fact that you and an inmate had been the ones to spot the scheme, and would testify in court if it came to that," she went on. "And I didn't."

"I know. I read your article. It was perfect."

"I even read back to him the notes I'd made," Gracie continued heatedly, "to be sure I'd got it right, and told him, 'this is what I'm going to write,' and he said, 'fine'," Gracie explained, feeling like if she had to repeat this one more time she'd scream.

"Well, I didn't know you'd gone to *those* lengths, Gracie," Jean admitted. "Kavenaugh was called into the Warden's office yesterday and now he's telling everyone that he only spoke to you off the record. I went to see the Warden yesterday afternoon after I'd heard what Kavenaugh was saying, and I told him that *you and I* had spoken off the record, but that Kavenaugh had agreed to talk to you *on* the record."

"Did he believe you? You're not in trouble, are you?" Gracie asked, concerned. "I didn't do anything wrong, Jean."

"Of course you didn't," Jean replied staunchly. "No, I'm not in trouble, and I think the Warden believed me: after all, he knows me, and knows I'm a straight shooter. And anyway, it doesn't make sense that you'd talk to me off the record, and then talk to Kavenaugh off the record, too: why? You wouldn't need to do that, you'd already talked to me. You needed to talk to Kavenaugh *on* the record, officially, so you could print the story," Jean summarized.

"Right." Gracie sounded relieved.

"But apparently the DA's the one who's really pissed about all of this. That's what Warden Jones said. Popovitch saw the story, and called your paper..."

"I know..."

"And he asked who your source had been, and I guess your editor told him?"

"Yes."

"And then the DA is the one who came down hard on Kavenaugh and on the Warden, " Jean continued. "Kavenaugh's saying he could be fired over this."

"But that's ridiculous!" Gracie returned.

"I know, and it probably won't come to that, but that's why Kavenaugh told the DA your chat with him had been off the record--to save his job."

Gracie sighed. "Well, I'm glad you're not in trouble," she told her friend.

Jean laughed. "Nah. They need me, for the case against the officers," she said brightly. "Look, Gracie, don't worry about it: you aren't to blame, Kavenaugh just doesn't want to be responsible for his actions because they pissed off the DA, so he's pinning it on you. It'll all blow over."

"I suppose it will," Gracie agreed reluctantly.

Chapter Five

Thursday evening, Gracie was still so upset about the phone calls from Dave, and Jack and Jean and the situation with her story on the Jail drug bust that she was almost surprised when Spears' name came up as her iPhone chimed to indicate an incoming call. She'd forgotten completely that she had been supposed to call him to find out about the preliminary results of Fred Jesperson's autopsy.

"Dr. Spears, I'm sorry," she said by way of greeting her caller. "I was supposed to call you."

"That's all right, Gracie," Spears replied mildly. "I can fax you the preliminary autopsy results, now, if you want," he suggested.

Gracie said she very much wanted the results.

"I'm sending them through now," Spears told her, and from her seat in the Oak Room, where she'd been staring into a small fire that was warming the spring evening's chill, Gracie could hear her fax machine whirr to life in the small alcove where she kept her desk. The Coroner's office, like many county offices, hadn't quite reached the level of using emails for correspondence, and still used faxes most of the time.

A few minutes later, Gracie was reading the autopsy report for the third time, and trying to make sense of it. Apparently, Senator Fred Jesperson had died from respiratory failure brought on by multiple organ dysfunction. According to the report, Maddie had told the ER doctors that her husband had been unwell for a couple of days, with vomiting and diarrhea. She had told the ER staff that she and Fred had presumed he'd caught a bad stomach virus, and that she'd tried to keep him hydrated with broth, water, and tea. However, it had been when Fred had had trouble breathing, and then gone into a convulsion during the early hours of Thursday morning that Maddie had called 911.

The autopsy stated that Senator Jesperson's liver, kidneys and lungs were almost completely necrotic, and noted that 'significant exsanguination' had hastened the organ failure. From what Gracie could gather, Fred's tissues had begun to deteriorate and he had, literally, started bleeding from his body cavities, first just a little bit, but then more and more.

"That explains all the blood in the treatment room," Gracie murmured to herself, recalling the scene at the hospital. "But why? What would cause this to happen?"

Frowning, Gracie dialed the ME's mobile number. It was only about 7 p.m.: not too late to call. And after all, he had told her to contact him if she had questions.

When the ME came on the line, Gracie apologized again for calling, but then asked him what could have caused the multiple organ dysfunction. "I notice you ruled the death accidental, so that's a relief, but I'm puzzled," she told him. "What would have made this happen?"

"Well, first, Gracie, the the tox screens should be back in a couple of days." He paused. "And to answer your questions, multiple organ failure, or dysfunctional syndrome as they now call it, or MODS for short, is usually caused by some kind of exposure to a toxin, or a severe traumatic injury," Spears told her.

"But Senator Jesperson didn't have a severe traumatic injury, did he?" Gracie asked. As the words came out of her mouth, something clicked in her brain, and she realized what had been nagging her about the Senator's demise. "Wait, Doc--multiple organ failure and all that blood--was it one of those weaponized inhaled toxins, like anthrax or ricin?" she asked, thinking that she'd seen reports of such things, but never had expected to encounter it in real life.

Spears whistled, low, on the other end of the phone connection. "Gracie, if you ever want to quit the news business, I'll hire you in a heartbeat!" he declared. "Exactly right--although we have to wait for the tox screens to tell us what the toxin was, precisely. Anthrax is caused by a bacterium, *Bacillus anthracis*. It can be transmitted to humans by exposure to infected animals, like sheep or cattle or goats, and of course, it can be weaponized, as you said, and inhaled."

"Oh my god!" Gracie interjected.

Spears continued: "Ricin, on the other hand, is not generally transmitted unintentionally. Like anthrax, it can be a powder that the victim inhales, or it can be ingested or injected. But it's made from the castor bean, and you can't just pick it up in a farmyard or a green house or something."

"Do you think the Senator was the victim of a terrorist attack?" Gracie squeaked in alarm.

Spears sighed. "I don't know. His wife didn't mention anything that would indicate that, like Fred getting any peculiar mail--"

"Oh, like opening an envelope and the powder goes poof up your nose?" Gracie put in.

"Yes. And she didn't say he'd been to any farms, although I suppose he could have been in the course of his duties, visiting agricultural sites and so on..."

"But wouldn't the farmers know their animals were infected with anthrax, if the latter scenario were true?" Gracie asked.

"You'd think so. But perhaps the disease hadn't really manifested itself in the animals yet. I've contacted the CDC and the Massachusetts Poison Control Center. I've also left a message at the Senator's office in Boston: they should be able to tell me if the Senator got any peculiar mail, and give me his itinerary for the past week or so, which would be the window for the infection to have been transmitted. That's in the case of anthrax."

"But you'd think if the Senator had got a letter with powder in it, he would have told someone, and it would have been on the news--I mean, don't they usually clear the building if an anthrax attack is suspected?"

"Yes, you're right about that," Spears agreed.

"And what if it were ricin?" Gracie breathed, solemn.

"You did notice Heather and I both had masks and goggles on, right?" Spears put in.

"Yes: I noticed," Gracie agreed, "but the significance of that didn't hit me until you called just now," she admitted. "I've had other--stuff--on my mind," she added grimly.

"The minute the transport called to say they were bringing the Senator's body down, we instituted universal precautions," Spears continued.

"But what about the people in the ER?" Gracie asked, concerned. "And what about Maddie? She'd been nursing Fred for a couple of days, while he'd been ill!" Gracie exclaimed.

"The ER staff were gloved and gowned, and put masks and goggles on when they noticed the condition of the Senator," Dr. Spears reminded her.

Come to think of it, Gracie recalled, she had noticed gloves and masks on the ER staff.

"Maddie had nursed the Senator, yes," continued Dr. Spears, "but I don't think she'd been close enough to have contracted whatever the agent was that had infected the Senator," Spears concluded.

Gracie was silent a moment.

"I suspect the Senator didn't tell his wife just how ill he was," Spears elaborated. "And since they thought it was a stomach virus, she probably washed her hands and kept her distance, even though she was tending to him, as anyone would who didn't want to become ill herself." He paused. "The sad thing is, Gracie, that neither anthrax nor ricin is communicable in the same way a stomach virus is: anthrax is much harder to contract and ricin nearly impossible. Still, we've put Maddie on a course of antibiotics, just in case she was exposed, even minimally."

"How horrible."

"It's all speculation at this point, Gracie. The symptoms could be either anthrax or ricin poisoning, or even something else similar to that. The implications differ depending on what the toxic agent was, and how it was administered or transmitted."

"The report says Maddie and Fred thought he had a stomach bug," Gracie repeated, sounding confused: this was proving very hard to comprehend, because it was hitting so close to home.

"Given the symptoms, the presumptive diagnosis of an intestinal virus of some kind isn't far off the mark. But the fact that the symptoms were so severe and didn't improve tells me that either Fred was hiding how ill he was from his wife, or that the illness progressed so rapidly, the level of his dehydration and infection wasn't recognized until it was too late," Spears said, regretful.

When Gracie was upset, she cooked, and Thursday evening between the confusing autopsy results and the debacle over the story on the drug bust, she was quite upset.

She had called Kavenaugh herself Thursday afternoon, but their chat hadn't given Gracie any satisfaction. Gracie had told Kavenaugh that she recalled their discussion on the drug situation as being on the record. She had told him she also recalled that he'd asked her to keep his name out of the story, and the manner in which the scheme had been uncovered out of the story, and that she'd done both those things. And, she had reminded him that she'd read the outline of her story back to him at the end of their conversation, to be sure she'd got everything right, and that he had said the story was 'fine.'

But Kavenaugh hadn't admitted that he was now changing the facts to suit his predicament and that he had, in fact, spoken with her on the record. He only told Gracie that 'it would all blow over,' and that he had a wife, two children, and a third on the way.

Gracie didn't know what his family status had to do with anything, unless it was Kavenaugh's way of excusing his behavior in the face of a possible reprimand or dismissal from his post. A part of her understood that, but the greater part of her still thought that Kavenaugh should be honest, and that, if he were honest, the DA would be shown for the ignorant, publicity seeking jackass he was. Popovitch, after all, was the one who had caused all this trouble, just because he had wanted to be the one to make the big reveal about the drug bust, and Gracie's article had prevented that.

So Thursday evening, after ruminating about the situation and then being perturbed by the autopsy report on Jesperson, Gracie retreated to her kitchen and baked several batches of apricot kiffle.

Baking had never been her strong point: she usually left anything fancier than quick breads to her childhood friend Joey's partner, Tyler, who was an amazing pastry chef. Tyler and Joey ran a trendy gourmet restaurant in Boston's Copley Square, called *Mange Tout;* Tyler was the accounting side of the partnership, and also responsible for the desserts and pastries served at the popular eatery.

But he'd recently given Gracie his 'foolproof' recipe for kiffle, the small oblong packages of sweet dough filled with preserves, and Thursday evening Gracie was just in the mood to lose herself in the challenge of making them.

The results were spectacular, mostly, Gracie thought, because Tyler's recipe was, indeed, 'foolproof.' And possibly because of beginner's luck.

Friday morning, Gracie was feeling a bit more cheerful, and then really pleased when Maddie returned her text of the previous day with a call, inviting her to stop by. After making sure her visit wouldn't be an intrusion, Gracie did just that, and packed up two dozen kiffles for Maddie and her family.

"Oh, Gracie, come on in!" Maddie said when Gracie had knocked on the back door of the pretty home. The yard behind the house was quite large, and Gracie could see the fence that surrounded Maddie's herb garden, as well as several large drifted plantings of crocuses and daffodils that were brightening the spring day. Throughout the beds were various garden ornaments of ladybugs: Maddie loved the little red and black insects and encouraged their propagation in her garden. She also used them as a decorating theme.

Maddie was wearing a fine dark grey silk jersey top and matching trousers, an Hermès scarf called 'Coccinelles,' or 'ladybugs,' knotted loosely around her neck. Her short blonde hair was frosted, attractively cut, and looked freshly styled. The diamond studs she generally had on winked in her ears, and she wore her wedding rings, and the series of varied bracelets she was known for on her slender wrists, just below the cuffs of the top. Italian charm bracelets, some Nepalese beaded bracelets and a few silver bangles mixed together, but each one told a story and held a memory, and Maddie was never seen without them.

"You look--you look great!" Gracie told her friend. She couldn't keep the surprise out of her voice.

"Oh Gracie, it's good to see you," Maddie said, accepting the platter of pastries with a smile. "What are these?"

Gracie explained about Tyler's 'foolproof' kiffle recipe. "They're pretty good," she told her friend. "So I thought, since you'll have family and visitors here, you could use them," she finished.

"Oh, thank you, Gracie: that's very kind." Maddie put the platter of goodies on a kitchen counter. "Would you like some coffee? Tea?" she offered with a small smile.

"No, I'm fine, Maddie," Gracie replied. "How are you doing?" she asked, concerned. "This must have been such a shock," she added as she and Maddie sat at the blonde wood kitchen table. There were lady bug patterned fabric placemats on the surface and a small, low container with white flowers of various types in the center.

"I am all right," she said firmly. "Really," she insisted at Gracie's doubtful look. "It was all just so quick! I—perhaps I haven't really had time to take it in. I don't know. He hadn't been well for a couple of days," Maddie told Gracie in a quiet voice. "We thought it was a virus he'd picked up somewhere, you know, he goes to so many functions and meetings and dinners and what not," she explained, babbling just a little bit. Her light blue eyes were expressive and her face looked regretful.

Gracie listened.

"Or we thought maybe he'd even caught something from one of the grand children, although Elizabeth--that's our daughter--said the kids hadn't been sick, but you know kids: stuff goes through them so fast you don't even realize but when adults catch it, it knocks us for a loop! So I tried to keep him comfortable, and gave him broth and tea and so on, but…" Her voice broke a little.

"Did he tell you how ill he'd become?" Gracie asked delicately. Her research and her chat with Spears had brought her to the conclusion that Senator Jesperson must have had a bloody nose and probably bloody diarrhea and bloody urine for at least a few hours before the convulsions had begun. She didn't want to come right out and say that to Maddie, hence her ellipsis.

Maddie frowned a little bit and her eyes lost focus as she remembered. "You know, he did say he had a nosebleed, but I didn't think that had anything to do with anything else," she murmured. "I—he wouldn't let me help him, really, except to bring him tea and water and so on. It all happened so fast," she repeated. "I did the best I could for him..."

Gracie smiled and shrugged. "Of course you did, Maddie. There wasn't anything else you could have done," she told her friend. "Beyond what you did do, I mean."

Maddie nodded and looked down at her hands, clasped in her lap.

"And they'll have the results of the tox screen in another day or so, and then we'll know more," Gracie finished reassuringly.

A tall, somewhat lanky young woman with long strawberry blonde hair and a slightly equine face entered the kitchen at this moment, and Maddie reached out to her with one hand. "Oh, Lizzie, this is my friend Gracie," Maddie said, making introductions. "Gracie: this is my daughter, Elizabeth." Her voice held a great deal of love and pride.

Gracie and Elizabeth shook hands and murmured politenesses. Then Elizabeth told her mother that Reverend Lovell had arrived, and that her younger brother, Edward, had also just got home.

"You've got a house full," Gracie murmured, standing up and backing towards the kitchen door. "I just wanted to drop the kiffles off, and give my condolences," she told Maddie.

Elizabeth left, and Maddie stepped over to where Gracie was standing and gave her a quick hug.

"I'm so glad you did, Gracie."

"Will you let me know if I can do--anything?" Gracie offered, feeling helpless. She imagined that despite her brave front Maddie must be devastated, and wanted her to know that she could count on her.

"I will," Maddie nodded. "The funeral notice will be in the papers," she added. "I imagine it will be Monday, to give everyone a chance to arrange their schedule," she said, thinking out loud. "And I think there will be something in Boston, too..."

"He was a good Senator, and he'd been a good Mayor," Gracie said honestly. "He did good things for this county, and for Pittsfield, and for the State."

Maddie nodded again. "Yes, you're right, Gracie: he was all those things," she agreed, smiling. "And more," she added, her voice quiet.

Chapter Six

"You'll never guess," Jean said to Gracie on Friday afternoon. She had called just as Gracie had got in the door from Maddie's.

"What?" Gracie asked, curious.

"I'm getting an award!" Jean announced, sounding both pleased and amused.

"That's great!" Gracie replied sincerely. "For what?"

Jean chuckled. "Apparently for uncovering the drug scheme," she said, her voice still merry. "And the inmate is getting an award, too, and I think the DA's petitioned Judge Cranston to shave some time off this sentence. Can you believe that?"

Gracie could, actually, and said as much.

"I figure the DA just wanted to find some way to get his ugly face in front of the cameras, and since your article blew his press conference idea out of the water, now he's decided to issue awards, so he can still get his publicity," Jean told Gracie.

Gracie, who agreed completely with her friend, was really glad Jean had outlined the theory first: if Gracie had, it would have seemed that she were belittling her friend's accomplishment, and she didn't wish to do that.

"You're probably right, but you do deserve an award, Jean," Gracie replied. "Be sure to let me know the details, I'll want to cover it for the *Intelligencer*," she added with a grin.

"Bring your wide angle lens, if Popovitch is going to be in the photos!" Jean laughed merrily, and the two hung up.

Monday as Gracie was drinking her morning coffee and half watching the television news programs while she checked her email and social media feeds, the police band scanner that she kept in her kitchen went off. This in itself was not that unusual an occurrence, but it was the transmission after the tones that caught Gracie's attention. A man had been discovered at the Hebert Arboretum, on the grounds of Pittsfield's Springside Park. Apparently, some early morning joggers through the Daffodil Hill section of the Arboretum had found the man's body, and called 911 on their mobile phones.

Gracie gulped down her coffee, shut the television off, and was dressed and out the door in under five minutes. It would take her about twenty minutes to get to the Arboretum, and she pushed the speed limit all the way, until she drove through the gates of the park and reached the parking lot.

Locking her Jeep, she headed, notebook in hand, in the direction that the rustic wooden sign indicated would bring her to Daffodil Hill. She'd chosen her 'go to' running shoes that had seen her through the Brazilian Rain Forest and the 6000 shop Grand Bazaar in Istanbul with nary a blister. They were the best 'work' shoes she owned.

She fairly flew along the gravel path in a trot half way between a jog and a speed walk, and in a couple of minutes saw several police in a tight knot ahead of her. She slowed, took a deep breath and noticed what a lovely spring morning it was, and then focused. About six police officers, some wearing the Pittsfield uniform in grey, and a couple of State Troopers in Massachusetts blue, surrounded a small area to one side of a drift of daffodils just past their peak bloom. The officers were standing on the grass, but Gracie stayed on the path: she could see enough from where she was.

It was quite clear that the police were attempting to shield the body at their feet from any curious onlookers. As it was still early, there were only a few people about, including the couple who apparently had found the body. These two, a man and woman in their early twenties, Gracie judged, were off to one side of the path, and being interviewed by the Berkshire County Sheriff, Ned Shermayne.

A minute passed while Gracie studied the scene; then she heard swift, purposeful footsteps crunching on the gravel behind her.

"Morning, Gracie," said Jack as he came up behind her. "Did you fly here?" he asked over his shoulder as he strode towards the knot of officers.

"Practically," Gracie smiled.

She earned a quirky half smile from Jack, who then continued on towards the body. Gracie watched as he asked a few questions of the officers surrounding the body: probably things like, 'did anyone touch or move anything?'. Jack pulled a small square of folded material from the pocket of his windbreaker and Gracie realized it was a very thin tarpaulin. He covered the body with it, and the officers still stood guard.

The coroner had been called, Gracie presumed, as she watched Jack go over to Shermayne and the couple who'd found the man, and join in with a few questions of his own.

There were a few more footsteps on the gravel path behind Gracie now, other nature lovers out for a morning walk at the Arboretum and a couple more State Police troopers. The latter helped keep onlookers at bay. Gracie didn't know the troopers personally, although they looked familiar to her, most likely from court appearances or from her weekly visits to the barracks for the newspaper. But they both gave her an approving nod when they realized she was staying firmly on the path, and had no intention of trying to approach the crime scene.

As one trooper was surveying the surroundings for good places to attach the well known yellow 'CRIME SCENE - DO NOT CROSS' tape, Gil Butcher from the *Gazetteer* came running at top speed towards the grassy area and the daffodils, camera hung from a frayed strap and bouncing on his belly, a shabby notebook in one grubby, pudgy paw.

The other trooper stopped Butcher's forward motion with a hand and a stern, "off limits, this is a crime scene."

Butcher reluctantly halted alongside Gracie, whom he noted with silent disfavor. Then, without so much as a 'good morning' or a nod for Gracie, Butcher addressed the trooper.

"I'm the Editor of the *Gazetteer*," he announced self importantly, flashing the press card he wore in the plastic pocket protector of his shirt. Gracie interpreted his tone to mean, 'the other paper just sent a lowly reporter, but I am of much more consequence and deserve special attention!' Butcher continued huffily: "I need to get the details of this situation! Do you have an ID? Is the man dead?" he asked, rapid fire.

The trooper just gave him a bland look, the way a block of concrete might look, if it had a face.

"This is a crime scene," the trooper repeated through tight teeth, "and no one is allowed beyond this tape--" which had now been stretched around the area courtesy of a few obliging tree trunks and shrubs-- "except authorized personnel." He paused. "That doesn't include you, Mr. Editor," he added with a gratuitous sneer that made Gracie giggle to herself.

Clearly, that particular trooper had had an encounter with Butcher in the past.

The editor, who was as out of shape as he was self important, was still gasping for breath. "But you must be able to tell me something!" he demanded on a wheeze. He panted like a dog after a long run. "Do you know who it is?" he asked again. His pencil was poised above his notebook expectantly, as though he thought an answer would be forthcoming. Gracie noticed the pencil had tooth marks on it, and its metal top was minus its eraser, and no longer round.

The trooper just shook his head in exasperation, and looked away.

Obviously wishing to distance himself from 'lowly reporter' Gracie, Butcher took a few steps along the crime tape in the opposite direction, all the while craning his neck to see what he could see. Then he spotted the couple being interviewed by Jack and the Sheriff, and immediately headed that way.

Gracie sighed. Poor people: she had no doubt but that Butcher would try to talk to them, completely disregarding their feelings and probably making an upsetting situation worse still.

"Good morning, Gracie," came Spears' voice a few seconds later. He had arrived at the crime scene along with Wilcox and another Morgue attendant Gracie didn't know. Between them, they were carrying a collapsible gurney and a large duffel bag that Gracie knew contained scene of crime materials like evidence bags, fluid collection tubes, etc. Heather had a large, expensive looking camera with a fine focus lens on it strapped around her neck.

"Hi!" Gracie returned brightly to the ME.

Heather smiled and nodded at her. "Hi Gracie!"

"Hi Heather: too pretty a morning for this, huh?" Gracie asked conversationally.

Heather rolled her eyes in agreement.

"I was just about to call you when this report came in," Spears told her with a nod towards the shrouded body.

"You got the tox results on Jesperson back?" Gracie asked, low.

Spears only nodded.

"I'll call you later," Gracie said quietly.

Processing the scene took about a half hour, during which time Gracie remained where she was, just listening and looking. The couple who had discovered the body was excused: they walked slowly away, talking in whispers to each other, and escorted by a trooper, whom Gracie thought would probably lead them safely back to their car. Butcher, although he took a couple of steps towards the witnesses as they departed, quickly retreated, since he realized he would not get within five feet of them.

After photographs, measurements and samples had been taken, and after Spears had done his field exam of the body and its immediate surroundings, Wilcox and the other attendant loaded the body onto the gurney's prepared 'body bag,' zipped it up, and trundled off.

Spears followed, walking towards Gracie, and avoiding the area where Butcher stood. He nodded to Gracie as he lifted the crime tape to pass under it. "I'll talk to you later," he said in a low voice.

She nodded back, and the ME left the area.

Gracie had taken a few discreet photos with her iPhone once the body had been covered, but these showed only the police standing in front of the tarp; a wide shot Gracie particularly liked captured the crime scene tape in the foreground, one end fluttering in the spring breeze.

Butcher had been snapping photos as well: it seemed to Gracie that he must have taken a hundred shots, mostly of the covered body and the police. But he'd also taken a few shots as the gurney had been wheeled away, and Gracie had noticed that the Editor had taken a couple of long range shots of the witnesses. She didn't know how well those would come out, but she hoped, for the sake of the couple's privacy, that they weren't useable.

Jack and Shermayne had checked in with all the officers at the scene, and most of the latter had been dismissed. The crime scene tape was removed. Finally, the Sheriff and Jack started to walk back towards where Gracie stood.

Butcher, a few yards to Gracie's right, scuttled over with a crab-like motion, and hailed the county officials.

"Do you have an ID yet?" he asked Jack and the Sheriff as they approached. Gracie said nothing.

"No names are being released at this time," Sheriff Shermayne said in an official tone.

"The Arboretum won't be closed, will it?" Gracie asked ingenuously.

Jack met her eyes knowingly and shook his head. "No: it'll remain open."

"When will you have a report?" Butcher pursued; he licked his thin lips beneath his scraggly mustache in anticipatory greed.

"The State Police will have a report," Jack returned mildly. "You'll have to go bother them," he added lightly.

Sherman and Jack both nodded to Gracie, then, and walked briskly down the gravel path back towards the parking lot.

Gracie sighed: not much else to do here, she thought to herself.

Butcher, again without a word to her, trundled off down the path after the Sheriff and Jack. He looked as though he might pester them with questions all the way back to the parking lot, Gracie thought as she watched his retreating back.

She wished him luck.

Once everyone had gone, Gracie slowly walked towards the area of flattened grass where the body had lain. Swiftly, she glanced around at the green blades, peppered with a few straggling daffodils that a couple of feet farther on swelled into an almost solid blanket of cream and yellow.

It seemed a peaceful, quiet place to have found a body, Gracie thought.

Especially as there was no blood. Anywhere.

Chapter Seven

Early Monday afternoon, the ME's name once again popped up on Gracie's iPhone.

"I was just about to call you," Gracie answered cheerfully.

"Ah--hmmm--Gracie, would you be able to come down here?" the ME asked in response. "I've called Detective Draper," were the ME's next words, and Gracie was confused.

"Jack?"

"Yes." The ME paused, clearly uncomfortable. "Gracie, I can't fax the tox report to you. But you can come down here and see it," he added cryptically.

It took Gracie a moment or two to reply: if the ME couldn't fax the report results to her, that meant that something pretty hinky must have popped up. And if he'd called Jack in...

"I'll be there in about a half hour," she told the ME, and hung up.

Strictly speaking, Spears should also have called the *Gazetteer* to let them know the tox report on Senator Jesperson was back, particularly as it appeared that the report must contain some unusual data. However, Gracie thought it unlikely that the ME had done this. Spears had had several run-ins with Butcher and maintained a healthy dislike for both the editor and his newspaper. Gracie knew Spears would do Butcher no favors. If the man showed up and asked for a copy of the tox report, he would be given one. But other than that, no.

Which was why Spears had asked Gracie to come to the Morgue and ask to see the tox screen results, she realized as she drove towards Pittsfield once again: this way, the *Gazetteer* couldn't claim favoritism. Spears couldn't help it, could he, if Gracie showed up long before the thought of doing so even occurred to Butcher!

Less than the promised half hour later, Gracie, Jack and Spears were gathered around the ME's desk in the far corner of the Morgue. Wilcox busied herself with paperwork at her desk near the doors. Spears was seated, and Jack and Gracie both stood to one side, waiting. The life sized, articulated skeleton that hung to one side of the ME's desk and always looked to Gracie as though it were grinning had one hand raised as if in greeting.

When Gracie had arrived, her appearance had not so much startled Jack as surprised him.

'You've got great timing,' he had told her with a wry grin. Autopsy results, including tox screen results, were public information. But Gracie's arrival just moments after Spears had notified him that the tox results were back made Jack wonder if perhaps Gracie hadn't had a 'tip.'

Now, Jack said, "We expecting anyone else, Doc?"

Spears looked at the Detective calmly. "I never know who will show up here, asking for something," he replied in a quiet voice. "But I should think not."

"We contacted the Senator's office as you suggested," Jack began, "and checked his itinerary for the past couple of weeks: the Senator hasn't visited any farms recently, and no one on his staff remembers him getting a letter or package with suspicious powder in it."

"I could have told you that," Spears said, and Jack frowned. "But only after I'd got these results back," Spears reassured him.

Then he opened the envelope containing the tox screen results and pointed to the graph on the top of the page. It was done as a bar chart, and one bar far exceeded the others, extending almost to the very top of the page.

Spears pointed to the high-reaching bar with one index finger. "See that?" he asked Gracie and Jack rhetorically.

They nodded in unison.

"What's that say? 'Toxalbumin proteopedia?'" Jack read from the chart. "What's that?"

"The common name is 'Abrin,' from the village in Iran, I believe," Spears answered.

"Iran?" Gracie echoed, intrigued.

"Mmm...it's a tropical thing, from the nut of the rosary pea," Dr. Spears continued in an informative tone. "Indigenous to Indonesia. The rosary pea is quite pretty, bright red. It can be fatal if ingested, but it's the inside of the pea that's toxic: the shell isn't, and generally it protects anyone who happens to swallow one from exposure to the inside. The dried peas are used in maracas and similar instruments."

Jack looked non plussed.

"Abrin, like ricin, isn't usually an accidentally transmitted toxin: one has to be deliberately exposed to it," the ME continued. He emphasized the word 'deliberately.'

"So the chances of the Senator accidentally inhaling or ingesting it are--" Jack asked.

"Mmmm...I'd say slim to none," Dr. Spears confirmed. "I mean, if he'd swallowed a bead, or pea, somehow, the shell would have kept him safe."

"Even if he'd chewed it?" Gracie put in, curious.

Dr. Spears shrugged. "If a rosary pea had been in some kind of food, I doubt anyone would have eaten it, or chewed it: it would have been very hard, almost rock like, and what do you do when you're eating something and you bite down on something that hard?" he asked rhetorically.

"You take it out," Gracie answered nonetheless.

Spears nodded. "But I don't think that's what happened."

"You have another scenario in mind?" Jack asked quickly.

The ME nodded.

"You think someone cracked open a pea, or a bean, or whatever it's called, and gave the toxic, inside part of it to Jesperson," Jack finished grimly.

The ME nodded again.

"So it's murder?" Gracie asked in a hushed voice.

Spears sighed, and nodded. "It certainly looks like it."

"I'll get a search warrant for Senator Jesperson's house, and his office," Jack said. "The timing stinks, with the viewing tonight and the funeral tomorrow," he added.

"But you need to see if you can find any evidence of rosary peas anywhere that Senator Jesperson might have been," Spears confirmed.

The funeral for Senator Jesperson would be in Pittsfield on Tuesday, a day later than Maddie had forecast, but the scheduling hadn't been left entirely up to her and had been done to allow as many politicians who had served with or who knew Fred to attend. The memorial service in Boston would be held on Wednesday.

Gracie had planned to go to the viewing Monday night, but not the funeral, and Dave had indicated that the *Intelligencer* would run a long profile/memorial on the Senator in the Friday edition.

Gracie was glad that she hadn't been assigned to cover any of the funeral services: since she was Maddie's friend, it would have been difficult for her to blend work and her private life in such an emotional and sorrowful situation. She also felt it would have been needlessly intrusive: if people wanted to see the funeral services, they should attend.

Jack got a search warrant and he and his team did a thorough search of the Jesperson home late Monday afternoon. He also contacted the Boston PD about getting a search warrant for the Senator's office, and was scheduled to drive out there Wednesday to execute the warrant alongside his Boston colleagues.

He was at the viewing on Monday night and approached Gracie after she had gone through the receiving line and paid her respects. It was a closed casket, but there were photos and documents recounting the Senator's life and work, and Gracie took some time examining them.

"I thought you'd like to know, we didn't find any rosary peas at the Senator's house," Jack said, low, as he walked Gracie to a corner of the large reception area at Pittsfield's classiest funeral home. "No funny plants, no maracas, no rain sticks."

She nodded. "It's a mystery, isn't it? I mean, if Fred couldn't have accidentally ingested the abrin, it seems clear that someone must have given it to him. But who? And why? And how?" Gracie queried.

Jack looked over at the receiving line where Maddie, Elizabeth, Edward, and Elizabeth's husband stood; the grandchildren were too young to attend, and had been dropped off at the home of a friend of Maddie's for the evening.

"Oh, Jack: you don't think it's Maddie!" Gracie whispered, her tone scolding. "Come on, be serious!" she added.

Jack shrugged. "I don't know, Gracie: she doesn't seem like a killer. But we always look at the spouse: you know that."

Gracie made a face. "Well, sure, but this is Maddie: she's my friend! She's in Club!" Gracie protested, as though being in Club automatically exonerated anyone from any sort of culpability. "The likelihood of her killing

Fred is--is--" she struggled to come up with something unlikely enough. "About as likely as me killing him," she finished.

Jack smirked. "Well, I don't think you killed him, Gracie: you have no motive, for one thing. And during the time the Senator would have been exposed to the abrin, according to what Dr. Spears says, you were still in England, I think."

"Ah. And, of course, where would I get a rosary pea?" Gracie asked rhetorically.

"You don't grow that plant?" Jack asked, only half kidding. Gracie grew a lot of what Jack would call unusual plants, including orchids, bromeliads, ferns and cycads. She'd been talking about putting in a conservatory, in fact, so she could give such exotics a proper environment, and grow even more of them.

Gracie made a face and shook her head. "No, I don't. And Maddie doesn't either," she put in defensively.

Jack's face was impassive. He looked over again towards Senator Jesperson's widow, and then stared out one of the large windows that looked onto the quiet side street in downtown Pittsfield where the funeral home was located. "So--how was England?" he asked, trying to make his voice nonchalant.

"It was--interesting," Gracie answered with a small smile. "I got involved in a murder, if you'd believe that!" she laughed, and gave Jack a précis of the case she'd stumbled on in her cousin's small village near London. She didn't mention David, the Detective Sergeant with whom she'd struck up a friendship--and perhaps something more. And she didn't mention the personal danger she'd been put in during the course of her own investigation into the murder.

Jack shook his head, but gave her a crooked grin. "Only you, Gracie, would go on vacation and land smack in the middle of a murder!" he told her. "Still, I'll bet you were very helpful to the police: I know you're pretty helpful to authorities here," he added sincerely. "And I'm sure Ben's glad you're back," he finished, affecting a lightness of tone that the look in his eyes contradicted.

Gracie hesitated: this was hardly the place to launch into the details of her love life. And she surely didn't owe Jack any explanation. But: "oh, erm, well, we broke up," Gracie informed him, her voice low. "Before I went away," she added.

Jack said nothing in response, but gave her a keen look from his dark blue eyes.

"So--who do you think might have wanted Senator Jesperson dead?" Gracie asked brightly. "Not including Maddie," she added sourly.

Chapter Eight

The award presentation for Jean and the inmate from the Jail to commend their roles in uncovering the drug smuggling ring was scheduled for Tuesday afternoon at 3 p.m. Gracie figured the hour was late enough so that Popovitch, who was running the award ceremony, could just take off once it was concluded, and not return to his office: why let pesky details like working a full day interrupt his life? Additionally, of course, the scheduled time would allow the news media, especially the TV media, to get the story prepared for airing on that evening's news broadcasts.

The ceremony was being held in the large courtroom at the Pittsfield Courthouse. Dating from 1871, the courthouse had both a formal courtroom, which was the larger one, and a smaller, less formal but no less legal courtroom. Family court was often held in the smaller courtroom, since its lower ceiling, modern windows, and blond wood upholstered furniture was less intimidating.

The large courtroom was, in a word, imposing. Paneled in dark mahogany with tall, narrow windows it was ringed by severe looking oil paintings of all of Berkshire County's previous judges. Maroon carpeting served to muffle footsteps while antiquated heating units generally meant the large, coffered ceiling trapped most of whatever heat there was, and the room itself held a persistent chill.

Tuesday afternoon the sun slanted through the tall windows and gave the somber space a bit of cheer. Additionally, the gaggle of media including TV on air reporters, camera operators, sound technicians, as well as Gil Butcher from the *Gazetteer* with a young trainee in tow, and of course Gracie, gave the awards presentation an almost circus like atmosphere.

It certainly was very jolly, Gracie thought, smiling as she entered the room and walked down the long central aisle towards the front. A couple of the on air reporters gave her a smile or a wave: they'd run into Gracie on previous stories, and since Gracie had always been helpful and informative to them, they liked and remembered her.

Gracie stood near the first row of seats while the TV crews set up. There were three of them, and Gracie wondered how hard Millie had had to work to get two Springfield stations as well as one out of Hartford, CT, to attend. Butcher was circling the TV personnel, and it looked to Gracie like he was introducing his sidekick to everyone as he briefed the young man on proper press procedure. The kid, who clutched a camera and notebook to his chest as though they were life preservers and he was in the middle of the open sea, didn't look more than fifteen, Gracie thought.

Surprisingly, when Butcher finished with the media encamped in the enclosure beyond the bar, the *Gazetteer* editor turned and approached Gracie.

"This is Gracie Barufaldi," Butcher told his young cohort, gesturing to her.

Gracie smiled and held out her hand. The young man fumbled to transfer his camera and notebook into his left arm so he could reach out with his right. His handshake was surprisingly firm, even if his hand was sweaty.

Gracie persisted with her smile and thought the young man must be nervous, particularly being dragged around by Butcher.

"You want to watch out for her," Butcher continued, nodding solemnly.

Was he kidding?

"She's with the *Intelligencer,* and they're out competition," he explained. "Most of the time we don't have to worry too much, though," Butcher continued in an superior, avuncular voice, "since Gracie here tends to jump the gun and write up stories before her information is official, or on the record," Butcher finished with a nasty smile.

Gracie bit her lip, hard. How dare he! She felt her face flush at the editor's taunts, but at least she didn't say anything. She couldn't: she didn't trust her mouth not to start defending herself and then begin ranting about his paper's constant inaccuracies.

She swallowed. "Is this a new reporter, Gil?" she asked through tight lips. At least her voice sounded normal.

"This is Stephen Antolik, our new intern," Gil said proudly.

"Oh?" Gracie managed a weak smile. "Studying journalism? What college?" she asked Antolik.

The young man smiled uneasily and shrugged. "Oh, I'm in 11th grade at the High School," he said, looking like he was thrilled to have been thought to be in college. "But I do want to be a journalist," he said, and Gracie mentally added, 'when I grow up.' " Pleased to meet you," he squeezed in before Butcher, scowling, led him away.

Gracie took a deep breath and returned her attention to the center of the room: Popovitch had just entered and was busy bossing everyone around, telling them where to stand and even telling the TV camera people what angle to use to shoot. He insisted they move from the center, where they'd set up, to one side, so that they could shoot more in profile.

Gracie chuckled to herself: shooting from the side wouldn't help anything, she thought: Popovitch would still look massive. Next to him, slender Jean and the skinny inmate looked Lilliputian.

Jean found Gracie in the crowd of press people and spectators—probably relatives of the inmate, Gracie thought—and rolled her eyes, giving her a conspiratorial grin.

The award ceremony was predictable, and quite short, with Popovitch making noises about how 'under his guidance' the prison staff was 'taught to recognize suspicious behavior.' Gracie thought to herself that it was more likely Warden Mick Jones' instructions and example that encouraged his staff to be vigilant and observant, not Popovitch's. If, indeed, the DA had ever had any interaction with prison staff.

A few kind words about the inmate's role in the discovery at which several spectators cheered quietly and clapped uncertainly, and the ceremony, such as it had been, was over.

Popovitch made his way over to the first of the TV on air reporters and launched into a one on one, clearly hoping that he would dominate whatever 30 second coverage the station gave the story. He left Jean and the inmate completely out of it. However, the inmate was probably just as glad, since the prison guard shepherding him allowed him a few minutes to chat with his friends and family.

Jean's children were in school and her parents lived in Florida, so she didn't have anyone at the ceremony especially for her, except Gracie. She made a beeline for her once she had the bronze and wood plaque in her hands.

"Let me get a shot of you with the plaque," Gracie told her friend, and posed Jean, in full dress uniform, below one of the oil paintings in the room.

"What about Inmate Carruthers?" Jean asked.

"I'll get the two of you next, but I want this one for Club," Gracie explained, taking the shot. "It's not every day one of our members gets an award for bravery and integrity!" she exclaimed.

The picture with Jean and the inmate was accomplished, and Gracie asked Carruthers what considerations the Judge had made towards his sentence because of his actions in uncovering the drug ring.

As the inmate explained, Gracie wrote, thinking that before she left the courthouse she'd see if she could catch Judge Cranston, get his comment and a quick photo, and write the story from that angle: the way prisoners can affect their prison experience and sometimes their sentences, through exemplary behavior.

She might not even have to run a shot of Popovitch at all, Gracie chuckled to herself as she said goodbye to Jean, thanked her and the inmate, and slipped out the back door of the courtroom.

The question Gracie had posed at Senator Jesperson's viewing had been the same one Jack had been thinking over since the ME had told them he now considered Jesperson's death a murder. Luckily, when Jack had explained the situation to Maddie at the same time he'd tendered the search warrant, she had taken the news calmly, and offered to help the Detective in any way she could.

'I don't know much about what Fred did when he was in Boston,' she had told Jack, sounding a bit regretful. 'But as far as who his friends were locally, and things like that, I can tell you. And if you need to look at our financials or anything, you'll have my permission,' she had added, sounding very cooperative indeed.

Because he did believe, firmly, in the adage of 'look at the spouse first,' Jack decided, after a cursory run through of the Jespersons' credit and bank accounts had seemed quite normal, to try and learn more about their relationship. He didn't see any overt reason Maddie would have wanted to kill Fred, but he knew next to nothing about them or their relationship.

So, how could he learn about it? The usual approach was to talk to their friends. He'd got a list from Maddie of the couple's social circle, even though Maddie had admitted a bit sadly as she gave over the list that she and Fred hadn't socialized much lately. He'd also obtained the names of each of their separate friends, and been gratified to see Gracie's name on Maddie's list.

Several of the other names on the lists were familiar to Jack, and he could probably ask them candidly what they had thought, if anything, about the Jespersons' marriage. However, the person he knew best on the lists was Gracie.

Late Tuesday afternoon, he gave her a call; she answered right away, and Jack, not wanting to play his hand too soon, asked if he could stop by that evening, if Gracie weren't busy.

Gracie's answer had pleased him: she'd said that no, she wasn't especially busy, and he should come over about seven that evening for coffee and dessert.

Chapter Nine

A moment or two before seven, Gracie heard the sound of Jack's truck coming up her driveway. She and Pumpkin had been enjoying another small fire in the Oak Room, warding off an unusually chilly night for May, and Gracie watched from a window as Jack hopped out of the truck, and then opened the passenger side door for Woof, his half wolf, half dog canine companion. Woof, who was now just over a year old, had been one of the rescues in a puppy mill / dog fighting raid. Gracie had been instrumental in getting Jack the location of the operation, which had enabled them to do the raid and shut the mill and fighting ring down. Gracie had gone with Jack when he'd told her he was adopting one of the rescued puppies. She considered Woof partly hers, and when she and Jack had been together, had even referred to herself as 'Mummie' to the handsome canine.

She hadn't invited Woof this evening, but she was happy Jack had brought him; even though he wasn't at her house as much as he had been in the past, Woof's bowl and dish and a bag of his kibble still lived in one of Gracie's kitchen cupboards.

She opened the front door with a grin, and immediately was engulfed in Woof's doggie hug.

"Woof, that's enough!" Jack said, sounding stern, but laughing: Woof was licking Gracie's face thoroughly, as if he wanted to own her--or eat her.

"It's okay--hi Jack, come in," Gracie replied, still smiling. "Pumpkin and I are in the Oak Room: why don't you guys go along in, and I'll bring out the coffee and dessert. After I wash my face!" she added wryly, and disappeared through the green baize door that separated her kitchen area from the rest of the ground floor.

Jack loved Gracie's house, and knew it almost as well as she did, he thought. He especially liked the Oak Room, which was basically a Great Room all done in blonde oak panelling, with a coffered oak ceiling. The central feature of the room was a huge field stone fireplace on the western wall. A small fire was, indeed, burning cheerfully in there as Jack and Woof entered the room. Pumpkin was lounging on the long chocolate brown leather sofa, but when she saw Woof, she jumped down and walked to the Kilim rug that Gracie had bought in Turkey and placed in front of the fireplace. Pumpkin looked over to Woof as if to say, 'well, come on, join me!'

Maybe that's what she had said, Jack mused, as he watched Woof walk over, touch noses with Pumpkin, and then curl up on the rug next to her, his eyes, like hers, mesmerized by the dancing flames.

"Here we go," Gracie said cheerily a few minutes later. She came back into the Oak Room via the Dining Room, which opened through a large arch made of thick glass cubes. Beyond the Dining Room was a big butler's pantry, and Jack realized that this was the reason for Gracie's route: she was carrying a pretty silver tray, loaded with a thermos carafe, mugs, plates and a platter of something he was sure would be yummy.

She put the tray down on the marble topped coffee table in front of the sofa, and sat next to Jack. "You go to Jesperson's funeral this morning?" she asked conversationally as she poured the coffee. "I didn't see you at the award thing for Jean," she added.

"No--I was busy all morning on the Richard Dawes case, the guy in the park," Jack answered bluntly. He presumed that Gracie had seen the preliminary police report, which included the fact that the man had been killed by a single gunshot wound to the forehead, and that the ID found on him identified him as Richard Dawes from south Pittsfield. The autopsy was scheduled for Wednesday morning.

"Yeah- that's weird, isn't it?" Gracie said cheerfully. "I mean, gunshot wound to the forehead: gotta be murder, right?"

"Probably--"

"That's what Dr. Spears said, too, when I asked him about that," Gracie broke in. She put a couple of the pastries she had brought out onto a smaller plate, for Jack. "I said that it couldn't be suicide for a couple of reasons, especially because no one shoots him or herself in the forehead," she declared authoritatively. "You put the gun in your mouth, or hold it to your temple," she explained, miming each example.

"Agreed."

"And then, of course," Gracie went on nonchalantly, and took a sip of her coffee, "there was no blood at the scene where the body was found."

Jack was silent for a second, then gave her a grudging smile. "You noticed that, huh?"

Gracie, grinning, nodded. "I did indeed. I waited until everyone, including Butcher, had left, and then went over to look closely at the spot where the body had been found," she explained.

"Well, all that means is that Dawes was killed somewhere else and dumped in the arboretum," Jack offered.

"Yep." Gracie gave him a look. "You talk to his wife yet?" she asked. Jack, of course, was under no obligation to tell her any details about his investigation. But maybe the fact that her questions indicated she'd been doing some digging, too, would encourage him to share.

"What are these?" Jack asked, changing the subject, and pointing to the pastries.

Apparently, no sharing, Gracie thought. Well, two could play that game, then. "Kiffle," Gracie answered, and explained Tyler's 'foolproof' recipe.

Jack took the proffered plate, selected a kiffle, and bit in. "Oh, wow, Gracie, this is delicious!" he told her honestly. "What's the filling?" he asked, scrutinizing the half pastry that was left in one hand.

"These are apricot. I could also make prune, raspberry and even apple. But I like apricot, so--" Gracie explained.

She took a kiffle for herself, and settled back against the dark brown surface of the sofa. "Well, Jack: not that I'm not delighted to have you taste my kiffle, but why are you here?" she asked with a smirk. She knew Jack had to have had a reason for asking if he could stop by. "Clearly it's not to compare notes on the Dawes investigation." She couldn't help the barb.

Jack polished off one kiffle, took a plate and put three more on it, and took a sip of his coffee. As always, it was very good coffee. He acted as though Gracie's words hadn't made any type of impact on him at all. "Well, Gracie, I'm trying to formulate a more complete picture of Maddie and Fred's marriage. Their relationship, including their friends here locally, and their activities." He paused, and bit into another kiffle. "I'm also going to be talking to his staff in Boston, and looking at his colleagues in the State House, to see if any of them might have had any kind of motive. The exposure time for the abrin indicates that Senator Jesperson might have—erm-- come in contact with the toxin in Boston."

"Oh? How do you figure that?" Gracie asked, curious.

"Dr. Spears said it would take three to five days for symptoms to appear. Fred was taken to the hospital early last Thursday morning," Jack reminded her. "Maddie told me, during our preliminary interview, that he had gone to his Boston office last Monday as usual, but had come home mid day on Tuesday, complaining of nausea and vomiting. His office confirmed that the Senator had cancelled his appointments for the rest of the week."

"Oh." Gracie hadn't known that: she hadn't discussed the timeline of Fred's demise with Maddie when she'd visited her: it had seemed too ghoulish to do that, even though the reporter in Gracie had wanted to.

"They heard from him Wednesday morning when he called to check in, and then didn't hear anything more until Maddie called to tell them on Thursday, and they saw the news of his death on Thursday's noon news."

Gracie nodded. "So--the timing?" she prompted. She was trying to recall what she'd read when she'd researched abrin.

"Dr. Spears said three to five days," Jack repeated. If symptoms appeared Tuesday, the Senator could have encountered the toxin the previous Friday, or even Thursday."

Gracie counted silently to herself. "Right. And maybe the symptoms really began Monday night, but Fred did a little work Tuesday, thinking he'd got some stomach virus and just shake it, and then when he couldn't, decided to throw in the towel and come home."

Jack nodded in agreement.

"So he could have been exposed at the end of the previous week," Gracie said.

"Which puts him in Boston." Jack paused. "The search of the Senator's office is scheduled for tomorrow, along with the Boston PD," Jack informed her. "I'm kinda hoping we find something, because as I mentioned before, we didn't find any rosary peas at the Jesperson home, or in the Senator's SUV."

Gracie sighed. "That's disappointing," she commented. "But clearly, whoever poisoned Fred did it, and took the evidence with them."

"Well, anyway, back to the abrin poisoning and the timing. If the onset was more in the three day range rather than the five day range, the Senator could have been exposed to the toxin some time over last weekend," Jack continued, polishing off the kiffle he'd selected, and taking another couple of gulps of coffee.

"Mmmm--true," Gracie reluctantly agreed. "But I still don't think Maddie killed him. I mean, why?"

Jack took a breath. "That's what I'm trying to find out, Gracie. And I was hoping you'd help."

"Maddie didn't really talk about Fred much," Gracie replied by way of answer. "She brought him to a few Club functions where spouses or partners were customary--you remember, you came with me to the Club Winter Dinner Dance one year, and he was there," Gracie reminded him.

Jack nodded. He remembered the dinner dance, and remembered that Fred Jesperson, making excuses about another political engagement, had left before dessert.

"Other than that," Gracie went on, "I didn't hear much about Fred, or see him. Maddie always seemed very proud of him, of course, but I didn't get the sense that she knew much about what he was actually working on in the State Senate. And when he was here, I don't think joint events crowded up their social schedule," she added thoughtfully. "It seemed that Maddie and Fred each kinda did their own thing. At least recently—in the past few years. And anyway, my friendship with Maddie was based on our shared love of herbs, and of cooking, and of gardening," she finished. "We didn't socialize with our partners."

Jack looked thoughtful. "Did you get the sense that Maddie was happy?" he asked carefully: Gracie was being really cooperative and very friendly and he didn't want to upset her.

Gracie nodded. "Yes. I think she was. Perhaps more so lately with her own life here: her friends, her garden, and of course, the grandchildren. But yes, I think she was happy. And I don't think she's a murderer!" Gracie insisted.

Chapter Ten

Tuesday evening after Jack left--and it hadn't been a late night, for many reasons, but chiefly because Jack had to be on the road very early Wednesday morning to get to Boston and do the search of Senator Jesperson's office--Gracie returned to the background checks she'd been running on Richard Dawes since obtaining the police report with the preliminary ID. Sitting at her little spinet desk in the hall alcove she used as an an office space, she discovered that Dawes had been an over the road truck driver. He'd been divorced twice, and had been currently married to his third wife. They had two children, a girl of seven and a boy of nine. Richard Dawes had been 45. His wife, Amy, 38, was a teacher's aide.

On Tuesday evening right after Jack left, launching a computer program she paid dearly for each year, Gracie launched a scan of the Daweses' employment and financial records. The scan wasn't a credit report, but it gave a detailed snapshot of the fiduciary well being of someone's life.

"Hmmmm..." Gracie murmured as she looked over the scan. Dawes' employment history was okay, although he seemed to change jobs frequently. But his credit cards were maxed out, and he was behind on a few payments. He also had a lot of credit cards: fifteen by Gracie's count.

The same scan run on Amy Dawes showed entry level jobs, a gap while, presumably, the children had been very young, and then her current job as a teacher's aide. Amy Dawes had five credit cards in her name, but three had been closed and the other two had small balances and equally small lines of credit, and hadn't been used in months.

Gracie suspected that Amy Dawes had taken steps to ameliorate her credit rating, and was trying to consistently pay down the cards she still had. Her husband, however, showed considerable recent activity on his cards. Their mortgage was two months behind, their municipal sewer bill had not been paid for more than a year, and they routinely used his credit cards to buy groceries and gas. Gracie checked on the alimony Dawes was paying out to clever ex-wives who apparently hadn't re-married: not huge amounts, but enough to put a dent in Dawes' monthly take home.

Gracie sat back in her desk chair and idly glanced out the narrow window in the little alcove. The window gave onto her walled herb garden, but of course it was night time, so the window embraced only darkness. Gracie involuntarily shivered.

"Feels like rain," she murmured to no one in particular. Pumpkin, her large orange and white female tuxedo/tabby, was still in front of the fire in the Oak Room.

Had Dawes been killed because of his financial situation? She wondered. Maybe: maybe he'd owed someone money, and hadn't paid up, and they'd shot him, she thought.

Although she couldn't see how shooting someone dead would get the money paid back: didn't unscrupulous money lenders usually beat someone up first?

What was niggling at Gracie about Dawes' profile, though, was his pattern of employment. Although the man always seemed to secure another job shortly after leaving one, he consistently worked only a year or two at each. In fact, Gracie realized, thinking back on what she'd just read, the longest Dawes had worked at any job had been a nearly five year stint as a driver for a local trucking firm. That had been about a decade before, around the time his two children had been born.

She stared out at the darkness that cloaked her back garden where raised beds stretched from the edge of her terrace down to tall trees that marked the end of her cultivated property. Soon she would get the hammocks out of storage, and install them between the largest, sturdiest trees there, in the deep shade.

Gracie let her mind wander onto the happy and more welcome subject of her garden. In another couple of weeks, she mused, the perennial beds would need to be raked and mulched and annual seeds would have to be planted. Every year, Gracie grew a variety of colorful annuals from seed, experimenting with little or lesser known flowers. Sometimes they were gorgeous, and sometimes they were quite disappointing. Occasionally, they didn't come up at all.

Her insurance was several types of zinnias and dahlias: these seeds reliably germinated and turned into sturdy little plants that produced a rainbow of vibrant color from June through the first hard frost.

Insurance.

Frowning, Gracie turned from her horticultural contemplations and quickly tapped a few keys on her laptop, and in another minute was regarding the screen with something akin to triumph. Huh.

"Draper."

"Barufaldi," Gracie replied humorously, echoing the oh so businesslike way Jack answered his phone.

"Yeah, Gracie, what is it?" Jack asked, sounding grumpy. He'd left her house about an hour ago, and had just been headed for bed when his phone had rung.

"You know Dawes took out a two million dollar life insurance policy on himself two months ago, right?" Gracie blurted, all in a rush. She knew Jack had to get up early, but frankly, she didn't really care: this was important. And despite her former thought of keeping her discoveries to herself if Jack wasn't going to share his, she hadn't been able to resist letting Jack in on this tidbit. And making it clear that she'd uncovered an important piece of information ahead of him.

There was a beat of silence on Jack's end of the phone. Then his voice came, slowly, sounding somehow inappropriately pleased. "No...Gracie, I did not know that," he told her.

The debate about what that two million dollar policy meant in the scheme of things would have to wait, however, as Wednesday morning, Gracie showered, dried off quickly, applied the minimum of makeup and a quick slash of lipstick, and pulled her glossy brown curls up into a high ponytail. A pastel print silk t shirt from Zara, her favorite jeans, a denim jacket and Sketchers flats were donned within five minutes, and then Gracie was galloping down the stairs as she inserted her favorite bezel set diamond studs in her ears, and clasped her Cartier Américaine tank watch on one wrist.

Gracie wanted to check in at the Morgue, and see if the ME had done the autopsy on Dawes, and could give her the report. If so, she decided, she'd treat herself to lunch at Bistro Adam, and then swing by the Dawes residence to see if Amy Dawes were available for a chat. The timing wasn't impeccable, as the widow would probably be preparing for the funeral, but Gracie wanted to at least stop by.

Then she'd go home and write up her article for that week's *Intelligencer*. She should just make the Wednesday evening deadline.

"Of course I'll give you a copy of the autopsy," Spears told Gracie cheerfully when she appeared at his door. Gracie knew her way to the morgue very well, as it seemed she stopped in frequently in the course of her job. While it did creep her out to some extent, she found she didn't really mind it.

At least it was quiet. All she could hear was the faint whirring of the coolers' compressors and the patter of rain up on the high windows. The deluge, thankfully, had just been starting as she had parked at the Hospital, so she had 'run between the rain drops' and been able to gain the Morgue and stay relatively dry. Outside, she knew, it was thunder, lightning and torrential downpours.

Spears had just finished the autopsy on Dawes, and although the tox screens weren't back yet, his examination had yielded enough information and evidence for the ME to declare cause of death as well as manner of death.

"Great, thanks!" Gracie smiled. She stood next to Spears' small desk on the far side of the large autopsy suite. The Morgue was not terribly modern, and didn't look a bit like the fancy sets on the popular TV shows. Some of the equipment was new, however: the autopsy tables had automatic drains and sluices, and the overhead halogen lights made even the tiniest freckle stand out. The room was tiled in plain white squares with a grey linoleum floor and a high ceiling from which fluorescent fixtures were suspended. The halogen lights were dotted between these and centered over the four autopsy tables that ran in a line down the center of the room's length. Equipment, cabinets, shelving, sinks, scales and other tools of the trade festooned the perimeter of the room.

Gracie found most of the details of autopsies and forensic science fascinating, and was very grateful she wasn't terribly squeamish.

Now, Spears moved over to his Diener's desk to make a copy of the report for Gracie, and then returned. Wilcox had already gone out for lunch; except for Spears and Gracie, the Morgue's only other occupant was

Dawes, whose body lay on the first autopsy table, tastefully covered with a pale blue sheet.

"Gunshot wound to the head," Gracie murmured, reading. "I knew that, we discussed it yesterday," she told the ME, referring to their short telephone conversation.

"Keep reading," Spears advised her with a knowing smile.

Gracie returned to the page, scanning the paragraphs and studying the sketches and photos. "GSR around the wound, means it was very close range," she deduced. GSR was gun shot residue and if that were found around the entry wound it meant the gun had been close enough for residue to land on the victim as he was being shot.

Spears nodded.

"Doesn't rule out suicide," Gracie judged, and kept reading.

There were peri mortem defensive wounds on Dawes' hands and arms, and Gracie again drew from this fact that there must have been some kind of struggle just before the victim had been shot. That, at least to her, cast doubt on the verdict of suicide. Also, Dr. Spears had not found any gunshot residue on the corpse's hands: to Gracie, this seemed a very clear indication that he had not killed himself. If he had, there would have been GSR on his hands.

According to the ballistics report that was attached to the autopsy, the weapon used to kill Dawes had been a .45. Maybe one person had subdued him and held him down while another shot him in the middle of his forehead, she thought.

Gracie advanced that theory to Spears who still looked inscrutable.

"So cause of death, clearly, a bullet to the brain," Gracie read aloud. "And manner of death, homicide," she read. "Huh." She looked at the next page, where a sketch preceded more paragraphs of findings.

"No blood at the scene," she read. "I knew that, too," she told Dr. Spears, and recounted what she'd told Jack.

"That's right," Spears agreed. "He'd been killed elsewhere and put in the park," he told Gracie. "Keep reading."

Gracie bent again to the report. A few seconds later she frowned.

"He'd been dead for about 48 hours?" she queried, looking confused.

Spears shrugged. "Since the body was dumped, the time frame isn't inconsistent," he explained. "I put his death at some time Saturday morning or maybe late Friday."

"But--" Gracie knew from the program she'd run earlier that day at home that one of Dawes' credit cards had been used early Monday morning at a gas station up near Williamstown. If he'd been dead for 48 hours, someone other than Dawes had used that credit card. And yet, the body had been found with Dawes' wallet and some credit cards and cash, so it clearly hadn't been a robbery. Who shoots someone and then takes only one credit card?

However, she was reluctant to share that bit of information with anyone just yet. Not that she didn't trust Dr. Spears: she did. But Jack was really the only one who knew what kind of software she had, and just how much information on someone she was able to acquire. She didn't think the ME needed to know that. And knowing Dr. Spears, he was probably just as happy not to.

Chapter Eleven

Gracie kept reading. At the bottom of the page was a diagram of human teeth. Notes alongside it explained fillings, crowns and a bridge that had been part of Richard Dawes' dental history.

On the next page of the report was a copy of the x ray of the corpse's teeth.

Gracie flipped from the x ray back to the diagram, then back again. Her frown deepened.

"The teeth aren't the same," she told Spears, who smiled widely in reply.

"No, they are not," he said, sounding quite jubilant, like a professor whose bright student had just made a great deduction.

"The body on that table," Gracie pointed, "is missing several back teeth and doesn't have any bridges or crowns."

Spears nodded, and then walked towards the autopsy table. He beckoned Gracie over, and folded the tarp down to expose the corpse's head.

It didn't look too strange, Gracie thought, except it was kind of greyish in color. You could barely see the incision where Spears had reflected the skin to expose the skull. The bullet hole looked almost fake, as though it had been done for a film, with latex and paint, by some skilled cosmetologist.

"This body," Spears began conversationally as he donned a pair of green latex gloves the color of pond scum, "also has severe decay in several teeth and advanced gingivitis," he told Gracie. Deftly, he lifted one of the body's lips and exposed the upper row of teeth: Gracie could see what Spears meant. Many of the teeth looked rotten, and all were blackened near the gum line.

Her nose wrinkled involuntarily, not so much at the smell of decay and decomp, which by now was very faint, but at the unsightliness of the teeth and the lifestyle it indicated.

"This decay is consistent with drug use," Spears said, closing the body's mouth and replacing the tarp. "I will spare you the sight, but the back teeth that are left are ground down severely," Spears explained. "Far more than would be normal in a man of 45," he added.

"And the decay: don't drugs cause dry mouth?" Gracie asked.

Spears nodded. "Yes, and the lack of saliva, and probably poor dental hygiene, encouraged the growth of bacteria, causing decay. Also, addicts usually crave sweet foods, so--"

Gracie nodded. "I see. But--how could Dawes' body have no bridges or crowns when his dental records show that he did?" she asked, lifting the autopsy report in her right hand again.

Spears only smiled slightly and raised his eyebrows. "Well, the answer to that is simple, although it then poses many more questions," he replied cryptically. "And to answer your next question, yes, we did take the victim's fingerprints."

"And?"

"Well, Dawes had been fingerprinted when he started working for one of the trucking firms, as a routine matter," Spears began.

They moved back towards the ME's desk.

Gracie nodded that she understood.

"The fingerprints on file for Dawes and the fingerprints of this victim do not match," Spears told her. "We'll run these fingerprints," and here he indicated the body on the table, "through AFIS to see if we can get an ID. But the long and short of it, Gracie, is, that the body on this table is not that of Richard Dawes."

Gracie had intended to visit the Dawes residence after lunch. When she had presumed Richard Dawes was dead, she had hoped to speak to his widow, Amy, particularly since when she'd asked Jack if he'd interviewed Amy, Jack hadn't given a response.

Now, having learned from Dr. Spears that the body in the park was not that of Richard Dawes, Gracie thought it would be interesting to see what the man himself had to say about his wallet turning up in someone else's pockets, and a dead someone, at that. She hoped he and his wife Amy would both be available, as she also wanted to find out if they had used their credit card, or if it had been used by someone else. In the latter case, Gracie's money was on whoever had killed the man in the park and planted Dawes' ID on him. Maybe Dawes, for some reason, didn't keep all his cards in his wallet and when he discovered it missing, as he surely must have over the weekend, he'd used the one card he still had?

Gracie planned to include anything she discovered at the Dawes residence in her article, which she still intended to have in by that evening's deadline.

A copy of the fingerprints of the corpse had been stapled to the end of the autopsy report. Gracie would run these through her own fingerprint matching software once she got home.

Although she didn't ask Dr. Spears, she assumed that Jack had been apprised of the same information regarding the corpse and Dawes, and thought the county's Chief Detective was likely running the 'John Doe's' prints through their own programs, too.

She didn't have time to stop for lunch as she'd planned, so she decided to call her friend Anne, and make a date for lunch for the following day. Meanwhile, she snacked on one of the granola bars that she always kept in her Jeep, and her trusty bottle of water. She noted happily that the thunderstorm of that morning had blown by, and she drove quickly to Hinsdale where the Daweses lived. According to her GPS, their house was on South Street, opposite one end of a big trucking depot. She found it with little problem, parked at the curb, and approached the front door via the large wrap around porch.

Puddles from the morning's rain festooned the concrete pavement leading to the porch, but under the overhang it was relatively dry.

Gracie rang the doorbell and listened to it echo inside the house. Then she knocked on the door with the knuckles of one hand.

Nothing. That was peculiar, she thought.

Frustrated, Gracie tiptoed around to one side of the porch and peered along the side of the house: a few medium sized clay pots stood in a neat row next to the porch rail, and several large plastic totes with small flap-covered holes in their sides were lined up against the house across from them. Some empty mismatched bowls beyond the totes spoke of a small colony of outdoor, possibly feral, cats, although Gracie saw no sign of the felines themselves. Probably still under whatever cover they had sought during the thunderstorm.

The other side of the porch was bare, and Gracie, with a quick look around, ventured quietly along the grey painted boards to the rear of the house. Steps led down to a small yard of grass with a few low maintenance shrubs and a large stand of tree rhododendrons that probably marked the property line. The back door of the house lay to her right: the nine-paned window was festooned with draped yellow curtains above a cross buck style panel. Gracie tiptoed over the worn black rubber mat that read, 'WELCOME' and glanced inside.

"They're not there," came an informative voice from somewhere behind her, and Gracie jumped. She turned, searching for the source of the voice.

Chapter Twelve

"Hello?" Gracie ventured, and noted with annoyance that her voice came out a bit squeaky.

"Took off Saturday afternoon," the disembodied voice continued, and as Gracie scanned the large rhododendron bushes that flanked the side of the porch her eyes caught a wink of reflected light.

"You saw them leave?" Gracie asked as she walked back along the rear of the house to the side, and towards that spot of winking light. She tried to avoid the puddles.

"Ayuh. Packed up the van and were gone," the voice replied, sounding cheerful.

Gracie wasn't sure why.

"Erm--can I come talk to you, then?" she asked, apparently, a large rhododendron whose buds were just starting to edge out in color. This one would be bright pink. Rain drops still glistened on its leaves.

"Certainly--come around the side of the hedge," the voice instructed. As Gracie complied, the voice continued. "You with the police?" It sounded eager and Gracie hated to disappoint whoever was addressing her.

"Erm--no, I'm with the *Intelligencer*. I'm Gracie Barufaldi, the news reporter for Berksh--"

The voice cut off her introduction as Gracie rounded the edge of the line of *ericaciae* that abutted the sidewalk at a ninety degree angle.

"Even better!" declared the voice's owner: a wiry human in khaki trousers, a bush jacket and a safari hat whose strap dangled down against a chest so flat Gracie couldn't tell the gender of the person. A pair of extremely large binoculars was grasped in one unguiculated hand, and a bright smile from obviously false and slightly overlarge dentures greeted her.

"Oh!" Gracie exclaimed, as the person took three quick steps in its hiking boots and extended a hand.

"Agnes Davis," the person said as Gracie took the proffered hand and shook it.

"Good to meet you," Gracie replied. It was a woman! Hard to tell given the unisex clothing and the woman's slender frame.

"Police were here Monday afternoon, and again early this morning, but they left," Agnes told Gracie. She sounded disappointed.

Gracie wondered what police that could have been, since Jack was in Boston this day. No doubt he'd come Monday, though, after the body that had been presumed to have been Dawes had been found. Maybe that's when he'd discovered that the Daweses had left and maybe, Gracie thought now, that was why he'd avoided her question the previous night.

"The police may be back to canvass the neighborhood," Gracie reassured Agnes now, and looked, as she did so, at the other neighboring homes. Agnes' house was the only one really near the Dawes home, and apparently, had the best view.

"See a lot with those?" Gracie asked with a grin, gesturing to the large binoculars.

"Ayuh, I do," Agnes agreed cheerily. "It pays to watch yer neighbors," she went on, glancing up at Gracie and shading her eyes against the watery spring sun as she did. Gracie was at least a foot taller than Agnes.

Gracie just smiled as she could think of no rejoinder, and was about to ask Agnes if she knew anything of interest about the Dawes family, when her informant beckoned with a knobbly finger and turned to enter her home's front door.

"Come in and have some tea. Or coffee. I'll tell you what I know about Dick and Amy," she added enticingly, so Gracie followed.

The flick of a long striped tail as she and Agnes set foot on that home's porch prompted Gracie to ask, "is there a feral cat colony here?"

"Ayuh," Agnes replied in the affirmative as she opened the front door and ushered Gracie through it. "Amy fed 'em, even had 'em neutered when she could catch 'em," she continued. "Since they left, I've inherited the job, I guess," she added, sounding slightly aggrieved. Paradoxically, she appeared happy to be aggrieved.

The interior of Agnes Davis' home resembled a research library: books marched in floor to ceiling shelving in the main rooms, periodicals and newspapers were neatly stacked on tables and atop filing cabinets that Gracie suspected held more of the same. A large desk top computer with an oversize screen adorned the living room's coffee table and a flat screen TV graced one corner. It seemed clear to Gracie that Agnes had been a researcher her whole life, and had embraced recent technology with a passion: a wi fi router glowed a steady green from a spot on one shelf.

The orderliness of the rooms was offset by the presence of four beautiful cats who lounged in various states of languor in sunny windowsills and comfortable looking chairs.

"Oh! What gorgeous cats!" Gracie exclaimed, and took a few steps so she could pet the cat nearest her. It was a long haired creature with deep grey fur and bright green eyes; it accepted a head scritch with friendly curiosity.

"Thanks! That one's Roquefort," Agnes said with a grin. In turn, she pointed to the other three. "The mostly white one in the window is Brie, that orange layabout is Cheddar, and the little Siamese is Sakura," Agnes informed her. Gracie spotted the latter curled in a tight ball atop a carpeted cat condo in a splotch of weak sun.

"Interesting names," Gracie offered as she followed Agnes to the kitchen at the rear of the house.

Agnes shrugged, but smiled. "I like cheese. And so do they!" she declared by way of justification. "I'm not sure they're delighted about sharing their food with the strays," Agnes went on, with a gesture out to the Dawes home and the cat shelters on its porch. Gracie saw a couple of cats of various breeds emerging from their shelters, now that the storm had passed. "And I'm not thrilled that Amy just up and left without giving a thought to those poor ferals."

"Mmmm...maybe she knew you'd take over feeding them," Gracie suggested. She was standing just inside the kitchen doorway: more books, mostly on gardening and cooking, were on long shelves that decorated the walls.

"Maybe. But she could have asked," Agnes retorted smartly.

"How long have you lived here?" Gracie asked then, as her hostess indicated she should sit at the white formica topped kitchen table. Agnes shifted a small rolodex and a neat pile of hand written documents, and put a pale green fabric placemat with brightly colored birds stitched onto it in front of Gracie. A spoon soon followed, and then Agnes answered her as she busied herself at the counter top.

"Did you say tea? Or coffee?"

"Actually, coffee if it's strong," Gracie answered truthfully.

Agnes chuckled. "Oh, it'll be strong," she answered. Then: "I was born in this house, lived here all my life," she said. Preparations for their coffee underway, Agnes turned, and removed her safari hat, then shrugged out of her bush jacket. She hung both on hooks just inside her back door; a well worn walking stick hung on yet another hook by a rawhide wrist strap. Agnes' grey and white hair was bluntly cut in a short, careless pixie style: Gracie would bet Agnes chopped her locks herself and subconsciously touched the waterfall of brown curls that brushed her shoulders.

"Dick and Amy bought that house ten years ago, just before their boy was born," Agnes told Gracie as she toed off her hiking boots to reveal thick grey wool socks.

Gracie nodded.

"Before them was some kind of house of ill repute," Agnes said, and for a moment, Gracie was confused. Then she understood what Agnes meant.

"A brothel?" Gracie asked, surprised. "Here?" It was a predominantly residential neighborhood, squarely middle class. Gracie wouldn't have located a brothel there. Then again, hiding in plain sight, perhaps? She wondered for a moment how long the trucking company had been across the road, and if that had had any influence on the brothel's location. In any case, it had been before she'd moved to the area and started covering news for the *Intelligencer.*

Agnes was nodding her head. "A high class operation," she continued. "The girls didn't come here," she explained, "the house was their main office, I guess you could say. They'd show up to get their pay, or sometimes for other things, like meetings. But all the-- ah--business was transacted elsewhere."

"Oho, so they were call girls!" Gracie deduced. "Escorts. And that house was where their Madam or pimp lived?"

The electric kettle boiled and shut off, and Agnes padded over to pour boiling water into two cups that already held generous spoonfuls of freeze dried coffee crystals. "Exactly right," Agnes confirmed. "When she was found out, they arrested her, seized her assets, and sold that house off for a song to pay back taxes and debts," Agnes revealed. "That's how Dick and Amy could afford it," she added, bringing the two mugs over to the table and setting them down. "Sugar or milk?" she asked Gracie.

"No, I'll have it black," Gracie replied with a smile.

Agnes settled herself at her own place, signified by a matching bird festooned placemat at the other end of the small white oblong table.

"Girl after my own heart," Agnes murmured approvingly. She lifted her mug in a salute and winked at Gracie from behind octagonal rimless glasses. "Bottom's up," she instructed, and took a deep draught of the dark brew.

Gracie sipped, found the coffee was indeed quite strong and had the usual slight saltiness of instant.

"Before that, a nice family lived there for decades: had kids my own age," Agnes revealed, and now she sounded wistful. "But we all grew up, and the kids moved on, and the parents died..."

"Mr. Dawes was an over the road truck driver," Gracie said then, bringing the conversation back on topic. It was a statement, but the tone of her voice invited Agnes to correct her if need be.

But her elderly informant nodded in agreement. "That's right!" She paused. "You surely do your homework," she commended Gracie, fixing her with an assessing stare. "I read your paper," she added, and smiled. "Always accurate, and always complete."

"Thank you!" Gracie replied, pleased. Even though most people liked the *Intelligencer*, it was still great to hear positive feedback. And especially now, given the debacle over the prison drug article.

"And his wife, Amy, worked at the Pittsfield Area Elementary School as a teacher's aide," Agnes said, returning to the Daweses.

Gracie knew that, so she just nodded companionably. "Did you ever notice anything, well, anything weird over there?" Gracie asked next, jutting her chin in the general direction of the Dawes home next door.

Agnes shook her head, then tipped it to one side and shrugged. "No, they were a pretty normal family, from what I could tell," she admitted, sounding as though she wished there were more she could say. "They didn't go out much, and they didn't have many visitors." She paused. "His uncle came visiting a few times," she said. "Nice man. Took the kids fishing."

"But nothing out of the ordinary?" Gracie pursued.

"Not until last week," she answered.

"What happened last week?" Gracie asked, trying to mask her eagerness.

Chapter Thirteen

Agnes explained that although the Daweses had occasionally had loud fights--loud enough for her to hear, and see, she admitted unashamedly--the previous week they had fought nearly every morning and every night. And there had seemed to be a lot of running around both inside the house and outside.

Gracie's new friend and informant cheerily explained that her upstairs bathroom afforded a clear view over the tall rhododendron hedge into the Dawes house, and as the family had eschewed all but the flimsiest of sheer curtains, Agnes had been able to see as well as hear whenever curiosity prompted.

Richard Dawes had worked an unpredictable schedule, at least in Agnes' view: he'd be gone for two or three days, then home for a couple, then gone again, in any given week. He usually slept during the day, as well, which Agnes thought peculiar until she told Gracie she'd researched over the road truckers and discovered that they preferred driving at night when there was less traffic and they could make better time.

Amy, on the other hand, was quite predictable, according to Agnes: she got the children and herself ready each day and then drove them to the Elementary School where she also worked. They all returned around 3 p.m. and the children would do homework or play outside until dinner time. Then it was more homework, or maybe television, until bed time.

The previous week, the schedule hadn't altered much, except for the increase in altercations. Agnes had noticed, however, that Amy had been unusually active during the afternoons and evenings, and said that she'd seen the woman load several suitcases, large totes and big cardboard boxes inside the beige van she generally drove.

Gracie took down the year, make and model of the van, which of course, Agnes could provide her with. "What about Richard Dawes," Gracie asked. "What did he drive?"

Agnes shrugged. "A pickup: dark green," she said informatively, and added the make and model and a good guess as to the year.

Gracie wrote the information again.

"And that activity was unusual, right?" Gracie asked Agnes.

The woman nodded. "Very. Amy doesn't generally carry much in that van besides herself and her kids and maybe some sports stuff if the kids have a game, or something," she explained. "I thought they must be getting ready to go on vacation."

"Did you ask them if they were?

Agnes shrugged. "I made a comment on Thursday when Amy and I were both out at the curb at the same time, collecting our emptied trash cans," she replied. "I said, 'looks like you're going on a trip,' to Amy, and she just gave me a strange look and told me she'd just been cleaning out the attic and was going to take some things to Goodwill."

Gracie frowned. "Did you believe her?"

Agnes shrugged again. "I had no reason not to, did I?" She paused. "That is, until she and the children took off and didn't return."

"She and the children?" Gracie parroted. "What about Richard Dawes?"

"Mmmm—haven't seen him since Friday, come to think of it," Agnes amended. "He left Friday evening, and I figured he was heading out on another job."

"Well, no reason to think he didn't," Gracie returned in a mollifying tone. "Now, Amy and the children left—you said that was Saturday?" Gracie checked.

Agnes nodded. "In the afternoon. About three o'clock, I think. I waited until Monday to start feeding the ferals," she added, sounding aggrieved. "I always like anyone who likes cats," she told Gracie, then, sounding as though she had to explain herself. "Amy seemed devoted to the small colony of ferals," Agnes had added.

"Seemed?" Gracie queried.

"Well, she abandoned them, didn't she? Without so much as a by your leave," Agnes responded tartly. "She could have taken them to the shelter, at the very least, not leave them to starve. She had no way of knowing I'd take over," Agnes put in firmly.

Gracie smiled, then took a sip of her coffee. The house was silent for a long minute.

"So, you 'researched' over the road trucking?" Gracie asked her informant, then, echoing her use of the particular verb.

Agnes nodded. "I did. This internet makes everything so easy. I wish the kids in school realized that: in my day, we had to research everything in books, in the library stacks!" she exclaimed.

"What's your degree in?" Gracie asked, hazarding a guess that Agnes was a college graduate.

"Library Science," Agnes replied with a chuckle. "Can't you tell?" she added with a grin and a gesture to the books.

Gracie had to hurry back home to have enough time to write her article and file it before the deadline for Friday's paper. She sent an alert to her editor to let him know that she was working on it, but that it would probably come in just under the wire, and got her notes out to begin.

Before she started writing, however, she scanned the fingerprints of the dead body in Spears' morgue into her own fingerprint ID software and launched a match search. She was only half way through her article when her computer 'pinged' to let her know the search was complete and a match for the fingerprints had been found: the prints belonged to a Ryan Colletti of Chicopee.

So--who was Ryan Colletti, Gracie wondered, and why had his body been found with Richard Dawes' wallet and ID? Gracie launched a background search on him. She had just begun to read the first page of the report as it populated her screen when her phone vibrated in her hoodie pocket.

She ignored it, and continued to read. Colletti was 42, had 'form' as her detective friend David in England would say, or 'a record' as was said in the U.S., and had been out of prison for about a year. He had convictions on several drug related crimes and a couple of robbery/burglary type incidents. The mug shot of Colletti matched, more or less, the face of the man Gracie had seen on Spears' autopsy table.

Frowning again, Gracie tapped a few keys on the laptop. Searching public records, she found Richard Dawes, and a few more clicks brought her to a photograph of the man. It was two years old, and had run in her very own paper of all places, when Dawes had been involved in a crash at a bridge in Franklin County. Apparently Dawes had been driving on a road that wasn't permitted for truck traffic. His violation, which he had clearly hoped would provide a short cut and would go unnoticed, had meant an inability to steer properly, and his rig had smashed into a bridge abutment on a hair pin turn. The fine had been more than $10,000 and although the company Dawes had been driving for had paid, Dawes' employee record had been besmirched with a reprimand and a percentage penalty of the fine.

Dawes had left that employer shortly after the incident, Gracie noted.

But it was the photograph more than the details of the crash that interested her. She pulled up Colletti's mug shot and put it along side that of Dawes. Close, she thought, regarding the two faces thoughtfully. They could be brothers.

Curious, she launched another high tech program she enjoyed owning and rarely got to use: facial recognition and comparison. It examined things like relative width between eyes, nose and mouth, forehead, cheekbones, etc. and could give a correspondence rating between two photographs. A rating of 20 meant the two faces were for all intents and purposes identical. 10 or below meant they were different people. Between 10 and 20 the probability increased that the persons in the photographs were related somehow and the closer one got to 20 the more likely it was that the photos were actually of the same person, although time and the camera angle could produce a score less than identical.

Colletti and Dawes scored a 16. Hmmm, Gracie thought. So--close. Not the same person, of course, but possibly related.

Her iPhone buzzed again. "Oh, all right, all right," Gracie chastised her device as she took it out of her pocket and gazed at the screen.

It it was David, calling from England. The missed call had been from Jack.

"Good evening!" Gracie said cheerfully to David as she touched the 'answer' button on her phone.

"Aye, Good Afternoon to you, mo duinne," David's voice came, warm and strong and reassuring across the miles.

After the pleasantries were exchanged, David caught Gracie up on his progress with the murder case she'd been involved in during her holiday in England.

Then he asked what she was working on, and she told him about the corpse in the park, as she called it.

"And they look alike, do they?" David asked, mulling over the facts Gracie had just presented, ending with the facial comparison.

"Remarkably so," Gracie affirmed. "I haven't found any relationship yet, I mean, I don't think they're cousins or anything," she explained."And I only have an hour to write my article before deadline, so I don't think I'll have enough time to do any more digging before I file it," she added, sounding regretful.

"Och, I don't know that it would even matter, Gracie, if they were related, would it now?" David queried. "Except as a detail, you know."

"It wouldn't?" Gracie frowned at her phone. What did he mean? She thought it would be important if she discovered that the dead man and the man whose ID he'd carried were somehow related.

"Aye, it doesna matter how they are related, or even if they are," David insisted. "Hundreds of people look like others," he went on. He pronounced 'look' as 'luick' and Gracie smiled. "And they're no more related than I am to you," David explained.

"That's true," Gracie admitted. She had always heard that everyone had a 'twin' somewhere in the world. "So you think the fact that they look alike is more important than whether they're related?" she asked.

"Aye. Ye might look for other types of relationships, though, Gracie: I mean, did the two men ('tew mayn') work together? Did they know each other?" David continued.

Gracie found that she'd missed hearing his voice in the few days they'd been apart. Even though they had texted each other, it wasn't the same. She smiled again.

"I'll see if I can find that out," she told David. "Thank you."

After a few more minutes of less business-like discussion, Gracie and David ended the call with plans to talk every couple of days and smiles on both their faces.

Sighing, Gracie returned to her computer. She missed David, but she was also glad to be 3000 miles away from him, at least for now. Although he clearly had wanted a relationship, she wasn't ready to begin one. Still smarting from the breakup with Ben and its disappointment, Gracie felt that she deserved--and needed--a good long time alone without any special man in her life. Work, friends, and her house and gardens should be enough for her for a while.

And then? Well, when she felt ready, she knew either things would progress with David, or they would each find happiness on separate paths.

Chapter Fourteen

Gracie's fingers flew as she typed her story on the body in the arboretum. Her headline read, 'Body of Ex-Con Found with Local Trucker's ID: Foul Play Suspected.' The article began with the identification of the corpse's fingerprints as Colletti's, then summarized the discovery of the body and Spears' autopsy findings. Her piece ended with the apparent disappearance of the Dawes family, supported by information gleaned from both the school where Amy worked and the trucking firm where her husband was employed.

A fast call to each as she had been getting ready to type had told Gracie that Amy had left work at the school on Friday without indicating that she would not return. Richard had been scheduled off on Friday, but had failed to report on Saturday night for his shift. And of course, come Monday, Amy had not arrived at the school for her job, and the children had not been seen, either. A message left on voicemail in the Superintendent's office related that Amy had gone out of town to care for an ailing mother; no details about when she might return had been given.

The article was emailed in to the paper with ten minutes to spare, so Gracie decided she had earned a glass of wine: 'Glass Slipper' was a seyval and red raspberry based creation from Sarah and Steve's winery that would be perfect as an aperitif while she tossed together a late dinner.

Before she started cooking, she launched a deep background program that would analyze both Richard and Amy Dawes as well as Ryan Colletti. The program would find points of comparison and similarities and provide more than just employment and credit history for the strangely connected trio: it should also give Gracie family backgrounds, census information, residential history, educational history and even what leisure activities had been enjoyed by the subjects, if they were traceable. Membership in clubs, for example, would pop up with this 'super search' software, even clubs as mundane and harmless as model airplane groups or church social organizations. The program would also identify mobile phones owned by the people in question; a different software program could trace calls to and from the phones, once Gracie had the numbers.

The greatest value of the program, Gracie thought, was its ability to contrast and compare, and link similarities in all the profiles searched. Gracie figured it would take an hour or more to run.

While the whole grain orecchetti were boiling and Gracie was chopping a small head of broccoli, she heard the distinctive alert tone that meant an email had arrived on her iPhone. She checked it, and saw that her editor had put her article on the body in the arboretum up on line already, with a news bulletin email to all subscribers. He'd added a note, 'good job!' and Gracie smiled.

Her success with this story didn't make up for the unpleasantness over the article about the drug bust at the jail, but it did help.

While her computer was churning away, Gracie enjoyed a quiet dinner at her barn board kitchen table with another glass of the distinctive wine in lieu of dessert.

After dinner, Gracie washed up her dishes, made sure Pumpkin had water and kibble, and went to check on the computer report: it was ready.

No familial relationship had been found between Dawes and Colletti. Well, that was fine, she thought, studying the findings. In light of David's suggestion, Gracie dismissed her initial hunch that the two men were relatives of some kind, and began to look for other connections. She took her laptop into the Oak Room, switched on the overhead track lights and one Tiffany table lamp with stained glass cats around its rim, and settled down on the chocolate colored leather sofa to compare Dawes' work history with Colletti's history.

Several minutes passed while she scanned the two lists, side by side on her computer screen, looking for anything that might have brought the two men together. Then, just as something caught her eye, her phone buzzed again.

"Aaaargh!" Gracie muttered, fumbling for her phone in her hoodie pocket. "Yes, Jack," she answered abruptly.

"Well, hello to you too," Jack drawled sarcastically.

"Oh, okay then I'll answer the way you always do," Gracie shot back: "Barufaldi."

"Draper."

There was a stiff silence for two seconds. Then:

"I read your article," Jack said. He sounded as though he were talking through clenched teeth. Maybe he was.

"That was fast," Gracie said. But she was really pleased. Did Jack have his phone set up so that it alerted him if a news bulletin went out from her paper? She wondered. He must. Either that, or he must check the *Intelligencer* website with remarkable frequency.

But she knew what was coming, and couldn't wait to remind Jack that she had many resources, and need not depend exclusively on him for information.

Jack sighed. "You saw the autopsy report," he said: a statement, not a question.

"More than that, I saw the body," Gracie couldn't help crowing. Well, Dr. Spears had a right to show the body to anyone he wanted, particularly after the autopsy had been performed.

"How did you come up with Colletti's name?" Jack queried, sounding grumpy.

Gracie explained quickly about the fingerprint software she owned.

Jack made an unintelligible noise from the other end of the phone connection.

"How was Boston? Find anything?" Gracie asked cheerfully, switching topics.

Jack sighed and for a moment Gracie felt sympathy for him: it wasn't an easy job, she knew, being a Detective. Particularly when you weren't finding any evidence to help you sole the crime.

"No, not really, nothing," came his reluctant reply. He detailed the interviews of Jesperson's staff, and the search of his office and Commonwealth Avenue 'pied à terre,' as Gracie put it, and repeated that they hadn't found any concrete evidence.

"How about not concrete evidence?" Gracie pursued, settling herself more comfortably on the sofa and inviting Pumpkin, who had strolled into the Oak Room, up on her lap.

"How do you mean?" Jack returned, sounding wary.

"Well, you said, 'not really' and then you said, 'nothing concrete' and I was wondering if, well, you know, your 'spidey sense' had picked up on something, erm, indefinite?" she elaborated.

There was a heartbeat of silence. Then: "well, it's not really anything, or at least nothing to do with the senator's death," Jack began. "I don't think," he qualified.

"What isn't?"

Jack explained that while he was chatting with the officers from Boston P.D. who were joining with him on executing the search warrants, one of the officers, a Detective Geene, had made a couple of comments that Jack took to mean that the senator wasn't especially well liked in the Department. When Jack had asked why, the Detective had revealed, 'off the record' of course, that the Boston P.D. had been asked, over the years, by one of the local magistrates to dismiss some 'indiscretions' on the part of the senator.

"Indiscretions?" Gracie repeated. "Like what, did the Detective say?"

Jack answered that, after a few more reassurances of confidentiality, the Detective had revealed that twice within the past 18 months the senator had been involved in a drunk driving accident. The first time, he had plowed his Cadillac SUV into the brick wall that divided his Commonwealth Avenue townhouse from the one next door. Since the damage had been to his own property, Jesperson had asked the magistrate to drop the charges. "They would have been DUI, certainly, and probably misdemeanors for damaging property," Jack explained.

"Who's the magistrate, did Detective Geene say?" Gracie queried.

"District Judge LeBron," Jack replied. "Why?"

Gracie made a murmuring noise, and with her free hand googled the magistrate on her laptop. "Carry on—you said 'the first time', what was the second coverup?" she asked, intrigued.

Jack continued, recounting that the second incident had involved the senator crashing into a parked police vehicle. "It was unoccupied, thank god, or I don't think the judge would have been able to overlook it. The car had been parked at the corner of Boyleston and Arlington streets, downtown, as a deterrent to speeders during the late night hours."

"Oh, I know where that is," Gracie replied brightly. "That's where the Hermès boutique is." Gracie collected the hand printed silk scarves and had turned a few of her more discerning friends on to them, too. She paused. "You said late night?"

"Yeah—both incidents happened around one or one thirty in the morning," Jack answered.

"Hmmm..closing time for the bars," Gracie suggested.

"Yes."

"Was the cruiser damaged?" Gracie pursued.

"Yes," Jack replied. "The driver's side door and the left front quarter panel, from what Geene told me. And the senator paid for it to be repaired, and then finagled some grant money for the Boston PD to acquire a couple new cruisers," he continued, sounding frustrated.

"Hush money," Gracie suggested again, in a tone that wasn't a question.

"Right, well, yeah, it seems like it."

"I wonder—Jack, have you ever heard of anything like that being done around here?" Gracie queried. "I mean, if the Senator likes to go out drinking when he's in Boston, maybe he likes to do that here at home," she offered.

"You have a point, and that thought crossed my mind, too, Gracie, but as far as I can remember, nothing like that has happened. At least not in Berkshire County. Not that I ever heard."

Gracie knew that Jack had been the Pittsfield Police Chief before becoming Berkshire County Detective: he'd been the Chief when they'd first met, a few years before. Prior to that, he'd been a Pittsfield PD Officer. So it made sense that he would know of any incidents, or coverups, involving the Senator.

After a few more exchanges that focused on the Dawes-Colletti case, Gracie and Jack hung up and Gracie almost immediately called her friend Anne. Asking if she were free the following day for lunch, Gracie fixed a date with her friend, and then returned to her laptop's findings on Dawes and Colletti.

What had piqued her interest just before Jack's call had come through had been a couple of addresses that had cropped up in her reports. Colletti's home address was listed as 'Milk Pail Lane' in Hinsdale, which was very near the trucking depot where Dawes worked, and also close to the Daweses' home. Of course, that didn't mean anything necessarily, but Gracie had a hunch the proximity of the addresses might be important. And sometimes, a hunch was enough.

The mobile phone records had shown no suspicious calls made by Richard or Amy Dawes, just the usual between the two spouses, an occasional one to the school or the trucking firm, and some to an address in a far northwestern part of the county a few miles west of Williamstown, on Berlin Road. When Gracie googled that, she discovered it was where a Lana Frisvold lived; given the fact that Amy Dawes' birth name was Frisvold, Gracie drew the logical conclusion that Lana Frisvold was Amy Dawes' mother. The theory fit what the school had told her, too, that Amy had left a message saying she was going to help out her ailing mother.

It appeared from the report that Ryan Colletti had not had a mobile phone, and Gracie had been disappointed. However, given his criminal history and the fact that she had been unable to find any current employment history, she supposed that Colletti might not have been able to afford even a cheap pay-as-you-go flip phone. Or maybe his lifestyle, whatever that had been, hadn't required one.

Chapter Fifteen

Gracie worked on her laptop for a couple more hours Wednesday night, trying to access traffic camera logs for the location of the gas station and convenience store where Richard Dawes' credit card had been used early Monday morning. The site of the gas station fit in, now that she had uncovered the fact that Amy Dawes' mother lived just a couple miles away.

Would the couple and their children have fled to Amy's mother's house? It seemed likely. Not very bright, perhaps, since it was a sure bet the police would check with any relatives of the family once their disappearance had been confirmed.

Had Jack already gone out to Mrs. Frisvold's Berlin Road residence to ask if she knew where her daughter and son in law and grandchildren were? Or to see if they were there? He hadn't mentioned it, but then again, Gracie hadn't told him that she'd discovered the use of one of Dawes' credit cards. Maybe each of them was holding back, a little.

After some finagling, Gracie was able to pull up the traffic cam data from the previous Monday morning. She limited her search to the fifteen minutes before the credit card swipe and the fifteen minutes after, and was rewarded when the dim, grainy traffic camera footage showed a medium colored Ford Windstar van approaching the intersection from the west, and turning left into the gas station's lot. The van matched the description of Amy Dawes' van that Alice Davis had given Gracie. Coupled with the use of the credit card, Gracie was quite sure that Amy Dawes and very likely her children had been in the Williamstown area.

She would have said that Richard Dawes might be there, too, except for the two million dollar insurance policy: that, coupled with the fact that Dawes' ID had been found on a man who wasn't Dawes, suggested to Gracie's agile mind that the trucker had attempted to fake his own death, substituting Colletti's body for his own and putting his ID on Colletti's corpse. That way, Gracie theorized, Amy Dawes could collect on the insurance money once 'Dawes' had been found and declared dead.

Or at least, that might have been Richard Dawes' plan. It was a flawed plan, Gracie considered Wednesday as she shut her laptop and went upstairs to get ready for bed. Had Dawes believed that a shooting death wouldn't be investigated? And why move the body? Why not stage it as a suicide in situ?

Too many questions, she decided as she slipped into her comfy queen sized bed and stretched out against the Frette sheets. It was still chilly in the evenings, even though it was May, and she snuggled under the cozy duvet. Pumpkin hopped lightly up and curled up in her usual spot next to Gracie.

She would take a drive out to Colletti's residence on Milk Pail Lane the next morning, Gracie decided sleepily as she drifted to slumber. She'd visited the Daweses' home, might as well visit Colletti's, too, and see what she could find out.

The next morning after an early breakfast, Gracie input 'Milk Pail Lane' into her Jeep's GPS and rolled out of her driveway. She drove south, skirting the town center of Pittsfield despite the GPS' advice to drive through the town, and continued on Route 8 until she came to Hinsdale. Route 8 now became Main Street, then River Road, and then South Street. She passed the town treasurer's office on her left, and then the Dawes residence on her right.

The trucking depot was now to her left as the road widened and became less residential. The depot occupied a large flat area with a big hangar like building in the distance. Several semi trailers were going in and out of the depot, Gracie saw: a service road that was unnamed on the GPS was apparently the main access point for the depot.

'In point four miles, turn left onto Buttermilk Road,' her GPS' calm female voice advised her.

Gracie turned. Buttermilk Road was mostly forested on both sides, with the occasional residence. She arrived at Route 143, aka Maple Street, and turned right as the GPS advised, and a few yards on turned right again, onto Creamery Road, again as her GPS told her to.

More deciduous forest lined both sides of the roadway: the branches were just starting to leaf out and the morning sunshine gave the tree tops a light greenish haze effect that Gracie thought was quite pretty.

'In 395 yards turn right onto Milk Pail Lane,' the GPS instructed.

"How am I supposed to judge when I've gone 395 yards?" Gracie retorted with a shake of her head. GPS systems were great, but sometimes they expected the driver to be as robotically precise as they were.

She noticed a dirt road leading off to the right, and turned in. This had to be Milk Pail Lane, though there was no sign. However, her GPS gave its customary approving double beep, so she knew she was correct.

The road curved around, leading back into the woods for about a half mile. It was rutted from winter snow and spring rains, and Gracie was once again thankful for a four wheel drive vehicle. The roadway branched off, appearing to circumvent a cleared area up ahead, but Gracie stayed on the main path and shortly arrived at a large open space.

'You have arrived at your destination, and your GPS guidance is now concluded,' her GPS' automated female voice told her. Gracie thought it sounded quite pleased with itself, but she didn't share the emotion: she had 'arrived' at what looked like a metal dump. The open area was full of piles of aluminum cans, heaps of scrap metal and a few junked cars.

"This is my destination?" Gracie murmured. Then she spied a rickety looking trailer half hidden by a large conical pile of cans. The trailer had cinder block steps leading up to a front door whose storm door had been repaired with duct tape. Wooden panels covered portions of some of the windows. A couple of metal trash cans were chained together next to the trailer, but they had been tipped over and uncovered, and refuse spilled out onto the packed dirt clearing. Bales of various types of paper were strewn about near the trailer as well.

This must be Colletti's residence, Gracie thought as she switched off her Jeep's engine. Maybe Colletti had been involved in some kind of recycling business, Gracie thought: although the background report hadn't listed an occupation, maybe Colletti collected metal and other recyclables and brought them in for cash. Maybe that's how he made a living, she thought, although Gracie wasn't entirely convinced Colletti had completely abandoned his previous habit of petty thievery and similar crimes.

The background report had also listed a 1989 pickup truck as Colletti's vehicle, and Gracie thought she saw a maroon vehicle matching that description parked at the far side of the trailer.

She exited the Jeep, shut the door, and began walking cautiously ahead: the entire place appeared deserted, but it paid to be careful. In the pocket of her jacket, she fingered the small can of pepper spray, just in case.

"Gracie what the hell are you doing here?" came a voice from behind the trailer, just beyond the old pickup truck. Seconds later, Jack emerged and walked towards Gracie, holstering his gun as he did so. He was frowning, and his lips were compressed into a tight line.

"Were you going to shoot me?" she asked, joking to cover her surprise. Darn it, he'd beat her to it.

He shook his head. Although Gracie couldn't see his eyes behind his sunglasses, she knew they were stormy; he was clad in his black leather jacket and jeans, with sneakers. He snapped his holster secure and as he re-positioned his jacket, Gracie could see his Detective's badge affixed to his belt.

"I wasn't sure who had driven up," Jack replied a moment later. He still was frowning. "Then I recognized your Jeep, and you jumped out and started wandering around without a care in the world," he admonished.

"I did not!" Gracie returned hotly. "I was very cautious, I wasn't 'wandering,' I was walking slowly, and I have this," she replied, brandishing the small aerosol of pepper spray.

Jack made a face. "Yah, right: fat lot of good that would do you if someone had been home, watching you from inside, and pulled a gun on you," he remarked sourly. "Why didn't you bring your gun?" he asked roughly. He knew Gracie had a handgun. He also knew she usually kept it in her bedside table, for self defense: she didn't generally carry it with her.

"Because I didn't expect to be jumped," Gracie answered in an annoyed voice. She put the pepper spray back in her pocket, and walked up to where Jack was, right in front of the trailer. "Colletti lived alone so I expected his - erm - dwelling would be empty. No one is home, I take it?" she asked with a chin jut at the trailer.

Jack shook his head. "No." If Jack were surprised that she knew the deceased's address, or that she had found the place, he didn't show it.

"Have you been inside?" Gracie asked, eyeing the door critically. It looked like just a thumb turn lock: she couldn't see a deadbolt or anything, although there could be a hook or a chain inside. But those wouldn't be fastened.

"Not yet. I was just about to--" Jack began, but Gracie cut him off.

"Good. I'll come with you."

"No, you won't."

"Why not? You have a search warrant, right?" she challenged.

Jack took a deep breath, and sighed. "Of course." Getting a search warrant hadn't been an issue once the corpse had been identified as Colletti; but that had happened the day before, when Jack had been in Boston on the Jesperson case. So it had been Thursday, this morning, before he'd been able to get a warrant and go out to Colletti's home to have a look around.

"Colletti has no known next of kin, so did you need a warrant?" Gracie asked now. "Did he own this place?" she added quickly, not waiting for an answer, and all the while casting an assessing eye over the dilapidated trailer. The tin roof hung out over the edge of the outside walls, and she wondered if this had been intentional, or just sloppy construction.

Jack nodded. "According to my info he bought the trailer a few years back in a county auction when they'd been selling off some old FEMA trailers from the floods in the 90's," Jack told her. "The land isn't his, but the land owner lets him live here for free," he added.

Gracie made a mental note to check in the courthouse to see who owned this parcel, since it was a fair bet Jack wouldn't make it easy and share that intel with her.

"So you got a search warrant in case the land owner were to raise an objection?" Gracie queried.

Again, Jack nodded. "Mmmm...he's in Arizona, so I mailed a certified copy of the search warrant to him, but I doubt if he will care," he said.

"Okay," Gracie responded cheerfully, and started for the cinder block steps. "Let's go in!"

Chapter Sixteen

"No, wait, Gracie--" Jack protested; he grabbed Gracie's elbow as she set foot on the first cinder block step. She turned, eyes blazing.

"Let go," she said flatly.

"You can't go in," Jack returned, but he released his hold on her jacket.

"Why not? You have a search warrant, I can go in with you," Gracie argued.

He shook his head. "No, you can't. You're not official personnel."

Gracie rolled her eyes and sighed. "Look, Jack, if you hadn't been here, I would be inside already," Gracie reasoned. "I just want to look around, see if there's anything here that might give a clue as to who killed Colletti and put Dawes' ID on him, and why." She glanced towards the dilapidated trailer again. "I don't think they killed him for his money," she murmured. "So let me go in, and then you can come in after me, and 'find' me inside: would that work for you?" Gracie asked, her tone sweet and sarcastic at the same time.

"If I 'find' you inside," Jack retorted, "you'd have committed breaking and entering, and I'd arrest you," he told her. His voice was serious but Gracie didn't believe him.

"Yeah, sure," she said, and went up the next two cinderblocks and opened the duct taped storm door.

"Gracie--" Jack's voice was full of warning.

"Oops! Looks like it's not going to be breaking and entering after all," Gracie said with a big grin on her face: the knob on the trailer's front door had turned easily in her gloved hand, and she opened the door a couple of inches.

"Gracie!" Jack's voice was reprimanding now, and cautionary.

"Hellooooo---" Gracie called as she creaked the door a bit wider. "Anyone here?" She paused. "It's Gracie Barufaldi from the *Intelligencer*. I have a few questions..." she called, properly identifying herself.

Silence.

She gave the door a slight push so it swung wide into the trailer, but she remained on the top cinder block. Jack was close behind her.

"I don't think anyone's home," Gracie said in a conversational tone to Jack. She took a quick step, and in a second was inside the trailer.

Jack followed, jaw tight, brow furrowed in anger.

Inside, the trailer was quite dark despite the sunny day. Tattered shades submerged the space in browned out gloom, and the plywood covered windows cast darkened pools throughout the interior.

Gracie pulled out her key ring and activated the small but very bright flashlight that she carried on it: she swung it around.

"Don't move," Jack said brusquely: he had pulled out his duty flashlight and was shining it inside, holding it in one hand, his gun in the other.

"I won't!" Gracie breathed, and stood rooted to the spot.

The trailer was sparsely furnished and largely unremarkable. Except for the big, red stain that was almost certainly blood in the middle of the living room carpet.

"Oh my god, Jack, we found the crime scene!" Gracie breathed. That hadn't been what she'd expected! She turned slightly to her left, located the light switch, and flipped it on.

"Gracie, I said, don't move!" Jack admonished. But he had to admit, the overhead light's glow was helpful.

"I only flipped the light switch," Gracie replied mildly. "And I still have my gloves on, see?" she added, waggling her fingers at him. "Leather: no fibers. So--what do we do now?" she asked eagerly.

Jack sighed and pulled out his Blackberry. "*We* aren't going to do anything, Gracie. *I* am going to call CSU and the Hinsdale police and we'll get this trailer cordoned off, and have the area swept. *You* are--"

But before he could tell her what she was going to do, Gracie interrupted Jack. "Presumably that is Colletti's blood," Gracie said, pointing at the big red blotch. She fiddled with the flashlight on her keychain and then hit the light switch, plunging the place into darkness again.

"WHAT—" Jack began, but stopped as Gracie aimed her small flashlight at the stain and was rewarded when it fluoresced faintly.

"Yep: blood," she commented matter of factly, and switched off the UV filter on the flashlight, flipping the light switch to 'on' once more. "Although until you test it we don't know that it's Colletti's, or even if it's human," she concluded. "If it is Colletti's blood, then this is probably where he was shot," she told him, speaking as though she hadn't heard anything he had said, and as though she hadn't interrupted him. She scanned the shag carpet quickly, then passed her flashlight's beam over an area to the side and behind the blood stain. Something gleamed.

"Colletti was shot once in the head, right?" she asked Jack rhetorically. "I don't think the shooter policed his brass," she went on. "Shell casing's over there," she told him, jutting her chin towards the glint in the carpeting.

She kept her flashlight trained on the spot while Jack walked carefully over, bent down, and retrieved the casing, using a small baggie to pick it up, and then secure it.

"Good catch," Jack told Gracie, his tone grudging.

She said nothing, only gave him a sweet, but gloating smile.

"You found what?" Anne squeaked about an hour later as she and Gracie found their usual table at Bistro Adam in Pittsfield, and Gracie shared her morning's excitement with her friend. Gracie had just made the noon lunch date, since the events at Colletti's trailer had held her up. But once she and Anne had been seated and had given Kyle, their server, their orders, Gracie had whispered in breathless, quick sentences, telling Anne what had occurred. Anne had pledged to say nothing to anyone, and Gracie knew she could trust her.

"You heard me," Gracie replied now, still whispering. "Jack's got the CSU team looking for evidence and all that, and he made me promise not to tell anyone I was there," she added.

"But you've told me," Anne offered.

"Yes, but you won't tell anyone, right?" Gracie asked again.

"Of course not!" Anne insisted.

"Technically, I suppose, I shouldn't have said," Gracie admitted, looking fleetingly rueful. "But it was just so exciting!" she crowed.

"Wait - so it was Colletti who was found in the park?" Anne questioned.

Gracie nodded. "Yes. With Richard Dawes' ID."

"But why?"

"Good question," Gracie agreed.

Kyle brought the caramel latte Anne had ordered and the 'dirty' vanilla chai ('dirty' was Kyle's term for a shot of espresso in chai) Gracie had requested, smiled, and left.

"This place is so cool," Gracie murmured, changing the subject for just a moment. "And I'm so glad it's doing well."

"The owner, Maureen, is a very smart woman," Anne noted. "She lives a couple houses down from me, and used to run a catering business—you know it: Delise? In North Adam?"

"Oh, yes, right: they're very good, I've been at functions they've done and their food's terrific."

"Well, she sold it a couple of years ago, and the people running it now are doing pretty much the same thing she did, so it's thriving," Anne related. "But Maureen wanted a place in town, closer to where she lives. She can walk to work, if she chooses!" Anne exclaimed.

Gracie realized that Anne was right: her house was about six blocks away, in a pretty residential street, not too far from where Jack's parents lived. If Maureen, who owned Bistro Adam, lived nearby then she could, indeed, walk to work.

"Maureen knows what she and her staff do well, and she sticks to that," Anne went on. "She doesn't try to expand her menu too fast or too much, and even though she'll have unusual stuff, she also has more middle of the road selections, so this place is popular with most people."

Gracie grinned. "You sound like you've made a study out of it!" she told her friend.

Anne grinned back and shrugged. "Those old psych instincts don't go away, no matter how different your life becomes," she told Gracie. Anne had majored in psychology and got her masters in behavioral psych before she met and married Marco Vioni, a chemical engineer with Solutions Technology in Becket, about a half hour's drive from Pittsfield down Route 8. The couple had settled in Pittsfield to be near their families. "So, tell me more about Colletti: what do you know?"

"Well, I haven't found out too much yet, except that he had a record: petty theft type crimes, and some drug charges," Gracie began.

Anne made a sympathetic noise and shook her head. "Shame."

"And he wasn't currently employed, at least, not that I found," Gracie continued. "But from what I saw at his place, I think he was into recycling, you know, picking up cans and bottles and so on and selling them for scrap."

"Can you make a living doing that?" Anne asked dubiously.

Gracie shrugged. "I don't know. I haven't checked yet to see if he's on assistance from the state." That was a different program, one she hadn't had time to run.

"Seems odd he would have had that truck driver's ID on him," Anne commented as Kyle approached with their orders. "And the trucker and his family have disappeared?" she asked again.

Gracie nodded. "Yes, the whole thing merits a much closer look," she admitted.

Kyle put down Gracie's roast vegetable wrap with pesto and red pepper dressing and Anne's mug of lobster bisque and her half tuna melt made with skipjack tuna, swiss cheese and horseradish mayo.

"Thanks, Kyle," Anne said with a smile. "I thought you liked their lobster bisque," she commented to Gracie as she took her first spoonful.

"I do, but if I have it, I can't eat an entire sandwich, and I didn't think about ordering a half," Gracie admitted. "I'll get a quart to go, maybe, and have it for dinner," she finished, thinking aloud.

For a few minutes the two friends ate. Then Anne said, "I haven't really talked to you since you came back from England. How was that? Anything new?"

Gracie filled her in on the highlights of her trip, and Anne didn't seem surprised that Gracie had stumbled straight into a mystery while visiting family. She commented that murder seemed to find her wherever Gracie went.

"And tell me more about—was it David? The police man?" Anne queried as she finished the bisque, and began on her sandwich. Gracie had told her she'd broken up with Ben, as that had happened before her trip to England. But in some Facebook posts she'd made while away, which Anne had followed, Gracie had mentioned David obliquely. Clearly, Anne's radar had picked something up, and now she pounced on it.

"He's a detective with the Essex police, yes," Gracie confirmed. She could feel, to her chagrin, her cheeks flush, and so tried to hide behind her mug of chai.

Anne teased her sweetly a bit more about her new 'beau' and then, suddenly, changed the subject.

"Wait a minute," Anne ordered peremptorily. "Amy Dawes? I thought that name sounded vaguely familiar: I know her. She's a teaching assistant at the Elementary School," she said with a revelatory gleam in her eye. "She's in Cara's class room," she added, naming her daughter, who was in first grade.

Chapter Seventeen

"She is?" Gracie queried, interested. "You haven't, well, heard anything about her, have you? I mean, there haven't been any notes sent home that said, 'Mrs. Dawes was going to be absent,' have there?" Gracie asked quickly. She doubted it. She'd already begun to form a theory in her head about the Daweses' apparent disappearance, and why Colletti's body had been found with Richard Dawes' ID. Her theory had a lot of holes in it, however, and she was looking for information that might fill some of those holes in.

Anne frowned, finished her half sandwich and shook her head. "No. But Cara did say when she came home from school, I think it was Monday, that Mrs. Dawes was 'sick.'"

Gracie shook her head, and revealed what the school had told her about Amy going to care for her ailing mother.

Anne shrugged. "So I guess that's what Amy must have done: called the school and told them she had to go take care of her mother. But you're telling me she's disappeared?"

Gracie finished her food and replied, choosing her words carefully. "Well, Wednesday I went round to the Dawes home," she began. "They weren't there, but their next door neighbor was, and she told me that Amy packed up the van on Saturday and left. I presume with the children," she added. "And she said that Richard

Dawes had left Friday evening: she thought he was just going to work. But he hasn't been seen since, and neither has his wife, nor his children."

"Well, I can find out exactly what Amy Dawes told the school," Anne told Gracie confidently. "And if they've heard from her since. My sister in law's the Assistant Principal at the Middle School." She pulled out her mobile phone as she spoke.

"Handy," Gracie replied, thinking that that might be a good contact to have. "What's her name?"

"Regina Vioni. I tried to get her to join Club, but she's too busy with grad school - getting her Ph.D. in early education administration," Anne noted with a proud smile, and tapped the phone's screen.

Gracie sighed.

Kyle came and took their plates and asked if they wanted dessert.

"Do you have any of those salted caramel brownie things?" Anne asked hopefully. She'd had a quick conversation with her sister in law and had hung up.

"Yes, we do," Kyle said cheerily.

"Have you had those?" Anne asked Gracie, who shook her head.

"Bring us one, but two forks?" Anne requested, and Kyle grinned and said she would.

"They're big," Anne cautioned Gracie.

"I'm not worried," Gracie replied with a laugh.

"Regina confirms what you found out: Amy called early Monday and left a message on the answering machine at the school that her mother was ill, and she and the children had to go take care of her," she informed Gracie. "But they have not heard from Amy since. Regina said she thinks her mother lives up north, close to the New York State line," Anne added helpfully.

"Aha!" Gracie said. She wasn't going to tell Anne the detail about the credit card use, nor was she going to tell her about securing the video from the traffic cam that showed Amy Dawes' van at the gas station where the card had been used at the time it had been used. But she did tell her friend about finding a Lana Frisvold in Williamstown, and that Amy's birth name had been Frisvold.

"Williamstown—is that up north, near New York?" Anne asked, and Gracie nodded, thinking that she would have to make a trip up to the small village where Mrs. Frisvold lived. Maybe tomorrow.

"Well, I know you, Gracie, you'll figure it out," Anne said reassuringly a moment later. "You're coming to the Banquet Saturday, right?" she asked then, changing the subject. The Banquet was the yearly Club Banquet, held in early May. Anne was the Membership Chair this year, and also head of the Banquet committee.

"Of course!" Gracie exclaimed as Kyle placed an oversized chocolate concoction in front of them with a fork for each woman. "Yum," Gracie commented, and dug in.

"Isn't it deadly?" Anne asked with guilty pleasure.

"It is—good thing we're sharing or we wouldn't fit into our outfits for Saturday night," Gracie joked. "What're you wearing?" she asked Anne.

Anne told her about a pretty peach raw silk sheath she'd found recently at a nearby Mall. "What about you?" she asked Gracie.

Gracie shrugged. "You know, I haven't even looked to see what I might wear!" she revealed, sounding surprised. "It seems I got back from England and then boom, we had the Jesperson thing, and then this Dawes-Colletti mess and I haven't thought much about it."

"Understandable—my goodness, we haven't even talked about Jesperson: wasn't *that* a surprise?" Anne asked. "I went to the funeral."

"I went to the viewing," Gracie said. "And yes, it was quite a shock: he seemed to be in good health," she agreed.

"I wonder if Maddie will be at the Banquet," Anne said suddenly. "She hasn't called or emailed to say she won't be," she added, sounding doubtful.

"Oh, well—she might not bother, figuring we'd know she won't come," Gracie put in. "Or, maybe she forgot all about the Banquet. Or, maybe she will come."

"I'd be surprised: I mean, her husband was just buried a couple of days ago, I can't see her coming to a Banquet this weekend!" Anne offered, sounding slightly scandalized.

Gracie shook her head. "I don't know. She might feel that being with friends would do her good," she put in. "I mean, it's Club Banquet, not an orgy!"

She and Anne laughed together. "More's the pity!" Anne joked. "She's at your table, along with Courtney," she informed Gracie, mentioning the woman who ran Planet Provisions.

"Oh, good."

"I was in Courtney's store a couple weeks ago, to get Marco some Echinacea. He thought he was getting a cold," Anne continued. "And Maddie was there, too, getting one of the supplements she takes. I wish I could shop there more," she admitted. "But the children are so picky about their food, they turn up their noses as at anything more interesting than turkey burgers and cheddar mac and cheese!" she laughed.

"Well, Courtney's store is doing okay," Gracie offered. "Did the Echinacea work?"

"I think so: Marco didn't get sick," Anne replied.

Gracie was quiet for a moment, then ventured, "you never heard anything, well, odd about Fred Jesperson, did you?" she asked her friend.

Anne looked dubious. "Odd? Odd how?"

Gracie finished her half of the brownie and took a final sip of her chai. "Ummm…anything about him drinking, maybe, drinking and driving?" she asked, keeping her voice low and thinking of what Jack had said the Boston PD officer had told him.

Anne finished her latte and took a deep breath. "Well, this was before you moved here, but when Fred was mayor of Pittsfield, he was a frequent customer at some of the city's watering holes," she began. "It was Pittsfield's best kept secret."

"That in itself is not a crime," Gracie put in. "I'm looking for something more, something involving him driving while under the influence," Gracie specified. "Maybe getting into some kind of accident?" she hinted.

"Mmmm…you might want to check into an incident that took place over near Springfield about a year ago,"Anne continued in a near whisper. The small restaurant had become quite crowded. "I only know about it because Marco was coming home from a late session in his lab, and had to make a detour because they had the road blocked. He didn't see much, but he did catch the license plate of the car that had caromed off the road and flipped onto its roof."

"Oh?"

Anne nodded. "It was distinctive. It said, '#1Man' and that's Jesperson's license plate."

Gracie just waited.

"That report never saw the light of day, and it was never in any newspaper,' Anne told Gracie. "That's pretty odd, given the fact that the road was closed," Anne noted. "But I guess since it was after midnight, not too many people were out, and it was probably only closed for an hour or so, till they got the wreck cleared. And I'll bet Marco was the only driver astute enough to notice the license plate. I don't know that the crash was drink related, but it may have been."

"Jesperson wasn't hurt?" Gracie asked. She knew the locale Anne was talking about was out of Berkshire County, so any report wouldn't have been among those she regularly received from the state police. That was presuming there had been a report, of course.

Anne shrugged. "If he was, it was minor. I mean, he didn't have to go to the hospital or anything. I've never heard of him having to go to any Drunk Driving classes, either, and I'll bet there's not a blotch on his driving record."

"I wonder why that crash was never reported?" Gracie asked, just for the sake of asking: it seemed she and Anne both knew the reason.

"Now he's in Boston all week," Anne continued, "I am sure he exhibits the same behavior," Anne reasoned. "You could ask the Boston police." She paused. "But of course, there might be a hush up going on there, too," she whispered.

"Maddie told me Fred golfed," Gracie went on in a more normal voice. "He said it was a great way to network," she commented, her voice even. Privately, she thought it was also a good way to do a lot of drinking on the '19th hole' and if Fred had been a drinker, which the evidence was suggesting, Gracie would bet that part of the allure of golf had been the alcohol that was ritually consumed.

Anne snorted in derision. "Yeah, well, maybe it's a good way to network, but it's a great way to meet other women, too," she commented.

Gracie looked a question: this was new. Anne explained that Jesperson's skirt chasing had been the other best kept secret in Pittsfield. "When he was Mayor, he had a fling with that Chamber of Commerce lady--oh, that was before you moved here," Anne revealed. "And everyone knew it. I'm sure even Maddie did."

"Then why did she put up with it?" Gracie asked, perturbed.

Anne shrugged. "I guess, because they had children together, and after all, she was the Mayor's wife, and then a Senator's wife, so I guess there was something in that…"

Then Anne revealed that Jesperson had, again when he'd been Mayor, aggressively pursued her sister in law, Regina. "He likes them young, and he likes them attractive, and Regina's a knock out, I'll admit," Anne explained. "But that doesn't mean she welcomes attention from any male out there. Actually, she's very picky, and always has been." Regina, Marco's sister, was still single.

The pursuit by Jesperson had come when Regina had been finishing up at Mt. Holyoke, getting her undergraduate degree in Education. Mayor Jesperson as he'd been then, had seen Regina at a local bar, bought her a drink, engaged her in conversation, and when Regina had said good night, had apparently accepted it. But, Anne told Gracie as they finished up their lunch, he'd found out her address, and had begun sending her gifts: flowers, and then he'd asked her to dinner. When she'd declined, he'd sent her jewelry, a bracelet. When she'd sent it back, he'd tried flowers again.

"Then he started showing up outside her dorm, on campus, asking her to coffee, etc," Anne continued. "I don't think he was used to being turned down," she added.

"How did Regina finally convince him to go away?" Gracie asked.

"She said she'd charge him with stalking if he didn't stop. So he stopped," Anne replied. "I guess he was afraid of the publicity." She paused. "And now he's in Boston all week. I mean, who knows what he gets up to there," Anne finished.

Interesting, Gracie thought. So Fred Jesperson, the apparently upstanding Mayor of Pittsfield and then Senator from Western Massachusetts, had been both a drinker and a womanizer. Huh. And according to Jack, and also Anne and Marco, the late Senator had been involved in drunk driving crashes more than a couple of times.

And yet, there had never been a report on any of those incidents.

Chapter Eighteen

Thursday evening, Gracie looked through her closets and chose a bright yellow silk jersey surplice dress with a flowing knee length skirt for the Club Banquet. Paired with beige pumps and a beige clutch, it would be perfect. A creamy pashmina would work, in case the evening were chilly.

She'd asked Anne who else was at her table, and was pleased to hear that in addition to Maddie, if she attended, and Courtney, her friend Jean was also seated with them. Two other women from Club would round out the six spot table.

Friday, Gracie tossed on jeans, a Yale sweatshirt and a scarf to keep her neck warm since it was chilly, hopped into her Jeep after a quick breakfast, and headed to North Adams. There, she'd go west on Route 2 towards Williamstown and find her way to Berlin Road, where she'd discovered Mrs. Frisvold, Amy Dawes' mother, lived. Berlin Road was just south of the Taconic Trail State Park, and Gracie had a fairly clear idea of where she needed to go.

The previous evening as she'd chosen her Banquet outfit, Gracie had reviewed what she knew, and tried to make sense of the latest information on Fred Jesperson. He had been murdered, using the poison abrin, which was uncommon, and made from the berries of an exotic plant, the rosary pea. No such plant had been found either at the Jespersons' home, or at the Senator's office or townhouse, or his SUV. It was still a mystery as to where the killer had obtained the abrin.

Gracie felt that if she could find out how, she would learn who. But since she couldn't find out how, at least not at the moment, perhaps she needed to turn that around, and identify who might have wanted to kill Fred Jesperson. Then, maybe, she'd learn where they'd obtained the abrin.

Another clue might be the way the abrin had been administered. Spears had said it had probably been added to the late Senator's food or drink. This narrowed the field of suspects, somewhat, because if that were so, whoever was the murderer would have to have had access to Fred Jesperson's food and drink. The poison could have been added to a gift of liquor, or added to food prepared and given to the Senator.

Given the fact that the late senator had been a drinker and a womanizer, and especially given the fact that it appeared that the authorities had looked the other way when it had come to Jesperson's indiscretions, Gracie felt there could be several people who might have wanted Fred Jesperson dead, and for a variety of reasons.

One of the women Jesperson had pursued, or perhaps had an affair with, might have wanted him dead because he'd been a threat, or because he'd tossed her aside for someone else, or because she had just felt used.

Additionally, a coverup always meant problems with blackmail and favors traded, so Gracie wouldn't be surprised if a magistrate, or even a police officer, had thought that Jesperson could become more trouble than he was worth, and had decided to obliterate the potential problem.

Gracie wondered momentarily if Jack had checked the liquor in the Jesperson home and at the Senator's pied à terre. She also wondered if he'd asked if the Senator had gone out to dinner, ordered food delivered, or otherwise been exposed to a means through which someone could have adulterated his food. Chances were, he had, she thought: the autopsy report had mentioned the likely routes of administering the poison, and Jack was smart: he would have followed up on food and drink.

Gracie was curious to know if Jack had discovered the late Senator's reputation as a womanizer, too. According to her friend Anne, it was one of Pittsfield's 'best kept secrets' but Jack had a good track record for discovering such things.

The plethora of possible murder suspects was reassuring in one way, and frustrating in another way. She went to bed Thursday night still ruminating over that.

Friday morning as she showered, Gracie pushed the Jesperson case temporarily aside and tried to piece the relevant facts in the Dawes case together since that case would occupy her morning, at least.

She knew Amy had packed her van and left, ostensibly to visit her ailing mother, the previous Saturday. She knew Amy had called the school early Monday and said she had to be out of work for a while to care for her mother, Mrs. Lana Frisvold. According to

Anne's sister in law Regina, the Assistant Principal at the Middle School, Amy had not given the school a range of time she'd need off. Gracie had also learned that Amy had been in the vicinity of her mother's home a couple days later, early Monday morning. It suddenly struck her that Amy could have used a pay phone at the little mini mart where she'd used the credit card, to make that call to the school since there had been no record of it on the phone details Gracie had pulled. She wasn't sure of the time the school's answering machine had received the call, but it had been before the secretaries got in, and they reported at 7:30 a.m. So it was likely.

Meanwhile, Gracie also knew that Richard Dawes had left his home Friday night. The neighbor lady had thought he was going to work. But Richard hadn't shown up for work on Saturday, his next scheduled day. He also hadn't called off. Given the fact that the body with Dawes' ID was discovered Monday, this seemed to indicate that 'Dawes' had come to some mischief and been killed Friday night or Saturday.

At least until Spears discovered that the body found in the Arboretum with Dawes' ID wasn't that of Dawes at all, but that of a shady ex con named Ryan Colletti.

Now, Gracie was on her way to see if she could find Amy Dawes, and maybe even Richard if he were with his family at his mother in law's. She wanted to find out what, if anything, Amy knew about her husband's whereabouts, and the two million dollar insurance policy, and if she'd ever heard of Ryan Colletti.

It was a pretty drive north, and in under a half hour Gracie was turning left onto Berlin Road. In another few minutes she arrived at Mrs. Frisvold's home, a large and well kept modular that looked to Gracie like it had at least three bedrooms and a full basement. It was painted a dark grey with white trim; a deep red door gave a splash of color to the front, which was landscaped with rhododendrons and junipers. The rhododendrons were currently bursting into swaths of pink, white and red that encircled the home.

A familiar looking car was in the long driveway: Jack's police cruiser. Disgruntled, Gracie slid out of her Jeep, and walked slowly towards the front door. If Jack was here, that meant he was already talking to Amy Dawes about her missing husband. Gracie thought this might make Amy less chatty to the press, in which case she'd driven out here for nothing. But there was always the chance that the news, if it was news, about her husband's disappearance and his ID being found on someone else's body might make Amy anxious to try to exonerate herself. In this case, she'd be eager to chat with the press.

Gracie rang the doorbell and heard the corresponding peal from inside the home. She saw movement through the narrow panes of frosted glass that flanked the deep red door, and then the knob turned and the door opened wide.

"You with the police, too?" asked the woman who had answered the door. Slight, and with long, greyish blonde hair, the woman wore bleached, fitted jeans, athletic socks, and an overlarge pink sweatshirt that read, 'Best Grandma.' Dark framed glasses adorned a face that was cheered by daubs of rouge and lipstick.

"No: I'm Gracie Barufaldi, from the *Intelligencer* newspaper," Gracie replied with a smile. She lifted the Press ID from the lanyard around her neck and showed it to the woman. "You must be Lana Frisvold, Amy Dawes' mother: are you feeling better?"

The woman gave Gracie a strange look. "You know my daughter?" she asked shortly.

"I don't know your daughter, no, but I heard from a friend that she'd called off from her job at the school because she had to come take care of you," Gracie answered honestly. Mrs. Frisvold looked pretty healthy to her, but what did she know? Maybe a few days of Amy's care had been a magic cure. "I wanted to talk to Amy about her husband, Richard," Gracie added.

"Ma—who is it? Is it more police?" came a voice from inside the house.

"No, not the police, it's the newspaper," Lana called back over her shoulder. She waited a moment. Then, having heard nothing from her daughter in response to the information that the newspaper was at the door, Lana returned her full attention to Gracie.

"Oh, Richard? He's not here," she said with a pat smile. "Amy's been trying to get in touch with him, but she hasn't been able to," she added. "We were just so relieved to learn that dead body wasn't him!" she added ingenuously.

Gracie nodded, but something bothered her about the woman's inflection: that last statement had sounded rehearsed. Also, although she'd looked Gracie in the eye when speaking at first, when she'd made the statement about Amy trying to reach Richard, Lana Frisvold's pale green eyes had looked downward, and to one side, and when she'd expressed joy about her son in law being alive, her face had been devoid of emotion.

"Well, could I speak to Amy for a couple of minutes?" Gracie pursued, deciding that she would contemplate Mrs. Frisvold's behavior later. "If the police are finished with her, of course," she added graciously.

At that moment, a thirty-something woman whose chunky frame was clothed in a two piece lavender sweat suit and sneakers, and whose short wavy brown hair was kept off her face by a white plastic head band, entered the hallway behind Lana Frisvold. The resemblance was enough, even given the differing ages and weights, for Gracie to know that this was her quarry: Amy Dawes.

The fact that Jack came sauntering out just behind her, closing a small notebook and giving Gracie one of his 'fancy meeting you here' looks, was all the confirmation she needed.

Chapter Nineteen

"Like I told the Detective, I don't know where my husband is," Amy told Gracie a short while later. They were seated in the front room of Lana Frisvold's house, the living room. The walls were painted a pale grey, and the carpet matched, and had flecks of green and blue throughout. A slightly worn velveteen sofa in a darker grey was flanked by two similarly upholstered arm chairs, one green and one blue. All three pieces were adorned with crocheted throws; small tables and ottomans were scattered in convenient places and a huge spider plant with dozens of 'babies' hung in the center of the white curtained bay window. There were only a few pictures on the walls, and these were mostly photographs of people, presumably family.

Amy's comments were accompanied by a wringing of her hands, and deep furrowing of her brow. "Me and the children, we came up Saturday to stay with Ma for a while, as she's been feeling sick," Amy elaborated, repeating much of what she had just told Jack. She fidgeted on her side of the sofa. "Richard went to work Friday, and I haven't talked to him since," she concluded. She fidgeted again, toying with her plastic headband.

"Didn't you think that was odd, that you didn't hear from your husband?" Gracie asked with a smile.

Amy shrugged. "A little, I guess. But sometimes his route takes him places where there's no cell phone reception. It's happened before," she asserted. But her eyes were shifting without purpose among the objects in the room, like a panicked mouse in a maze.

"And now that it's been several days?" Gracie pushed. "Have you called the trucking company? Maybe they've heard from him."

"Yes, I did!" Amy replied, sounding relieved that she had accomplished that small thing, "but they haven't heard from him either, and now I *am* beginning to be worried," she admitted, sounding stagily concerned.

"Amy, do you and Richard have life insurance?" Gracie asked, changing the subject and smiling in what she hoped was a reassuring way.

Amy nodded. "I have $10,000 through the school," she said. "And I think Richard has some through his work," she added, sounding unsure, but looking a bit more relaxed.

"You don't know anything about a larger, separate policy your husband took out on himself just a short time ago?" Gracie queried.

Amy batted her eyelashes and looked up at the corner of the room, as if seeking answers in the white painted ceiling. "No, no I don't really know what insurance he's got through work," she replied vaguely.

"Okay—just one more thing, Amy, because I'm sure you're very busy,"
Gracie put in.

Amy smiled sweetly.

"Have you ever heard of a man named Ryan Colletti?"

Amy's frown of confusion was instant and genuine. "No." She shook her head. "The Detective asked me that too. Ryan Colletti? No. At any rate, I hadn't until the news said this morning that that was the name of the man found in the park. With Richard's ID. I can tell you, like I told the Detective, I was just so happy to receive the call from the police that the body wasn't Richard's!" she finished, placing a chubby, be-ringed hand over her chest in an attitude of profound relief.

Gracie was certain the woman wasn't being completely truthful with her. For one thing, the body had been found Monday morning and thought to be Dawes. Gracie was sure the police, or Jack's office, would have tracked Amy or her mother down to tell them the sad news. Why wouldn't Amy have returned home at that point? Her mother didn't appear to have been at death's door. Then again, Gracie thought quickly, maybe Amy would have wanted to remain with her mother, for moral support during such a difficult time? But it still seemed peculiar, at least to Gracie, that Amy hadn't begun any of the expected arrangements for a funeral, and attendant events.

And now that Amy knew the dead man wasn't her husband, why wasn't she more concerned that several days had passed without her hearing from him?

Unless, of course, she had, and just was keeping that a secret.

"Your mom looks much better," Gracie commented, changing the subject again as she rose to leave. "Your nursing must have helped."

Amy gave a fleeting smile. "Oh, it was just the 'flu, but you know, it helped to have someone here. And she enjoys seeing the kids," Amy added in an innocent tone.

"You'll be going back to work soon, then?" Gracie asked as she headed for the door, followed by Amy.

"Probably Monday," Amy confirmed.

Again, no mention of being concerned that her husband had disappeared. Gracie thought if she were in Amy's place, she'd be distraught, and certainly not thinking about returning to work.

"I'm sure Detective Draper asked you to call him if you hear from your husband," Gracie said, "but could you also call me?" she requested, handing Amy one of her cards. "I'd like to be able to print that he's all right," she said kindly.

"Oh, yes, I hope he is," Amy replied earnestly. She squinted at the card. "Okay."

Gracie thanked Amy and Mrs. Frisvold for their time, and returned to her Jeep, wondering just exactly what kind of article she could turn that vague interview into. She had no doubt that Amy was lying to her on most of the points they'd discussed. She had seemed to be sincere, though, when she'd denied knowing Ryan Colletti.

Gracie had just turned off Berlin Road and back on to Taconic Trail Road when she found that familiar dark blue cruiser in her rearview mirror. Jack flicked his lights once, and Gracie obligingly pulled to the shoulder of the roadway as the approach to Route 7 south appeared ahead.

Jack got out of his car and came up to Gracie's driver's side window.

"People are going to think I got stopped for speeding," Gracie joked as she rolled down the window.

"You think people know your vehicle that well?" Jack returned with a sarcastic grin.

Gracie shrugged. "Maybe. What's up?"

"Uhm—I thought maybe we should compare notes on what Amy Dawes said to us," Jack said.

Gracie was surprised. He wanted to 'compare notes?' "She told me she thought her husband had left for work Friday night and hasn't talked to him since," Gracie summarized.

"Yeah, she told me that too," Jack responded, looking glum. He cocked one eyebrow at Gracie. "You believe her?" he asked.

It seemed clear to Gracie that he valued her opinion. Nice to know he still did.

"Frankly, no," Gracie replied. "I mean, it's been what—" she held up slim, manicured fingers one at a time, "Saturday, Sunday, Monday, Tuesday, Wednesday, Thursday—six or seven days since she's heard from her husband, in the midst of which she thought he'd been found dead, and she's yet to contact the police or file a missing persons report?" Gracie made a derisive noise in the back of her throat.

"Yeah, I don't believe her, either," Jack agreed.

It was a pleasant enough spring day, but clouds scuttling across the sun made it chillier than it could have been and Gracie wanted to shut her window against the lively breeze.

"Anything else, Detective?" Gracie asked.

"Well, I did hear back from CSU: the blood we found in the trailer? It was Colletti's, almost certainly," Jack went on. Gracie had been the one to spot the shell casing, and she'd been with him when he'd investigated the trailer: he felt she deserved to know the results of CSU's investigation as soon as possible.

The CSU team had worked quickly Thursday and Friday to get the blood sample from the Colletti trailer analyzed. The chunk of shag carpeting they'd cut and bagged as evidence had been typed and cross matched to Spears' samples from Colletti's corpse in just a few hours. Comparison with Colletti's blood with regard to specific DNA would take at least two weeks.

Jack had the results he'd expected by Friday afternoon when his Blackberry buzzed and pinged that a new text message had just come in. He was just leaving the Frisvold residence, and had decided to wait for Gracie, so he could share the information with her.

"The blood on the carpet was a match for Colletti's blood as far as typing goes: B positive," Jack told Gracie now, leaning one hand on the roof of her Jeep. "Since that's not a real common blood type, it put the odds that the blood was Colletti's at a pretty favorable level."

"What about the shell casing?" Gracie asked quickly.

"Preliminary tests show it was fired from the same make and model gun that killed Colletti: a snub nosed . 38."

"That's the gun Richard Dawes has," Gracie returned, sounding excited. "At least, that's what's registered to him."

None of this meant that Dawes had been the one to shoot Colletti, of course, and both Gracie and Jack knew that. However, it was strong circumstantial evidence, enough to bring Dawes in for questioning: except that Dawes could not be found.

"So that's my next step: trying to find Dawes. Any ideas?" Jack asked. "Since Amy Dawes was less than helpful," he added wryly.

Gracie shrugged and shook her head. "Nope. No ideas at the moment. But if I get inspiration, I'll call you," she promised. "Look, Jack, I've got to get home," Gracie said. Well, that was true: she and David had planned a Skype 'dinner date' for four o'clock her time, which would be nine o'clock in England. Gracie was looking forward to it and wanted to have time to dress up a bit and do her hair and makeup: just like a real date. Also, she thought chatting here at the side of the road was silly.

Jack just gave her a keen look.

Gracie sighed.

Chapter Twenty

Thousand Treasure Rice was a recipe Gracie had stolen from Joey and Tyler's restaurant Mange Tout. It was based on Indian cuisine, and like an Oriental dish with a similar name, it was basically rice with various meats, veggies, nuts and dried fruits in it. The Indian version added onions and carrots that had been caramelized before being mixed with the rice and the fruits in a Korma type sauce and baked, whereas the Oriental dish didn't have fruit and stir fried the mixture. Gracie, who had sampled the Indian style dish at Mange Tout, had thought it was quite tasty and had decided to make her own version of it.

On Friday afternoon, once she returned from visiting Amy, Gracie added a healthy slug of Sriracha sauce to the basic Korma before she mixed everything together: she wanted a spicy kick. She also added some chopped smoked turkey thigh meat she had, as well as a handful of frozen peas, chopped celery, string cut carrots and thinly sliced red onion; the latter two she caramelized, then tossed in the celery to let it release most of its water. For the fruits she chose golden raisins and a teaspoon of grated lemon rind; the nuts were walnuts.

Gracie spooned the mixture into a greased casserole and slid it into her convection oven: it looked very pretty, and smelled great. She'd toss together a salad of fresh field greens in a light soy sauce vinaigrette, and that would be dinner.

She sighed. Sometimes, she really missed having someone to cook for. Since she and Jack weren't together any longer, and she'd broken up with Ben, and David was an ocean away, and her girlfriends were either with their families or working, Gracie was becoming accustomed to solitary dinners, at least for the time being. Cooking for herself was all very well and good, and she enjoyed testing new recipes. But it was more fun if someone else were involved.

Well, at least with Skype, David could see what she'd cooked. She wondered what he'd be eating, and then laughed to herself: they probably wouldn't really eat much at all. The 'dinner date' was just an excuse to talk together for a while in a slightly more personal way than emails and phone calls.

Gracie changed into a pretty cotton twinset printed with colorful butterflies against a creamy background and re-brushed her shoulder length brown curls, adding a mist of spray. She freshened her lipstick and blush, and smiled at herself in the mirror: she liked what she saw, and hoped David would, too.

Returning to the kitchen, Gracie could smell the rice dish, and despite the fact that it was early for her to be eating, the aroma made her stomach growl. She poured a half glass of Apothik white wine and plated the rice along with the small salad.

Pumpkin strolled into the kitchen at this moment and looked pointedly at her food dish: a scattering of kibble remained on the bottom of it. Time, the feline seemed to be saying, for Gracie to remember her priorities.

"Would you like some fresh crunchies?" Gracie asked the beautiful orange tabby, smiling.

Pumpkin miaowed.

Gracie dug in the proper bag and put a shallow scoop full of kibble in the bowl, along with two treats that were supposed to be good for keeping cats' teeth clean. Pumpkin squeezed her gooseberry green eyes shut for a moment in pleasure, then stuck her face in the bowl and tucked in.

Gracie smiled again and recalled a saying she'd seen recently on Facebook: 'whoever lives with a cat will never be lonely.' Well, that was true. And she wasn't exactly lonely. It was just that sometimes she wished she had someone to share certain things with, like a new recipe. Or a beautiful sunset. Or even a murder case!

The distinctive tones that heralded a Skype call sounded from the laptop, which Gracie had placed in the center of her barn board table in the kitchen. She quickly brought her plate over to a spot in front of it, and clicked the answer key.

Jack pulled into his driveway and drove slowly up the crushed stone incline until his truck was parked neatly in front of the new double wide he called home. He sighed. Maybe it was time to start thinking about building, he considered as he exited his vehicle and walked towards his front door. He could hear Woof's paws scrabbling on the back of the door, eager to greet Jack at the end of his day. And also, no doubt, eager for a quick visit to his favorite rhododendron bush.

Jack opened the door, greeted the large half dog, half wolf who was his roommate, and watched as the canine trotted to the shrub, anointed it, and quickly trotted back inside.

Jack collected his mail, flipped on the lights and shrugged out of his jacket.

It wasn't that the trailer wasn't nice: it was. But it had been meant as a temporary dwelling, until he met 'the right woman' and together they would build their home. He had a few acres of land, and already knew exactly where he would want to locate a home: the question had been, in his mind, what kind of home would the woman in his life want?

For a time he had thought that woman was Gracie. Despite the fact that they'd broken up, quite horribly in fact, and it still hurt Jack to think about it, he continued to have a sneaking suspicion that Gracie was still 'the one.' This, however, seemed foolish, as she did not appear to feel the same way.

Jack freshened Woof's water and opened a can of premium dog food, emptying it into a stainless steel bowl and putting it on the floor, where Woof attacked it with gusto. Then Jack looked through the cupboards in his kitchen and the shelves in his refrigerator, and began to assemble his own meal.

"*Och, mo duinne,* its lovely to see you!" David exclaimed by way of greeting once the Skype connection completed and both were live on each other's computer screens. "Is that your kitchen, then?" he asked, taking in Gracie's surroundings.

"Yes," Gracie answered with a smile. "I can give you a tour after dinner if you like," she added. She'd told him about her house, of course, and the ongoing renovations as well as the home's history. But this was the first time since meeting, and since she'd left England and returned home, that she and David had had a chance to see each other, more or less in the flesh. Well, virtual flesh, at any rate.

"What's that for dinner, then?" David asked, and Gracie told him about the dish she'd made. "Sounds a fair bit better than mine," David replied genially, holding up a newspaper cone of fish and chips.

"Oh, I miss the fish and chips over there!" Gracie exclaimed.

The two began by discussing small topics of little consequence while they both ate. Then, saying that at the moment his case load was remarkably light, David asked how Gracie was coming with the truck driver investigation.

Gracie explained about her friend Anne's sister in law's information from the school where Amy worked, and told David that her research had shown that one of Dawes' credit cards had been used Monday morning. She also told him that surveillance videos—she was unspecific as to which ones exactly, or how she got them

—had revealed that Amy had been the one to use the card. Then she told him how she'd located Amy's mother's house and gone there to speak to her.

"But she claimed she didn't know anything," Gracie told David disconsolately as they each finished their meals. Gracie drained her wine glass and considered pouring a bit more. However, since it wasn't even five o' clock yet, she decided to wait.

"And the mother, had she really been ill, or was that a ruse?" David asked, interested in the way the case was unfolding.

"She didn't look especially ill to me," Gracie replied honestly. "And even if she had been ill, I still question the timing, since no one has seen Richard Dawes since last Friday evening."

"When you talked to Amy Dawes, did you get the sense that she knew where Richard is?" David asked Gracie a few moments later. "Did she seem happy that the body in the park hadn't been him?"

Gracie made a face. "Yes, and no. I think she knew he was going to disappear because she didn't seem upset that she hasn't heard from him in several days. But I don't think she knows where he is. Maybe he didn't tell her, to protect her and the kids. Or maybe he didn't know where he'd go, he just ran." She paused. "Amy sounded very 'rehearsed' when she was talking about how relieved she had been to learn the real identity of the body, and she kinda overacted when she said she was worried because she hadn't heard from Richard."

"What about the blood tests from the trailer?" David asked. Gracie had emailed him when she'd 'found the crime scene' and told him about the spent shell casing and the blood.

"I just heard today that although it will take time for the DNA match to come back, preliminarily it looks pretty conclusive that it's Colletti's blood," she told David.

The English detective nodded slowly. "And it makes sense the killer moved the body," he noted. "It's easier to fudge the corpse's identity out in a park somewhere, if he plants someone else's ID on him," David went on, thinking aloud.

"Well, yes: if he'd left Colletti in his trailer, even with Dawes' ID on him, it would be kinda obvious that the body was Colletti's," Gracie agreed.

"Or at least more obvious," David rejoined. "Do you think Dawes killed Colletti?" David asked keenly.

Gracie nodded. "I do. Why would someone else have killed Colletti and put Dawes' ID on the body?" Gracie questioned. "Unless, of course, Dawes hired someone to kill Colletti for him. But I don't think he had the money to do that," she concluded, and reviewed for David the sorry state of the Daweses' finances.

"Ah, well then, especially with the insurance policy, it seems like Dawes wanted to fake his own death so his 'widow' could collect the insurance money, yeah?" David asked, smiling.

"Mmmm. But didn't Dawes think that the authorities would run tests, do an autopsy on the body, to confirm identity?" Gracie queried, asking David the question that had been bothering her.

David gave her a wry grin. "Ah, sure now, Gracie, criminals aren't rocket scientists! Clearly, this Dawes isn't very smart, and he also didn't think his whole scheme through."

"I haven't found any links between Dawes and Colletti," Gracie returned thoughtfully. "Except that they look alike, as I told you before, and Colletti's trailer isn't far from the trucking depot where Dawes worked and the Daweses' house."

David nodded. "The superficial resemblance might have been all Dawes really needed to choose Colletti as his body double," he commented.

"Yes, but how did Dawes know Colletti? Where had he seen him? How did he gain access to Colletti in his trailer?" Gracie asked, fast.

David nodded again. "All good questions, *mo duinne,* but I think your theory is a good one, even if it doesn't stand up yet to much scrutiny. And I agree with you, I think the wife has known all along that Richard is alive, and that he's gone off somewhere but I don't think she knows where."

"What do you think their plan is?" Gracie asked. She thought it likely that Amy and Richard would meet up again together, some time in the future, and somewhere distant from western Massachusetts.

"D'you know if the authorities have put a trace on anyone's phones, in case Amy were to try and call

Richard. Or the other way 'round," David asked, sounding very much like the detective he was.

"Probably," Gracie answered, thinking that she should have asked Jack about that while they were having their roadside chat. "And Amy and Richard aren't too bright, but they're bright enough to probably use burner phones," Gracie amended, adding that no suspicious calls had appeared on the phone records she'd accessed. "Or pay phones," she added, recalling that she'd seen a pay phone outside the mini mart that morning as she'd driven by it on her way home. "They're harder to trace."

David thought for a moment. "Well, Dawes, once he gets to wherever he's going, will contact his wife, I think. Remember, *mo duinne,* he probably doesn't know his ruse hasn't worked."

"That's true!" Gracie replied, sounding excited. She'd been so immersed in what Amy might have known or not known, she hadn't thought about the situation from Richard's perspective. "But once Amy tells him that we know the body in the park is Colletti's, not his, do you think Dawes will return?" Gracie asked, curious.

David shook his head. "Och, no: I wouldn't. Would you? I mean, yeah, his plan failed but now he's the main suspect in a murder case, and wanted for other crimes as well, like attempted insurance fraud," David reminded Gracie. "I'd stay disappeared."

"Hmmm...I think the plan was that Amy and the children would re-join Richard after she got the insurance money, and after a few months had passed," she said, advancing her theory.

David nodded. "You're likely right about that."

"I wouldn't be surprised if, even once Dawes knows the insurance plan has gone bust, he and Amy will still plan to reunite. Maybe in a few months, maybe sooner. But her movements bear watching."

"Och, aye, Gracie, they do. I hope your friends in law enforcement are doing just that. At least put a trace on the phones."

"Even a burner phone?"

"There are ways to monitor any phone activity, even if you can't trace it very easily," David explained obliquely. "And if the wife goes anywhere, your police should be able to ping her location pretty easily," he added, sounding confident.

Gracie nodded.

After discussing a few more details on the case, David and Gracie turned to the other murder investigation: that of the late Senator Jesperson.

Gracie ran through what Anne had told her about Fred Jesperson's drunk driving and womanizing, and the more important fact, at least to Gracie, that some kind of coverup appeared to be taking place. What Anne had said about her sister, Regina's, pursuit by Jesperson, as well as other details her friend had revealed, confirmed what Jack had been told by the Boston PD.

David seemed quite impressed with Gracie's ability to pull information from disparate and unrelated sources and wished her well in trying to find Jesperson's murderer.

"But be careful, *mo duinne*," he concluded. "You know only too well how ruthless politicians can be if they feel threatened," he warned her.

Chapter Twenty-one

Saturday, Gracie spent the early morning examining her iPad Air's Google maps and running Fred Jesperson's driving record. She and Anne had been correct: the late Senator's driving record was clean.

She had pinned Anne down to the exact location of the crash involving the late Senator that Marco had witnessed: along Route 112, just north of a small town called Huntington, west of Springfield.

Marco's company, Solutions Technology, was near the Barnes Municipal Airport west of Springfield, on North Road, just off Route 10. Anne had said he usually came home on back roads rather than the turnpike, because it was less boring and in peak tourist season, less crowded. She had told Gracie that Marco generally drove up Montgomery Road, or Old Main Road, which was a fairly straight two lane highway that led right into Route 112. From there it was a short jog to Route 20 and that led directly to Route 8, and home.

Gracie, examining the detailed map closely, could see that this was so. The accident Marco had witnessed had blocked the small section of Route 112 Marco had wanted to take, the road that would have led him south to Route 20. But Anne had said the road had been blocked to clear the accident, which she'd described as the Senator's car having flipped in the roadway. Marco had then taken 112 north and eventually got home that way.

Gracie pinpointed the small section of Route 112 where the accident had taken place. It was very close to Huntington, so she suspected the Huntington PD, such as it was, would have handled the crash. And the coverup.

Next, Gracie did a search to find bars in that area that Fred Jesperson could have been coming from. There were a couple of likely candidates: The Whitewater, right on Worthington Road that was also Route 112, and The High Street Pub which, as its name indicated, was on High Street, right in town. There was also the Springfield Country Club, a bit farther east, but still a possibility.

Thinking that she should put the sunny, pleasant day to good use, and knowing there were several hours before that evening's Club Banquet, Gracie decided to take a drive out to Huntington and see what the two bars looked like.

She arrived in Huntington just before lunch time. The High Street Pub was unimposing from the outside but inside sported warm wood paneling and a large open seating area. There was also a small antiques and gift section featuring a number of items from local artists.

Gracie wandered around here, idly examining the things on offer until a friendly woman in black trousers and a black short sleeved 'henley' type shirt with a name tag that read 'Jessika' approached her.

"Help you find something?" she asked.

Gracie smiled. "Actually, I'm just out for a drive, and stopped in because a - a friend told me about this place," she hedged.

"You hungry? We just started lunch service, and we have the lobster sandwich today. It goes fast, so—" Jessika said, waving one arm towards the restaurant proper and looking enthused.

Gracie shook her head. "I'm not really hungry, not yet," she admitted. "But I was looking at these—" she pointed to a selection of sketches of area beauty spots, of which there were several.

Jessika nodded. "They're nice, aren't they? Local guy does them, artist who lives just out of town."

"Mmmm…" Gracie studied one of the Knightville Dam on the south end of the Westfield River. "My friend said you can rent a kayak and shoot the rapids on the river near here," she prodded.

Jessika nodded again, and recommended two places where Gracie might rent a kayak and go white water rafting. She looked dubiously, however, at Gracie's jeans, loafers, shirt, silk scarf and linen blazer: it didn't look like rafting gear to her!

"Oh, I didn't mean now, I was just thinking maybe some time I'd do that, but—but not with my friend," she said, affecting a sombre tone. "You probably know him—Fred Jesperson? The State Senator?"

Jessika's brow furrowed a moment. "Oh, yes, the one who—he died, didn't he, last week? He was your friend? I am so sorry!" she said sincerely.

"Well, he's been in here, surely?" Gracie pursued. "I mean, he told me all about your place, and he raved about the—erm—the sweet chili meatloaf," she said, recalling what she'd read in the google search results.

"Oh, yeah, that's really good," Jessika replied, but shook her head. "I work most afternoons and evenings, and I don't remember any Senators eating here," she told Gracie. "And I think I would have heard, even if I hadn't served him myself." She paused. "Are you sure it was this place?"

"Yup," Gracie confirmed. "High Street Pub. That's what he said." She took a deep breath. "Well, anyway, thanks for your time. I'll stop again—when I'm hungry!" she told the young woman, and beat a hasty retreat.

In truth, she was getting hungry. However, she wanted to check out the second Huntington bar, the Whitewater, and maybe even the golf club if she needed to, so she hadn't wanted to stop and eat at the first place she tried.

As Gracie maneuvered her Jeep towards Route 112 and the Whitewater, she thought that despite Jessika's statement that the Senator had never been to The High Street Pub, it was still a possibility. However, with such a small place, and with the notoriety that Senator Jesperson had probably called to himself, Gracie thought Jessika was probably right.

She arrived at the Whitewater and despite its somewhat unfriendly façade entered to find a cozy, stone-walled bar with mirrors and glass: it was intriguingly dark despite the sunny day.

"Here for lunch?" asked the pert red haired hostess, bouncing up to Gracie with a menu in her hand.

The smells emanating from the kitchen area were tantalizing, and Gracie succumbed: she was really hungry now.

Nodding, she said, yes, and then yes again when the hostess asked if she wanted to sit on the deck.

"First time here?" the hostess asked, pronouncing 'here' like 'hee-yuh' which marked her as a native.

Again, Gracie answered in the affirmative.

"Oh, well, then, the deck is the place for you!" declared the hostess. She led Gracie to a table along the railing, overlooking the Westfield River. In the sun, it was pleasantly warm and Gracie accepted the menu with a smile, and took a moment to appreciate the scenery before deciding on her lunch.

Her eyes fell on a familiar figure.

"Chet?" she called over to the man seated at a table two over from her own.

The man, who had been staring out at the river from behind his sunglasses, turned and waved.

"Gracie! Hi! What brings you here?" he asked genially. He got up and came over to where Gracie was seated.

Gracie grinned, and decided to let Chet in on what she was doing in Hampshire County. Chet, after all, was the Worcester County Detective, Jack's counterpart in the larger region near the center of the state.

"I'll tell you all about it if you'll join me," Gracie offered. "Have you ordered?" she asked. All she'd seen on Chet's table was a coffee mug.

"Just did," Chet replied. "Getting the rainbow platter," he told her, and explained that it was grilled rainbow trout with 'rainbow' coleslaw made from carrots, red cabbage and celery, and 'rainbow' fries made from sweet potatoes, yellow fleshed red skinned potatoes, and blue potatoes.

"Oooh, that sounds great!" Gracie agreed.

The server approached at this point, and Gracie explained the change in tables and said she'd have the same thing Chet had ordered.

"I've heard they make the best fries around," Gracie said to Chet as he sat down and the server brought his coffee over, along with Gracie's order of iced tea.

"Well they sure sound good, don't they?" Chet replied companionably. "So, what brings you here: can't just be the great fries," he asked again.

"I could ask you the same," Gracie returned.

Chet shook his head. "Well, I was supposed to run out on the Harley to get Jean and we were going to take a ride," he told Gracie, mentioning her friend. Jean had been dating Chet for a while. They had met through Gracie, while she'd been covering a series of bizarre murders in Berkshire and Worcester Counties the previous year.

"Oh? What happened?" Gracie asked, hoping Chet wasn't going to say Jean was ill: Gracie was looking forward to seeing her at the Banquet that evening.

"She texted me this morning and said she had too much to do at home, and that we'd have to re-schedule," Chet answered carefully. From his tone, Gracie could tell that he didn't really believe Jean's excuse, and also that there might be more, that he wasn't saying. "So I just took a ride myself, and I ended up here: it's pretty nice," he added happily. "Great spot, great view."

Gracie nodded agreement and then explained that the Club Banquet was that evening, and said that maybe Jean was busy with that. "She *is* on the Banquet Committee," Gracie told him.

Chet's brow cleared a bit and he looked relieved. "I'm glad to know that, Gracie," he said. "For a while, now, I've been thinking she's gone off me," he admitted, adding that Jean had cancelled a couple of other dates in the past few weeks, although they had also gone out a few times, too.

"I'm sure it's nothing," Gracie said kindly, but she determined to ask her friend about it that evening. Not that Gracie had any say, or wanted any say, in Jean's love life. But since she'd been back from England, what with two murder cases and the usual post vacation errands, not to mention trying to conduct her own love life with the Atlantic Ocean between her and David, Gracie hadn't had a chance to really talk to Jean.

"So, now, tell me what you're doing out here?" Chet asked. Their food arrived, and they both tucked in. The trout was succulent and sweet, and the slaw had been dressed with a mustard sauce that was unusual as well as pretty on the plate. But the fries were great: Chet smeared his with ketchup and Gracie sprinkled hers with malt vinegar and both started to eat.

"I'm checking into some rumors I've heard about the late Senator Fred Jesperson," Gracie told him honestly.

"Rumors?" Chet asked, but his face said he knew all about whatever it was Gracie was 'checking into.'

Chapter Twenty-two

Gracie explained about the crash on Route 112 the year before that had never been reported. Then she mentioned that some of the Boston PD cops had said something about the late Senator being in a couple of 'incidents' that had been DUI related.

"But again, there's nothing on his record, and neither of those incidents was reported," Gracie said. She paused. "I think there must also be others, but I don't know for sure."

Chet chewed a forkful of trout slowly. "Well, now that he's dead—"

"Yeah, I know, 'don't speak ill of the dead,'" Gracie chimed in. "But he was murdered, Chet. I have to find out what was going on in his life if I'm going to have a shot at figuring out who might have wanted to kill him."

Chet grinned. "Sounds like you're a Detective, now, Gracie," he said. "And how is Jack, by the way? And — Ben, is it?"

Gracie said Jack was fine; she knew Chet was aware that she and Jack no longer dated. She explained about breaking up with Ben, and about visiting her cousin in England, and gave a précis of the murder she had run into there.

By that time, they had finished their meals and were just chatting and enjoying the atmosphere and their beverages.

"So, Chet: what do you know about the late Senator's DUI record?" Gracie asked bluntly. He wasn't going to get her off point that easily! "I know that should have been a reportable crash: the guard rail was mangled, and the road was shut down, so there should have at least been a police report. But there was nothing," Gracie said, and waited. She remembered that Jack had told her Detective Geene from the Boston PD had said a local magistrate had asked the department to trash the reports on Jesperson's 'incidents' in their jurisdiction. Gracie wondered if something similar were occurring out here.

Chet leaned over the table a bit and lowered his voice. "I had nothing to do with any of that," he said just above a whisper. "And you're talking Hampshire County: that's not me."

"I know," Gracie nodded. "But—have there been incidents in Worcester County?" she queried, and looked directly into Chet's grey-green eyes. She gave him credit that he didn't look away. "This is off the record, Chet: I'm not writing a story, at least not right now. I'm just doing leg work. I want to know if the late Senator had a habit of drinking and driving, and if his indiscretions were covered up. If so, that might lead to, erm, some people like, oh, like magistrates, for example, who might have felt the Senator was becoming a liability. And that could be a motive."

Chet sighed. "Like I said, I had nothing to do with any of it," he repeated.

"So—there is an 'it'?" she asked, matching Chet's near whisper.

He looked away at the scenic river, glanced up at the blue sky, then looked back at Gracie. "Yeah. There's an 'it.' Several, actually. And a couple in Worcester County, as well."

"And you didn't *do* anything about it?" Gracie hissed, sounding more harsh than she'd intended: Chet was talking. She didn't want to piss him off and have him clam up.

But it appeared her shock had the opposite effect: Chet began to defend himself by way of explaining what had happened.

"It was out of my hands, Gracie," he protested, still whispering. "I don't get involved in DUI stuff, anyway, and I can't tell you about Hampshire County. But in my county, it *was* the local magistrate who ordered everything expunged."

"Which local magistrate?" Gracie asked, holding her breath. This was the same story Detective Geene had told Jack: a magistrate was behind the cover ups. Gracie wondered if the late Senator had had a string of magistrates in every county in his pocket. And, she wondered where else such influence might have been felt.

"Aw, Gracie, I can't tell you that," Chet began to protest. He leaned back in his chair, and shook his head, his body language clearly showing his desire to separate himself from the conversation.

Gracie leaned back, too, and tried to relax her shoulders. "Oh, well, that's okay," she began quietly. "There aren't that many magistrates in Worcester County:

I'll just assume they're all guilty and go from there," she murmured, and affected disinterest, looking down at her hand bag next to her in the chair. She'd tied one of her favorite scarves on the handle: an Hermès 'Bolduc' pochette in bright spring tones. It fluttered in the breeze.

People came and went, and Chet and Gracie were both silent for a long minute.

Then Chet relented. "There are eleven district justices in Worcester County," he told Gracie through tight lips, and Gracie looked suitably impressed. Berkshire County had three, Hampshire two. "It's a big county," Chet noted with a small smile.

"I'll say!" Gracie rejoined companionably.

Chet bent towards her, over the table again, and she leaned in as well.

"Concentrate on the district court near the turnpike," Chet advised in his now familiar stage whisper.

That made sense, Gracie thought to herself. "Okay." She paused. "Do you know if Jesperson ever had to pay a fine, or do any community service or anything?" she asked. It was one thing to cover up behavior like the Senator's, and quite another to let him off without any type of penalty as well.

Chet nodded. "I don't know," Chet said carefully. He cleared his throat. "If he did pay a 'fine,'" he went on, enunciating slowly, "it was never documented."

Gracie stared at Chet, hard. Both had removed their sunglasses to eat and she could see his eyes, and he hers, clearly. "A payoff to the judge," she whispered.

"Mmm....your words, not mine, Gracie," Chet replied obliquely.

After they had paid their bills and said goodbye, Gracie slipped into the ladies' room to freshen up and re-apply her lipstick. Then she headed straight for the bar in the grotto like cocktail area within the Whitewater establishment. Her initial goal in coming here had been to see if Jesperson had ever frequented the place; running into Chet, while it had given her even more information, hadn't supplied her with the piece of the puzzle she had originally set out to find.

Since it was by now just 2 p.m., no one was at the bar drinking. But because it was a Saturday, early traffic from about 4 p.m. would be the norm, and Gracie was happy to see a middle aged man in a Metallica T shirt behind the bar. He had a gold earring in one ear, and a black and blue bandanna around his neck. His neatly trimmed beard was shot with grey, but his eyes and brows were dark.

Gracie wondered briefly if the bandanna were a gang related symbol but then pushed the thought aside in the interests of her investigation. So what if the bartender was a member of a gang: she was just asking for information. Not threatening at all.

She approached, and gave the man a big smile. "This is a great place you have here," she told him by way of opener.

"Your first time?" he asked, smiling back. He was filling little dishes with peanuts and chex mix and pretzels and stationing them strategically along the bar top.

Gracie admitted that it was. "But I'll be sure to come again. A friend of mine used to come here," she said, injecting a bit of sadness in her tone.

"Used to?" the barkeep, whose name tag read 'Jerry,' questioned. He gave Gracie the obligatory once over and apparently approved of what he saw.

Gracie looked down at the dark wood bar. "He—he died, just last week."

The barkeep stopped in mid-fill and just stared. "Geez, hon, I'm sorry," he said sincerely. His accent marked him as a transplant from New Jersey.

"You probably knew him," Gracie said eagerly. "Fred Jesperson? The State Senator?"

This time, unlike the negative answer she had got from Jessika, Gracie received a smile of recognition from Jerry. "Yeah, sure, of course. I did hear that, on the news: that he died, I mean. Heart attack, wasn't it?"

That, indeed, had been what the initial reports had theorized. Apparently Jerry hadn't heard any subsequent updates.

Gracie leaned over the bar and whispered, "no, Jerry: Fred was murdered," she told the barkeep, trying to make her tone sorrowful and shocked at the same time.

"No, shit!? Murdered? Someone killed him, you mean?" Jerry asked, matching Gracie's furtive whisper.

Gracie nodded solemnly.

"Geez, he was such a nice guy, you know? And he was your friend?" Jerry paused, and gave Gracie another look. "I mean, he had an eye for the ladies, but ya can't hold that against a guy, right?" Jerry commented.

Gracie, in spite of her firm opinion that yes, you could 'hold that against a guy,' nodded in apparent agreement. For an uncomfortable moment she wondered if Jerry thought that she had been one of the late Senator's 'ladies.' Then she decided that if Jerry thought that, she'd let him keep thinking it, as long as he talked to her.

"He was a big tipper, too," Jerry was saying now, in a normal tone. "Always drank top shelf stuff," he added. He turned, and, eschewing the array of liquor bottles that sat in front of the mirrored wall behind the bar, bent and retrieved a tall, slender bottle from a small freezer. He put the clear bottle in front of Gracie on the bar. "I carried that just for him," Jerry said mournfully, but with a touch of pride in his voice.

The bottle said Stolichnaya, which name Gracie knew. But it was 'Elit- Himalayan edition,' and Gracie had never seen that.

"What makes this so special?" she asked, frowning at the label.

Jerry told her the vodka was distilled using snowmelt and water from only one spring in the Himalayan mountains, and was one of the smoothest on earth. "Each bottle runs me three grand," he said. He squinted at the bottle's contents: it was about three quarters full. "With Fred gone, I wonder who will drink this?"

Gracie looked at the vodka bottle critically: it was hand blown Czech glass, which accounted for some of its priciness. "What do you get out of this bottle, like, 15 shots?" she hazarded a guess.

Jerry gave an appreciative nod. "Yeah, just about that. The Senator liked full shots, though: two ouncers, on the rocks, so it was more like a dozen."

"He diluted something that costs $250 a serving with *ice*?" Gracie asked, shocked. Maybe Fred Jesperson had appeared to like expensive vodka, but he obviously really just liked throwing money around: what genuine vodka connoisseur would put ice with something that precious, and purportedly so pure? It would ruin it!

Jerry shrugged. "Cost more than that per drink: you're forgetting my markup," he commented. "So I didn't ask him why he wanted Massachusetts ice in something that came from a Himalayan spring: the man was paying. I gave him what he asked for."

Jerry appeared to be enjoying having Gracie to talk to while the bar was empty, and Gracie was happy to engage the voluble barkeep in conversation.

At one point Jerry told her that the Senator would routinely have at least three drinks in the course of an evening visit to the Whitewater bar. "I had a standing order for a bottle of this stuff every two weeks, with my supplier," Jerry said. "Guess I'll have to cancel that, now," he added.

"Wow: three full shots?"

"Sometimes doubles."

"Three doubles?" Gracie asked. Never mind the cost, probably $600 a drink, but the alcohol! "I'd be on the floor asleep if I drank that much. Or puking my guts up," she added with a grin.

Jerry laughed companionably. "Oh, the Senator could hold his liquor all right," he told her. "He'd stop off here on his way home, most Fridays," he said.

"Wow," Gracie breathed ingenuously. "Could he drive okay?" she asked, feigning concern. "I mean, did you ever have to take his keys?"

Jerry gave her a look. "C'mon, the guy was a State Senator! I wasn't gonna cut him off, or take his keys. Besides, he usually could walk pretty good when he left, so I figured he'd drive okay."

They chatted a little bit more about Senator Jesperson, and about vodka, during which time Gracie learned the difference between grain fermented vodka's taste and that of potato fermented vodka. Jerry offered to set up a couple of 'tasting' shots for Gracie, but she refused, explaining that she had to drive, and unlike the late Senator, she couldn't 'hold her liquor.'

"Well, you got a point about that," Jerry admitted. "But you come back some time, with a designated driver or something, and I'll do a tasting for you," he urged.

Gracie smiled.

Chapter Twenty-three

The Pittsfield Junior League, or 'Club' as Gracie and her friends referred to it, had been established over 100 years before and was one of the more socially prominent organizations in Western Massachusetts. Its nearest rival was the Springfield Women's Club which belonged to the General Federation of Women's Clubs and boasted over 50 members. PJL had 34 members at last count, which Gracie thought was quite impressive for an association centered in the most rural county in the state.

Despite its name, PJL accepted any woman over the age of 18 who lived in either Berkshire or Hampshire Counties. Members had to be sponsored by a current member, and had to be vetted by the Membership Committee. This year, Gracie had been elected Membership Chair; her friend Jean, who'd been inducted into Club three years before, was also on the committee along with three other members. Gracie's friend Anne, also in Club, was the outgoing Membership Chair.

Gracie had been in England for Club's April meeting, held on the second Tuesday of every month. By tradition, the May meeting was the Annual Banquet at which Club's new Executive Board and Committee Chairs took office, and those who had made outstanding contributions to Club or the community were recognized. As always, it was held on a Saturday evening, and as always, it was one of the highlights of the social calendar and usually received good press.

The Banquet was always held at the swank Pittsfield Country Club. Despite its prosaic name, the Country Club was private and memberships started at $55,000 a year. Its restaurant was one of the best in the region, but it too was reserved for members and their guests. The only reason PJL could hold its Banquet in the Club's beautiful Green Room was that the founder of the PJL had been married--eons ago--to the President of the Country Club. Although now there was no such association, the tradition continued, and the PJL always made a generous 'contribution' to the Country Club's scholarship fund in return for the use of the facility for its Banquet.

"Let me show you to our table!" Jean said merrily as Gracie entered the Green Room on Saturday evening. Jean was on the Banquet Committee this year, and had been busy most of the day making sure everything at the Country Club was ready for that evening's festivities.

She greeted Gracie with a hug, and led her to a table set with fern green and cream linen, with a centerpiece of candles and ivy. Each place also featured a hand made nosegay of herbs and dried flowers: Maddie had agreed to provide the favors, which she had tailored to each Club member, months ago when the Banquet had been in the planning stages. Gracie was just a little surprised to see that, despite the upheaval of the previous week, Maddie had come through with the promised favors.

"Wow, this looks amazing!" Gracie remarked, surveying the large banquet room. It was in a separate, glass conservatory type wing away from the Country Club's Members' Dining Room. The room's chandeliers and candles sparkled as the PJL Members arrived for their Gala. Everyone was dressed in semi formal cocktail dresses in pastels and brights: they reminded Gracie of butterflies as they entered and greeted each other, going from table to table laughing and talking.

Gracie was very glad she'd joined Club. When she'd first moved to Pittsfield, she had known no one: the first 'friend' she'd made besides her neighbors Bob and Anna had been Larry, her contractor.

A couple of months after her arrival, once she'd settled in to her 300-plus year old Colonial farmhouse and had essentials like the furnace, the wiring and the plumbing upgraded, Gracie had started writing for the *Intelligencer,* a weekly newspaper which covered Berkshire and Hampshire Counties. She was given the job of Berkshire County news reporter, and quickly had established her 'beat' and made contacts in downtown Pittsfield.

The County Prothonotary, Paula, who to this day remained both a trusted source and a friend, had been Vice President of the PJL at the time, and had put Gracie up for membership. There had been a bit of discussion, because Gracie was not native to the area and no one knew much about her: there were concerns that she was not settled in the community permanently, or that her past might have been an unsavory one from which she was running.

However, Paula had put a stop to such xenophobic suspicions by providing the Membership Committee with a detailed history of Gracie's life to that point: her youth in South Boston; her outstanding academic careers at Yale and then Harvard where she'd earned an MA in Journalism; her work as fact checker and then junior copy editor at the prestigious Boston Globe; her parents' tragic death; her move to Berkshire County and finally, her considerable inheritance.

Although none of its members would ever admit that they were influenced by money, the fact that Gracie was 'comfortable' as they liked to say, as though she were an armchair or a sofa, and could thus be counted on to support a number of Club's charitable activities, hadn't hurt her membership application. And as Paula told them when she spoke on her pledge's behalf, Club needed new blood, young people with fresh ideas who could energize the century old organization.

And so, Gracie had been inducted into Club, and ever since had found she made fast friends there from all sorts of backgrounds. Some she'd found an instant kinship with when they'd worked together on a Club project, and others she had just naturally gravitated towards. Now, although she might not see each of her particular friends very often, they all at least got together once a month, and so stayed in touch.

Anne was a stay at home mother with four children at last count and planning on six. She and Gracie had taken kickboxing classes together, and met for coffee or lunch occasionally as well as seeing each other at Club events.

Jean was a Correctional Officer at the Berkshire County Jail. Influenced by Gracie's culinary skill and by her son, who was in the Culinary Arts program at the local college, she had started to explore more adventurous menus on her own. Her son Chris had spent the previous summer interning at Joey and Tyler's restaurant *Mange Tout* in Boston. Jean and Gracie also met frequently to discuss local courthouse and criminal news from their differing perspectives.

Courtney Proulx, the owner and operator of Planet Provisions, had been thrilled to be inducted into Club earlier that year. Her husband's family was from the area and her mother in law had been a member before her early death. When Gracie and Maddie Jesperson sponsored Courtney, the Club's older members who had known Violetta Proulx, were particularly pleased.

These women: Anne, Paula, Jean, Maddie and Courtney, were Gracie's closest pals in Club. Only Anne was sitting at a different table for the Banquet: as outgoing Membership Chair, she was at the table with the other outgoing Committee Chairs. To round out the table of six, Hilda Senter joined Gracie and her friends; she and Gracie had worked together a couple of years before for the Club's Fall Fest Fundraiser. Hilda was the Head Librarian at Pittsfield's Berkshire Athenaeum, one of the largest libraries in the western part of the state.

Everyone except Maddie had arrived and appetizers were being served: mushroom ravioli in a light green herb sauce topped with crispy fried scallions and a quenelle of crème fraîche. By mutual unspoken agreement, everyone at Gracie's table kept Maddie's chair free, 'just in case.'

"I doubt she'll come," offered Courtney. "Although she was in the store yesterday," she added thoughtfully.

"And she dropped off the favors this morning," Jean put in. "They were waiting for me when I got here."

"She just buried her husband," Hilda put in. "I doubt she would really feel up to coming. I know after Walt died, I didn't go out for weeks," she added softly, referring to her late spouse. Hilda had been one of the early Club members, like Maddie: both were about two decades older than Gracie and her friends.

"True," Paula put in sympathetically. Paula bridged the gap between the 30-somethings and Hilda's 50-something, being in her 40's. "But she may also feel like being with her friends, and I know that sometimes after the funeral and all the la dee dah is over, people forget, and it gets really lonely. My mother in law told me that."

"Oh, I do hope she comes, it would be good for her to get out and be with us, be with her friends!" commented Gracie with a smile.

"I wonder if I could get the recipe for this," Jean remarked, changing the subject as she tasted the appetizer. "It's really good and I'd like to make it for Tom."

"Tom?" Gracie queried, giving her friend a puzzled glance. "I thought it was Chet?" She had yet to tell anyone, let alone Jean, of her day's activities, or of her informative lunch with Chet Sullivan.

Jean had been dating Chet since the summer before but given Chet's conversation earlier in the day, and Jean's comment just now, Gracie wondered what was going on.

Jean gave her a sly look. "See what happens when you go away?" she taunted.

"You broke up with Chet?" Gracie exclaimed. No wonder he'd been a bit glum at lunch.

"Wait—who's Chet?" put in Courtney, taking a sip of her pinot grigio.

"Who's Tom?" echoed Paula with a wicked smile.

"Chet is the Worcester County Detective. I met him last summer through Gracie and we've been dating…" Jean began by way of explanation. "Tom is Tom Woleski. I met him in high school. We were kinda going steady then, but stuff happened…"

"And now you've met up with Tom again?" Courtney surmised with a lift of one eyebrow.

Jean nodded.

"And you've broken up with Chet?" Gracie asked again.

"Not exactly--but I've started dating Tom." She sighed. "It's complicated."

"Ooooh, tell us about Tom!" demanded Courtney.

Jean explained that Tom Woleski had been her high school sweetheart many years before. He was recently divorced and had relocated from upstate New York, where he'd moved to attend Eastman College and where he'd settled down with his now ex-wife. Originally from Lanesboro, just north of Pittsfield, he had returned and of all surprising things, looked up his old high school girlfriend, Jean.

Gracie considered for a few moments. "Well, we'll have to have a chat about all of this," she said with a grin, but her friend looked quite happy about her current situation, and Gracie decided to say nothing about having run into Chet that day. "And as for this dish, I can tell you how to make it," she said with certainty.

"Even that little twirly thing on top?" Jean asked, meaning the quenelle.

"Yeah, sure: you make it with two teaspoons--" she broke off as Maddie Jesperson, wearing a violet silk sheath with a matching jacket approached the table. "Maddie! You're here!" Gracie exclaimed happily, but unnecessarily.

"Did you save a seat for me?" Maddie asked with a smile.

Chapter Twenty-four

Gracie and her friends welcomed the very recent widow to their table and included her in their small talk. Paula got a server's attention and made sure Maddie was given her appetizer and a tall glass of water with lemon. Gracie finished explaining how to make a quenelle. Jean chatted about her son's most recent adventures in the culinary world. Everyone said how much they liked their nosegays, and Maddie looked really pleased. Gracie noticed she had sprigs of lavender and rosemary in hers, along with some other herbs she would have to look up since she didn't know them by sight. Courtney's little bouquet had red yarrow in it and Jean's had, among other things, the pearlescent honesty plant.

"I'm amazed you had time to do these," Gracie murmured to Maddie, gesturing to her favor.

"Oh, I started assembling the herbs I wanted to use weeks ago," Maddie explained calmly. "I worked on them a bit at a time, and they were actually finished last week." Maddie looked like she was recalling something troubling, and Gracie put a hand on her arm.

"You okay?" she asked solicitously.

"Oh yes," Maddie replied brightly. "I was just recalling that Fred hadn't liked me working on the herbs in the kitchen," she explained. "I'd cleared some appliances from one of the work tops in front of a window, where the light was best. When he came home that Friday night and saw the herbs, he told me they were messy and smelled—oh, I shouldn't really say. It doesn't matter now," she broke off suddenly. Then she shrugged. "Anyway, I tidied everything out of sight when he was home, and worked on them during the week when he was away. I enjoyed making the favors."

"Each one's different, too: that took a lot of time and effort, Maddie. And they're beautiful," Gracie replied, thinking to herself that it was rather a shame that one of Maddie's last recollections of Fred was such an unpleasant one. Then again, no one had created that recollection except Fred.

While Maddie and Gracie were having their private conversation in lowered tones, Hilda had begun to tell everyone about that year's 'One Book, One County, One Film' initiative: Thomas Hardy's *Tess of the d'Urbervilles.*

"That should be fun!" Courtney said with delight: the tale was one of her favorites. "Which film are you using? Roman Polanski's?" she asked Hilda.

Hilda made a face. "Actually, none of the films really was thought to be suitable," she said, sounding quite prim, "although we considered using Bidyut Chakrabarty's *Nishiddha Nadi,*" she explained, referring to a Thai film maker's 2000 adaptation of the classic novel.

"I've seen that," Gracie put in. "With subtitles, of course: my Thai is limited to hello, thank you, yes, no and goodbye," she joked.

"Yes, exactly!" Hilda rejoined. "Subtitles. The committee decided that no one wanted to read their movie."

Paula nodded. "You have a point."

"So what did you choose?" Maddie asked. She had finished her appetizer and was sipping at her water. Gracie, seated next to her, thought she looked very good —great, in fact. Better than she had in a long time. Maybe the rumors about how difficult it had been to live a political life, or to live with Fred Jesperson, had been true, Gracie thought to herself. Maddie looked more relaxed than she had ever seen her.

"It was a close vote between the one from London Weekend Television and the BBC one," Hilda said.

"But the BBC one has Eddie Redmayne," Courtney piped up with a grin. "He's cute."

"I saw him in The Other Boleyn Girl," Maddie put in. "And he's going to be in that new film about Stephen Hawking, that comes out in the fall," she added, sounding enthusiastic.

"I don't remember having seen either of those *Tess* adaptations—were they shown here?" Gracie frowned. Normally she watched a lot of PBS, and a lot of costume dramas. She had even recently started streaming programs you couldn't get in the US directly from the UK on her laptop.

"Yes: the first one is three hours long and from 1998. The BBC one, which is the one we chose, is four hours," Hilda replied. "It's from 2008."

"Four hours?" Jean asked dubiously.

The servers brought out the main course now; members had chosen either vegetarian, chicken, or beef, and all three choices were represented at the table.

"We decided to do something a little fun and different," Hilda said brightly. "We'll show the first two hours, then we'll have a break for people to get up and go to the lavatories, and in the theatre lobby we'll have hors d'oeuvres and specialty coffees," she explained.

"That sounds great!" Gracie commented. She thought it would also be a good story for the paper, and made a note to write down the date of the film showing so she'd be sure she wouldn't miss it.

Hilda nodded. "Delise is doing the food and coffee," she put in.

"None better!" Courtney chimed in. "They do gluten free, too."

"Yes, and they've promised to have a selection," Hilda assured her. "Then we'll show the last two hours."

"It should be a great evening! I'll have to download a copy of the book for my iPad and re-read it," Gracie murmured.

"I remember reading that in high school," Paula put in. "I'll do the same, re-read it on my Kindle."

Conversation slowed while everyone ate, then picked up again as dessert and coffee were served.

"Did you like your dinner?" Courtney, who was on Gracie's right, asked. She had ordered the gluten free vegetarian lasagne, and had pronounced it excellent.

"I did," Gracie replied. She had chosen the Pomegranate Chicken in Pastry, and not only had she liked it, she'd surreptitiously written down what she thought the ingredients were, and determined to give it a try. The puff pastry wouldn't be hard: it was the pomegranate sauce over the chicken pieces inside, teamed with portobello mushrooms, that might be a bit of a challenge.

Hilda was the only one at their table who had chosen the beef, a petite filet mignon which she said was so tender she hadn't even needed her knife to cut it. All the entrées had been plated with spring vegetables (peas, arugula, asparagus, and artichokes in lemon butter) and a basket of whole grain rolls was on the table for anyone who needed bread.

Dessert was another great creation from the pastry chef at the Country Club: a graham cracker crusted cheesecake topped with a strawberry rhubarb confit and finished with shavings of white chocolate.

"That was so good, I just didn't eat the crust," Courtney smiled: even graham crackers had gluten, which she avoided. "But that cheesecake!" she rolled her eyes.

"Yeah, I could have licked my plate," Gracie confided.

"Maddie, you enjoyed the chicken?" Gracie asked. It appeared her friend had: there was nothing left on her plate but a couple of artichoke bits in a tiny puddle of lemon butter.

"It was delicious," Maddie said in a voice that sounded satisfied and calm. "And it's so nice to have company for dinner," she added, and Gracie bit her lip and looked concerned.

"You must miss Fred," she said quietly.

Maddie gave Gracie a stunned look, and then smiled. "Well, yes, I mean, of course, I do, yes," she stumbled over her words and appeared to be trying not to laugh. "But he wasn't home for dinner very much." She sighed. "I haven't had company for dinner on a regular basis in years."

Gracie didn't know what to say to that, so she asked Maddie if she wanted tea or coffee, and busied herself pouring. Maybe she shouldn't feel so happy for her friend. After all, Maddie's husband was dead. That was supposed to be a sad thing, wasn't it? And yet, Gracie thought, slanting a glance at Maddie sipping at her tea, her friend seemed just fine. Maybe not all departures from this life were deserving of great mourning.

After a short break, it was time for the yearly awards, and the introduction of the following year's Officers and Committee Chairs.

"So, Maddie, you look good, you doing all right?" Hilda asked as the table was being cleared.

Maddie turned to look at the librarian. "I am doing all right, Hilda, I really am," she said in a sure voice.

"I'm glad," Hilda rejoined, and put a hand on Maddie's arm.

"Oh, you're wearing the mala bead bracelet you bought at the store!" Courtney put in. From her spot on the other side of Gracie, she'd noticed the beaded rose quartz bracelet on Maddie's right wrist as Maddie had turned to speak to Hilda. It made a colorful addition to several others of similar types that the woman always wore on one hand. On her other, she wore a few Italian charm bracelets with links that stood for hobbies, grand children and favorite things, and about seven slender silver bangles, all different, that made a pleasant tinkling noise as she moved her arm.

Maddie looked down, and fingered the rosy pink beads. "They're so pretty," she said, smiling.

"All the way from Nepal!" Courtney put in.

"You sell those at your store?" Jean asked. "I thought you only did natural food?"

"I have a small jewelry line, all fair trade, all from Nepal and a couple of places in South America," Courtney explained. "You should come check it out."

"I should," agreed Jean. "I bet Sarah would love those," she noted of the bracelets, thinking of her teenaged daughter.

"They each mean something, don't they?" Hilda asked, curious. "I've read about them."

Of course, Gracie thought: she would have. She ought to introduce Hilda to Agnes Davis, the Daweses' bookish neighbor: they'd get on great!

"Yes. That is, I guess so. I buy them sometimes for their meaning, but also because I like them," Maddie replied.

Gracie looked at Maddie's bracelets then, since they were the topic of conversation and Maddie was displaying them and chattering away about what they meant. As she looked and listened, Gracie's smile slowly faded. Maddie wore a bright turquoise bracelet supposed to bring balance, the new rose pink one for love and friendship, a dark brown almost black one with white notations on the larger beads that was said to protect the wearer from harm, amber colored beads for happiness, a Turkish 'good luck eye' bracelet that Gracie herself had brought her friend from Istanbul a few months back, and a bracelet made from bright red oblong shaped beads with a black tip, clasped with a standard jeweler's lobster clasp. The other bracelets were all on elastic thread to fit over the hand and snugly on the wrist: they didn't have clasps. But the red one did. And the red beads looked familiar to Gracie.

"What's this one called?" she asked Maddie, her heart in her throat. She pointed to the red and black bracelet.

"Oh, that's Jequirity," Maddie answered. "I like it because it reminds me of ladybugs, and you know how I love ladybugs," she replied, smiling. " And ladybugs are lucky," she added happily.

"You got that one from my store, too!" Courtney exclaimed. "That was from some cooperative in England and the money from the bracelets went towards an ecological initiative of some kind," she said to the table at large.

"You always try to make a difference," Jean told Courtney with a smile. "I admire that," she added.

"Thanks!" Courtney blushed at the praise. "But, Maddie, did you change the clasp?" Courtney asked, then. "I don't remember the bracelet having a clasp, actually," she admitted.

"Oh, it didn't," Maddie replied easily. "The beads were on an elastic thread, but it broke and I didn't have any elastic so I just re-strung the beads on some fishing filament we had in the basement." She looked down at the pretty bracelet. "I got the clasp in the notions department at the fabric store in the mall," she added.

"Oh, well, I'm sorry it broke: you should have brought it in and I would have replaced it free for you!" Courtney protested.

"Oh, that's all right, Courtney," Maddie insisted. "It's fine, and it's nice and sturdy now, won't break again."

'Jequirity,' Gracie thought, not really listening to the introductions of the new Officers and Committee Chairs. She'd never heard that name before. But the 'jequirity' beads looked just like the pictures she'd seen of the rosary pea when she'd been researching it, and she could hardly wait for an opportunity to google 'jequirity' and find out.

Chapter Twenty-five

Gracie could hear Jack in her head: 'we always look at the spouse, Gracie.' Well, yes, but this was *Maddie* they were talking about! Maddie wouldn't hurt anyone, let alone her husband. Fred Jesperson's murderer had to be someone else.

A short while after the announcements concluded, the Banquet attendees began to say their farewells, and Gracie seized the opportunity to slip into the ladies' room and google 'jequirity.' She hadn't wanted to do that in front of everybody.

To her dismay, the results popped up on her iPhone's screen, and Gracie felt her stomach clench: jequirity was, indeed, another name for the rosary pea or rosary bean.

She sighed. She knew she should tell Jack, but she also knew what he would say, and what it would mean, particularly for Maddie. And yet, not telling Jack would be obstruction of justice, for sure. She could try to say she hadn't known jequirity was another name for the deadly rosary pea, but she couldn't really live with herself if she did that. And, Jack knew her too well: he knew that if Gracie came across a term she was unfamiliar with, she'd look it up. So even if Gracie made the excuse that she didn't know the connection, the excuse wouldn't hold water.

But she couldn't bear to tell Jack. Not just yet. Maybe not until he had a break in the case that might point to someone else as Fred Jesperson's murderer.

Driving home from the Banquet, Gracie had a brainstorm, and fairly ran into her house once she arrived. Glancing at the clock, she realized it was nearly 11 p.m., which meant that it was close to 4 a.m. in England, where David was. But he had mentioned when they'd had their Skype date that he had some night shifts coming up, to accrue points towards his upcoming vacation.

So Gracie thought he would probably be working the overnight shift this night. She wanted to get another opinion on the discovery of Maddie's deadly bracelet, and she wanted to ask David, since he was objective.

"Hallo."

"David, it's Gracie. You're on night shift, right?" she asked in a rush, her voice tense. "I mean, I haven't woken you up or anything, have I?"

"*Och, mo duinne!*" David replied happily. "What a wonderful surprise to hear your voice."

Gracie allowed as how she was happy to hear his voice, too, and then got right to the point. "Remember the Senator I told you about, who'd been killed with that weird poison, abrin?"

"Aye, it's like ricin only stronger, and your ME said it was certainly not accidental," David replied, his tone serious.

Yes, he remembered.

Gracie explained about Jack searching the Jespersons' home, and the Senator's office and townhouse and finding no trace of rosary peas or abrin. Then she told him about Maddie's bracelet.

"The thing is, David, she's always worn a bunch of bracelets," Gracie finished. "I don't know if that red and black one with the rosary pea beads is new or what," she explained. "Courtney said she sells them in her store, too, and that she gets them from some environmental place in Cornwall or Devon or something," she continued, becoming more and more upset.

"Oh, Gracie, that does look bad for your friend," David admitted. "But you said she seemed completely unaware of how poisonous her bracelet could be?" he queried.

Gracie answered in the affirmative.

At this moment, Pumpkin came walking into the kitchen and began to miaow, sitting forlornly next to her empty bowl.

"Och, I hear the wee beastie," exclaimed David, his Scots accent pronounced as he chuckled.

"Yes. She wants her snack, since I'm home now," Gracie explained.

"Well, Gracie, it's circumstantial evidence, the bracelet, I mean," David said then, trying to reassure her.

"But don't you think I should tell—erm—the authorities?" Gracie asked.

"Aye. You probably should. But if your friend Maddie is as innocent as you believe, then it's likely that they won't discover anything when they question her." He paused.

Pumpkin miaowed again.

"Have ye not thought, Gracie, that if your other friend is selling those bracelets in her shop, then that's *really* what ye should tell the police?" David said, sounding like the Detective Sargent he was. "Anyone could have bought one of those bracelets and used the beads to poison the Senator, anyone who had gone in that shop and knew what the bracelet was made of and wanted to kill Fred Jesperson, that is," he amended.

"Oh, David! Of course, you're right!" Gracie exclaimed, relieved. "I couldn't see that, I was just so focused on trying not to implicate Maddie," she explained. "Oh, David, thank you so much!"

He laughed, and they had another brief exchange that was much more pleasant than the earlier part of the conversation.

Then Gracie said she had to go and feed the cat, who was now pacing back and forth in front of her bowl and casting beseeching glances up to where Gracie stood.

"Aye, feed the wee beastie, *mo duinne*. I'll speak with you soon," David agreed, and they hung up.

Chapter Twenty-six

Gracie waited until Monday to tell Jack about the jequirity/rosary pea bracelet. Because it was something she thought she could explain better in person, she drove into Pittsfield Monday morning, and ran up the two flights of stairs to the DA's suite on the third floor of the courthouse.

"Hi Millie!" Gracie greeted the long time secretary. "Detective Draper in?" she asked breezily.

"Yes, he is, Gracie, go on back," Millie said with a big smile; she waved one hand in the general direction of Jack's office.

Gracie stopped and knocked on Jack's open office door. "Got a minute?" she asked.

Jack must have heard her voice, because he was already standing behind his desk, smiling in greeting. "Good morning!" he said happily. "Have a seat."

Gracie did as he requested, then fixed him with a curious look.

"Why is everyone so happy?" she asked. "I mean, everyone is always very cordial and polite, but today you're all grinning—even Phyllida was humming in her office as I passed by!" Gracie declared.

It was a lovely, sunny morning and all the windows in the suite seemed to be open, flooding the space with light and birdsong. But it was more than that.

Jack chuckled. "Popovitch is on vacation," he revealed, still smiling. "Not that it makes a bit of difference to the work load, but it does to the morale around here. We all feel like our sentences have been commuted. At least for a few days."

Gracie nodded. "Ooooh, I see," she replied.

"Millie even shut the door to his office," Jack chuckled again. "I heard her muttering that as long as he was away, she didn't want to be reminded of him more than she had to be," he finished with a grin.

Gracie's smile was conspiratorial. "Where'd he go?" she asked, not really curious, but making conversation, the better to ease into her report.

"He and Tammy went to one of those all inclusive resort places, I think" Jack replied, referring to Popovitch's wife.

"Oh they're supposed to be nice, if you like that kind of thing," Gracie answered evenly.

"They went to the one in Grenada," Jack continued, his tone dubious. "I think it's another attempt to get Tammy pregnant," Jack added, his voice dropping lower, so quiet Gracie could barely hear him.

"Well, I suppose.." Gracie began, but trailed off as the image of the corpulent DA on the beach rose unbidden in her mind's eye. "Oh, god, Jack, can you imagine Popovitch in a bathing suit?" she blurted, giggling.

Jack's face underwent a swift series of changes, but he, too, ended up grinning. "I wonder if he wears a speedo?" he queried.

Gracie looked momentarily nonplussed. Then: "no, probably a really loud pair of surfer's shorts, you know, with, bright red crabs on a fluorescent yellow background or something," she offered, still giggling. Then she caught her breath and composed herself. "So you're super busy, I'm sorry to barge in, but I need to tell you something."

Jack gave her a keen look. "Okay…"

"It's about the Jesperson case," Gracie began, and filled Jack in on the Club Banquet the previous Saturday evening, and on Maddie Jesperson, and her bracelets, and the fact that Courtney sold those bracelets in her shop, Planet Provisions.

When she was finished, Jack just sat back in his chair and stared at her.

"Wow, Gracie: that might just break the case wide open," he said to her, sounding amazed.

Gracie cringed. "You—you don't think it was Maddie, do you?" she asked, desperately wanting Jack to reassure her that no, he didn't think her friend was a murderer.

Much as he might have wanted to do that, however, Jack told Gracie the truth.

"Well, like I always tell you: look at the spouse," he began slowly. "But the fact that these bracelets are being sold locally does spread the blame around," he admitted. "And, if your friend is selling them here, they are probably being sold elsewhere, too," Jack added.

"So, it could have been someone other than Maddie," Gracie insisted.

Jack nodded. "Yes. It could have been. Even though she is top of my list of suspects, and really always has been." He paused and took a deep breath. "First, I need to have a talk with Courtney, and let her know about the bracelets and how deadly they can be. I'll ask Millie to see if she can turn up other stores that sell those bracelets, too, or have sold them. Then, I'll be talking to Maddie again, and seeing if I can find out anything more about her particular bracelet," he said, thinking aloud. "Gracie —can I ask you not to tell anyone about this, not yet, I mean. Until I've had a chance to talk to everyone? It should only be a couple of days."

Gracie shrugged, and nodded her head. "Sure. I mean, it's not enough to run a story on it, and I can keep the link between jequirity bracelets and rosary peas and abrin to myself," she agreed.

Jack arrived at Planet Provisions mid morning, and as it was his first time at the shop, although he knew Gracie went there quite a bit, his eye was caught by the clever displays and the range of items sold. There were two people staffing the shop, one of whom was the owner, Courtney Proulx, Gracie's friend. Jack introduced himself, and asked Courtney if they could talk privately, so she led him to her small office behind the cash desk at in the shop, and shut the door.

"It's nice to finally meet you," Courtney said, moving a stack of display baskets off a chair so Jack could sit down. She slipped into her own chair behind the small desk she used to keep track of orders and sales at the store, and looked expectantly at Jack. "Gracie's always spoken so highly of you," she told him with a smile.

"Nice to hear," Jack commented. Then he asked her about the jequirity bead bracelets.

"Sure, I ordered six in, and I've sold—um—three I think, let me check," Courtney answered promptly. She 'woke up' her laptop that sat on her desk, at the ready, and navigated to a sales report. "Yes, three."

"You don't happen to have listed who you sold the bracelets to, do you?" Jack asked with hope.

Courtney shook her head, and her thick, wavy chestnut colored hair swung around her shoulders. "No, I'm afraid my sales information isn't that detailed," she apologized. "I know Maddie Jesperson bought one: we were just talking about it Saturday night at the Club Banquet," she said.

Jack nodded, and explained that Gracie had already filled him in on Maddie's bracelet and the Club Banquet, and that was why he was here at Planet Provisions.

"Is it important to find out who bought the other two?" Courtney asked, concerned. A thin vertical line appeared between her brows.

"I'm afraid so, yes, Courtney. And—you need to pull the other three from the sales floor," Jack began. "Could you bring them in here, please?" he asked.

Courtney excused herself and, looking worried, disappeared for a scant few moments, then reappeared holding three bright red beaded bracelets. Each bead had a single black end, and they were threaded onto elasticized string. She handed the bracelets to Jack, who took them carefully, and looked at them closely.

The elastic string was knotted at the beginning and end of each bead, and the holes through which the string ran were very small: just enough to admit the string. However, a bracelet that had been drilled improperly could, he theorized, leak some of the deadly abrin that was inside each bead.

Jack slipped the three bracelets into a clear baggie he'd brought with him, and then asked if he could wash his hands at the small sink he spied in a corner of the office. He encouraged Courtney to do the same and she complied, but looked more and more agitated.

"Detective, I've had those bracelets in my shop for months," she said as they returned to her desk and sat. "You're scaring me: what's going on?"

Jack explained that the bracelets contained the deadly poison abrin inside each of the pretty beads. "It's unlikely anyone would be poisoned by just wearing the bracelet, or handling it, unless it was a damaged or defective one, maybe with a crack or a drill hole that was too big," Jack explained. "That's why I wanted us to wash our hands: just in case."

Courtney had paled. She knew Fred Jesperson had died from abrin poisoning, but had had no idea that abrin was found inside the jequirity beads. She'd heard about something called a 'rosary pea' but she hadn't made the connection.

"So you see why it's important that I find out who bought bracelets from you. And if you could, will you give me the name of the company you bought them from?" he asked.

Courtney returned to her computer and tapped several keys. "I don't have the names of who bought the bracelets, I just have the dates they were sold. But—" she tapped a couple of other keys, "one of them—no, both of the others, besides Maddie's, were bought by the same person, and they charged the purchase along with a bunch of other stuff they bought." She quickly wrote down a name and address on a small piece of paper and handed it to Jack. "I think I remember her, too: she bought the bracelets as holiday gifts. The sale was the week before Christmas."

"Oh, Courtney, that's great, thank you," Jack said, looking at the information, then tucking the note in his pocket.

"Let me get the name of the company for you, too," Courtney went on, and moments later she was writing that information down for Jack as well.

"I'll be contacting them about any other shops they may have sold the bracelets to, at least the ones in this region," Jack said grimly. "They'll probably want to recall them from everyone they sold to, given the risk they carry."

Chapter Twenty-seven

Upon returning to his office, Jack contacted the Genesis Project in Devon, England, and let them know about the concerns he had about the jequirity bead bracelets they were selling. He was finally connected to the gift shop manager, and she told him she would look into the matter immediately. She also agreed to email him a list of stores in the U.S. that had purchased the bracelets from the Genesis Project, to help with the Project's environmental and educational goals.

Jack also called the woman who had purchased the other two bracelets from Maddie's shop. She wasn't in, but he left a message for her to contact his office as soon as possible; then he instructed Millie to explain to the woman that the beaded bracelets could be potentially harmful, and tell her to bring them into his office at her earliest convenience.

Rather than wait for the email from the Genesis Project, Jack decided he'd try and catch Maddie Jesperson at home, and talk with her more about her bracelet. The first thing, of course, was to alert her to the danger it might pose, and encourage her to give it to him. He didn't have enough to subpoena the bracelet, but he hoped it wouldn't come to that.

It was just after noon by the time Jack rang the Jespersons' front door bell. Seconds later, Maddie answered, looking surprised, but pleased to see Jack.

"Come in, Detective!" she said happily, and ushered him into their foyer. "I spent all morning in the herb garden, and I'm afraid I'm a bit of a mess," Maddie continued, gesturing to her shabby jeans with soil stains at the knees. "Do you have news about Fred's murder?" she asked eagerly.

Jack looked at her, scrutinizing her face. If she was faking being a concerned widow, she deserved an Oscar. "Yes, Mrs. Jesperson, I do," he said.

"Oh, Detective, please call me Maddie," the woman returned, pushing a lock of blonde frosted hair away from her face. "I changed my shoes and washed my hands, and I've just made lunch—may I offer you some? There's plenty," she asked kindly.

"Oh, no, no that's all right, but I'll come speak with you while you eat, if that's okay?" Jack replied. He'd stopped *en route* at his favorite fast food outlet and demolished a large, loaded burger and small fries. "It shouldn't take too long," he continued, as he followed Maddie down the hallway and into her bright, sunny kitchen. It was painted white, with touches of red and black and decorative lady bug themed items throughout: the valances on the windows, the placemats on the kitchen table, even the potholders were all festooned with ladybugs.

Maddie saw him taking it all in and laughed lightly. "The ladybug has always been a favorite of mine," she said by way of explanation. She gestured for Jack to sit. "Would you like some coffee or tea?" she asked.

"Coffee would be great, thanks," Jack answered, sitting.

Maddie switched on the coffeemaker, which apparently had already been set up. "I don't normally drink coffee mid day, but I had rather a demanding morning in the garden, so I thought I might like some," Maddie told Jack convivially.

"Oh? What were you doing in the garden?" he asked, trying to imagine what tasks might have been 'demanding' as Maddie had said.

She explained that she had been removing the picket fence that had surrounded her herb garden. "I plan to expand it, you see, and have walkways constructed that run throughout the lawn, and through and around the herb garden, to integrate it more into the overall design of the backyard," she told him.

Jack smiled, and mentioned Gracie's herb garden that was chiefly against an old rock wall that caught the southern sunshine.

Maddie nodded. "Yes, I've been to Gracie's house, and seen her garden, and it's lovely the way she has tied all the various areas of her plantings together," Maddie said, fetching two mugs out of a cupboard. "That's what I would like to achieve here," she added, smiling.

Jack wondered silently why she hadn't just integrated the herb garden into the backyard and the other flower beds and shrubs in the first place, but didn't feel comfortable asking.

"Are you sure you don't want some lunch? It's nothing fancy: just a sandwich," Maddie asked again.

Jack smiled. "I grabbed something on my way here, so I'm set, but coffee will be nice," he answered.

Maddie brought over two mugs of coffee and her sandwich, and sat opposite Jack at the table.

Jack looked out the nearest widow, and wondered how he should begin. He could see a corner of what must be a substantial herb garden: sections of picket fencing lay neatly next to it on the lawn.

Initially, Jack had thought to just tell Maddie the truth about the bracelets, demand hers, and be on his way. But when he was confronted with Maddie in the flesh, Maddie herself, not on display as the Senator's wife, or in any kind of official capacity, just Maddie, her genuine sweetness disarmed him. Jack could see why Gracie was so fond of Maddie, and, like Gracie, he was beginning to doubt Maddie was a viable suspect.

Still, he had a job to do. He eyed the bread of her sandwich. "You got that at Planet Provisions, didn't you?" he asked. "It's that seven grain gluten free bread, right?" he asked. Gracie used the same bread, not because she had gluten issues but because she loved the taste. Jack had to admit, it was pretty good.

"That's right, Detective!" Maddie exclaimed. "Do you use it, too?"

Jack mentioned that Gracie did, and Maddie nodded. "Oh, yes, I know the two of you used to date, but now you're —still friends, yes?" she asked, looking hopeful.

"Yes," Jack confirmed.

"I always think that's—important," Maddie returned in a gentle voice. "If people can remain friends." She gave a small chuckle. "Let's face it, Detective, romance only lasts so long, but friendship, well: that endures."

Jack nodded, and they were quiet for a few moments as Maddie ate her lunch. Then Jack mentioned the jequirity bead bracelets sold at Planet Provisions. "I notice you're not wearing yours," he said.

As a matter of fact, Maddie didn't have any jewelry on: just some kind of religious medal around her neck. That made sense to Jack, if she'd been gardening as she'd said.

"I don't usually wear any jewelry when I'm just home, and especially if I'm in the garden," Maddie replied. "This," and here she fingered the medal around her neck, "I never take off. But I put everything else on when I dress to go out," she explained. "Why, Detective?"

Jack sighed, and told her about the danger the bracelets could pose if one were cracked or defective. "You'd have to ingest the abrin that would leak out, and that's a fairly unlikely scenario," he admitted.

"But—but it could happen," Maddie put in. She put her half eaten sandwich down, and her blue eyes opened wide. "Oh, my god, the grandchildren!" she breathed, and put a hand to her lips.

Jack was confused. "Grandchildren?"

Maddie explained that her grandchildren could have played with the bracelet, even sucked on the beads.

Quickly, Jack put Maddie's mind at ease by noting that if the grandchildren had ingested any of the poison from her bracelet, they would have shown signs of illness by now.

Maddie took a deep breath. "I just talked to Elizabeth, that's my daughter, this morning," she told Jack. "The children are fine." She sighed again.

"Can you tell me who would have had access to your bracelet?" Jack asked next. Maddie's concern for her grandchildren had been so immediate and so great that he was becoming more and more convinced that she wasn't her husband's murderer. Still, he had to dig deeper: she could just be a very good actress. Or she could be a psychopath.

Maddie shrugged. "Well, no one, really: the bracelet, along with the other bracelets I generally wear, and my rings, and earrings and other necklaces and such, are in my jewelry box on my dresser in my bedroom." Her voice had cracked on the word 'rings' and Jack knew she meant her wedding set.

"And if they're not in your jewelry box?" Jack asked.

"Then they're on me," Maddie said definitely.

"And you mentioned the grand children—when might they have had access to the bracelet?" he queried, sipping his coffee and keeping his body language casual and non threatening.

"Well, I have two grandchildren: Billy, who is four, and Martha, who is five, nearly six," she answered. "They have played 'dress up' with some of my things, and—and

Fred's," she said, her voice getting very quiet again. "But, Detective, although I can't recall each and every instance, I think most of the time they would have been visiting, I would have had my bracelets on. And I don't recall them playing with the bracelets specifically, although they visit once a month at least and after so many visits, they all kind of run together, so I suppose the children could have played with my jewelry," she admitted.

Jack nodded and then, since Maddie had finished her sandwich, he asked if she could bring him her bracelet.

It took her only a few minutes to retrieve it from her second floor bedroom; she handed it to Jack, who looked at it critically.

"This isn't the same as the ones in Planet Provisions," he said, his tone unemotional.

"No: I bought it there, last December, when Courtney got them in," Maddie explained. "But the elastic string broke and I—I repaired the bracelet using fishing line we have, and a clasp from the fabric store," she finished, her voice sounding disbelieving. "I took the beads off the string and re-strung them," she went on, sounding a bit panicked. "But I—I've never been ill," she finished, frowning down at her hands as though she expected to see evidence of the poison on them somehow.

Jack nodded. "Right. You probably washed your hands when you were finished repairing the bracelet," Jack said easily, wanting to calm her. "So any abrin that might have got on your hands was washed away." He paused, and was glad to see that Maddie looked less worried.

Jack fingered the bracelet. "May I have this, Mrs. Jespers—Maddie?" he asked.

"Of course!" Maddie exclaimed. "Do you think it's linked to Fred's death?" she asked in a hushed tone. "I mean, he died from abrin poisoning, and that's abrin," she gestured to the bracelet, which Jack was now securing in a baggie. He tucked the baggie in his pocket and then stepped over to the kitchen sink and washed his hands. Even the soap dispenser was in the shape and coloring of a lady bug. And the hand towel.

"I don't know the answer to that Maddie," Jack answered kindly. "You said the elastic broke?"

Maddie nodded.

"Do you remember when it broke? Where you were, for example? Were you wearing it, or..." he prompted.

Maddie thought a moment, gazing off at the back door of the house, which led from the kitchen out to the yard and garden.

"No, Detective, I wasn't wearing it. I went to put it on one morning, oh, maybe a month ago? I don't really recall. And when I picked it up, it came apart! So I slipped the beads off the elastic string, tossed the string in the trash, and re threaded the beads onto the fishing line, as I've explained."

Jack nodded and leaned against the sink. Maddie remained at the table, but turned in her chair to look at Jack.

"I don't remember what else I did that day, specifically, but I know I made a special trip out to the fabric store in the mall because I knew they had a notions and craft supply department where I could get a clasp for the bracelet and finish the repair."

Jack recalled the original bracelets didn't have a clasp, they just stretched to fit over the wearer's hand.

"You said this happened about a month ago?" he asked.

Maddie nodded. "I think so."

"Did you find it odd that the bracelet just broke, like that? I mean, you weren't wearing it or doing anything that might have caused it to break," he suggested.

Maddie shook her head. "No. I really didn't think anything of it," she admitted. "I guess I just assumed that I'd inadvertently snapped the elastic or pulled it too hard when I'd taken it off the night before."

That seemed reasonable, but despite that, and Maddie's innocent appearance, Jack still wasn't ready to completely rule her out as a suspect.

"It would be good if you could pinpoint the day you went to the mall to get the clasp," Jack told her gently. Given everything that had happened in the past couple of weeks, he doubted she'd be able to.

She sighed. "I'm sorry, Detective, I don't remember when, exactly: I just went there and came back, and I paid cash so I won't have a charge receipt...wait," Maddie sat up straighter in her chair. "I think—I think it was a Monday, because I remember now, I had a yoga class in the morning and had to teach a Master Gardener class that afternoon, so the only time I had to run to the mall was the middle of the day." She paused, thinking, then got up and went to a calendar that hung on one wall: it had a picture of—what else?—a ladybug on it.

Maddie flipped the calendar back to the previous month, then she took it off the wall and brought it over to where Jack stood. "Here," she said, pointing. "That's the Monday I taught the class in the afternoon, and in the morning I had a yoga class," she said. She explained that the Master Gardener classes rotated instructors so that each week the students had a different teacher and a different subject and a different perspective.

"So that would have been the only Monday recently that you had both the yoga and the class?" Jack asked, examining the calendar.

Maddie nodded in the affirmative. "The next time I teach a Master Gardener class is the first Monday in June," she added, flipping to that date, and showing Jack the notation. "I take the yoga class most weekday mornings," she added.

"Okay, so we're pretty sure the day you repaired your bracelet was April eighth," Jack confirmed.

"Yes, I think so," Maddie agreed. Then she smiled. "I remember I had really been looking forward to the yoga, to relax," she continued, "because Elizabeth and her husband and the children had come for Sunday lunch the day before and, well, it had been a little tense."

Chapter Twenty-eight

While Jack was visiting Maddie, Gracie had made her courthouse rounds for that week's *Intelligencer* and returned home. When she switched on her laptop to start typing up her reports for the paper, a notification badge popped up on her home screen: it was telling her that there was new information on the background program she'd run on Amy and Richard Dawes.

Frowning, Gracie pushed her notes aside and launched the program and discovered that the Daweses' credit card, the same one that Amy had used at the convenience store and gas station near her mother's house, had been used again. This time, however, it had been used in Bloomingdale, NY, just a few hours ago. The time stamp was 1:42 a.m that morning.

Muttering to herself, Gracie input the town on her map app and was surprised to see its location: in the middle of the Adirondack region of New York State. Bloomingdale was a hamlet in Essex County, NY. It had just over a thousand residents and its biggest claim to fame was that it was at the junction of five roadways in upstate New York.

Now why, Gracie wondered as she pondered the information, would that credit card have been used way out there? She made another quick calculation and realized the location was about three hours from where Amy's mother lived. Hmmm…She let her eyes wander northward on the map. The Canadian border was another three hours north. She wondered.

As she typed up the fairly rote reports of arrests, car crashes, and cases logged in the past week with the local magistrates, Gracie let her mind churn away in the background on the question of the Daweses' credit card. She finished all the write ups, and emailed them in to the paper. Then she sat back in her chair at her spinet desk and thought some more.

The spring sun was still high and strong in the sky even though it was now late afternoon. Gracie gazed out at her herb garden, which was directly beyond the small window next to her desk. She could see several green shoots and newly unfurled leaves, early perennial herbs that were poking through the chilly soil. She ought to get in touch with Maddie, and see what herb cuttings she wanted to exchange this year.

Maddie. Gracie wondered how her friend was doing: had Jack already talked to her? What had he discovered, she wondered? She was tempted to call Jack, but decided against it: he'd likely tell her soon enough, if he had made any concrete connections between Maddie, her jequirity bead bracelet, and Senator Jesperson's death.

Gracie gazed again at the map. Amy had been the one to use the credit card before, so it was logical to think she was the one to have used it again. But why there? And where was Richard?

The card had been used to purchase quite a lot of gasoline, Gracie noticed, more than $300 worth. That suggested a very large gas tank, much larger than the one in Amy's Windstar van; or it could indicate additional gasoline containers.

Or another vehicle?

Gracie thought most vans and trucks like the vehicles Amy and Richard Dawes drove had twenty or twenty five gallon tanks. That would mean, at the current price of gas, a fill up would run around $85. Even if both of them filled up both their vehicles, there was still money left over. Gracie thought it was likely that extra gasoline containers had been involved.

Inspired by her success before in accessing traffic camera recordings, Gracie spent the next half hour getting into the New York State traffic cam system. Fortunately for her, the little hamlet of Bloomingdale had two traffic cams, one at each end of the main road of the town near the major intersections. Also fortunately for Gracie, the gas station was located at one of these intersections, the junction of Saranac Avenue or Route 3, and St. Regis Avenue, or Route 55.

As she had before, Gracie narrowed her search to the minutes before and after the use of the credit card and was rewarded by a grainy black and white vision of a van matching the description of Amy Dawes' arriving at the intersection and driving into the parking lot of the gas station. Although Gracie ran the footage back prior to Amy's arrival by almost fifteen minutes, and after her departure by the same margin, she never saw a vehicle that could have been the truck Richard Dawes was last known to have driven. As a matter of fact, no other vehicles entered the gas station lot, from what she could see, during the time Amy Dawes' van, and presumably Amy Dawes herself, had been there.

This didn't mean that he hadn't been at the gas station, which is what Gracie had conjectured. He could have changed vehicles. He could have come much earlier and left much later. But Gracie wasn't going to spend hours looking through traffic cam footage: she was lucky to have got the snippet she needed without having been detected.

She ran the footage, which she'd downloaded to her laptop, again, and this time she spotted something she hadn't noticed before. After Amy drove into the gas station and out of frame, she didn't exit for more than thirty minutes, driving away in the direction she'd come from. Even if she had been filling up several gas cans, this seemed to Gracie like a long time. The station was self service 24 hours with credit card payment only, and no attendant. The google earth image showed a kiosk to one side that Gracie thought might be bathrooms. No mini mart. So what had Amy been doing? Even a trip to the bathroom wouldn't take that long!

A shifting blur on the far edge of the picture seven minutes before Amy's van reappeared in the frame as it departed piqued Gracie's interest. She couldn't clean up the image very well and it wasn't even an entire person— it was just an elbow and the edge of someone's left hip.

There was no way Gracie could say that shadowy half figure was Amy Dawes. The fact that the traffic cam hadn't noted any other vehicles turning into the gas station during the time Amy had been there strongly indicated it, however. And whoever it had been had appeared to have arrived at that spot on foot, not in a vehicle, and have stood there for about a minute, and then disappeared.

What would someone do standing practically still for about a minute at the side of a gas station kiosk in the middle of the night?

It was nearly time to close the bank for the day when Gracie arrived, breathless and apologetic.

"I'm sorry, I'm sorry, but I need a favor!" Gracie told Judy, the Branch Manager of her bank in Cheshire.

"That's all right, you have five minutes!" Judy replied cheerily, but she would stay a few extra minutes for Gracie. Not only was she one of the bank's best customers, she always helped out with Judy's colony of feral cats who lived behind the bank in and around a small shed. Judy trapped, neutered and released the cats, and vaccinated the ones she could. The population was always shifting, of course, with new cats finding their way to the colony and new kittens being born, and at least one or two cats a year dying from either illness or from being run over.

So Judy had a soft spot in her heart for the lively reporter.

Quickly, Gracie explained what she needed to know.

"I don't know if we have an ATM in Bloomingdale, NY," Judy said, frowning at the computer on her office desk.

The other bank personnel said good night, turned off the lights and locked Judy and Gracie in.

"I'm so sorry, I'm keeping you…" Gracie murmured.

"No, that's all right, this'll only take a minute," Judy reassured her, tapping a key. "Or, it should only take —aha, here we go." She studied the list of ATM locations for their bank, one of the largest in the northeastern U.S.

Gracie had made a deductive leap that the shadowy half figure had been using an ATM: the length of time was about right, as was the relatively still, standing posture. Few other things would have fit that profile.

Gracie hoped that the ATM in question was owned by her bank; it could have been owned by any bank, of course, including New York State banks. But she knew from the background checks she'd run on the Daweses that they used the same bank she did. So perhaps they would choose to use ATMs associated with their bank to avoid fees.

"Yes, we have one in Bloomingdale, NY," Judy told her a moment later. "It's at a self service…"

"…gas station," Gracie finished for her, "at the intersection of Routes 3 and 55."

Judy gave her a look. "How'd you know that?" she asked. Then she grinned. "Maybe I don't want to know."

"Judy—is there a camera at that ATM?" Gracie asked quickly.

Judy nodded. "There are at all our ATMs, why?" she asked with a bit of trepidation.

Gracie took a breath. "Could you pull up some footage for me if I give you a date and time?" she asked pleadingly.

Chapter Twenty-nine

Judy couldn't help Gracie with that last request. "I don't have access to the ATM footage, I have no need to, really," she explained. "I'm sorry."

Gracie nodded and thanked her anyway. "You've been a huge help: I never would have been able to know that ATM was yours without driving up there myself, if it weren't for you," she told Judy honestly.

"The police could subpoena the footage from our main office," Judy suggested next.

Gracie nodded. Yes, she supposed they could. Well, maybe she'd call Jack and see what he thought about her theory. She called him as she got back to her Jeep, and left a message as his phone went directly to voicemail.

Jack's phone went directly to voicemail because he was in Egremont, south of the Turnpike and far enough west to be a stone's throw from the New York border. He had made the journey to Maddie's daughter's home to re-interview her as well as her husband; Jack's conversation with Maddie had raised more questions that he felt only Elizabeth and Roger could answer.

When Elizabeth answered the door with four year old Billy in one hand and five year old Martha lurking behind her, she recognized Jack from the initial interview he'd done with her immediately after the Senator's death. The interview had been fairly standard, and Jack, by way of introduction, now explained that he wanted to ask

Elizabeth more 'in depth' questions, as some new information had come to light.

"Of course, come in," Elizabeth told him. She was polite enough, but Jack didn't sense any of the warmth that he had from her mother. Well, Elizabeth had two young children, Jack thought to himself as he followed the tall young woman into the living room. And if the bulge he had just noticed beneath her floral shift was any indication, she was expecting a third child in a few months. Perhaps she was just very busy and stressed, and so stuck to the essentials.

Elizabeth told the children to go play in a corner of the large living room where there was a large blue plastic laundry basket full of toys of all descriptions. They obeyed with startling alacrity.

"Your kids are very well behaved," Jack told Elizabeth with a grin.

"Thank you, Detective," she answered, and gave him a fleeting smile. "We try."

Elizabeth said her husband should be home from work within the half hour, and Jack replied that he would speak with her and then with Roger, if that was okay. Elizabeth really didn't have a choice: Jack was the law, and if he wanted to speak to Roger the moment he got home, he would. But Jack always tried to be polite.

Elizabeth nodded, and Jack began.

His initial questions were about her mother and father, and any other relatives who lived nearby and with whom they visited on a regular basis. All quite unexciting, the questions served their purpose, and relaxed Jack's subject so he could get to more focused queries.

"Did you ever suspect any, well, trouble between your Mom and Dad?" Jack asked quietly. "I know this might be disturbing, Elizabeth, with your father gone, but it's important to know. If it helps, I've asked many of your mother's friends and your father's colleagues and friends, the same thing," Jack added.

Elizabeth sighed, and her response came slowly. "Well then, if you've talked to Mother's friends, I suspect what I will tell you will sound familiar," she began. "I think it was very—different—from what Mom had expected, being a Senator's wife," she told Jack quietly.

"Different how?"

"There were more people," Elizabeth said. "People around Dad all the time, wherever he went. He and Mom were never alone. Even when he came home, the phone would ring, or he'd have some meeting or other." She paused. "It was very difficult to have a private life," she finished. Her tone was even and unemotional.

Jack didn't reply. While he didn't doubt what Elizabeth was saying, it wasn't exactly what he was looking for. He had heard the reports about the late Senator's skirt chasing, as well as his drinking, from several of Maddie and Fred's friends as well as from others, and had been hoping Elizabeth could confirm that.

He hadn't asked Maddie about these things: it had seemed to him beyond callous to do so, at least this soon after the Senator's death. But, if Jack could get someone within the family, i.e. Elizabeth or Roger, to confirm what several friends and colleagues had obliquely referred to, then he would talk to the widow, to see if she had been aware.

"You and Roger and the children visited often?" Jack asked. He also wanted specifically to ask her about their visit on April 7, which Maddie had characterized as 'tense.' He'd asked Maddie why, and had got her impressions and recollections of what had gone on, but he wanted Elizabeth's, and later, Roger's.

Elizabeth nodded.

"When was the last time you all visited your Mom and Dad, before he died, I mean," Jack asked.

Elizabeth frowned, thinking back. "Early May, I think," she replied. "I can get you the exact date if you want…" she leaned over and picked up a smartphone in a Hello Kitty case, and tapped at the screen. "It's generally a Sunday—yes, Sunday, May second," she confirmed.

"What about the month before?" Jack asked. Did you visit in April?"

Elizabeth nodded, flicked at the screen of her phone, and said, "Sunday, April 7," she confirmed.

"Can you tell me what you'd all done that day?" Jack asked, listening intently. That was the visit he wanted to know about.

Elizabeth thought for a moment, then related that they had arrived fairly early in the morning, before 10 a.m. The children had gone outside to play with their grandmother, who had been gardening. Elizabeth and

Roger had, as they often did, begun to do a few chores around the house that were either too strenuous for Maddie, or that required two people.

"Too strenuous?" Jack asked, frowning, and wondering why the Senator wouldn't help out with chores needing two people. Hmmm…Maybe he thought things like that were beneath him?

"Yes, Detective, my Mother has had Sjogren's Syndrome for years, although lately she's been a lot better," Elizabeth told Jack, who looked surprised. He hadn't heard that, and wondered if Gracie knew. "But we still try to help out with the heavy stuff: Roger and I cleaned out the gutters, I remember, that morning, and Mom had some curtains and bedspreads waiting to be laundered, so we did that, too. Spring Cleaning, you know."

Jack nodded.

"I remember Mom really wanted to take the fence around her herb garden down, and talked about doing some new landscaping in the yard, but we didn't start on that."

"Why not?"

Elizabeth made a face. "My father thought my mother's herb garden was ugly, Detective, that it spoiled the entire yard. He insisted that she install that picket fence, to hide it. So several years ago—I think Roger and I were just still dating, in fact—we put it up for her."

Jack didn't feel it was the moment to mention that Maddie, that very morning, had been handily taking that selfsame fence down.

He cleared his throat. "So...that Sunday, April 7, when you are Roger were doing the spring cleaning and so forth, where was your father?"

Elizabeth's face became hard, and her expression closed. "When we arrived, he was—taking a shower," she replied evenly, with just a tiny hesitation. "I think he'd been out at a fund raiser or something the night before, and had got to bed late." Her voice was calm, but Jack noticed that she was becoming flushed: her fair skin looked quite pink. He wondered why. Maybe it was just because it was an uncomfortable subject for her to talk about? Roger would probably be more prosaic.

"Did he join you all?" Jack asked, "your father?"

Elizabeth nodded. "Oh, yes, he did: he came downstairs, and called the children inside and visited with them for a while." Her flush paled and she looked more normal.

"Elizabeth, did you think your father should have been the one to help your mother with household tasks, rather than you and Roger?" Jack asked frankly. "Did you resent that he didn't?"

Elizabeth's face grew hard again, and she looked to one side before answering. "I think, that is, I thought, he should have helped Mom more, in general," she told Jack quietly a moment later. "I can't say I resented that he didn't, I just didn't think it was right. And Roger and I didn't mind helping, but that wasn't the point: we shouldn't have had to," she explained earnestly.

Jack nodded. "And then, back on April 7, what was next after playing with the children and doing the gutters?"

Elizabeth thought for a moment. "Then we had dinner," Elizabeth went on.

"What did you have?"

Elizabeth shook her head and gave a wry smile. "It was a really nice day, so Dad wanted to barbecue," she told Jack. "What is it about a spring Sunday that makes every man think he can barbecue?" she asked with a half laugh, but the remark was laced with sarcasm, and an undercurrent of bitterness.

"Your Dad wasn't a good barbecuer?" Jack rejoined.

Elizabeth shrugged. "I guess he was all right. But it just seems like so much trouble to me, to barbecue, and all that charred meat isn't good for you, anyway," Elizabeth put in. "And Mom had a ham ready to go in the oven and had all the vegetables and sides ready, but didn't have anything to barbecue, of course, so Dad and Roger had to run out to the store to get, oh, ribs I think, and other stuff."

"I see."

"Mom had gone to all the trouble for a perfectly lovely meal, but it wasn't good enough for Dad: he had to go get things he could throw on a fire and be all manly about," Elizabeth muttered. She tried to laugh it off, act as though she thought the incident had been funny, but Jack suspected she didn't really think that.

"Was your Mom offended?" he asked Elizabeth. He didn't have to ask if Elizabeth had been offended, it was clear she had been, at least on her mother's behalf.

From outside, they heard the sound of a car in the driveway, and then the sound of the automatic garage door.

"Roger's home," Elizabeth said quickly. "Yes, Detective, I do think my mother was offended, and hurt," Elizabeth said frankly. "But she didn't say anything. Honestly, sometimes she is a saint! She just smiled, and put everything away, the vegetables and the ham and so on, because Dad brought back potato salad and a vegetable tray with dips, and chips. The only thing we ate that day that my mother had made was dessert."

"And what was that?"

"Strawberry trifle. We had that later, with coffee, before Roger and the kids and I left to drive back home."

Chapter Thirty

Roger Colcannon's arrival home caused his two children to erupt with joy. Shrieking with laughter, they rushed their father as he entered the living room, still in his raincoat and carrying his briefcase. Martha dragged the latter item out of his grip and put it firmly in a corner of the room while Billy tugged at his father's sleeve until he was lifted high in an embrace.

Elizabeth quickly explained to her husband that Jack was there to ask them more questions about the late Senator, and divested her husband of his coat, pecking him on the lips and snatching Billy out of his arms. She marshaled the children into the kitchen with her, leaving Jack and Roger alone in the suddenly silent living room.

It seemed clear to Jack that Elizabeth was the disciplinarian of the family.

Jack quickly zeroed in on the visit in April and as he'd suspected, Roger was more comfortable discussing his in laws than Elizabeth had been discussing her parents. That made sense, of course.

Roger told Jack that yes, he and Elizabeth had done some heavy laundry, cleaned the gutters out, and that he had also turned the compost in the composter Maddie kept in a far, sunny corner of the yard. Jack didn't bring up the herb garden fence.

"Did you resent having to do those chores for your mother in law?" Jack asked Roger. "I mean, you have your own home to keep up with." Jack noticed that Roger looked very tired: circles were under his eyes behind his thick rimmed glasses, and his face was drawn. Perhaps he was feeling the strain, or perhaps he was grieving more for his father in law than Jack had suspected.

Roger shook his head. "No, Detective. I didn't mind. Maddie —and Fred—have been very good to me." He sighed. "My parents both died when I was in my teens, and I kicked around the foster care system until I was out of high school and into college. Maddie has been my surrogate mother." He smiled warmly. "I'd do anything for her."

Roger then confirmed for Jack what Elizabeth had said about her father wanting to barbecue, and about the late Senator and him going to the store.

"You look unhappy," Jack said as Roger related that part of the story.
"Is there something else? Something you want to say?"

Roger frowned, his dark brows coming together. "Well, yes, Detective: my father in law had been drinking," he said flatly.

"This was the morning of April 7?" Jack asked, to be sure.

Roger nodded. "It was about 10:30 when he came down and brought the children inside from the yard. He played with them in the living room I think, for a while, and then poured himself a drink. It was maybe 11 a.m."

"What type of drink?"

"His usual: some fancy vodka," Roger explained shortly.

Jack waited.

"Thing is, Detective, when he decided we should barbecue, well, first he started berating my mother in law because she didn't have any of the proper stuff in the house to barbecue. She explained, quite calmly as a matter of fact, that she hadn't prepared for a barbecue, but she'd fixed an entire meal."

Jack nodded. "Right. And then?"

"Well, then Fred—my father in law—said he would go to the grocery store and get some meat for the grill."

"Uh-hunh," Jack put in.

"But I didn't think it was a good idea for him to drive," Roger explained.

"So you went with him," Jack finished. "And you drove?"'

Roger looked uneasy again. "Well, yes, Detective. Only," he gave a sort of chuckle, "that wasn't an easy thing. I mean, my father in law insisted on driving, and taking that behemoth he drives," Roger told Jack, referring to the Senator's black Cadillac Escalade. "I finally convinced him we should take our car, the Subaru we'd come in, and that I should drive."

"And how did your father in law react to that?" Jack asked. This was new: perhaps Elizabeth hadn't known? Or maybe she hadn't wanted to say. Or maybe she'd blocked it out.

"He 'allowed' it, but he was in a pique the rest of the day." Roger reflected a moment. "Kinda spoiled the visit, really. I don't think the kids noticed, but I know Lizzie did, and I did, of course, and Maddie."'

Jack asked about the remainder of the visit, and Roger said his father in law had done the barbecue while he'd continued drinking, straight through to when he'd retreated to his study to watch basketball. "I guess that's what he was doing," Roger commented. "I don't go in there. I stayed with Maddie and Martha and Lizzie; she put Billy down for a nap, and we sat in the kitchen and chatted, and when Billy woke up, we all had dessert and coffee and then we left."

"Did the Senator come out to have dessert and coffee with you?" Jack asked.

Roger shook his head. "He came out, but didn't have anything to eat."

"Was he still drinking?"

Roger nodded shortly, and looked uncomfortable again.

"About how many drinks would you say he'd had throughout the day?" Jack asked, curious.

Roger shrugged. "I don't really know. As I said, he was in his study for a time, and I'm sure he had a drink or two in there." He paused.

Jack waited.

"Maybe—five or six?" Roger suggested doubtfully.

Jack thought Roger was erring on the side of caution, but went on with his questions. "And when Elizabeth put Billy down for a nap, where was that, I mean, where did Billy take his nap?" Jack asked, making notes.

"There's a crib in one of the guest rooms, we use that. If Martha has to have a nap, or on the rare occasions that the children stay over, there's a twin bed in that room, too," Roger explained.

Jack drove back to Pittsfield mentally drawing up a timeline for that critical day, April 7. If Maddie had discovered the broken bracelet the morning after that, Jack's theory was that the bracelet had been tampered with, and possibly a bean removed, the day before.

The Colcannons' insights had been valuable, particularly Roger's, and Jack had now developed a more complete picture of the late Senator. Sure, he had been firm and commanding and statesmanlike as needed, just as he had been the genial glad-hander when occasion demanded. Those had been the public personae of the Senator. But with the input from Jesperson's immediate family, Jack was now able to see the flip side of the deceased Senator: the querulous, argumentative man when he did not get his way, and the almost hermitical inebriate he became when he was home.

It was not a happy realization.

Jack drove home from Egremont by way of his office, because he wanted to secure Maddie's bracelet, which he still had with him, in the evidence locker. He also wanted to count the number of beads on the bracelets Courtney had given him, and on Maddie's bracelet to see if they matched.

They didn't: Maddie's bracelet was one bead shy of the sixteen beads that the other bracelets had. Jack supposed Maddie wouldn't have noticed. But it was an extremely important detail that almost certainly revealed the means by which the Senator had been poisoned.

The question, however, was still, who had done the poisoning, and when. If Jack's theory were correct, and it had been someone who had taken a bead from Maddie's bracelet on April 7, the list of people who had had access to the bracelet was a short one: Maddie herself, her daughter Elizabeth, her son in law Roger, the two children and Fred himself. Jack discounted the children as suspects because although children had been known to kill, of course, it seemed beyond even the older child's capacity to know about the jequirity bead, crack it open, and adulterate the late Senator's food or drink.

Before leaving his office, Jack quickly typed up a request for another search warrant for the Jesperson home: this time specifically for the bottle or bottles of vodka Roger had mentioned. He emailed the request to Judge Cranston. If he was lucky, the approved warrant would be waiting for him Tuesday morning. He fired off an email to the Boston PD, as well, suggesting that they obtain a warrant for any vodka at the late Senator's condo or office.

Then he went home, to Woof, and a late dinner.

Tuesday dawned bright and clear and Gracie presented herself at one of the local magistrate's offices practically when they opened. In a small historic brick building that also housed attorneys' offices on the second floor, District Justice Anton Kregliewicz had his offices and small courtroom. He was probably Gracie's favorite, if one could be said to have a favorite magistrate.

Responsible for cases in the southern part of Berkshire County, Kregliewicz had been on the bench in the lower court for more than a decade, and brought his good sense and experience from having been a business man to his adjudications. He didn't tolerate silliness or rudeness in his court, but he did take the time to listen. And unlike some other magistrates whom Gracie felt rubber stamped practically every case that came before them, Kregliewicz seemed to genuinely weigh the merits of the arguments he heard, and deliberate on each case with thought and admirable sensitivity.

Gracie didn't know who else to ask about the cover up she suspected may have gone on with regard to the late Senator's drinking and driving. But she knew that if she talked to Kregliewicz, he would at the very least say nothing about her query. And perhaps he knew something: judges all talked to each other, from the lower court through to the supreme court. They had their own little club, Gracie knew, and she felt that if Kregliewicz had ever heard anything about a cover up in Berkshire or surrounding counties, he just might tell her.

"I brought gifts," Gracie said to the magistrate's two secretaries, Lucy and Sophie, as she entered the foyer of their office suite. "Is he in?"

The foyer had a few chairs and a long wooden bench with a cushion on it. A schifflera plant stood by a window, and a hat stand graced the corner. Prints of Massachusetts wildlife and landscapes dotted the walls, all of which helped to alleviate the chill lent to the room by its steel grey paint.

The secretaries sat behind a large sliding window made from bullet proof security glass; a steel door that could only be unlocked from inside was the way through to Judge Kregliewicz' chambers, a conference room, and the courtroom.

Sophie jumped up from her chair and came to the window. She was grinning, and slid the window open, happily accepting the two flavored lattes Gracie handed through.

"Wow, thanks! You know we love this stuff!" said Sophie, a petite woman with ash blonde hair and bright blue eyes. "Look, Lucy—Gracie brought us lattes!"

Lucy, a slender red head, grabbed one of the tall cups. "Are these from Bistro Adam?" she asked.

Gracie nodded. "I stopped there on my way into town," she said. "I'm really early, so I thought I'd better bring coffee," Gracie laughed.

"Oooh, yummo they're the best, thanks, Gracie!" Lucy exclaimed.

"That was really sweet of you," Sophie added. "And yes, he just got in," she finished, answering Gracie's question. "And he doesn't have court 'till this afternoon, so now's a good time."

Sophie buzzed the door to unlock it and Gracie stepped through. She heard Sophie go into the judge's chambers, and they had a quick murmured conversation. Then she came back out.

"You can go in," she told Gracie.

Chapter Thirty-one

Judge Kregliewicz stood up behind his desk as Gracie entered, and took the hand she offered, shaking it in a firm grip.

"Gracie, nice to see you," he said. "Sophie tells me you wanted a word?"

Gracie nodded, and took one of the curved back Colonial style chairs in front of the magistrate's desk. She gave him a solemn look. "I need some information," she began. "I don't know if you can give it to me, or if you even would. I don't know if you even know about what I'm looking into," she continued. "But this conversation never happened, it's totally off the record."

Kregliewicz looked puzzled, his piercing blue eyes curious. He was in a regular business suit, this one charcoal grey, with a pink shirt and a grey and pink tie with little fish on it. Or maybe they were whales: it was difficult to see from where Gracie sat, and she could hardly begin her chat with the judge by demanding to examine his neck tie up close!

"If you want it off the record, that's fine, but I have no idea what you're talking about, Gracie, so perhaps you'd better tell me?" Kregliewicz said.

"Have you ever heard—even rumors—of Senator Jesperson being involved in a drunk driving incident?" Gracie asked, keeping her voice low. She had shut the office door, but she still didn't want to risk being overheard.

"The late Senator?" Kregliewicz asked, surprised. "Well, I can tell you that such a case has never come before me," he answered. His straight grey hair was an attractive shade of silver and he'd had it cut fashionably; it complemented the neatly trimmed beard he sported that lent his regular features a slightly Mephistophelian air.

Gracie nodded. "I know that, your honor," she said, extremely polite. "But I meant maybe you heard about something that happened in another county, before another judge, or involving another magistrate?" she suggested.

Kregliewicz frowned, and put his two hands together in front of his face, steepling the fingers and taking a deep breath.

"And why do you want to know this, Gracie: I mean, the man is dead and buried. What good would it do to dredge up unsavory incidents from his past?" the magistrate asked.

Gracie bit her lip: was that a confirmation, albeit oblique, that there had been 'incidents'?

"Well, the Senator was murdered," she told Kregliewicz bluntly. He should know that, it had been all over the news.

He nodded.

"I'm just thinking that the more we know about the Senator's life, the more likely we are to discover someone who might have wanted the Senator dead, and thus find his murderer," she explained.

The judge nodded slowly.

"I've heard about a couple of DUIs the Senator was involved in from two other sources," Gracie continued. "But nothing was ever filed, or brought to court. I figure, if someone were covering up—erm—things for the Senator, maybe they got tired of doing it, or maybe the Senator wanted something else done for him, and whoever it was got tired of taking those risks, and…"

"And killed him?" Kregliewicz asked. Then he shook his head. "I don't know that that would be any sort of motive," he said, but Gracie didn't believe him and from his tone she wasn't sure he believed his own words.

"I'm just trying to get corroboration," Gracie pleaded. "Like I said, I've heard it from two disparate sources. If I can just confirm it with one more reliable source, then I can bring my suspicions to Detective Draper and he can take it from there." Gracie paused. "I'd feel a fool talking to him if there was really nothing to any of it. I know I can trust you. That's why I'm here," she finished.

Everything she had said was true. But it never hurt to parcel out praise, especially if you wanted someone to confide in you.

The magistrate nodded. "You do hear talk, you know, but the whisperings and mutterings I've heard, well, they've all been second or third hand," he protested. "I never really gave them any credence: someone's always trying to rouse a scandal, it seems, especially if it's about someone in high public office," he added with distaste. "I wish people in judicial capacities would focus on what they're elected to do instead of getting involved in stupid nonsense like this," he added.

"Like what?" Gracie pounced.

Kregliewicz pursed his lips and shot Gracie a glance that said, 'you've got me there.' Then: "Like doing favors for people," he answered finally.

"You heard about some other judge somewhere doing favors for Senator Jesperson?" Gracie asked flatly.

"I heard someone tell someone else that they had heard that, yes," the magistrate revealed. "As I said, third hand at best."

"Did you believe it?" Gracie asked.

"I don't know that whether or not I believe it has any bearing…" Kregliewicz began, but stopped as Gracie interrupted him.

"It doesn't, but I trust your judgement," Gracie told him frankly. "If you think there might have been something to the rumor, well, that's good enough for me. I don't know what to believe: that's why I came to you," she finished. Appealing to his chivalrous nature might work, too.

Kregliewicz paused, and scrutinized his hands, which were immaculately manicured. He was buying time, Gracie knew, either that or he was really deliberating what to tell her, if anything. But she wasn't going to give up, or get tired, or just go away. If he knew something, anything, she wanted him to tell her.

"I did hear something, yes. There wasn't a lot of detail, but it was some kind of DUI crash the Senator had been involved in, as you said. No injuries, so he asked for it to not be processed."

"And a judge would do that?" Gracie asked, annoyed at how gullible she sounded.

Kregliewicz just shrugged. "I wouldn't. But I'm not every judge," he added.

"But what about the police, surely they would want to file a report," Gracie began, but at Kregliewicz' look, she stopped. "No? They wouldn't?" she asked him.

He sighed. "If there were to be such an incident, the police could perhaps wish to keep the peace with their local magistrate and do as he or she asks, if you see my meaning?"

Gracie thought she understood. "This crash you heard about, where did it occur, did you hear that?" Gracie queried, intent.

"I heard about one near Springfield," the magistrate answered slowly.

Gracie thought that must have been the one Marco Vioni saw when he'd had to take a detour home. That had been in Hampshire County.

"And I heard about one over near Hadley," Kregliewicz went on.

Another one? In Hadley? Gracie thought. That was new. But that was in Hampshire County, too, she thought. Hmmmm.

"And there have been rumors for years that the late Senator had the police down in Boston in his pocket." He paused. "Maybe you should ask them."

Chapter Thirty-two

Following her visit to Magistrate Kregliewicz, Gracie treated herself to her own latte at Bistro Adam, along with a wholegrain bagel with butter and cream cheese. Kyle had seated her in a back corner of the small boîte, where she wouldn't be disturbed, and Gracie had pulled out her new iPad to do some work. It was far more conducive to transport than the laptop, as the iPad fit in her handbag. And it was larger than the iPhone, so it was easier to do online research.

Which was precisely what Gracie had in mind.

She had been disappointed that Judy couldn't access the ATM camera logs. But that had started Gracie thinking: what if Amy's presumed visit to the ATM in Bloomingdale hadn't been the only one? What if Amy had engaged in other ATM activity, or even made withdrawals from their bank account?

Gracie's initial background check on the Daweses had included current bank balances, but that had been all. She recalled they hadn't had much in the bank, less than $5,000, which made sense given their financial picture.

However, Gracie didn't have information on any transactions since that initial report, and she thought it very likely that Jack hadn't run any recent checks on the Daweses either. If he ever returned her call from the day before, maybe she would suggest he do that very thing.

Since she'd loaded the same program she had on her laptop onto the iPad, Gracie was able to pull up a report of the latest activity on the Daweses' bank accounts by the time she'd finished half her bagel.

The report showed that the checking account was down to just over the $50 minimum required, and the savings account, to which the checking account was tied, was down to $200, also the minimum. Several withdrawals for the maximum allowed per day were shown over the course of the past week, and Gracie had no doubt that Amy had been collecting money, most likely to give to Richard.

But why not just write a check for as much as they could spare, cash it, and be done with it? Why do all the surreptitious cash withdrawals at various ATMs, Gracie wondered.

Possibly so the withdrawals wouldn't be flagged, Gracie theorized, starting on the other half of her bagel. It would look suspicious if a newly widowed woman withdrew what amounted to the couple's life savings just days after her spouse's death. And even more suspicious when it was discovered that her spouse wasn't dead after all, but missing.

The other bit of work Gracie wanted to do was to pinpoint exactly where the rumored DUI crashes involving the late Senator had occurred. Pulling up a map of Massachusetts that showed the counties, Gracie dropped virtual pins at the locations she'd heard about.

First, Jack had said Detective Geene in Boston had told him about a crash at the Senator's brownstone on

Commonwealth Avenue, and another one downtown, across from the Hermès boutique. That was Magistrate LeBron, he'd said. Gracie dropped two red pins for the crashes and one purple pin for the judge's offices, which she located easily, since it was in the Boston Municipal Court Department on New Chardon Street, right near Government Center, downtown.

Chet had mentioned no specific incidents that he knew of when Gracie and he had lunched at the Whitewater. But he'd told her to focus on magistrates in Worcester County whose offices were close to the turnpike. A quick comparison of the list of magistrates in Worcester County and the map showed only one near the Massachusetts Turnpike: Judge Dennis O'Dea in Westborough. She dropped a purple pin on Judge O'Dea's location.

Marco Vioni had made his detour near Huntington, in Hampshire County: Gracie dropped a red pin on Route 112, at its intersection with Pine Street.

Anton Kregliewicz had told her he'd heard of that crash, but also about another one that happened near Hadley: also in Hampshire County. Gracie didn't know exactly where in Hadley, but she dropped a red pin in its general locale and then found where the Hampshire County magistrates' offices were.

There were two magistrates in Hampshire County, one in Belchertown, and the other in Northampton. Gracie learned with a couple more taps of the iPad's screen that the court in Belchertown had jurisdiction for

Hadley and Huntington. The magistrate was Tonya Ragans.

Gracie thought it was a fair bet that Judge Ragans would have been the one who had made the late Senator's accidents disappear, as long as no one had been hurt and no property had been damaged.

So it appeared from her map at any rate that the late Senator had had Judge LeBron out in Boston, Judge O'Dea in Worcester County, and Judge Ragans in Hampshire County in his pocket. What had Chet said? Or actually, not said, Gracie thought to herself as she chewed the last bite of her bagel. He'd told her that if Jesperson had ever paid a fine, it hadn't been recorded. And Gracie had said, 'he paid off the judge,' to which Chet had responded, 'your words, not mine.'

Gracie hadn't heard any rumors about incidents in Pittsfield, or in Berkshire County, or at least, not DUI incidents. The skirt chasing that Anne had told her about, particularly regarding her sister in law Regina and the former head of the Chamber of Commerce, that had happened in Berkshire County, albeit a while ago. Maybe Jesperson had decided to 'cool it' closer to home, particularly once he was a senator, and had freedom to do and act as he wished all week in Boston.

She wondered, as she finished her latte, about how the Senator had gone from being a small town mayor to a State Senator. Gracie walked out to her Jeep and got in, still thinking. Who would know about that, and more to the point, whom could she ask about it?

"We have all the newspaper accounts from that time on microfilm," Hilda Senter, the Head Librarian at the Berkshire Athenaeum and one of Gracie's friends from Club, said that afternoon. Gracie had had the good idea of contacting Hilda about the late Senator's background and rise from local mayor to State Senator: not only would she, as librarian, know where to find records from that time, she was about the same age as Maddie and a Pittsfield native. Gracie thought Hilda would very likely remember Fred as Mayor, and maybe even as a political science professor. It was his early years Gracie was interested in.

"You doing a background tribute-y type article?" Hilda asked with a smile as she led Gracie into a small side chamber where the microfilm machines and cassettes were stored.

Gracie debated: she had not given a reason, just greeted Hilda and asked if the library had records that could give her some insight into Fred Jesperson's early days as mayor. She could agree with Hilda's presumption, even though it was incorrect, or she could tell Hilda the truth.

Gracie opted for the truth. She generally did. She knew Hilda to some extent because the two had worked together on some Club projects. What she didn't know was how the librarian, who appeared quite strait-laced, would take to Gracie poking around in the late Senator's less than snow white past.

"Well, not exactly, Hilda," Gracie began, then launched into her strategy that the more information she had on the late Senator, the easier it would be to uncover the murderer, by identifying people who might have wanted the Senator dead.

Hilda nodded. "That makes a lot of sense." She cocked a well groomed eyebrow at Gracie. "You doing this research for the Detective?"

When Gracie shook her head 'no' Hilda rejoined, "he hasn't been in to ask about this stuff, and I should think he would have been."

Gracie smiled. Apparently, her approach pleased the librarian who seemed to share Gracie's opinion that most things could be solved if one did enough research.

Hilda indicated a microfilm reader for Gracie to use, and Gracie put her things down; the room was deserted. She guessed there wasn't much call for microfilm research, at least not in the middle of the day. Maybe once school let out, students would be in here. Sure, you could find a lot on the internet, Gracie thought, but most local papers' archives weren't on line yet: not this far back. And more than the documents, Gracie wanted to talk to someone who would remember Fred in those early days, and give her a fairly objective picture of him.

"Hilda," Gracie said, following the older woman into the stacks as she located the proper cassettes for Gracie to view, "you remember Fred, of course, when he was Mayor?" she asked, curious.

"Of course: I knew Fred and Maddie socially, sure," she replied. "And can I tell you, Gracie, I'm so glad you and Maddie have become friends? She is just one of the sweetest, kindest people, and she—" Hilda hesitated, biting her lips, which were slicked in an attractive shade of rosy lipgloss. It flattered the woman's silvery hair and dark eyes. "It's wonderful that you're friends," she finished, sounding as though she had wanted to say more, but had held back. "Maddie and I joined Club within a year of each other, and Fred came to several of our Dinner Dances and such, early on," Hilda continued chattily.

"When he was Mayor?" Gracie asked.

"Oh, before that, when he was an instructor at the community college," Hilda said.

"He was an instructor, not a professor?" Gracie clarified.

Hilda nodded. "Yes. He was working on his doctorate, but decided to leave academia for the political arena, and never finished," Hilda explained, sounding slightly accusatory about the late Senator's choice. "You have to have your Ph.D. to be called 'Professor,'" she explained.

"What was he like then?" Gracie asked bluntly. After all, she had said what she was looking for, she didn't need to be coy.

Hilda brought over five cassettes and laid them on the desk Gracie was going to use. Then she sat down in a chair next to the desk and Gracie sank onto the hard wooden chair in front of the desk. Hilda looked off into the distance, remembering. She had slender sterling earrings in the shape of delicate dragonflies in her ears and they caught the light and twinkled.

"Fred and Maddie were a lot of fun to be around," Hilda began. "We were all young, just starting our lives. I remember Maddie couldn't wait to have kids: she's from a big Catholic Polish family out near Springfield, so that was top of the list of what she planned for her life," Hilda noted, smiling.

"Her birth name was Yankovic, wasn't it?" Gracie murmured. She had done some preliminary research, and recalled that detail.

"Yes that's right," Hilda said, looking pleased at Gracie's studiousness. "Anyway, Walter and I had John the same year Maddie and Fred had Elizabeth. Elton and Marilyn Draper's twins—"

"Laura and Jack?" Gracie put in helpfully.

"Yes, Laura and Jack, well of course, you'd know that, wouldn't you?" Hilda said with a grin. "They were born that year, too. We were all in the same play group, that is, the kids were. But it's how I met Marilyn, who brought me into Club, and Maddie, as well."

Chapter Thirty-three

"How did Fred go from being a poli-sci instructor to Mayor?" Gracie asked, interested.

"Well, Fred is—was—a genius at networking," Hilda said frankly. "Even when he was at the college, he got in with a local group of businessmen and such, young guys, like himself, and they all played golf every Saturday. Sometimes the wives would go along."

"Was Walter in that group?" Gracie asked, referencing Hilda's late husband. Before his retirement, Walter Senter had been one of the better known general practice physicians in the area. He had also been a good bit older than Hilda, and Gracie wondered tangentially if Hilda had been thought to have made quite the catch when she'd met and married him.

"He was. He didn't golf very well, but he went along for the companionship, I think. And it was good exercise," she added. "In those days, they walked from tee to tee, none of this golf cart nonsense. And they caddied their own clubs!"

"And the wives went along?" Gracie asked, fascinated. This all sounded like something out of the *Donna Reed Show.*

Hilda nodded. "We did. We'd pack a picnic lunch and after the guys played their nine holes in the morning, we'd all have lunch together. We used to go to a little course out in the middle of nowhere near a county park, so it was convenient," Hilda explained. "I remember, we all had matching red and white checkered tablecloths we'd spread out on the grass. Thermoses of soup if it was chilly. Sandwiches. Sodas. Cookies, and sometimes a cake…"

"Who else was in the group, do you recall?"

Hilda rattled off names of couples who had been prominent in Pittsfield three decades before: Gracie recognized some of the surnames. The wives had been on Boards of charities and some had been or were still in Club; the husbands had been businessmen, contractors, restaurateurs, attorneys, physicians, and similar movers and shakers. A former County Commissioner had been among them, too, but Fred Jesperson had been the only one from academia, as Hilda called it. "We all hung out socially, of course: Club Dinner Dances, fundraisers for various charities, and sometimes we'd go to the symphony in Albany, or just to the movies," Hilda reminisced, her voice unusually sentimental.

Gracie thought that Hilda must feel that those had been the 'golden days of youth' as the saying went.

"Anyway, Fred got to be a pretty good golfer," Hilda continued in a brisker voice, "and before you know it he was asked to play in charity games and the like, all over the state. He kept on networking, and got to meet some influential people from the area," she explained.

Gracie nodded.

"Then—well—then we all started having children, and one by one, we all stopped going on the golf excursions, since most of us were needed elsewhere on Saturdays," Hilda said.

Behind her words was a sadness. Gracie knew that Hilda and Walter's only child, John, had died quite young, from cystic fibrosis. They had never had any more children.

"And the guys started going on weekend golf trips around that time, too," Hilda went on a moment later. "You know, farther afield, so they'd all carpool and stay at some resort or hotel, usually attached to the golf club where the tournament was being played, and then they'd come home late Sunday."

"Ah," Gracie said. This might be a good moment to ask Hilda about Fred's skirt chasing, Gracie thought, but then decided to let Hilda finish her recounting of Fred's political rise. "Go on, this is great," Gracie told her friend.

Hilda smiled, and, warming to her tale, sat forward in her chair. Although they were alone in the small microfilm room, Hilda's voice lowered.

"Well, then the Big Plan was hatched," she began. "Fred's friends and their friends, all lawyers and business people and developers, as I told you, they all put up a lot of money and mounted a campaign to elect Fred as Mayor. A couple of other people threw their hats in the ring," Hilda told Gracie, "but Fred won. He does have a natural charm, and he wasn't hard on the eyes, as the kids say, particularly when he was young," Hilda commented with a cheeky smile.

Gracie recalled that the late Senator had been what she would call a distinguished looking older man, with nicely greying fair hair and blue eyes that were still bright and clear. His genes and his bone structure had given his face a perennially youthful appearance, too, and Fred Jesperson had looked about a decade younger than he actually had been. Gracie could understand that women would have found him attractive: money and power aside, he had been a good looking man.

"His education and experience all helped, of course," Hilda went on, "and teamed with his connections through his coterie of golfing buddies, and the considerable 'war chest' his election committee had amassed, he had everything he needed to win handily."

"He was a good Mayor, by all accounts," noted Gracie. Jesperson's terms as Mayor had ended just after Gracie had moved to Berkshire County, so she had to rely on other people's opinions of Jesperson's mayoralty.

Hilda nodded. "He was," she agreed, but there was reservation in her voice. "But he had, again, lots of friends and a lot of backing." She stopped. "This isn't on the record, is it, Gracie?" she asked, concerned.

Gracie shook her head. "Absolutely not: I'm not out to write any kind of exposé, as I told you. I just want to know what Fred was like, in the hope it will lead me to a suspect, or suspects, with motive to kill him," Gracie assured her.

Hilda nodded assent. "Okay, then, well, Fred had contractors in his pocket—although nothing could ever be proven, or if it could have been, no one ever bothered because the outcome for the town was so positive," she added, her tone sour. "Fred had friends and acquaintances in every walk of life, and on every rung of the ladder and could tap just the right person for any job going. So yes, Fred Jesperson was a genius mayor for getting things done." She paused. "But I have no doubt that favors were exchanged," she said, nearly whispering now. "That is, unfortunately, the way things are, at least in most places. And that was a time of tremendous growth here, with Western Massachusetts coming into its own," she added.

"So—what made him want to be a State Senator?" Gracie queried

"Oh, I'm not sure at all that that was Fred's idea," Hilda replied. "The same group that had got him elected Mayor spent much of his mayoralty raising and saving money: they had decided early on that Fred would go farther than the Mayor's office. And if he hadn't died, I think Fred would have gone from State Senator to Congress and perhaps even higher, who knows?" Hilda shook her head. "I'm not saying Fred didn't do good things, he did. At least for Pittsfield, he did. And once he got to the State Capital, he didn't forget us: Berkshire County always got its share of any state or federal money coming down the pipeline, Fred was good about that."

"But?" Gracie prodded.

"Well, it just seems wrong to me that the people who get elected are the people who have money, or who have money behind them," Hilda replied with a frown. "That's not right. Beyond anything else, it always puts the person who is elected in the position of being beholden to his—or her—backers, and owing favors isn't conducive to sound, objective government," Hilda analyzed succinctly.

Gracie nodded.

"Sometimes they do an okay job, anyway, and sometimes they maybe do a good job. But there are undoubtedly people out there who could do a much better job, but they don't have the 'war chest' as it's called to mount a successful campaign. And they haven't made the right connections, which may not, as I said, always be the most savory ones."

"Savory?" Gracie asked. Maybe this would be what she was after.

Hilda sighed. "Well, Gracie, if people put a great deal of money up to get you elected, you owe them, whether you actually agree to anything or not. So, of course, in Fred's case, there were favors exchanged: at first in business, or even on the golf course, testing the waters as it were. You know: 'I'll overlook that double bogie if you overlook my water penalty,' things like that. Then it progressed to, 'I'll get you building materials at next to nothing left over from a job that I've billed to someone else, if you make my parking tickets disappear,' stuff like that."

"Oh…"

"And then, once Fred and his cronies knew whom to trust about what, it developed into, 'I'll get you that contract if you fund such and such an initiative,'" Hilda continued. Her fair skin had become slightly pink as she began to get worked up about her subject. "Even the money for this new building, I'm sure, had some of that type of money in it, huge contributions that no doubt were done tit for tat to pay off some other favor," she added, sounding angry. The Athenaeum's expansion project had run into the millions, and had been completed two years before. Gracie remembered having covered the Grand Opening.

"But what can one do?" Hilda asked rhetorically. "I can't prove anything."

Gracie sighed companionably. "I'm afraid that's a very common situation in politics, Hilda: political favors."

Hilda nodded, and then looked perturbed.

"What?" Gracie prodded again.

"Well, that wasn't—all," Hilda answered reluctantly.

Chapter Thirty-four

"I really shouldn't say any more," Hilda replied, and made a move to rise from her perch.

Gracie took a shot. "Oh, I understand, but if it's about Fred's womanizing, I know all about that," Gracie murmured, affecting unconcern. She was extremely eager to hear more about it, but felt instinctively that showing how interested she was would put Hilda off.

She was correct.

"Oh, you do?" Hilda said, sounding relieved.

Gracie shrugged. "Yeah, some of it anyway: Regina Vioni from Mt. Holyoke, and that Chamber lady…" she trailed off as though she could recall other names too numerous to list.

Hilda sat back in her chair. Apparently, she was relieved to unburden herself, as long as Gracie already had knowledge of the subject, and had promised it was off the record.

"Well, that started when they all used to go away on those weekend golf trips I told you about," she whispered, and explained that her husband, Walter, had gone on a couple of trips but had become disenchanted when the others in the group had visited strip clubs, and then met up with, "they called them 'escorts'" Hilda snorted. "Right. We knew what they were, and Walter wanted no part of that."

Hilda mentioned that during this time, the group's membership had shifted somewhat, with a few men—

and their wives—dropping out of the inner circle, and others—without their wives—entering. "We still saw Fred, of course, from time to time, usually with Maddie, and usually at a Club function. But the group from the old days was gone," she said with regret.

"And Fred, erm, continued that behavior, do you think?" Gracie asked. "I mean, when he became State Senator," she amended.

Hilda nodded, gave Gracie a look as if to say, 'of course!' and explained, "When he was in Boston, who knows what he got up to: we would never know. I've even heard that back when he was at the college, he had a fling with one of his grad students." She sighed. "Some men just aren't monogamous, whether by nature or by choice or by discipline," she theorized. "For Fred, being with other women besides his wife was part of who he was."

"Do you think Maddie knew?" Gracie asked. Other people had told her that of course Maddie had to have known.

Hilda nodded sadly. "I think she did. How could she not? Fred was always discreet, but when he really started getting in with that crowd of movers and shakers, as I call them, they'd all go drinking and chasing after women, and I think Fred's discretion suffered."

"Heavy drinking?" Gracie put in, affecting curious surprise.

"Oh, yes, quite," Hilda confirmed, looking severe.

Gracie frowned, then said, as though just having the thought, "you ever hear of Fred being involved in a DUI or anything?" she asked innocently.

Hilda sighed. "Remember what I told you about political favors?" she answered in a non answer.

Gracie looked uncertain.

"I've heard," Hilda's voice dropped again, "that Fred generally does his drinking over in the next county, because he's got the magistrate down there in his pocket," she told Gracie, who tried hard to keep her glee from showing.

"How've you heard that?" Gracie asked, breathless.

"The woman who works in Judge Ragans' office in Belchertown is in the Morris Dance group I'm in," Hilda replied.

Gracie recalled having heard Hilda talk about the dance group which met every other week to engage in the traditional English Country dancing.

"You know, I've always wanted to ask you about that," Gracie told Hilda honestly, adding that she'd seen Morris Dancers a few times during her visits to England.

"You should come along some time, I think you'd like it," Hilda said enthusiastically. "I can email you and we could even ride together, if you'd like," she added.

"I would love that, thank you Hilda!" Gracie said, excited. Well, she was, actually, and her enthusiasm wouldn't hurt here. "So your friend in the Morris Dancing group is the Magistrate in Belchertown?" Gracie followed up, affecting confusion.

Hilda laughed shortly. "No, no, she's the administrative secretary to the Magistrate. The Magistrate is Tonya Ragans."

"Oh—and you think Fred had her in his pocket?" Gracie repeated what Hilda had claimed.

Hilda gave another short laugh, and not an especially nice one. "More like she had Fred in somewhere else, if you know what I mean," Hilda rejoined with surprising rudeness. "But my friend, Maureen, she's told me about it."

"Maureen is in the Morris group," Gracie verified.

"Yup. The Northampton Ramblers," Hilda explained. "We're lucky, because we have a mixed team, men and women, and enough people we can do all women and all men in addition to mixed dances. It's because we're near all the colleges," she added, and Gracie recalled Anne having mentioned that her sister in law, Regina, had been bothered by the late Senator when she had been at Mt. Holyoke. That was very near Northampton.

"And she told you that Fred and Magistrate Ragans, was it? were having an affair?" Gracie asked bluntly.

Hilda nodded again. "Yes. For years, on and off."

"And you think Maddie knew?"

"Oh, I don't think, first off, that the magistrate was the only woman Fred had on the side," Hilda told Gracie. "I think he very likely had one or more in Boston, and maybe a couple others stashed away all over the state whom he could call upon should the need arise," she said in a prim tone. "And yes, I think Maddie figured it out. She's a smart woman and she's observant and on top of things."

"She is," Gracie agreed.

"In spite of the Sjogren's," Hilda said, and Gracie looked a question.

Hilda explained, again in a whisper, that Maddie had suffered from Sjogren's Syndrome for years. "I know they say it's a real thing, a real diagnosable illness, but I somehow can't help thinking it's tied, at least in part, to the situation between Maddie and Fred," she pronounced, explaining that Maddie's diagnosis had come shortly after Fred had begun going away most weekends, after their second child, Edward, had been born. "I'm sure there was some post partum depression, too, and I think she was treated for that. But then the Sjogren's came, and, well, as I say, she's quite a woman and she's done an admirable job given that she's been virtually a single parent," Hilda finished hotly.

So, Fred Jesperson didn't win any parenting awards in Hilda's book, Gracie thought with a nod to her friendly informant.

"But anyway, I've gone on way too long and you want to get to your research," Hilda concluded brightly. Maybe she had realized she'd been chattier and more revealing than she had intended, or perhaps than strict ethics allowed. "You won't say anything to anyone, especially Maddie, about our talk, will you?" Hilda asked. She seemed satisfied that Gracie wouldn't write about anything she'd said, but talking to a friend was something else.

"Of course not," Gracie shook her head.

"I'm surprised she never told you about the Sjogren's," Hilda put in thoughtfully, as she stood to leave Gracie to her microfilm research. "That's why she's always running to Planet Provisions for herbs and such: she says they help with her illness."

Gracie smiled. "Actually, she did tell me she had chronic fatigue, I think she called it, one of the first times we really talked. We were in Courtney's store, and discussing various herbal supplements, and she mentioned that curly dock had really helped her. But she never gave her illness a name. Actually, she passed over it so quickly, she made it almost a non-issue. I remember her saying that she tried not to let it get the best of her," she recalled.

Hilda smiled. "That sounds like Maddie: always looking on the bright side, spying the silver lining, doing her best in spite of whatever might be against her."

"Like Fred?" Gracie asked.

Hilda made a face. "Yes. Like Fred."

Chapter Thirty-five

Gracie spent two solid hours scanning old newspaper articles about Fred Jesperson's rise in politics. She made copies of a couple of items, but the majority of information was stuff she already knew.

She also hopped onto the Athenaeum's free wi fi for library patrons and looked up Sjogren's Syndrome. Many of the symptoms that she read about fit the way Maddie had looked and behaved as long as Gracie had known her. Although Maddie rarely complained, Gracie had sometimes seen her look as though she was in pain during Club meetings or events, or like a particular movement or task was difficult for her. Also, if Sjogren's was an inflammatory auto immune disease, Maddie's consumption of Tart Cherry capsules as well as the Curly Dock and other herbs available at Courtney's shop, made sense: these were well known anti-inflammatory substances.

Although the websites Gracie consulted admitted that the cause of Sjogren's was still not known, they all pointed to stress as a trigger. Some of the symptoms listed led Gracie to wonder if the illness had really put a strain on Maddie and Fred's marriage. Perhaps it had created a vicious circle, with Fred's infidelity being sparked by Maddie's physical condition, which in turn was exacerbated by the stress of Fred's infidelity and so on and so on. It wasn't an excuse, of course, for his straying, and Gracie thought back to what Hilda had said: that some men just couldn't be happy with only one woman in their lives. Gracie didn't know about that, but her job wasn't to judge the late Senator's character: she wanted to learn all she could about him in order to identify possible murder suspects.

So—Tonya Ragans, the magistrate down in Belchertown. She could have a motive, particularly if the 'favors and gifts' relationship she'd had going with the late Senator had become too risky, or if he'd asked for something she hadn't wanted to agree to.

Who else? Maybe one of his political cronies, for similar reasons? Quite possible.

Gracie glanced at the Cartier tank Americáine she always wore and was surprised to see it was three o'clock. No wonder her stomach was rumbling! Well, since she was finished at the library, maybe she'd swing by Antonio's and get a pizza to go, and have an early dinner. She could pick at the pizza all evening and she could relax, too, maybe, and give both the current murder investigations a night off.

Despite Gracie's best intentions, her evening of relaxation was not to be. However, it got off to a good enough start: she arrived home just before four p.m. bearing a fragrant anchovy and garlic pizza—her favorite. She intended to eat a good part of it over the course of the evening, and save the rest for the following day: pizza was one of her favorite 'leftovers.'

Antonio's had recently begun offering gluten free pizza crusts as well as whole grain pizza crusts, and it was the latter that Gracie had chosen. In her opinion, Antonio's sauce was the best, other than her own, and their cheese mixture included the usual mozzarella and parmesan but also tangy locatelli and mouthwatering asiago.

Pumpkin, of course, arrived in the kitchen as Gracie was tucking the pizza in an oven to stay warm and sorting through her mail: a couple of bills, some catalogues she didn't really want, the newspaper circular she never read. Quite dull.

She processed the mail, placing the bills in the holder on her desk and slipping the other items in a flat, tray like basket near the door to the basement; next time she went down to clean out the litter box or empty a dehumidifier, she'd take the unwanted mail down and shred or stack it for recycling.

Pumpkin miaowed.

"You smell the pizza?" Gracie asked, smiling at the pretty orange and white cat. Pumpkin's fur was longish, and she was a large cat for a female, close to fifteen pounds. Gracie wondered if she had some Maine Coon in her.

In any event, Pumpkin replied with another miaow that clearly said, 'yes, and I should like some, please!"

Gracie just laughed lightly, and ran upstairs to change into jeans and a cotton canvas sweat shirt, perfect for these transitional May evenings. She had just returned to her kitchen, and was opening the oven door to get the pizza when her iPhone rang.

She sighed, and glanced over where she'd placed it on one bluestone countertop: 'Jack Draper' appeared on the lock screen.

Gracie shut the oven door, grabbed the phone and answered the call.

"Hello?"

"Gracie, hi, it's Jack."

"Yes, Jack…" Well, it wasn't evening, precisely, yet: it was still part of the business day. She shouldn't be miffed that he called: how was he to know she'd worked through lunch and was starving? And he was obviously —finally—returning her call from nearly 24 hours before.

"I—um—how are you?" Jack asked, sounding extremely unsure of himself. "I got your message about Amy Dawes using the credit card up near Bloomingdale, NY," he added quickly.

"I'm fine, but I'm starving: I worked through lunch," Gracie explained, hoping Jack would take the hint and make the call a fast one.

"Oh. Erm—you want to meet me in town for dinner? We could get a pizza at Antonio's…"

Great minds.

Great minds, just a little bit out of sync.

Gracie quickly explained that she was already home, and had picked up a pizza.

"Ah—I see," Jack replied.

Gracie sighed. "I won't guarantee I'll wait for you, but if you want to share the pizza, come on over, as soon as you can," Gracie said. "We can talk about Amy. And Fred Jesperson, too, if you have any news on him."

Jack agreed, and said he would be there as fast as he could, and yes, he wanted to talk to her about both of the major cases on his desk.

Gracie figured it would take Jack about twenty minutes to get to her place from his office, even if he stopped off en route to get Woof, which he probably would. She trotted downstairs to her wine rack for a bottle of Noiret, a dry red from her friends' winery.

Sarah and Steve used to call their place Double S Vineyard and Winery. Then for a very brief while they toyed with a couple of other names, because Sarah said that 'Double S' sounded too much like the name of a ranch in some B rated Western film. Just this past summer Sarah and Steve had settled on the name Sunset Creek Vineyard and Winery and were now in the process of registering that with the state.

Gracie found the bottle she was looking for, and returned to her kitchen.
The Noiret bottle still had the Double S logo on it, Gracie noted as she opened it, and retrieved two red wine glasses from a cupboard.

She dug in another cabinet for the bowls and kibble she kept for Woof's visits. She put a few pieces of kibble in one bowl, and set it next to Pumpkin's food dish, which also contained kibble. Then she filled another bowl with water and put it next to Pumpkin's water bowl, which was a few feet away from the food bowls.

Chapter Thirty-six

When the doorbell rang a few minutes later, Gracie met Jack and Woof with a half eaten slice in one hand.

"I told you I was starving," she said by way of hello, and beckoned both of them into the kitchen.

"That's all right: I invited myself, I'm not going to complain," Jack replied easily.

"I did wait for you to pour the wine, however," Gracie conceded, and while Woof went over to check out his bowl, Gracie filled the crystal stemware with the dark red wine. Then she took the pizza out of the oven again, opened the cover, pointed to plates and napkins, and told Jack to help himself.

With their pizza and wine, they settled in the Oak Room on the long leather sofa. Woof followed and flopped down in front of the fireplace, although Gracie hadn't lit a fire.

"So, what's up?" Gracie asked, biting into her second slice.

"I interviewed Maddie again," Jack began slowly between mouthfuls of pizza and wine. "Oh, this is really good wine—from Double S?" he asked, tasting it.

Gracie nodded. "Yes, only it's called Sunset Creek Winery now," she informed him. "Go on, you interviewed Maddie again, and?" she prompted.

Jack took a deep breath. "I think you may be right, Gracie: maybe she didn't kill Fred," he admitted.

Gracie broke into a huge grin. "I told you she never could have done that!" she crowed. "So, who do you like for it?" she asked eagerly.

Jack told her about pinpointing the bracelet's location and who would have had access to it, and about speaking with Maddie's daughter Elizabeth and her husband Roger.

"They seem like nice people," he said of Elizabeth and Roger. "She's a bit on the, oh, I don't know: she doesn't have any of Maddie's softness or warmth," Jack characterized. "But Roger's really—kind, I think."

Gracie shrugged. "I don't know them at all. I met Elizabeth the morning I went to visit Maddie, right after Fred died," she told him. "She wasn't especially friendly, but then again, there was no reason that she should be."

Jack explained about Roger, in particular, talking about the late Senator's drinking. "I didn't have the heart to ask Maddie about that, or about any other women," Jack confessed. "I wanted to hear about those things from another source before I brought them up with her. But Roger mentioned that Fred often drank, and drank quite a bit," Jack noted.

Gracie had yet to tell him about her sojourn to Huntington and the Whitewater bar, but Jack wasn't finished yet so she waited, and had another sip of wine.

"Even on a Sunday morning the late Senator drank, Roger said, so I got a search warrant specifically for the vodka Fred kept at his house. This morning, I went back to the Jespersons' house and just caught Maddie on her way out. I told her I had a warrant to search and seize

Fred's vodka and she told me to go ahead. I didn't have time to speak to her about Fred's alcohol consumption, but I did ask her if we could talk tomorrow."

"Oh!"

"Anyway, Gracie, I found a bottle of Stolichnaya Himalayan Vodka in the kitchen refrigerator-freezer. I also found two bottles in the chest freezer in the garage and another bottle in Fred's study: he has a small refrigerator in there. CSU had dusted for prints, of course, during the initial investigation, and I reviewed those today while I was waiting for the results of the vodka analysis. The vodka from the kitchen and the chest freezer has tons of prints, including Fred's and Maddie's. The bottle in the study had only Fred's fingerprints on it, which I find odd."

"That *is* odd," Gracie agreed, intrigued.

"When will you get the results from the lab on the vodkas?" Gracie asked eagerly.

"Well, we know what we're testing for, so, maybe by tomorrow," Jack replied. He paused. "Elizabeth didn't say anything about her father's drinking,"

"Well, she may not have wanted to make him look bad, I mean, he's dead, and he is—was—her father," Gracie put in sympathetically.

Jack nodded. "Maybe. But Roger mentioned it. So I'll talk to Elizabeth again, see if she can corroborate Roger's statement. And then I'll talk to Maddie."

"You going to ask her about the other women? Did Elizabeth or Roger mention that?" Gracie asked. "I've got something to…" she broke off as Woof suddenly huffed and pricked his ears, sitting up, and looking towards the dining room.

The sound of paws thumping purposefully up the basement stairs was heard, followed by the faint jingling of the tags on Pumpkin's collar. Seconds later, the large orange cat entered the Oak Room and trotted directly to Gracie: a small grayish brown mouse was clasped firmly in her jaws.

She set it down at Gracie's feet, and miaowed triumphantly.

"Oh, Pumpkin, thank you," Gracie said evenly, trying not to disturb the shell shocked, motionless mouse on the oriental carpet. Gracie handed her plate to Jack and quickly drained her wine glass. She was about to upend it over the mouse to trap it when Woof came over to see what Pumpkin had found. He whuffed at the mouse, who squeaked, and ran.

Both cat and dog took off after the mouse who, not very cleverly, had darted across the Oak Room floor towards the front windows, seeking refuge in the skirting. Gracie and Jack laughed as they watched the chase around the room until Pumpkin again successfully snagged the prize with a fast, clawed paw, and once again brought it over to Gracie.

The few moments had allowed Gracie to grab what she called her 'mouse apprehending apparatus' which she kept handy: an old wide mouthed plastic tumbler and a piece of stiff cardboard. This time, when Pumpkin dropped the mouse and miaowed her victory, Gracie plopped the tumbler firmly over the mouse.

"Thanks again, Pumpkin," Gracie murmured as she deftly slid the cardboard under the tumbler, and under the mouse. Then, carrying the 'gift' Gracie made her way out of the room. "I'll be back in a few minutes," she told Jack.

"Be sure and wash your hands!" he called as Gracie left, moved through the kitchen, out into the mud room, and out to the back yard to take care of her furry intruder.

Chapter Thirty-seven

"Did you know Maddie had Sjogren's Syndrome?" Jack asked a short while later. Gracie had returned from mouse disposal duty, and they had resumed eating and talking. Pumpkin had been fed a couple of treats as a reward for her hunting skills and she and Woof were sitting in front of the fireplace. There still was no fire in it, but they were accustomed to that spot nonetheless.

"I just found that out," Gracie replied. "Do you think that has anything to do with the murder?" she asked.

Jack shook his head. "Not really, do you?"

Gracie advanced her thought about some of the illness' symptoms perhaps making Maddie and Fred's marriage difficult. Then she shared Hilda's opinion with Jack, that some men just always needed to have more than one woman in their lives.

Jack gave her a look. "Well, maybe, Gracie, I suppose some men might be that way. But not me," he added.

Gracie bit her lip. "I know, Jack," she told him softly.

They were silent a minute or two.

"More pizza?" Gracie asked him. "I never had lunch, I'm going for another slice," she added with a grin.

They filled their plates and topped up their wine and continued the discussion on the Jesperson murder.

"Hilda—Hilda Senter? She's in Club and she's the librarian at the Athenaeum? You remember her, you've met her at some Club things," Gracie told Jack as they settled back down on the sofa. Jack nodded. "Well she told me a lot of stuff about Fred when he was young, and about his cronies, and how he got elected Mayor and then to the State Senate," Gracie began, and gave Jack a summary of Hilda's information. "I know it's not a first hand account of his extramarital affairs, but it's good information," she concluded. "Maybe you should talk to Regina Vioni: Anne told me Fred had chased after her, quite some time ago, though."

Jack nodded thoughtfully. What Gracie had just told him was fascinating, and the kind of background information that often helped investigators look in the right places, and at the right people, to solve a murder case. Or any case, for that matter.

"I'd like to find someone more recent," Jack admitted. "Maybe I'll talk to Magistrate Ragans, see if she'll open up to me," he told Gracie.

"Good idea." She paused. "Or I could?"

Jack looked at her thoughtfully. "You could."

"I would tell you anything significant I found out," Gracie assured him.

Jack nodded. "Anyway, about the bracelet, the one you saw on Maddie's wrist?" Jack began, changing the subject slightly.

Gracie nodded.

"She gave me hers, only too happy to help, Gracie, and again, I'm beginning to really think she didn't do it," he put in. "And I compared it with the ones I got from Courtney's store." He'd told Gracie about visiting Planet Provisions, and also about his conversation with the company in England that Courtney had bought the bracelets from. "Maddie's bracelet had one fewer bead than the others, and of course, they were on the elastic thread that Maddie said had broken," Jack continued. He filled Gracie in on Maddie's recollection of the date that she'd found the broken bracelet, and her trip to the mall to get a clasp to repair it.

"So back in April, someone removed a bead from Maddie's bracelet and left it in her jewelry box so it would look like it had just broken?" Gracie responded.

Jack nodded. "Looks that way. And then, some time before the late Senator's sudden illness and death a couple weeks ago, they crushed the bead and put the abrin in something the Senator ate or drank."

"And you're thinking it was the vodka?" Gracie asked again.

Jack nodded. "It makes sense, especially if the murderer is one of the family. The vodka is something only Fred drank. No one else in the family touched it. In that way, it was a safe thing to adulterate, because it was almost guaranteed that the intended victim would be the only one to ingest it."

"And I found out that Fred specifically drank that vodka, and only that vodka," Gracie put in, and gave Jack a fast summary of her sojourn to the Whitewater restaurant and bar where the barkeep had kept Fred's favorite vodka in stock. She also mentioned running into

Chet, and told Jack what his Worcester County counterpart had said with regard to the late Senator's DUIs.

Jack nodded his head as he listened to Gracie's story. "All good information, Gracie. You do realize that we are talking premeditation, planning—this is Murder One."

She nodded. "And access to the bracelet gives us the means, and access to the vodka gives us opportunity."

"Right. And right now, while Maddie, Elizabeth and Roger all had access to the poison and the vodka, others might also have, since those bracelets were sold all over the place. The English company that was selling them emailed us the list, and there are tons of little shops throughout New England that sell them. And the vodka —"

"You contacted Boston PD to seize any vodka from the townhouse or office, too?" Gracie asked quickly.

"I contacted them to obtain a search warrant," Jack clarified. "They'll probably have it tomorrow, Wednesday, and seize any vodka they find then," he surmised. "So, anyway, the availability of the bracelets and the distribution of the vodka widen the field of possible suspects," he concluded.

Gracie nodded.

"I talked to Detective Geene again when I called Boston," he noted. They had finished their pizza and were now just sipping the delicious wine: it was smooth and dry, a perfect foil for the spicy gooey pizza. "Boy, she really doesn't like Jesperson," Jack said, shaking his head.

Gracie frowned. "How do you mean?" she asked.

Chapter Thirty-eight

Jack outlined for Gracie the conversation he'd had with Detective Geene from Boston, but more than that, he shared with Gracie the impression he'd got from the female Detective.

"She's fairly new to the Boston PD, only been there 18 months, I think she said," Jack noted. "She used to be in the Bethlehem, PA, PD, but transferred to Boston."

"That's odd," Gracie put in. "Maybe she moved because of a relationship?" she wondered, thinking about Ben's proposal that had been contingent upon her moving with him to Washington, D.C.

Jack shrugged. "I don't know. At any rate, her issues with the late Senator might just be a case of the new person coming in and seeing stuff that people who have been there longer have come to accept as part of the way things are," Jack said carefully.

"Surely, the Boston PD isn't that corrupt!" Gracie exclaimed.

Jack gave her a smile. "Sometimes you really are so naive, Gracie," he said, still smiling. "Not the whole department, no, but maybe just a couple of officers, and the magistrate: Leo LeBron," he noted.

Gracie nodded. "I guess you're right. If Fred Jesperson had had an—agreement—with LeBron and a couple of cops, if he got into trouble, he called them, and they, erm, handled it," she murmured. "And their payoff would be—?"

Jack shrugged. "Who knows? IA would have to look into that," he told her, referencing Internal Affairs. "But it could be anything from money, like the payoffs you and Chet talked about, to tickets to sporting events and other perks the Senator might have had access to."

Gracie finished her wine. "Hmmm. Golf junkets to exotic locales?" She cocked an eyebrow at him. "You should ask Maddie about that," she advised and sighed. "The picture I'm getting from Hilda and a few other people I've talked to is that Maddie and Fred weren't particularly intimate or close in these last few years," Gracie said, sounding a bit sad. "She seems to have made the best of things, and kind of made her own life, if you know what I mean. People seem to think she was aware of Fred's womanizing, and probably of his drinking, but stayed out of both issues. Maybe she felt she had enough to do just keeping the peace, as it were, at home?" She paused. "And now that I know about the Sjogren's, maybe that took most of her energy, dealing with the symptoms," she finished compassionately.

"You never had a clue she was ill?" Jack asked, sounding doubtful.

"I knew something wasn't right, I mean, sometimes she looked like she was in pain, and she often looked very tired. But she never complained, only mentioned that one time in Courtney's shop that she had issues with chronic fatigue," Gracie answered.

Jack nodded. "Well, your impression of the Jespersons agrees with what I've learned from his colleagues and friends," Jack said. "His staff in Boston didn't know much about Maddie, of course, and neither did his political pals out there, but they all told me Jesperson liked his drink, and loved to flirt, and sometimes more: a case of when the cat's away the mouse will play, or something like that," he noted wryly. He gave a long sigh. "Anyway, I don't know that we can do much more now, until the vodka analysis comes back from the Jesperson home and from Boston," Jack said.

"But you said you're talking to Maddie again tomorrow?" Gracie queried.

Jack nodded. "That's the plan. I'm going to have to ask her some pretty difficult questions, I think," Jack said, then, sounding regretful. He sighed. "There are parts of my job I really don't like, you know?"

"I know, Jack. But hey, look, let's talk about the Dawes case: we haven't even started on that one!" Gracie said brightly. She told him about her chat with Judy at her bank, and the confirmation that the bank that the Daweses used did have an ATM at the location where Amy's credit card had bought more than $300 worth of gasoline. She also mentioned that a recent pull of the Daweses' financials showed several withdrawals over the past few days.

"I won't ask how you know some of that stuff," Jack began slowly, but his mouth was quirked in a half grin. "But I will ask you what your theory is, because you obviously have one," he said.

Gracie, beaming, nodded. "I think Amy's been making small withdrawals so they wouldn't be flagged," she said quickly. "And I think she brought all the money, close to $5000, to Richard up in Bloomingdale. And I think when she was there, she or she and Richard filled up a bunch of gas cans so Richard would have gasoline for his truck," Gracie finished. "That way, he'd have cash to live and gas to travel and he could stay off the grid," she added, happy with her theory.

"Okay, that all makes sense," Jack agreed. "But why Bloomingdale?"

Gracie chuckled. "I don't actually think Richard is in Bloomingdale," she said slowly. "I think he's in Canada," she said, and flipped open her iPad to show Jack, pulling up the map app. "See? Bloomingdale's about half way between Amy's mother's place and the Canadian border." She pointed.

Jack whistled. "Geez, Gracie, that's a stretch, but you're right," Jack replied, sounding surprised. He looked closely at the map on the screen. "Straight up Route 30 and he's over the border," he murmured. "But why Canada?"

Gracie shook her head. "I'm not sure. I just keep thinking that…something I read, or saw or…" she shrugged.

Jack looked off into the middle distance and Gracie watched, silent. "If my math is right— you said they bought $300 worth of gas?" Jack said a moment later.

Gracie nodded.

"If Richard's truck gets, oh, say, 20 to the gallon…"

"And if gas is about $3.60 a gallon," Gracie chimed in, seeing where Jack was going with his mental calculations, "and if my theory is correct," she put in, trying to sound humble.

"Then that would mean about 80 or so gallons of gas was what they purchased. Give or take," Jack added with a smile.

"And Richard probably had gas in his truck already, anyway," Gracie said. "He had to have driven to Bloomingdale."

"Right. And if you're right, he and Amy had chosen a half way point, then he'd only have a three hour drive back, so that's what, 150 miles or something like that?" Jack put in.

Gracie nodded.

"But why would he need all that gas? Where's he going?" Jack asked rhetorically, and then answered his own question. "If you assume most of that $300 gas purchase was for whatever trip he was taking, wherever he was going, how far would it take him?"

"Eighty gallons of gas? At twenty miles to the gallon, that would take you 1600 miles," Gracie answered, excited.

"Or thereabouts. Maybe a little less. Let's say 1500 miles. Where does 1500 miles from the Canadian-US Border near Ottawa bring you—pull up that magic map of yours again," Jack requested, and Gracie touched her iPad's screen.

She touched a couple of spots on the map, then: "Winnipeg's about 1400 miles or so."

"Hmmm…" Jack looked unsure. "If I were going to try and hide, it wouldn't be in a big city, and it wouldn't be so close to the border."

"Agreed," Gracie said. "But there's something…" she taped the side of her head and looked frustrated. "Something I heard, some connection with Manitoba, but not Winnipeg…oh, I wish I could remember!" she groaned in frustration. Then she sighed.

Jack had a bemused smile on his face. "You heard something about Manitoba in connection with Dawes?" he queried, trying really hard not to laugh. It was rare to see Gracie at a loss, and he was enjoying it, actually, though he knew just how she felt.

"Yes, but I don't remember what!" she answered, still frowning. "Oh, never mind: it's gone."

"Maybe you'll remember later," Jack said soothingly. Meanwhile, he thought, he might just put in a call to the Canadian Mounted Police in Manitoba, just to see how cooperative they might be in searching for a fugitive.

Gracie made a face.

"And meanwhile, I think I'll have Amy Dawes brought in for further questioning," Jack said.

"Gee, Maddie, Amy, and you should get the results from the vodka analysis: you're going to have a busy day!" Gracie declared.

Jack smiled grimly. "Looks like it."

Chapter Thirty-nine

Wednesday morning just after nine a.m., Jack received the analysis of the vodka bottles collected from the Jesperson home. The two bottles in the chest freezer and the one in the kitchen refrigerator's freezer were both just vodka. But the bottle in the small fridge in Fred's office showed a remarkably large amount of abrin: more than three times the lethal dose.

Pending the results from the Boston PD on any vodka bottles found at the Senator's condo or office, this put the scene of crime in the study of the Jesperson home.

Jack grabbed the CSU report from the initial sweep of the home, and flipped to the page detailing findings in the study. Yes, his recollection and what he'd told Gracie the evening before was correct: most of the fingerprints in the study itself were Fred's, understandably. Some smudged over ones were Maddie's, and there were more too fragmented to identify. He flipped back to the report on the vodka bottle from the study fridge: only Fred's prints. Jack looked back at the CSU report. The mini fridge showed only Fred's fingerprints, as well.

Something bothered Jack about that: something wasn't right. The prints on the fridge and the bottle were too few in number, compared to the prints everywhere else in the room. It almost seemed to Jack as though someone had...wiped the bottle and the door of the fridge at some point in the not too distant past. After which, Fred had touched those surfaces and left his prints. And only his prints.

It was a hunch, and it couldn't be proven, but Jack felt very strongly about it. He contacted the CSU department and asked if he could meet them that afternoon at the Jesperson home to go over the late Senator's study again, making sure they checked every surface for prints. They agreed, although Jack could tell from the tech's voice that she thought another visit there was redundant.

"It's been identified as the crime scene," Jack told her grimly.

That seemed to make a difference, and Jack said he'd meet them at the Jesperson home at four o'clock.

Then he called Maddie, and let her know he and the CSU techs would be visiting her home again. He explained that the study appeared to have been the crime scene, but didn't go into detail, particularly with regard to the vodka. He asked Maddie if it would be inconvenient for him to question her there, at her home, about a few more things and she agreed that he could come earlier in the afternoon, as she would be home all day.

Before he put the Jesperson case aside, Jack also called Elizabeth and asked very quickly about her father's drinking.

"Yes, Dad drank," Elizabeth admitted. Her tone was brusque.

"Did he drink a lot, Elizabeth?" Jack asked softly.

"How does one quantify 'a lot,' Detective?" Elizabeth shot back.

Sarky.

"Did your father as a rule have more than two drinks during one of your Sunday visits to your parents' home?" Jack asked deliberately, biting off the words as he enunciated.

"As a rule?" Elizabeth echoed, still prickly. "Yes," she admitted.

"About how many?" Jack pushed. He wasn't going to be nice if she wasn't.

Elizabeth was silent, thinking. "Probably six to eight, Detective, I am not sure because he did a lot of his drinking alone, in his study. And no one bothered him when he was in his study," she added firmly. "No one went in there."

That was similar to what Roger had told him.

Once that delightful conversation was over, Jack checked and discovered that the police had brought Amy Dawes in for questioning. When he was available, Jack ran downstairs to the Sheriff's Office where Amy was being held in the small interrogation room and turned his attention to that case.

Wednesday was a beautiful spring day and Gracie woke with two things still churning through the back of her mind: first, why was she so convinced Richard Dawes had fled to Canada? And why did she think Manitoba was somehow involved? Second, why was that Boston PD Detective so eager to discredit the late Senator's memory by telling Jack about his indiscretions? It was more than just a newcomer wanting to right an established wrong, more than just whistle blowing. It seemed to Gracie, at least from what Jack had said, that the Detective could have a personal reason...

"Jack!"

"Gracie, I'm about to go into an interrogation, can't this wait?" Jack answered his phone because he'd seen who was calling, but he was literally steps from the interview space at the Sheriff's Office.

"It can, but not for long. Please call me when you have a break: I've had an epiphany about Detective Geene and Fred Jesperson," Gracie told him.

Jack sighed and said he would. Then he smiled to himself: only Gracie would say she'd had an 'epiphany' about a murder case.

After speaking to Jack, Gracie got busy on her laptop and pulled up the Boston PD website. Under a section that listed all the officers and their official photos —except for the undercover detail, of course—she searched for Sidney Geene and found her: a petite red haired woman of about thirty with soft hazel eyes and a generous mouth. Hmmm.

Well, she wasn't about to drive out to Boston to try and see Detective Geene and ask her if part of her reason for wanting to set the record straight with regard to the late Senator was because she herself had been a victim of his unwanted advances. She'd run that idea by Jack first: he had met the Detective in person, at least, and might be a better judge of how likely that was. But from what she could see of Detective Geene in her official photo, she was pretty enough and young enough—and in a position, perhaps, being a Detective, to be of aid to the late Senator —to have been a target for Fred Jesperson.

Since she'd filed her items for that week's paper, Gracie decided after breakfast to drive to Belchertown and see if Magistrate Ragans was available. She knew from the information she'd gathered from Hilda that Ragans, one of two magistrates in Hampshire County, was thought to have been involved in coverups of the late Senator's DUI accidents. She also had heard from Hilda that Ragans had been having an affair with the late Senator. Gracie thought a trip there to introduce herself to Maureen, Hilda's friend from the Morris Dancing group, and perhaps to speak with the magistrate if she were available, might prove a good use of the morning.

As she drove out of Cheshire, Gracie formulated her premise: she was doing a follow up on the late Senator Jesperson, and interviewing some of the people he had dealt with over the years.

Belchertown was a good sized town that used to be called Cold Spring. The eponymous name of the settlement was for Jonathan Belcher, who had owned large tracts of land in the area and who had been an early Royal Governor of Massachusetts. Belchertown was one of the oldest settlements in the western part of the state, having been incorporated in 1761 but settled thirty years prior to that. The Metacomet Trail, the Clapp Memorial Library and the scenic Swift River were all postcard perfect sights of rural New England.

Once Gracie arrived at the Magistrate's office, she decided to find a good place for lunch after she'd spoken to Maureen, and with any luck, Magistrate Ragans. Maybe then she'd do a little exploring of the quaint historic town, Gracie mused. She hadn't really had a day 'off' or even an afternoon 'off' since returning from England.

Maureen Kimmins was a slender middle aged woman with short, dark blonde hair and snapping black eyes. Gracie introduced herself to her, and Maureen unlocked the door leading from the lobby of the office to the office proper, and shook her hand.

"Hilda mentioned she might have found another member for our side," Maureen said happily to Gracie, referencing the Morris Dancing team, called a 'side.'

Gracie demurred, saying that she didn't know how graceful or good she would be at dancing: "I'm a bit of a klutz, but I'd like to at least come to a practice," she told Maureen.

"I'll give you the dates and times," Maureen said swiftly, and started writing on a slip of paper. "We just shifted our practice sessions to the Community Hall on Main Street in Northampton," Maureen explained, adding the address.

"I've got a GPS, I'll find it," Gracie returned cheerily.

They chatted a bit more about Morris Dancing and its history and popularity, and then a door to an office at the rear of Maureen's territory opened and a young woman came out.

Magistrate Tonya Ragans had thick auburn hair styled in a slightly teased Jackie Kennedy type flip. She wore rather a lot of makeup, Gracie thought, perhaps to hide a bad complexion, or perhaps to give contour to her somewhat flat, Persian-cat-like face. The feline resemblance was furthered by Ragans' use of thick liquid eyeliner to enhance and highlight her light blue eyes. This day, she wore an aqua suit with gold buttons, black heels and a white blouse with a jabot collar. Small gold button earrings and a gold Rolex completed her ensemble. Gracie noted that she had no beaded bracelets of any sort on, and neither did Maureen.

Introductions were made and then Gracie said, "actually, your Honor, if you have any free time, I was hoping to speak with you." She paused. "I could always make an appointment, but I took a chance…"

Tonya Ragans laughed lightly. "As you see, Miss Barufaldi, we aren't very busy today," she declared. "I was catching up on some paperwork and I don't have court until tomorrow."

"Does that mean you could spare me a few minutes?" Gracie asked humbly. She did humble quite well when it suited her, and she had a feeling from Magistrate Ragans' appearance that humble would get her further than assertive. "I'm doing a follow up on the late Senator," she added in a somber voice. "I'd really appreciate a few comments from you, if you could." Better not to indicate she thought Ragans had known Jesperson any better than any other magistrate in his district might have. Not yet. Not unless she needed to.

Ragans looked Gracie up and down, and seemed to consider for a long minute. Then, "yes, I'd be happy to," she said. "Won't you come into my office—if you and Maureen have finished chatting, that is?" she finished, sounding very gracious, but Gracie heard an edge in her voice, and suspected a chastisement in store for Maureen because she'd been visiting during working hours.

Chapter Forty

"What do you mean, I have to call the AG's office?" Jack blustered later that day. Gracie had just called him: it was lunch time, and he was taking a break from questioning Amy Dawes, and eating a hoagie at his desk. Funny, when Popovitch was in the office, everyone took every moment of every lunch break they were entitled to. But with him on vacation, people had started bringing lunch or ordering in. In spite of the amount of pressing issues he had to deal with, Jack found himself really enjoying the picnic like atmosphere.

Gracie had just suggested that he call the AG's office and ask them to investigate Magistrate Tanya Ragans in Belchertown.

"Well, I know you can't do it, it's Hampshire County, not our county," Gracie said reasonably. She, too, had stopped for lunch and was presently awaiting her roast turkey on whole grain cranberry bread sandwich at The Korner Kafé. She'd smiled at the name, and thought of Ben, who had always made fun of what he'd considered the 'countrified' monikers of restaurants in the rural area where Gracie lived.

"I could contact their DA's office," Jack reasoned.

"Yes, I guess. But I wonder if the DA's not in on it too, somehow," Gracie murmured. She was sitting at a small round table near the bay window of the restaurant and had a good view of Main Street and the commons. It was quite pretty, and Gracie smiled. "That's why I thought the AG's office might be the way to go."

Jack made a non committal grunt.

"I don't want to go into too much detail on the phone, but I also wanted to tell you my thoughts on Detective Geene," Gracie went on.

"Oh?" Jack queried, sounding doubtful.

"Yes." Gracie nodded. "Is she pretty? I mean, I was thinking over what you told me she'd said about the late Senator, and I couldn't help feeling, in my gut, that it was more than just wanting to right a wrong. I wondered if Detective Geene might have been the recipient of unwelcome advances by the late Senator?" she asked. "You know, like Regina Vioni, and others we have learned about?"

Jack thought a moment and took a bite of his Italian sub. It was delicious. And he was extremely hungry. "She's cute, yeah, I guess you'd say she was pretty," he admitted after he chewed and swallowed. "I wasn't really thinking of her that way, Gracie," he added wryly.

'Good to know,' Gracie thought to herself. "Well, maybe it would be something to ask her about?" she suggested aloud. "You could maybe call her, or talk to her, maybe once you get the results of their vodka analyses? And you could mention the DUIs and then segue into the womanizing rumors, and she what she says," she outlined.

Jack sighed. "I suppose so. I'll wait for the vodka analyses come back and take it from there," he said. "And

I'll give a buddy of mine at the AG's office a call, let him know what we think may have been going on about the DUIs being swept under the rug by Ragans, and see what he says," he concluded.

Gracie supposed it was at least a start. Sometimes she wanted to go in all guns blazing, but Jack took a more balanced approach. Mostly, it worked out okay.

After lunch, which was very good indeed, Gracie decided to head back home rather than shop and sightsee. She wanted to continue working on the murder cases and didn't want to break stride.

She knew the story of Regina Vioni's pursuit by the late Senator from a reliable source: her friend Anne, Regina's sister in law. Gracie knew the story of Magistrate Ragans' involvement with the Senator from Hilda via Maureen and what Gracie herself had seen that morning. Although she and Ragans hadn't discussed her personal relationship with Fred Jesperson, the district justice had revealed that the Senator had been 'instrumental' in pushing her appointment to the bench through. In Massachusetts, judges were appointed by the Governor with the help of the Governor's Committee; the late Senator had been on that committee and from what Ragans had told Gracie, had been very determined to see her be approved.

As Ragans had related the story, Gracie had observed her fingering her Rolex. Gracie had nodded to the watch and said, 'that's a gorgeous time piece, your Honor…' and let the implied question hang in the air.

Ragans had taken the bait, smiling coyly and telling Gracie that it had been a gift from the late Senator to commemorate her appointment to the bench. Gracie had privately thought that it sounded to her as though Ragans should have been the one giving gifts to the late Senator. Then, she realized that perhaps the magistrate had done exactly that, albeit in another way.

The third local woman who was said to have had an involvement with the late Senator was the woman who had run the Berkshire County Chamber of Commerce before the current Director. Gracie didn't know who that was, since the new Director had taken over about the same time Gracie had moved to Berkshire County. And in any case, Gracie's focus during her first couple of years here had been on her house, almost exclusively.

But a quick search on her iPhone gave her the name of a Sandy Cocker who was formerly the Chamber Director and another search using some specialized software yielded Cocker's current address and employment. Apparently, she was now the Facilities Manager at the Pontoosuc Lake Athletic Club.

As she approached Pittsfield, Gracie had another brainstorm, and on a hunch, she made a detour to the funeral home where Jesperson's viewing had been held.

"It's a good thing we're friends," commented the Funeral Home Director, Tony Wilson. Wilson had been a county commissioner when Gracie had first begun reporting for the Intelligencer, but had retired to run his funeral home business full time. He now had three locations, and was planning more.

Gracie beamed. "I know I'm a bother," she said apologetically. "And I'm lucky to find you in," she added with a smile.

"We have two viewings this afternoon, so I'm here making sure it's all ready," Wilson told her. "What can I help you with?" he asked, smiling.

"Could I have a look at your master Guest Book?" Gracie queried.

"Sure…" he led her over to it.

Wilson's Funeral Homes kept two guest books: an individual one that the family got, and the comprehensive permanent one that the Home kept, using photocopies of the family books' pages.

Together they found the right section. Gracie scanned it and discovered 'Sandra L. Cocker' in a kind of scrawl about half way down on the fourth page. She also noted a flowery 'Tonya Ragans, Esq.' on another page, and smiled to herself.

"Thanks, Tony," Gracie said happily, and left. She thought that Ms. Cocker would likely be at work on a Wednesday afternoon. Anyway, the woman's home address was north of Pittsfield, almost in Lanesboro, on Narragansett Avenue, right on Pontoosuc Lake, and just a stone's throw from the Athletic Club. So Gracie figured either way, she'd be able to find Ms. Cocker. She just hoped the woman would be willing to speak with her about the late Senator.

Gracie thought she would use the same excuse she had with the magistrate for wanting to speak to the former Chamber Director: writing a follow up profile of the late Senator. Cocker had been Chamber Director while Fred had been Mayor of Pittsfield. Undoubtedly, the two had worked together. It was good enough to start with, at any rate.

"I'd be delighted to talk to you," Sandy Cocker told Gracie once Gracie had found her. The Clubhouse at Pontoosuc AC was a bit like a rabbit warren, but an inquiry at the front desk had provided directions and with only one wrong turn, Gracie had presented herself without preamble at the Facilities Director's office door.

"Thank you, Ms. Cocker," Gracie replied, taking the chair indicated. The office was rather small, and crowded with plaques and pictures, trophies and memorabilia. There was no secretary, but sequestered as she was back in the far end of the Clubhouse, Cocker probably didn't get a lot of foot traffic.

"Oh, call me Sandy, please," noted the strawberry blonde. Although she was what Gracie would call a bit on the chunky side, Sandy Cocker was still a very attractive woman. Curly ringlets crowned her open face; a snub nose and bright blue eyes gave her the look of an irrepressible Raggedy Anne doll, only not raggedy in the least, Gracie thought. And she had a fabulous smile. This day, Cocker was attired in a bottle green trouser suit with a plain jewel necked t shirt in a soft yellow color.

"Sandy, thank you," Gracie agreed, and launched into her premise about a follow up piece on Fred Jesperson. "I want to focus on his years as Mayor, with you, because you were Chamber Director then, right?"

Sandy nodded enthusiastically. "That's right. Fred —I mean, Senator Jesperson—was a wonderful Mayor. He was instrumental in so many *leaps* made by Pittsfield and the surrounding area during that time!"

"Can you tell me about some of the projects you worked on with him?" Gracie asked, pen poised above her notebook.

"He worked very hard to expand Tanglewood," Sandy told her. "Even though that's not in Pittsfield, of course, he was connected to the people who were doing the expansion," Sandy explained. "With that came a need for top quality accommodation near by, and I worked with him on several hotel upgrades and developments," she went on, and named a couple of the better hotels in Pittsfield.

Sandy continued to be a fount of information, all of it positive and most of it radiating approbation for the late Senator. She told Gracie about the way Mayor Jesperson had made land acquisition problems 'disappear' if they'd run into them. About how he'd 'magically' been able to get funding for different projects through various state funding streams. Some of the programs Sandy mentioned were, Gracie was quite sure, not the type of programs meant to fund things like luxury hotels and golf courses. One in particularly, the Community Block Grant program was, Gracie knew, targeted at helping low to moderate income residents. Had funds been diverted from Pittsfield's considerable CBG pot to fund Fred Jesperson's pet projects? She'd have to look into that, Gracie thought, and made a note to herself.

After about a half hour, the gushing slowed to a trickle, and Sandy, surprisingly, choked up. She reached for a tissue and dabbed at her eyes. "I'm sorry," she said to Gracie with an apologetic smile. "It's just that, talking about all of that, it's made me realize what a wonderful man we have all lost," she said.

Gracie waited a heartbeat while deciding just how to respond. Then, "Yes, he was quite an amazing man, from all accounts. I'm just sorry I didn't know him better. Of course, I know his wife, Maddie," Gracie murmured evenly.

"Oh, yes, Maddie," Sandy said. But when she repeated the name, it would have been difficult for her to have sounded less enthusiastic. Odd, Gracie thought. When she had brought up Mrs. Jesperson in her chat with Magistrate Ragans, the young judge had just smiled in a cat-that-got-the-canary manner and continued the conversation. But Sandy Cocker's voice was distinctly dismissive.

Gracie closed her notebook and put away her pen. "You don't like Mrs. Jesperson?" she asked slyly.

Sandy blinked twice, then fixed Gracie with an aggrieved look. "I hardly know her. But I think she held Fred—Senator Jesperson, that is— back. I think, without her dragging him down, he could have done great things!" Sandy declared. The implication and the longing in her voice and on her face was clear, even if she hadn't confessed to anything more than desiring the late Senator's political advancement and success. Sandy patently thought that *she* would have made a far better partner for the late Senator than Maddie had. That could be motive.

"I've heard that, if he'd lived, Fred might have gone on to Washington," Gracie whispered, purposely using the decedent's first name. "At first in Congress, and then, well, the White House wouldn't have been hard to believe for a man like him, would it have been?" she whispered excitedly.

That's what Hilda had told her the group of Fred's backers had intended for him. Let's see what Sandy thought about it, Gracie mused.

Sandy looked surprised, then pleased, and then she smiled. "You're absolutely right, Gracie," she said, adopting first names all around. "Fred would have been amazing in Washington!" Her silent, 'with me at his side!' was the obvious subtext.

Gracie nodded agreement. She couldn't really push any more, not without being heavy handed, and finding out about an affair between Sandy and Fred was way beyond the scope of writing a testimonial article for the paper. So she decided to quit while she was ahead, and let Jack in on what she'd discovered. He could carry the investigation forward.

She thanked Sandy for her time, expressed again her regret at the late Senator's death, and left. It was nearly four o' clock. She'd interviewed two likely former mistresses of the late Senator, and given Jack her thoughts about a possible link with Detective Geene in Boston. A good day's work, Gracie thought as she got into her Jeep.

Something occurred to her, though, as she went to start the Jeep, and she placed a hasty call to her friend Anne.

"Sorry to bother you, Anne, but I have a quick question," Gracie said, fast, when her friend picked up on the second ring.

"Sure," Anne said cheerfully.

"What color hair does Regina have?" Gracie asked. Marco, Anne's husband and Regina's brother, had dark hair and dark eyes.

If Anne thought it a strange question, she didn't say. "Marco always said she was his Titian haired sister," Anne giggled. "She's got red hair, Maddie, and dark brown eyes, like Marco. As I told you, she's quite stunning."

Chapter Forty-one

Regina, Magistrate Ragans, Sandy from the Chamber and Detective Geene all had red hair. Varying shades, from strawberry blonde to dark auburn, but all red. While this in itself didn't mean they had all been the late Senator's mistresses, it was too much of a coincidence to overlook. And Gracie didn't believe in coincidences, anyway. Particularly since redheads were only two percent of the population or something.

Maybe the Senator just liked redheads. If he'd had other 'women' over the past several years, maybe they had all, or mostly, been red heads, too, Gracie mused. She didn't think she'd realistically be able to find that out. However, it was an interesting detail and one that gave more credence, she thought, to her theory about why Detective Geene might have it in for the late Senator.

Gracie drove home Wednesday afternoon, while Jack drove out to Maddie Jesperson's house. The results from the Boston PD on the vodka bottles seized from the Jesperson condo and office had shown nothing but vodka in the bottles. Jack had been impressed by the swiftness of the test, and supposed there were some perks to working in a big city.

He could now confirm to Maddie that the crime scene was the study in the home she'd shared with her husband.

He wondered what the widow would make of that. He pulled into the driveway, and Maddie met him at the door.

"Prompt as usual, Detective," she said, smiling, and ushered him into the kitchen. "Is this all right, or do you prefer a more formal setting?" she asked.

"This is fine, Mrs. Jesperson, as long as we won't be disturbed?" Jack replied. He noticed that she had no jewelry on at all, except for the religious medal around her neck, and recalled that she had said that when she was gardening, she didn't wear jewelry.

"No. I'm alone here, and if your CSU people aren't coming until later..."
she trailed off and Jack confirmed they'd be arriving in about an hour. Then he explained about the vodka testing positive for abrin.

"Only the vodka bottle from the mini fridge in your husband's study had abrin in it," Jack said. "We can rule out the Boston condo and his office," he added, wanting to be clear.

Maddie looked stricken. "Then, he was really— murdered—*here*?"

Jack nodded. "I'm afraid so." He paused. "Mrs. Jesperson: some of your prints were found in the study," he began gently.

Maddie nodded. "I suppose my prints would have been in the study, although I didn't go in there very often," Maddie said.

"No?" Jack asked.

"No," Maddie said softly. She sighed. "The political life in reality is very different to what it is seen from the outside. As you might guess, much of what you observe, and think you know, is a front, and it isn't the whole picture."

Jack nodded. He wasn't sure where she was going with this. "When was the last time you were in your husband's study, Mrs. Jesperson," he asked softly. "Can you recall?"

Maddie took a moment. "I'd have to say, it was probably a couple of months ago, Detective," she replied.

Her answer surprised him. "Months?" he asked: it just came out, he couldn't stop it.

Maddie got a sad, wry smile on her face. "Yes, Detective. Fred's study is his *sanctum sanctorum*," she explained. "That is, it was. I learned several years ago that Fred needed to have his own, inviolate space where he could retreat and do—what he enjoyed doing," she finished obliquely. "Around the time just after Eddie was born, I was quite ill," she elaborated. "It was a place Fred could go to escape the chores and the illness and, well, the difficulties we were encountering."

Ok, Jack thought: a man cave. Lots of guys had those. He didn't think they were a bad idea, but Maddie's face suggested that at least in Fred's case, his study had been more than just a 'man cave.' "What do you mean, Mrs. Jesperson, 'what he enjoyed doing?'" Jack asked, harkening back to an earlier comment. Well, he'd warned her when he'd set up the appointment that some of the questions he now had to ask her would be difficult.

"It started with him having a couple of drinks, and then smoking cigars in there," she answered. "Hideous, disgusting smelling things," she added with a *moue* of distaste.

"Anything else?" Jack asked. "Why did you go in so rarely, weren't you welcome?" Jack pushed.

"No, actually, Detective, I wasn't welcome," Maddie answered forthrightly. "To be honest, no one was. Fred stopped just short of locking the door, I think." She was completely serious. "But no one, and I mean no one, went in there. Particularly when he was inside. I only peeked in every couple of weeks when he was gone, to see if the place absolutely needed cleaning. But Fred was quite good about collecting any used glasses, emptying the waste basket and so on. I just checked, and maybe vacuumed. But that was all."

Jack found himself surprised that Maddie did her own cleaning, and asked if she didn't have a housekeeper.

Maddie shook her head. "No. I like to do it myself. I do a little bit every day, and I can pretty much keep up with the light work," she said in a satisfied tone.

Jack looked around the immaculate kitchen, and recalled the sparkling appearance of the rest of the home. "You do a great job," he told her sincerely.

Maddie smiled, and told him that Elizabeth and Roger helped with the heavy chores. Jack was glad to have that confirmed, but then he asked Maddie what he'd asked Elizabeth and Roger.

"Did you resent the fact that your husband didn't help you out at home?" Jack queried.

Maddie bit her lip and looked down for a moment. Her hands were loosely clasped on top of the kitchen table. "I suppose I did, a little bit, although I couldn't help feeling that if I were, well, completely healthy, I would be able to tackle most things myself." She paused. "I was diagnosed with Sjogren's Syndrome shortly after the birth of our son," Maddie told Jack. "I'm much better now, but there have been days when I could barely move," she said.

"Your daughter mentioned that to me," Jack revealed in a sympathetic tone. "I'm sorry."

"Oh, that's quite all right, Detective. As I said, I'm much better now. And getting back to the chore question, I did hire professionals: landscapers, roofers, painters, for certain things. But I also understood that Fred worked very hard all week and didn't really want to have to do house chores on his weekends," she added reasonably. "And, of course, he often had work related events on the weekends, too."

"So—did you dust in the study?" Jack asked, getting back to the scene of the crime.

Maddie shook her head. "No. You've seen it, Detective: papers everywhere, and files. I didn't dare. No, I just collected dirty glasses, although as I said, Fred was quite good about that, actually. And if he'd told me he was out of something—tonic water, ice, whatever, I'd re-stock that," she explained.

Jack nodded. "So, your husband worked in his study?"

"Oh, yes, Detective, he did."Maddie nodded.

"But it wasn't all a work space," Jack continued. "I mean, there was a television in there," he added. It was a huge flat screen HD television. "Do you know what else your husband may have done in his study? Did he watch sports?" That's what Roger had said.

Maddie smiled. "Yes, all the time: we have the premium sports package and there was literally always some kind of sporting event or game to view," she replied easily.

"How much time did your husband spend in his study when he was home?" Jack asked next.

"Fred was almost always in his study, when he was home," Maddie replied softly. There was a distinct tone of regret in her voice.

"How do you mean, Mrs. Jesperson?" Jack asked, his voice matching the softness in his subject's.

"Well, since becoming Senator, of course, Fred was mostly only home at the weekends," Maddie began. "He'd come home Friday, late, and he'd have eaten dinner. He'd go directly into his study and stay there till the early hours of the morning. Saturday he'd be out, usually golfing or at some kind of public appearance, or sometimes both. Again, he'd come home late, after dinner. He'd spend the balance of his evening in his study. Sometimes he'd make phone calls that I presumed were business related. Occasionally I would overhear a comment, even though the door was closed, and that's what it sounded like."

Jack just nodded. They had subpoenaed the phone records, but nothing strange had popped up. Given the new information, however, he'd have to look at them again. And maybe he'd subpoena Magistrate Ragans' phone records, too. "And all that time, your husband was watching sports?" Jack asked. There was no delicate way to ask what he really wanted to know, and he hoped Maddie would give him the answer without him having to ask the question.

Maddie got a peculiar look on her face: a bit of distaste, a little regret, and a bit of knowing. "We also have all the *other* premium channels, Detective, although I have them blocked on the televisions in the other rooms," she explained. "I don't want my grandchildren watching Playboy!" she declared, almost making it sound funny.

Jack made a note to check on the Jespersons' satellite television viewing history: that would be an easy way to find out about the late Senator's taste in late night programming. And he wouldn't have to ask his widow.

"When Fred was Mayor of Pittsfield, and before that, did he still spend so much time in his study?" Jack asked, switching gears a bit.

Maddie shook her head. "Oh, no. At first, I mean, when we were first married, he would only go in there if he wanted to watch sports and I wanted to watch something else on the living room television. But then, he started golfing after work, and having dinners out with his business associates, and then with his political cronies," she explained.

"And that's when he started…"

"Retreating to his study, yes." Maddie paused. "To be fair, Detective, I really think it began as a way for him to not disturb me," she said. "The Sjogren's made me, among other things, very tired. So I would go up to bed by nine o'clock every night. Fred would often still be out, and when he would return, rather than put on the television in the living room, where I might be disturbed by it, he started going into his study and watching television there," she explained.

"And lately? You said it started out as a way not to disturb you. So—later?" Jack queried.

"It became a habit. And his study became Fred's private sanctuary."

"Did he have friends over?" Jack asked.

Maddie shook her head. "No. He'd go out, or go to their houses, but he never brought friends home, not that I can recall," she murmured. "And certainly never in his study."

"And you said you would already be in bed when he'd come home?" Jack asked.

Maddie nodded. "Yes. Even now, when I am much, much better, Detective, I still go to bed by eleven o'clock," she said.

"And Fred?"

"He often doesn't—I mean, didn't— get home until well after that. And then, by the time he came up to bed, I was soundly asleep. And he never disturbed me," she added; the slightest of hesitations suggested to Jack that she was using 'disturbed' in a euphemistic sense. "He was just on the other side of the king bed, but he might as well have been on the other side of the world," she said sadly.

Chapter Forty-two

It was a relief to Jack when the CSU team arrived at the Jesperson house, and he could leave his questioning of Maddie and join the team in the study. Although they had delved into Maddie and Fred's relationship enough for Jack to know that a lesser woman might have considered the coldness between the couple motive for murder, Maddie clearly had not felt that way. Jack was more convinced than ever that she was not the person they were looking for.

He had remembered to ask her about Fred's golf trips, specifically any where he had played host to others, not so much ones where Fred himself had been a guest. Maddie had told Jack that she didn't have details on who went on these golfing 'junkets' and Jack accepted her answer.

A review of the late Senator's financials had shown that several of the trips in the past few years, whether golfing, or to a big sporting event like the Superbowl, had claimed as many as four 'guests' attending on Fred Jesperson's ticket. However, no names were listed.

Further questioning of political allies as well as other friends of the late Senator's might fill in those blanks.

Joining the CSU team in Fred's study, Jack was gratified to see that they were, literally, going over the place with the proverbial fine toothed comb. They had vacuumed and searched for fibers on the initial pass, but now, gloved and gowned, they were even moving books and files to search around, below and between them. Although they'd dusted for fingerprints on the obvious surfaces, they were now dusting on less likely areas, including the back of the television, and inside the desk's drawers.

"Detective?" a young CSU tech tapped him on the shoulder. "I think we missed this before," she said contritely and pointed to the wand at one side of the room's mini blinds. The wand controlled the angle of the blinds; at the moment they were open. The tech was pointing to a print she had just uncovered when she had dusted the wand.

"I can see how that might have been overlooked," Jack murmured, but he was smiling. "Get that print up to my office asap," he told the tech.

She nodded, pulled out her smart phone, and a minute later said, "it's in your email inbox, Detective."

It was probably Fred's again, but there was always the chance…

Wednesday evening, Jack worked late at the office, partly because he still had to go over Amy Dawes' videotaped interviews and partly because once he had returned to the office he had printed out the fingerprint from the window blind control and pulled the file containing the family's fingerprints to compare it.

The visual comparison hadn't been enough, and Jack had fed the new print plus the captured print from Roger Colcannon into the fingerprint analysis program and was really pleased when it turned up a match. Then, Jack felt frustrated: finding Roger's fingerprint on the wand meant next to nothing. It put him at the scene of the crime at some point in the past, sure. But it didn't link him in any way to the vodka bottle, which was how the poison had been delivered. So it wasn't even really circumstantial evidence.

And as for Amy Dawes, a review of her interviews yielded only a late day admission by her that yes, she had met Richard in Bloomingdale, and yes, she had given him money and bought gasoline for him. Jack was pleased to learn that Gracie's gas can theory had been correct, and thought how happy she would be when he told her. However, Amy Dawes had said repeatedly that she did not know the whereabouts of her husband, only that he had 'gone north.' Whether she truly did not know where her husband was, or was just an extremely strong willed liar, Jack was unsure.

Because he considered Amy as having aided and abetted in a fugitive's disappearance, and possibly in the murder of Ryan Colletti, Jack sent Amy, at the close of the long day of interviewing, to one of the two small holding cells in the basement of the courthouse. They were not used very much any more, as the Sheriff also had an area within his office suite where suspects could be detained.

But the holding cells were more primitive: with the rest of the basement used only for storage now, the cells were isolated. They were also very old, being original to the courthouse, and done in whitewashed brick. A small 'eyebrow window' allowed a little light into the small cells, and wooden pallets folded down from the wall for beds. These last had thin pads on them to serve as mattresses, but no pillow. The place was highly evocative of the most stringent of Victorian punishments.

Amy was allowed one phone call, which she made to her mother, telling her she was being detained and making sure Lana Frisvold would take care of the children. Then she was ushered into a cell, given her dinner, and locked in for the night. A Sheriff's Deputy would check her cell on the hour throughout the night.

His hope was that the Spartan conditions might prod Amy into being more cooperative. He couldn't hold her more than one night: on Thursday, he'd have to charge her, or let her go. Jack was considering offering Amy a deal of some kind, if she told him where her husband was. But he thought he'd wait until the following day and gauge Amy's mood, first.

Gracie was also concentrating on the Dawes case on Wednesday evening. After she got home from her visit to Belchertown and the athletic club, she decided that the only way to recall what it was that she wasn't quite remembering about Richard Dawes and Canada was to go through all her notes again. She had notes about the case, notes from her research, and notes for the articles she'd written on the subject.

After dinner she began, sifting slowly through the printed items first, but finding nothing. Then she checked her laptop's search history for the days immediately following the discovery of Ryan Colletti's body. She had done her background checks, of course, and—

She zeroed in on one document in particular: as a matter of routine, Gracie's program had produced a copy of Richard Dawes' employee file from the trucking firm where he had last been employed. In that file was his original employment application. Gracie recalled having scanned the application when she'd first seen it, and found nothing of great interest: Richard Dawes' school history and work history were listed along with Amy as his next of kin, and…

"Eureka!" Gracie shouted. "I knew I'd seen that somewhere!" she crowed, nearly dancing around the little alcove where she had her desk.

Richard Dawes had listed under 'alternate contact' a William Dawes, whose address was Lockport, MB, Canada. She remembered wondering where Lockport was, and searching for it on her map app. She had discovered—and then apparently forgotten—that it was about 25 miles north of Winnipeg.

Inspired, she googled William Dawes of Lockport and discovered that he was a professional fishing boat captain. Sport fishing was big business in that region. Gracie flipped back through her interview notes from her chat with the helpful neighbor, Agnes Davis. Davis had mentioned Richard's uncle who had visited and while she hadn't said anything about him being from Canada, she had said the uncle had taken the children fishing. Interesting.

Gracie couldn't wait to tell Jack, so she called his mobile, and was gratified when he picked up on the first ring. Despite Jack's rather abrupt greeting, Gracie forged ahead with the story of Dawes' uncle from Lockport, Manitoba, Canada and was rewarded when Jack gave a low whistle.

"That's great, Gracie: thank you for checking on it," Jack told her sincerely.

"So, now you'll call the Mounties?" Gracie giggled. She couldn't help it: she felt it in her bones that Richard Dawes was staying with his uncle. He was probably working on the fishing charter boats. She was equally sure that Amy and the children intended to join him, either in Lockport or nearby, after a few more months had passed.

Although Gracie's theory was mostly conjecture except for the concrete listing of William Dawes as Richard's next of kin, Jack had to admit it made a lot of sense. He told her about Amy Dawes' interview and that he was detaining her in the basement holding cells.

"Ehew! The basement cells!" Gracie chimed in: she'd seen them, and thought that a night there might just make Amy very willing to cooperate.

"Now, tomorrow morning, when she's had her fill of solitude and darkness down there," Jack told Gracie, "I can try one last time to break her and see if she'll tell me where Richard is. I know, thanks to you, that he's very likely in Manitoba, but I'm hoping that if I spring 'Lockport' on her she'll be so shocked she'll blurt out anything she may know."

"Good luck with that," Gracie told him sincerely. "How did the interview with Maddie go?" she asked next.

Chapter Forty-three

Jack sighed and admitted it had been one of the most difficult interviews he had ever had to do, but that he'd emerged from it more convinced than ever of Maddie's innocence. Then Jack told Gracie about Roger's fingerprint in the study.

"How did they miss that?" Gracie huffed.

Jack didn't make excuses, but he did point out that the wand was easily overlooked.

"But what motive would Roger have had for killing his father in law?" Gracie asked.

"Well, he didn't like the late Senator's drinking: remember I told you about his comments to me regarding that?"

"Yes. But that's not enough reason to kill the man!" Gracie protested.

"Well, maybe there was something else," Jack returned cooly. "Something we don't know about. Which is why I need to talk to the guy again."

"The fingerprint just puts Roger at the SOC it doesn't mean he was there at the time the vodka was adulterated," Gracie continued.

Jack, as always, appreciated her astuteness. "Yes, that's true, but it's enough to ask him to come and talk to me again." Then he told her about the peculiar lack of other fingerprints on the front of the refrigerator and on the vodka bottle.

"Someone wiped them," Gracie said immediately, giving voice to what Jack had thought. "The vodka bottle should have had a bunch of strange prints on it, too, besides Fred's: the person who sold him the vodka, the person who packed and shipped it, I mean, lots of people. The fact that only Fred's showed up on it, and on the door and the front part of the mini fridge, tells me that someone wiped the fridge and the bottle after handling it. Probably the person who put the abrin in the vodka."

"I think you're right, Gracie, but why not just wear gloves?" Jack asked sensibly.

"You and I think that way, Jack, but most people don't," Gracie answered. "Particularly if they're under stress, and the murderer had to have been under stress. Maybe, although I'll admit there was an element of premeditation, maybe they were apprehensive about what they had planned to do. And that made them stressed." She paused. "How about the doorknob to the study?"

"Ah, yes, also, like the fridge and the bottle, just a few of Fred's prints," Jack told her. He'd forgotten that: the door was another suspiciously clean area. If, as Maddie had told him, she went in every month or so to check if the study needed cleaning, her prints should have been on the door knob, too.

But they weren't.

"So it looks like Roger murdered Fred?" Gracie asked.

"Well, I think he's worth questioning again, certainly, but I wouldn't jump to any hasty conclusions,"

Jack cautioned. "If he's the murderer, then he just forgot to wipe the wand: that's understandable. But he could have gone in the study for some completely unrelated reason, which would explain his print on the wand. And if Roger is innocent, then whoever wiped the surfaces down to eliminate his or her prints didn't wipe the wand because they hadn't touched it."

Gracie was silent.

"By the way, no one's claimed Ryan Colletti's body yet. He's going to be buried in the Potter's Field, next week."

"Ah," Gracie said. "That's sad." She paused. "Did you ever track down the owner of the land where his trailer is?" she queried.

"Yeah, he called here, oh a couple days ago I think, said he didn't care what we did with the place and that now that Colletti was dead, he would probably just hire some company to come and bulldoze the trailer and all the scrap on site, and put the property up for sale."

"Did you get a chance to talk to Detective Geene today?" Gracie asked then, swinging back to the Jesperson case.

"No," Jack admitted.

"Well, you were awfully busy," Gracie told him sympathetically. "I was thinking, maybe, erm, in order to complete the research on this alleged follow up profile on the late Senator I am writing for the *Intelligencer*, maybe I should go to Boston, and talk to some of his staff there, and such?" Gracie suggested slowly.

"That sounds logical, Gracie," Jack replied, wondering what else she had in mind, because he was certain that talking to the late Senator's staff wasn't the end of it. "And?"

"And...and I was thinking maybe I could talk to Detective Geene. D'you think she'd talk to me?" she asked bluntly. "I mean, I'd have to reference you, and let her know you had told me about her suspicions regarding the late Senator's DUIs...I could stop off in Westborough on the way."

"Westborough? Why there?" Jack asked, confused.

Gracie reminded him about the magistrate near the turnpike that Chet had suggested she look into.

"Well, yes, I guess you could, but Gracie, you can't just ask the magistrate if he's done favors for the late Senator," Jack protested. He sounded anxious.

Gracie sighed. "Of course not. Give me more credit than that," she demanded. "I'll continue to use the excuse about the story, and just ask the magistrate if he'd known the late Senator and if so, how well and in what capacity. It's innocent enough. And you never know, something might turn up."

Thursday morning, Gracie got up early, had breakfast, gave Pumpkin extra kibble in her bowl and made sure she had plenty of water.

"I'll be back tonight, but I'll be late," Gracie assured the large orange cat who was sunning herself in the window of an upstairs bedroom.

Pumpkin didn't seen fazed by her announcement, so Gracie trotted downstairs and out to her Jeep. She'd stop to fill up her gas tank on the way out of town, and also swing by Courtney's store to pick up a sandwich and a drink for the road. It would be better than stopping at the roadside restaurants, and faster, too, since she could eat when she wanted, and not when she was near a stop. Then, if she were successful in talking to Judge Dennis O'Dea, the late Senator's staff and Detective Geene, Gracie thought she would have earned herself dinner at *Mange Tout*. It would be a nice surprise to pop in on her good friends Joey and Tyler, who owned the chic restaurant. After dinner, she'd drive home.

Gracie was choosing a 'steddatuna' whole wheat wrap with soy mayo and greens when she heard her name being called.

"Hi Maddie!" Gracie said when she turned and saw her friend. "How are you?" she asked, concerned.

Maddie smiled. "I'm doing okay, Gracie, thanks for asking."

"I hear the investigation is getting some breaks," Gracie murmured, and Maddie smiled again.

"Yes, Detective Draper seemed very upbeat yesterday when he left."

"I hope they figure it out soon," Gracie told Maddie sincerely, making no mention whatsoever of her own involvement in the investigation. Or of her destination and intent for that day.

"Oh, so do I," Maddie rejoined. "Seems I'm waiting to get back to normal—but meanwhile…" she gestured with the box of hair rinse in one hand. "Life must go on."

Gracie nodded and smiled, but then reached out for the hair rinse. "What's this?" she asked.

"Oh—it's my vanity, really," Maddie explained. "My hair went completely white with the Sjogren's. I was in my late 20's, but I looked ancient, or so I thought. Anyway, I didn't do anything to it for years, because of the chemicals in all the hair colors. But this one, this has…" and she read off a list of ingredients that not only were pronounceable and familiar, but also sounded like they would actually be good for the hair.

"That's great, Maddie: I didn't know they made all natural hair coloring," Gracie admitted.

"Well why would you?" Maddie rejoined. "You don't have to worry about it, not for years," she chuckled.

"So you're a natural blonde?" Gracie asked, looking at the rinse color on the package in Maddie's hand.

"No, actually not. But this seemed the—least drastic—color for me to use, if you know what I mean."

Gracie thought she did, but she couldn't help asking. "What—what is the natural color of your hair, Maddie?"

If Maddie thought it an odd question, she didn't say. Just smiled, and answered, "coppery red. Fred always said that he first saw me walking through a patch of sunlight, and my hair looked like it had caught fire."

Chapter Forty-four

The nearly two hour drive to Boston gave Gracie plenty of time to ruminate about Maddie's red hair and Fred's apparent penchant for mistresses who had the same hair color. If she thought about it from one point of view, it even seemed kind of tragic, that Fred had really been paying tribute to his wife in his choice of other women. The timing of the end of the 'golden times' of Fred and Maddie's youth, the birth of their children and her illness fit with the start of his philandering, too, Gracie thought: at least the majority of it. And the red hair detail it fit neatly with Gracie's theory about Maddie's illness making intimacy between her and Fred difficult.

It wasn't hard to find the Westborough Magistrate's office, but unfortunately, Judge Dennis O'Dea was not in his office.

"He's never here on Thursday afternoon, or on Friday, mostly," his helpful secretary told Gracie, once Gracie had explained the reason for her visit.

"How does he manage that?" Gracie asked with an ingratiating smile.

The secretary explained that Judge O'Dea scheduled all his cases all day Tuesday and on Wednesday mornings. "That way, he has Monday to prepare, and Thursday morning to review, and the rest of the time is his own, unless there's an emergency. And he's on call once every month, for the whole weekend," she added, her tone suggesting that this inconvenience justified O'Dea's creative time management the rest of the week.

Gracie knew the magistrates' positions weren't considered full time, but it seemed to her that O'Dea had taken this to new heights. Or depths.

She thanked the secretary and left her name, but didn't ask for the judge to call her back. "It's not critical," she told the secretary. However, Gracie took the time to scan the walls of the outer office, and was rewarded by a large, framed photograph of the late Senator with, presumably, Judge O'Dea. They were somewhere warm, on a dock: a large yacht type boat was in the background, and they were holding up a bluefish the size of a five year old child. Both were grinning like fools.

"Is this the judge?" Gracie asked the helpful secretary, pointing to the photograph.

"Oh, yes: he's a big sport fisherman," she replied happily. "That's him with Senator Jesperson. The late," she added, sounding woeful.

"Oh, he went fishing with the Senator?" Gracie asked, sounding purposely thick.

The secretary nodded eagerly. "Yes, they went a few times a year, up in Maine, down in Florida, sometimes even to an island somewhere… The Senator always paid, too, treated the judge just like royalty, the judge said." Her tone was full of approbation.

"Hmmm…when was this taken, do you know?" Gracie asked of the photo.

"About three years ago, I think," the secretary replied. "Why?"

"Oh, no reason, really: just any insight into the Senator's, erm, relationship with his colleagues, is so helpful," she murmured vaguely, and said her goodbyes.

Gracie drove into the state capitol with a sense of familiarity: it was where she'd been brought up, after all, and she still had friends here. She chose to travel straight down Commonwealth Avenue, and thought herself lucky to find a parking space not too far from the late Senator's condo. Jack and the Boston PD had already interviewed the neighbors and had found nothing remarkable. But it was a short and very pretty walk around the edge of the Public Garden and up Beacon Street past the Common to the State House.

She had phoned ahead, and the late Senator's staff was expecting her.

As Gracie headed for the Statehouse, she couldn't help glancing down River Street where she could just make out the corner of Mount Vernon Street, a few blocks to the north. Ben's brownstone was there, but he was in Washington. She remembered several good times in this area with him, when they'd been dating, and experienced a sense of nostalgia as she finished her walk and arrived at her destination.

The late Senator's staff: a chief, two assistants and a secretary, all seemed very willing and eager, almost, to speak with her. Gracie collected a lot of really good information on the projects the late Senator had been involved with. Most of them had seemed genuinely productive and aimed at improving the lives of Massachusetts residents, especially those living in the western part of the state. Fred Jesperson, after all, had been elected to represent them.

The financial records of the late Senator, though, were closed to her. Gracie knew Jack had them, and she'd have to remember to ask him to check on the Community Block Grant dispersals. Something that Sandy Cocker had said led Gracie to believe that the Senator's 'miraculous' way of finding money for certain projects might actually have been more 'mishandling' than 'miraculous.'

After what she considered a successful chat with the staff, none of whom appeared to have a motive for killing their former boss, and none of whom wore beaded bracelets or had red hair, Gracie hailed a taxi outside of the statehouse and proceeded to her next stop: the Boston PD on New Sudbury Street, near Government Center.

The desk sergeant at the New Sudbury station appeared confused as to why Gracie wanted to speak to Detective Geene. However, seeing no reason why she shouldn't, he gave Gracie a large white and red 'V' for Visitor badge to clip onto her blazer, and instructed her on where she might find the detective.

Two floors up, and one hall down, and Gracie was in a medium sized open plan office with five desks. Two were empty. At one sat a wiry African American Detective: she was studying a long printout with great concentration. At another, a chunky man with closely clipped grey hair was on the phone, speaking in low but deliberate tones. He rolled a toothpick between his full lips. And at the last desk was Gracie's quarry: Detective Sidney Geene. She was scrolling through some kind of report on her desk top computer, and she looked up as Gracie approached.

"Miss—Barufaldi?" she asked, pronouncing the surname with just a tiny hesitation.

"Yes—Detective Sidney Geene?" Gracie asked, smiling.

"You found me," Sidney said. "You wanted to talk to me?"

"Yes…" Gracie grabbed the back of a straight wooden chair. "If I may?" she asked, and sat without waiting for an answer. "I just wanted to chat with you briefly, Detective, about the late Fred Jesperson."

Sidney's hazel eyes looked frankly at Gracie. "Long way to come for a chat," she said evenly.

Gracie smiled in a friendly way. "It is. But I know from Detective Draper that you believe there were some —irregularities, shall we say?—with regard to the late Senator's driving record," Gracie murmured. "I was hoping we could talk about that."

Chapter Forty-five

Whether it was the invocation of Jack's name, or the presentation of her press credentials, or just Gracie's smile, Detective Geene agreed to speak with her about the DUI irregularities she had heard about. Gracie promised not to use her name, and told the Detective honestly that, if her investigation showed that some kind of cover up had taken place, she would turn the whole thing over to the state Attorney General's office.

This seemed to please Detective Geene, who nodded her approval.

It was lunch time, and the Detective apologized when a delivery person from a nearby deli brought her sandwich.

"Oh, that's okay: if you want, go ahead and eat," Gracie replied with a smile. "I appreciate your time, and actually, I brought my lunch with me," she added.

"Then join me!" Detective Geene urged. After bringing over two mugs of coffee, the Detective unwrapped her sandwich while Gracie unpacked hers, and they continued their conversation.

Detective Geene confirmed what Jack had told Gracie he'd heard from her before about the two DUIs. However, she said, she hadn't heard about any more.

"How about, erm, any unsavory behavior?" Gracie asked as she started on the second half of her wrap.

The Detective cocked a quizzical eyebrow at her.

"Like, oh, drinking too much at a local bar, that sort of thing…" Gracie suggested. "I mean, if he drove drunk, he had to drink somewhere," Gracie added logically.

The Detective named a couple of bars in the Government Center area that the late Senator had been known to frequent. "They stocked that special vodka that the Senator always drank, from what I hear," Detective Geene continued. "The one your Detective wanted to have us run tests on," she noted. "The bottles we collected from his office and condo came back clean. Do you know if he found abrin in the bottles he seized from Jesperson's Pittsfield house?" she asked Gracie.

Obviously, Jack had shared that information with the Detective, Gracie thought, possibly when he had called to explain why he thought they should get a warrant for any vodka bottles at the late Senator's office and condo. The question sounded nonchalant, but Gracie thought the Boston Detective was keenly interested in the answer. It was part of the ongoing investigation, and it was information Gracie probably shouldn't share with just anyone, but the Detective wasn't just anyone, she reasoned.

"I think abrin *was* found in the vodka from the Jesperson home," she answered, deliberately imprecise. She didn't feel comfortable saying that it was the bottle from the study fridge. "But you should ask Jack, I mean, Detective Draper," she told Geene.

The woman smiled. "I'll give him a call later today, maybe. I'm just curious," she shrugged.

"Well, Boston PD is part of the investigation, you've a right to be curious," Gracie replied supportively. "Erm—what were the names of those two bars again?" she asked.

Geene told her, and gave her directions. Both were within walking distance of the Police Department, so Gracie thought she might stop in to both when she was finished.

"So…any other sleazy behavior on the part of the late Senator you've heard about?" Gracie asked next. "If he was a bar fly—I know you're not supposed to speak ill of the dead, but it's less his conduct and more the coverup that I'm concerned with," she hedged. "But to investigate the latter I need to know about the former," she explained.

Detective Geene looked at Gracie, and then looked down at the remains of her chicken club. "He, uhm, he liked the ladies," she said euphemistically.

Gracie waited.

"He would meet women at those bars, sometimes."

"That's not a crime," Gracie said softly.

"It is if they're prostitutes!" Geene replied shortly, and Gracie sat up straight.
This was new.

"Oh!" Gracie waited a heart beat. "Was the Senator ever picked up for soliciting a prostitute?" she asked, low.

Detective Geene made a face. "That's what I've heard." She pushed her chair back from her desk and took a deep breath. Then she scooted forward again and leaned in to speak in soft tones. "Look, I've only been here not quite two years. I'm still the new kid on the block. But I heard a lot of things when I first came, stuff about how things were done, and I was told, on the 'QT' as they say around here, that if I ever got a call involving the Senator, I should handle it discreetly and report it directly to the Chief, and he'd take care of it."

"The Chief?" Gracie echoed.

Geene explained that she meant the Chief of Detectives. She also told Gracie that she had been told that the Chief 'protected' some of the better-looking and exclusive prostitutes in the area, in addition to protecting the late Senator.

Gracie nodded again. The Chief had probably been the late Senator's fixer, then, when it had been a question of a police matter.

"Did the Chief ever fix the late Senator up with, erm, female companions?" Gracie pursued, her voice low.

Geene frowned. "I've heard that. I never witnessed it. But I have heard that, yes. And my sources are good ones."

Gracie thought to herself that the sources might be good ones, but unless this investigation were handled very carefully, she knew only too well what 'good' sources could do if faced with reprisal. Another reason to call in the AG.

"And what did you say, or do, when people told you these things?" Gracie asked. She made her voice curious, not judgmental.

Geene sighed. "I didn't like it, but I wanted to keep my job. So I just played along and hoped I would never be involved in an issue with the late Senator, so I wouldn't have to confront my conscience," she answered.

"And were you?" Gracie pushed.

Geene frowned. "Not exactly in the way you might think," she answered. Then she looked around at the squad room. It was deserted, the wiry detective and the chunky one having gone out to lunch. The Detective seemed to make up her mind about something, and then began to speak, quickly, and in a low voice, but Gracie caught every word.

"I was right about Detective Geene," Gracie said a little while later to Jack. She'd found a coffee bar on the far side of Government Center in a little shop she remembered from when she'd been a child. Now, although it had retained the iconic teapot over the door, the place had catapulted into the twenty first century, complete with wi fi.

"How so?" Jack queried. He was in his office, starting on the paperwork for Amy Dawes' plea agreement: she had been desperate to talk by that morning, and although she really did appear not to know exactly where her husband was, she'd told Jack enough about their scheme for him to begin the preliminary paperwork on a plea agreement.

"She did have a run in with the late Senator," Gracie told him. "Did you know, she was born in Australia? That's where her first name, Sidney, comes from! Anyway, her parents settled in Bethlehem, Pennsylvania, and as you told me, she came up here from the Bethlehem PD a couple years ago. She said she had relocated and requested the transfer because of her boyfriend, who works here. When she got here, she apparently was 'told how things were done,'" Gracie related, adding some details.

Luckily, the coffee bar was not crowded in the middle of the afternoon, so Gracie was sure she wouldn't be overheard. Still, she spoke in generalities and figured she could leave the particulars for later. "She says she wanted to keep her job, so she just hoped she'd never run into the Senator in a situation where she'd have to sweep an indiscretion under the rug," Gracie went on. "But apparently, it was well known that the Chief of Detectives was the late Senator's buddy, and helped him out of tight situations," she added wryly. "And got him in to other ones, if you get my drift?"

"Hunh." Jack understood.

"And it turns out that about a year ago the Senator was at some shindig in Boston and there was some kind of security kerfuffle, and Detective Geene responded along with a couple others."

"Unh huh," Jack murmured.

"Well, the Senator propositioned her!" Gracie crowed in a gleeful whisper. "He had, of course, been drinking, and Geene told me he came up to her after the security incident had been resolved—I don't think it was anything major—and asked her how a pretty little thing like her came to be a Police Detective."

Jack cracked a grin. Trust Gracie to get the story.

"And then…" Gracie went on, sounding even more enthusiastic, "he told her that he had been wanting to hire a personal bodyguard, and maybe she would like to change jobs, because it would be a lot nicer for her than being with the Boston PD, and he was sure she could meet his requirements, and he would do his best to meet hers."

Jack whistled. "He said that?"

Gracie nodded. "Yes. That was what Geene told me were his exact words. Accompanied by a suggestive run of his hand down her back."

"She said no, I imagine?" Jack asked wryly.

"Yes, of course. Actually, she told me that although she'd been surprised and pretty grossed out, she'd had the presence of mind to just step away from the Senator and tell him, firmly, that she was very happy where she was, thank you, and that for his own sake he'd better pretend that what he'd just said and done had never happened, because if she heard that he'd breathed a word of it to anyone, she'd rat him out," Gracie concluded.

"That was very professional of her," Jack noted. "And Senator Jesperson went along with that?" he asked. His experience of drunks going after women was that they were generally more persistent.

Gracie nodded. "He did. Geene said he's sort of a bumbling drunk, anyway, and quite possibly felt that she could do him more harm than good by squealing on him if he made trouble, or if he persisted. So he didn't. Like Regina Vioni: when she told him she'd call the police if he didn't stop stalking her, he stopped," Gracie reminded

Jack. "He is—was—very concerned with his image. Well, he would be: he's —he was—a politician," Gracie finished. "And he probably thought that if one woman turned him down, he could probably find another who would say 'yes' pretty easily."

Jack sighed.

"Anyway, I told Geene that I would likely turn all of the information over to the AG's office, and she said she'd be glad to talk to them," Gracie went on. "She confirmed the DUI stuff, too, and I'm going to check with the local bars she told me about, see if they'll tell me if the Senator used to frequent their establishments."

"What about Westborough?" Jack queried.

Gracie told him that O'Dea hadn't been in, but mentioned the photo of him with Jesperson on the wall, and told him what the secretary had said.

"I think there's enough with all of this to get the AG's office involved, for certain," Jack decided. "But I sure would like to have the murder solved before I bring it to them," he added.

"Aren't you going to talk to Roger?" Gracie asked.

Jack told her that he'd contacted Roger and asked him to stop by his office after work. "So another late night for me," Jack sighed.

Chapter Forty-six

Gracie stopped in at the two bars once she'd left the coffee shop, and had brief but successful conversations, confirming that the late Senator used to be a 'very good' customer at both locales. She was also told that both bars carried the expensive vodka the late Senator had preferred. More small pieces of the puzzle found and put in place.

It was only late afternoon when she was finished with that, so Gracie took a taxi to Newbury Street, a couple of blocks from where she'd parked her car. She stopped in at one of her favorite shops, the Crush Boutique, and was happy to find a cute pair of Dolce Vita sandals in an almost iridescent acid yellow. A top from the same designer nearly matched in shades of the same acid yellow and grey, and was more dressy than the tailored T shirt and linen blazer Gracie had worn for the day.

She changed into the top and sandals, putting her shirt, scarf, blazer and loafers in the Crush bag. She kept her jeans on: teamed with the top and sandals they looked fancier, anyway, in that great way that jeans had. Gracie spritzed on some perfume from the sample rack, fluffed out her curls, and decided she would wander down Newbury Street towards *Mange Tout,* which was a couple blocks over, until it was time for dinner.

If she was going to surprise her friends, she wanted to look nice. And the sandals and top would work well in her wardrobe this spring and summer, so they'd be put to good use.

Actually, she admitted to herself, she could do with a bit of a makeover: she'd been in a small funk ever since returning from England, what with breaking up with Ben, and then leaving David. The *pièce de résistance* had been the nonsense over her Jail drug ring story and being accused of not doing her job properly. Not to mention the pain of having a source burn her, in spite of all her precautions.

So maybe she'd see what other little goodies she could find on her way to *Mange Tout*, to cheer herself up: after all, Ben was behind her, as was the unpleasantness over that article. And as for David, well, although the distance between them was a hindrance, it didn't seem insurmountable.

Gracie's stroll down Newbury Street brought her to Lalo Treasures, where a sea glass and silver abstract necklace in all shades of yellow caught her eye: that would look great with the top, she thought. It was reasonably enough priced, so Gracie bought it and put it on.

Continuing her 'progressive makeover' as she had decided to call it, she popped in to Spa Newbury and was delighted to learn that yes, they could squeeze her in for an immediate mani/pedi. She chose a 'French' varnish for both manicure and pedicure. Mani/pedis weren't things Gracie often indulged in, but on occasion (and this was one of them), they were very nice indeed. And since the sandals showed off her feet, it would be great to have them looking as pretty as possible.

When she was finished, it was time for dinner, so she walked to *Mange Tout* and breezed in the doorway just on the stroke of six o' clock. When she gave the hostess her name, the young woman smiled, discreetly pressed a button under her podium, and seconds later Gracie's long time friend Joey Battafaglia came rushing up. He'd known Gracie since grade school when their surnames had placed their desks adjacent to each other.

"Gracie! What on earth are you doing here?!" Joey exclaimed, kissing her on both cheeks. "You don't have a reservation, do you? I mean, I didn't forget something, did I?" he asked, concerned suddenly.

Gracie shook her head. "Nope. I was in town on business, and I just thought I'd stop in. Do you have a table?" she asked, hoping that they did.

"Of course—for you? Of course!" Joey exclaimed, his brown eyes sparkling and his short brown hair almost electric with excitement.

Tyler Koch, Joey's partner and co-restaurateur arrived at the hostess' podium seconds later, and greeted Gracie nearly as effusively as Joey had.

"How did you guys know I was here?" Gracie asked, suspicious.

They explained that there was a 'short list' of VIPs at the hostess' station. If someone who was on the list showed up, they were to press the call button that sounded in the kitchen and also sent a text to each of their phones.

"Wow, that's pretty hi tech!" Gracie said admiringly. "And I'm on the list?" she squeaked. She didn't think of herself as a VIP. Just a friend.

"Of course. So's the Mayor, a couple of other politicos, some people from the art world, and depending on who's playing a show or concert in town, other names too," Tyler explained.

Gracie, knowing that Tyler was the 'money and gadget' guy of the duo while Joey was the chief creative person, thought the VIP list had been his idea. She smiled.

"We are pretty booked tonight," Joey murmured a second later, having reviewed the reservation list. "Will a chef's table do?" he asked cheekily, knowing Gracie would love the idea.

"A chef's table? When did you start doing that?" Gracie asked in delight as they led her back towards the kitchen area. She had been to *Mange Tout* just a few months before, prior to heading off to England, as a matter of fact, and found it hard to believe so much had changed in such a short time.

"Well, we've been thinking about it for a while, but we only just started two weeks ago," Joey revealed.

A 'chef's table' was a small table for one or two people in, as the name suggested, the kitchen of a high end restaurant. Guests at the chef's table could choose to sample anything and everything the chef was creating that evening and could order something from the menu as well. Specific wines were usually paired with each particular course, and the guest could also, of course, order anything special he or she wanted. Restaurants usually charged quite a bit for the chef's table service, generally double what the standard dinner would cost.

Gracie remembered when she and Ben had first started dating, he'd taken her to a very ritzy restaurant called Espadrille in Boston's Back Bay, and they'd had the chef's table. It had been Gracie's first experience of the fairly new trend, and she'd loved it.

She reminded Joey and Tyler of that, and Tyler happily admitted that her experience at Espadrille had been the spark that eventually urged them to offer the Chef's Table Experience at *Mange Tout*.

This evening, Gracie was the only dinner guest enjoying the chef's table; this meant she could visit with Joey and Tyler exclusively, whenever they had the time.

Joey was quite a hands on restaurateur, so he was alongside his chef de cuisine, Paolo Vermici, as the man supervised three sous chefs and two kitchen workers, what Gracie called 'scullery maids,' since both were female. They had the lowest jobs like cleanup and rubbish removal. Gracie had to admit that the kitchen at *Mange Tout* was spotless; the small corner where her table for one was situated was out of the way enough to allow for a free flow of traffic in the kitchen, but nearby enough for her to hear and see everything. Additionally, Paolo chattered away to her in Italian for much of the evening, explaining what dishes were being created.

Mange Tout's cuisine was Mediterranean influenced French, but far from a hodge lodge. Focusing on new takes on classic recipes sourced from southern France and

Morocco, the restaurant had grown steadily from its first location in Brookline to trendy Copley Square. Its reputation was very good, and several food critics had repeatedly pointed to *Mange Tout* as a place to watch.

As Gracie was starting on an appetizer plate put together by one of Paolo's sous chefs for her, Joey scooted into the empty chair opposite her.

"So, what've you been working on? Still on that Senator's death?" he asked eagerly.

Gracie nodded, as she had a small spoonful of lemon dressed artichoke soup in her mouth, and she wanted to appreciate it. It was garlicky and she thought she detected summer savory in it as well. Very nice. The adorable demitasse cup it had come in was cute, too.

Before she moved on to the next appetizer— grilled melon with prosciutto studded halloumi—Gracie quickly filled Joey in on the latest developments in the Jesperson case. She didn't mention the specific connection between the vodka bottles and the abrin: that was still privileged information.

"He never ate here, did he?" Gracie queried. It had never dawned on her before now to even ask.

Joey shook his head. "No. Not that I know of. We're probably too experimental for him," he added, sounding pleased about the possibility.

Gracie finished the melon creation, pronounced it very tasty despite the fact that melon wasn't one of her favorites, and moved on to the next fragrant morsel on the appetizer platter: a single mushroom cap stuffed with a kibbeh type mixture of squash, bulgur, kale, onions, and garbanzos, all finished with a drizzle of pomegranate syrup.

"Oh my god, this is great!" Gracie said through her first mouthful of this appetizer. "What's in the stuffing???" she demanded of Joey, who just smiled.

"You'll have to tell me," he teased her. He knew only too well how refined Gracie's palate was: she was quite good at figuring out ingredients and then re-creating a dish in her own kitchen.

Gracie finished the small bite, concentrating on the flavors.

"You going to make that for your Memorial Day shindig?" Joey asked. "We could have a whole Mediterranean theme."

Gracie usually gave three big house parties a year, one on Memorial Day, one on Labor Day, and another at Christmas. Joey, Tyler and Gracie's friend Susan all came for the long weekends and stayed with Gracie; local friends and neighbors were invited for an all day 'Open House,' generally on the Sunday. Each party had a different theme, particularly the summer ones. Sometimes it was tropical. Sometimes it was Asian. Sometimes it was North American…it just depended on Gracie's mood and inspiration.

At Gracie's blank look, Joey started.

"You are having a party, right?" he asked anxiously.

Chapter Forty-seven

"Oh my god, I forgot all about that," Gracie blurted, mortified. "What with getting back from England at the start of the month, and then being plunged into two murder cases, I haven't had a chance to even think, much less plan a party," she told her friend.

"No worries: if you're up for it, you've still got two weeks, and we can help," he said enthusiastically. He and Tyler always offered, but Gracie usually only allowed them to do a little plating and a little cleanup. Sometimes she would ask Tyler to handle dessert, too, as his specialty was pastry.

Gracie nodded. She had pulled house parties together in less time, but still, she couldn't believe she'd forgotten. She supposed, as she'd told Joey, she had had a great deal on her mind.

She returned to her appetizer plate to attack the last offering: a tiny piece of lamb skewered on a sugar cane stick the size of a kitchen match and finished with a basil mint sauce. Divine. She drained the small glass of Moët Tyler had poured for her and looked up expectantly.

Joey had vanished with a quick apology, but Paolo himself was en route to her, bearing the next course: 'insalata.' A blend of quinoa, strawberries, almonds and feta, the tablespoon sized serving was plated on fresh baby spinach leaves arranged in a star shape, and garnished with 75 year old balsamic vinegar.

This was extremely tasty, too, Gracie thought as she chewed and swallowed. A small glass of light, crisp white wine was poured for her to accompany the 'insalata.' Maybe she should have a Mediterranean theme this year: it wouldn't be hard to do, and the cuisine would please all her guests. She'd have to look up traditional Mediterranean cocktails, since she always offered a 'signature' cocktail in addition to the more usual beverages and libations. But it was a great idea, and Gracie found herself looking forward to the planning.

It was a good thing that Jack was close to wrapping up the Jesperson case, Gracie considered. It appeared that the murderer was Jesperson's son in law, Roger, although Gracie still didn't think he would have had a sufficient motive. Still, Jack knew best about that.

And as for the other murder, Jack had mentioned only briefly when they'd spoken earlier in the day that he would be drafting a plea agreement with Amy Dawes. He had promised to tell Gracie all about it, but said he'd have to wait to file it until Popovitch returned from vacation. That would be Monday, so Gracie planned that the disposition of that case would be her 'big story' for the following week's paper.

She had found it ironic that Jack wanted to offer Amy a deal, because he hardly ever chose that route: Popovitch was the one who sought plea agreements, because they meant less work and less time in court for him. But in this case, Jack had told her, Amy had some really good information, and her data, coupled with her testimony about how she and Richard had planned the scheme, was invaluable.

Gracie was anxious to hear all the details.

But first: the main course was on its way to her. Paolo had asked if she wanted to order anything specific, and she had just shaken her head and opted for a 'tasting' serving of whatever he was making for the regular diners ordering in the main restaurant. The 'insalata' she knew had been a one off: Paolo and Joey had only just put this on the menu, and wanted Gracie's opinion of it. She suggested cutting the amount of almonds, but said otherwise the dish was, in her opinion, tasty and well balanced.

For the main course, Paolo sent over an oversized oval platter with about two bites of five different creations. Alongside it was a smaller dish with a selection of that evening's vegetables: baby green beans, baby carrots and new asparagus, all thinly sliced, blanched, and then finished with a yoghurt based cumin dressing. Yum.

The sample servings of the entrees were arranged in a specific order, and Gracie was instructed to eat them right to left. The first was a single, perfect, scallop ravioli in a delicate spring onion butter sauce. Next was a little nest of capelli d'angeli pasta topped with a spring mushroom reduction. Following that was a bit of grilled saffron chicken, then two meltingly soft bites of a European flounder fillet that had been marinated in tomatoes and onions, and finally, a portuguese dish called 'vina dosh' which was wine, olives and garlic marinated pork.

"I know, Portugal isn't on the Mediterranean," apologized Joey, who had returned and taken his seat opposite Gracie again. "But this dish is just soooo good!" he exclaimed.

Gracie agreed. "This is amazing," she agreed. "Everything was amazing," she added with a smile. With the main course, Gracie had enjoyed a small glass of a dry rosé, something she normally didn't drink, but which played well against all the various flavors of the sampler platter.

To her shock, Gracie realized it was nearly eight o'clock, but *Mange Tout* was still hopping, which surprised her on a Thursday night.

"We're really doing well," Joey said, sounding grateful and pleased. "There's hardly a night we aren't fully booked. Maybe Tuesdays. But since we do Brunch now on Sunday and nothing past three p.m., and we are shut Mondays, our regulars are always eager to get back to us by Tuesday!" he declared.

Gracie opted for a double espresso and a small serving of Paolo's signature tiramisu for dessert, which she savored while she continued to visit with Joey and Tyler. Then, at about half past eight, it was time to leave and drive back to Cheshire.

"I've had a fabulous time, you guys have been so good to me," Gracie told her friends, who refused flatly to let her pay for her dinner.

'Think of all the meals we have had at your house,' Tyler had exclaimed when Gracie had tried to settle her bill. 'No way are you ever paying for a mouthful here.'

She protested once, and then graciously accepted their generosity. And then, fortified and full, she took a taxi back to her Jeep and made the drive home.

Roger Colcannon was a title searcher with a small abstract company in Pittsfield, so it was easy for him to stop by Jack's office once his business had concluded on Thursday. He was an even featured man, but his thick rimmed glasses gave him a boyish air. Jack noticed he still looked tired and strained.

Roger put his briefcase on the floor in Jack's office, and at Jack's invitation, sat in one of the two chairs facing the Detective's desk. Jack asked if Roger would like something to drink, water, or coffee, and Roger declined.

Then Jack got right to it.

"Roger, we found a fingerprint matching yours inside your late father in law's study," he said without inflection.

Roger blinked, then nodded. "I suppose you could have, Detective."

"You mean you have been in that study? I thought when we spoke initially you said you never went in there," he reminded his subject.

Again, Roger nodded. "Yes, I recall saying that, but I think I meant more as a general rule." He paused. "I'm sure I've been in there a couple of times, at least, over the course of the past several years."

Roger and Elizabeth had been married for seven years, Jack recalled. He supposed Roger's explanation was as good as any, and he had no means to disprove it, so Jack moved on.

"Can you tell me, Roger, as near as you can recall, when you were last in your father in law's study?" he asked.

Roger looked surprised, then thoughtful. Then: "you know, Detective, I really don't remember." He shrugged. "Maybe sometime around the holidays?"

Jack took a deep breath. "The holidays," he repeated.

Roger said, "yes, maybe. I mean, I don't remember a specific instance, but there's always a lot going on at the holidays. Maybe Maddie asked me to tell Fred it was time for dinner, or maybe she asked me to help her clean up and I offered to check the study…I don't recall. I'm sorry, Detective."

But something in his tone didn't sound genuine, and Jack didn't think Roger was especially sorry.

Chapter Forty-eight

"Tell me again about April seventh," Jack said. He'd been talking to Roger Colcannon now for nearly an hour. They'd danced around Roger's visits to the late Senator's study and Roger had become more and more agitated.

"I really need to call Elizabeth back and tell her I'll be later than I'd expected," Roger told Jack now, for the third time. His phone had pinged and buzzed every few minutes at the start of the interview, and Jack had asked him to turn it off. Roger had, reluctantly, and now his voice sounded almost frightened when he repeated that he had to call his wife.

"You can call her after we discuss April seventh," Jack returned, firm.

It was nearly six o'clock and most of the other people had left the courthouse for the day. Other than the occasional footfall of a Sheriff's Deputy or other official working late, there was complete silence. Jack liked it, but it seemed to unnerve Roger.

"What is so important about April seventh, Detective?" Roger finally burst out. "I've already told you: Lizzie and I went with the children for our usual monthly visit. The children played with Maddie while Lizzie and I started on some chores. I'm not sure where Fred was but he appeared later, played with the children and then wanted to barbecue."

"And he was drinking."

"Yes."

"And you didn't like that."

"It's not my place to judge."

"Yes it is, Roger: you exposed your children to Fred. You have the right to judge. It *is* your place," Jack insisted.

Roger shook his head. "I didn't like it. You're right. But he wasn't *my* father," he said in an apparent non sequitur.

Jack waited.

"Elizabeth…" he began.

"What about Elizabeth?" Jack asked softly.

Roger's inner torment was very clear on his face: his even features had become distorted, the pleasant mask he generally wore was gone. Roger was clearly exhausted. His guilt had probably allowed him little sleep, Jack thought as he watched Roger's face: he was probably tired of pretending not to have hated his father in law. Tired of pretending that he hadn't decided to do something about it, to rescue the women in the family from the monster, like some knight in a mediaeval pageant, Jack thought.

While he didn't condone what Roger had done, Jack thought he understood his motives.

Then suddenly, Roger's face crumpled, and he looked down.

"Elizabeth didn't like that her father drank so much, either, did she?" Jack asked sympathetically.

Roger shook his head.

"So you did something about it, didn't you?" Jack suggested, sympathetic. "Something that would keep Lizzie, and Maddie—whom you thought of as a second mother—and your children safe?" Jack's voice was gentle.

Roger looked up as quickly as he'd dropped his head, and blinked twice behind his glasses. "Me?"He looked surprised.

Jack waited.

Roger shook his head. "No, Detective. It wasn't me. I didn't do anything."

Wrong-footed, Jack was silent.

"It was Lizzie," Roger whispered.

To Jack's surprise, Roger told him the entire story once he'd begun, almost without taking a breath. He related that he and Elizabeth had known for years about her father's drinking, and even about his drunk driving and how he'd made his DUIs disappear. Apparently during one visit early in Roger and Elizabeth's courtship, Fred had bragged to Roger that should Roger ever have any sort of trouble with the police, even a parking ticket, he, the State Senator, could make it go away. And he'd told Roger that he'd had what he called 'a little fender bender' the week before but that no report would ever be filed on it.

Jack was hastily scribbling as Roger talked, and made a note to find out exactly where that fender bender had happened, if Roger knew.

Roger continued by saying that he and Lizzie had known about her father's 'philandering' as well. "Lizzie told me practically when we first started dating that her father had cheated on her mother for years," Roger said. "He kept it quiet, mostly, but she was sure her mother knew, although for reasons of her own, she preferred to just ignore it." He paused. "Lizzie never understood that: we both thought Maddie was something of a saint."

Roger told Jack he had not known anything about his wife's plans to kill her father until a few nights after the Senator died. Elizabeth, he related, had been very calm all day, even when she was called to her mother's side at the hospital, and when she told him, and when they told their children. Roger told Jack that of course he had known his wife had detested many things about her father, but he had still been surprised that his death hadn't saddened her more. After all, she must have remembered good times from her childhood, at least. And he *was* her father.

Roger related that throughout the funeral services and the family and friends who gathered during and after, Elizabeth had remained serene, so much so that Maddie called her 'my brave girl', at which, Roger recalled, Elizabeth had smiled.

"But I finally asked her about it, because I thought she was just keeping it all in, and that's not healthy, Detective. So I told her, 'go ahead, let go, have a good cry' the day after the funeral: the children were at a neighbor's house for a play date, and we were alone in the house. And do you know what she told me?" he asked Jack, who shook his head. "She said, 'cry? Roger, I'd dance in the street if it wouldn't look suspicious.' And then she told me what she'd done, and how she'd done it."

"She killed her own father?" Jack asked. Patricide was more suited to Greek tragedy than Pittsfield politicians, he would have thought. But apparently not.

Roger nodded. "I couldn't believe it. She swore me to secrecy…"

Jack wanted to put in that such an oath didn't stand up against the law: Roger should have called the authorities, immediately. But then, Jack thought: would he have done that? To his surprise, he found himself unsure.

"She 'swore you to secrecy?'" he asked, repeating Roger's phrase.

Roger nodded. "Yes. She—she told me that if I said anything, she'd take the children and disappear," Roger whispered.

Jack had to make some hasty arrangements. The children of Roger and Elizabeth were his first priority: he needed to contact Child Services and explain what had happened, and what was going to happen. While Roger waited anxiously—still forbidden to call Elizabeth, of course—Jack first telephoned the Sheriff, asking him to go to Egremont, take Elizabeth into custody, and bring her in for questioning.

Then Jack called Child Services and spoke to the on call case manager. Once he had explained the situation, the case manager agreed to meet the Sheriff at the home of Roger and Elizabeth in Egremont, and to give Maddie temporary custody of her grandchildren if she were willing. Roger would probably have custody returned to him eventually, but the charges against him would have to be filed first, and then he'd have to plead guilty, and serve whatever sentence the judge imposed.

Jack planned to be lenient with Roger in return for his information—albeit a week late—revealing his wife as her father's murderer: he would be given immunity from any felony charges, at least, although lesser charges might still apply. He probably wouldn't do jail time, but he could have community service or some form of house arrest, and that was why Jack needed to find the children a temporary home.

Jack's next duty was to place Roger in one of the Sheriff's holding cells and make a fast trip to Maddie Jesperson's home. He estimated that he could be back at the courthouse by the time the Sheriff would bring Elizabeth in, as long as things with Maddie went well.

Chapter Forty-nine

"I can't believe it was Lizzie," Maddie uttered, shattered, to Jack a short while later. She had answered his knock on the door and ushered him into the living room where she'd been doing some needlework and watching television. They had sat down, side by side, on the beige chintz sofa, and Jack had quietly explained first his suspicions of Roger, and then Roger's startling revelation.

Now, Jack put one hand over the older woman's in a comforting gesture. "I'm sure this comes as a real shock, Mrs. Jesperson," he said gently. "I have to tell you, I was thrown for a loop when Roger told me, too," he added in commiseration.

Maddie took a deep breath and gave a quick smile. "You're certain?" she asked, sounding both hopeful and resigned.

Jack nodded. "I still have to interview Elizabeth, and get her confession. But yes, I'm sure."

Maddie bit her lips and sighed, "oh, dear, but what about the children? I mean, I assume, Detective, you're going to arrest—" her voice broke here, "Elizabeth? And Roger?"

Jack outlined his plan, admitting that yes, Lizzie was on her way down to the courthouse now, courtesy of the Sheriff, and that Roger was being held, and would be charged shortly as well. He explained that he planned to charge Roger as lightly as his conscience and the law would allow, but agreed that the children would need a place to go, at least for the time being.

"Children's Services is meeting the Sheriff in Egremont, at Roger and Lizzie's house," Jack said. "I was hoping, Mrs. Jesperson, that they could bring your grandchildren, well, here."

He waited.

Maddie's eyes were tear filled, but at Jack's words, her face lightened and she gave him another smile. "Here?" she asked, her voice breaking again.

Jeez, this was tough, Jack thought.

He nodded. "If you'll have them. It will likely only be temporary custody, Mrs. Jesperson, until Roger's finished serving his sentence and the court deems him fit to resume care of the children…"

"But of course I'll have them, Detective!" Maddie had put in happily. "I—they're my grandchildren! I would love to have them here with me."

Jack smiled. "I was hoping you'd say that."

With the children assured of a good home with their Grandmother, Jack returned to the courthouse. The Sheriff had not returned with Elizabeth yet, so Jack typed up the charges he planned to file against Roger while he waited.

Massachusetts law allowed considerable latitude on the crimes of obstruction of justice and accessory after the fact, the two offenses of which Jack felt Roger was certainly guilty.

The level of crime, whether a felony or a misdemeanor, depended on the nature of the actions of the defendant, as well as the timing. In severe cases, a criminal charged with obstruction and accessory could receive the same sentence as the person who actually committed the crime. In Roger's case, however, he had not known what his wife had done until she told him. For a week after that, however, he had kept her secret, and that made him guilty of both obstruction and accessory. As far as Jack had been able to ascertain, Roger had merely kept silent: he hadn't helped his wife cover up the crime or in any other way made a material contribution to the subterfuge. Additionally, while a week was a long time in some ways, it could be argued that it was a very short time for Roger to come to terms with the shock of his father in law's death and his wife's crime.

There was also the further question of Roger and Elizabeth's relationship. Although Roger hadn't said anything overt during any of the interviews, Jack was beginning to suspect a darker side to the couple. He had observed that Elizabeth was the disciplinarian in the family. That was not unusual, but coupled with other details and especially in the light of Roger's almost frantic pleas to be able to call his wife earlier that evening, Jack wondered if Elizabeth was emotionally or physically abusive to her husband. Her threat to 'take the children and disappear' was particularly telling, Jack thought.

And it would explain a lot.

Jack charged Roger with a second degree misdemeanor on both obstruction and accessory: while these carried significant fines and possible jail time, they also allowed for alternative punishment programs. He suspected Judge Cranston would lean towards the latter option.

The Sheriff finally did return with Elizabeth, about 10 p.m.

"Tried to run," Sheriff Shermayne told Jack shortly as he brought Elizabeth into the interrogation room. His tone held satisfaction that Elizabeth's escape had been foiled. "Had the kids' stuff all packed and hers, too, and was loading up her car when we arrived," he continued as two Deputies brought the prisoner, in handcuffs and shackles, through to the interrogation suite. "Gave us a bit of a tussle, but we got her manacled all right, and the Child Services lady got there right on time."

"I called her, and she's bringing the kids to their Grandmother's house," Jack told the Sheriff, who nodded.

"That's what she was telling the children when we left," Sheriff Shermayne added of the case worker.

"Were the kids upset?" Jack asked, low. Those little children had had rather a lot to deal with in the past several days: he hoped this evening's activities wouldn't scar them for life.

The Sheriff shook his head. "Nah. They didn't see what was going on with Mrs. Colcannon: the Child Services caseworker was there talking to them in the front of the house while we were out the back, wrestling the little lady into our transport van." He chuckled

"Thank god for that, I'm glad, Sheriff," Jack put in.

Sheriff Shermayne smiled. "The caseworker told them that Daddy and Mommy had some very important things to do for a while, and that they would be staying with their Grandmother, and that she'd explain it all to them." He shrugged. "They both seemed really happy about going to Granny's."

The on call Magistrate arrived just about the time the Sheriff and Jack were concluding their conversation, so Jack handed him his hastily-typed charges and affidavit and Roger was taken to the Magistrate's courtroom on the ground floor of the courthouse for his preliminary arraignment. It took less than five minutes, and Roger was released on his own recognizance. The Magistrate also signed off on the temporary custody arrangement. It specified that Roger could have supervised visits with the children, for now, and also call them on a regular basis, as long as Maddie was with the children while he spoke with them, and as long as the conversation was on speakerphone, so Maddie could hear it, or listen in on an extension.

Roger was advised to go home and get his affairs in order. Jack told him further court proceedings would likely take place in the next couple of weeks. He counseled Roger to be up front about the situation with his employer, and said that if the employer wished, he would write a letter on Roger's behalf, urging that the Title Company retain him.

"I have a good employment record," Roger told Jack humbly.

Jack nodded. "Let me know if there's anything I can do," he assured the man.

Just before 11 p.m. Jack finally entered the interrogation room where Elizabeth Jesperson Colcannon had been waiting. When he opened the door, she looked up at him quickly, and her features became resolute.

"Mrs. Colcannon, your husband told us some very disturbing things earlier this evening," Jack began, "and I need to ask you about them." He plopped a fairly thick file down on the table between the two chairs in the room. The file did contain details of the Jesperson case, but it also contained a lot of blank paper. Its heft was meant to suggest a weighty amount of evidence against the defendant.

Elizabeth gazed at him levelly. "I knew he wouldn't keep quiet," she said of Roger, but there was only resignation, no bitterness, in her voice. "I knew when he didn't come home from work on time, and didn't call, that something had happened." She gave a small, sad smile. "And, of course, Detective, I knew what that something had to be."

Chapter Fifty

"Tell me about your father," Jack said after a few minutes of conversation with his quarry. Elizabeth had already admitted to planning to flee the area with her children that evening, and admitted to killing her father, and now it was time to find out her reasons.

She gave a sad, sarcastic smile. "I think you know all about my father, Detective," she answered.

"But I would like to hear about him, from you," Jack urged, his voice firm but not without compassion.

Elizabeth nodded, and began to outline a relatively happy early childhood, one that fit with the 'golden times' Hilda Senter had told Gracie about. The Jespersons sounded like they had been quite happy, and quite typical of nuclear families of twenty five to thirty years before: days out at amusement parks, picnics, exploring historic sites, trips to the beach, and more. Elizabeth said that she'd taken tap dance as a youngster, and that for the first several years both her mother and her father had proudly watched each recital. Even her father's interest in golf was, in those early years, something the whole family shared. "After my Saturday morning dance class, we would go out to lunch: nothing fancy—fast food usually, but it was better then, I think. And then Mom and I would go with Dad while he spent the afternoon at the driving range," Elizabeth reminisced. "She'd listen to the opera broadcast on the radio in the car, and I usually had a book to entertain me, but Dad always chose a spot to hit his bucket of balls where we could see him, and we'd wave and cheer if he hit a really good shot."

"You were happy?" Jack asked.

"Yes, Detective. We all were."

"Go on," Jack encouraged.

"Well, then my brother was born, and Mom became ill. I was only five, so I didn't understand, I just knew that Mommy was always very tired and that a nurse came in every day to help with her, and with the baby." She smiled a little bit again, a soft smile. "And I helped too. I loved bathing Eddie, and dressing him, and playing with him. I don't know if I thought he was some kind of animated doll or really comprehended that he was my own flesh and blood at first, but I loved him. I read to him, and sang to him, taught him his numbers and letters before he was three," she continued.

"You two were very close," Jack assessed.

Elizabeth nodded. "We still are." She paused. "Mother did get better, slowly, but I sensed she still needed help, so I continued to be the best big sister I could as Eddie and I both grew up. When Eddie started school, I'd help him with his homework. Then I started helping Mother with the meals, and so on, but I didn't mind." She sighed. "By then, Dad wasn't around very much and—" she frowned, recalling, "I think that was about when he was elected Mayor."

Jack did the math in his head and agreed: Jesperson had served two six year terms as Mayor, and been in his second four year term as a State Senator when he'd died. He nodded to Elizabeth that she was correct.

"I was about fourteen when I figured out just why my father wasn't around much, and what was going on," she said.

"What was going on?" Jack echoed.

Elizabeth nodded. "When I was fourteen, Eddie was nine, and he was in cub scouts. It was his troop's first big overnight camping trip, and it was on Father's Day weekend: the cub scouts and their fathers were supposed to all go camping together. My father had said he would go—" She paused again. "But—"

"He didn't show up?" Jack guessed. He remembered a similar cub scout event when he had been a child, and he remembered still how much it had meant to him to have his Dad with him, along with all the other boys, and their fathers.

Elizabeth shook her head. "No." Her voice was small. "Eddie was crushed. It meant that he couldn't go, either, and I think he cried the whole weekend. I don't even remember what excuse my father gave, but whatever it was, I think I saw right through it. I think finally, what had been going on for the past few years at last made sense to me. Or maybe I was just old enough to understand."

She paused again, and took a sip from the bottle of water Jack had kindly provided.

Jack mirrored her action with his own water bottle, creating sympathy and reinforcing their connection.

For the next half hour or so, Elizabeth enumerated other instances similar to the one she had begun with where her father had disappointed her, her brother and her mother: family events where her father was either absent, or left early 'on business;' important occasions, in particular her dance recitals, which her father consistently began to miss; Eddie's 'graduation' from Elementary School—"it's kinda silly to have graduation for fourth graders, but Eddie was so proud, and it would have meant the world to him for his father to be there," Elizabeth explained. She told Jack that in the past couple of decades, her father had even been remiss about her mother's birthdays and their wedding anniversaries. "He always gave her something, and usually they went out to dinner, but it was always a week or two later, when he could fit it into his schedule," Elizabeth explained, her voice tinged with anguish for her mother. "It was never on the day, or near the day. He never even sent her flowers—that would have been easy enough, I imagine! I remember some birthdays when he didn't even call her," she whispered.

Jack nodded. "Go on," he invited.

Elizabeth recounted how she had been looking forward to a long standing tradition at the elite all female prep school she had attended: the Father-Daughter Dance, in the spring of the girls' junior year. "My father was supposed to escort me, of course," she said, outlining how she and her mother had shopped for just the perfect gown. "I even had a wrist corsage, ostensibly from Daddy, but mother told me later that she had ordered it."

"And he never showed up?" Jack asked, hating to, and understanding what a blow that would have been to the young girl.

"No," Elizabeth answered in a small voice. "He didn't. He didn't even call. Mother—Mother was so distraught, but she called her friend June Spears and asked if her husband, Tom, could stand in for my Dad."

"And did he?" Jack asked, imagining the County ME hurriedly donning his tuxedo and rushing over to the Jesperson home to escort the teenaged Elizabeth.

She nodded. "He did. He'd gone to his daughter's dance the year before, so he knew how important it was. He is a very kind man," she finished.

After more exposition of what Jack came to characterize in his mind as a pattern of willful disinterest on the part of Fred Jesperson in the lives of his family, Jack asked Elizabeth about her mother's bracelet.

"When she bought it, she naturally told me about it, and showed it to me," she said. "And while I can understand that the herbal supplements my mother takes might, in fact, help her condition, I frankly didn't see how just wearing a bracelet that was supposed to make you feel good could really be of any help," she told Jack, very nearly rolling her eyes. "I don't believe in sympathetic magic, but my mother did, and since the bracelet appeared harmless I didn't say anything. But later, I googled 'jequirity' and found out about the use of the beads by shamans, and how a weak tea can be a kind of stimulant, but that even in those traditions medicine men are reluctant to use the beads because their toxicity is so unpredictable." She sighed. "I don't think I planned anything—specific— then," she murmured. "But I knew what the beads in those bracelets could do, and that knowledge stayed with me."

"Tell me about April seventh," Jack urged.

Elizabeth took a deep breath, and then recounted what Jack already knew: that she and Roger had begun doing some of the heavier chores around the house, a usual occurrence during their visits. She said that she had collected some laundry that needed to be done—curtains and a duvet—and brought everything down to the laundry room in the basement. However, she had discovered soiled clothing in a basket on top of the washer that needed to be laundered, and told Jack she had decided to do these first, and then wash the heavy items.

"I was sorting the soiled things when I smelled perfume. It was coming from one of my father's dress shirts: it reeked of it. And it wasn't my mother's. If she wears any scent, she wears L'Air du Temps, quite distinctive, Detective: light and floral. This was heavy, musky, totally different."

Jack nodded: this was what Roger had told him.

"I have to say, Mrs. Colcannon, I'm a little surprised that your mother still laundered your father's dress shirts: why not send them out to the dry cleaner's?"

Elizabeth gave a small smile. "My mother is very environmentally conscious, Detective, and dry cleaners use all kinds of toxins. And, frankly, I think she enjoyed starching and ironing my father's shirts just so. It was something she was still able to do, even when she was quite ill, and over the years she's become an expert, and quite quick about it: she can do a shirt perfectly in just over seven minutes."

Jack smiled encouragingly.

Elizabeth went on to explain that she had noticed stains on her father's clothing that morning, as well, stains that she said clearly were evidence of an assignation.

"And all I could think about was, what if my *mother* had been the one to do the laundry? What if *she* had seen, and smelled, what I had?" Elizabeth demanded, angry.

Jack didn't ask if Elizabeth hadn't realized that her mother had very likely encountered similar 'evidence' before: he wanted the young woman to finish her story. "And what did you do? Did you confront your father?" Jack asked instead.

Elizabeth shook her head. "No. What good would it have done? He didn't care if I knew, I don't think he even cared if mother knew. I don't think he cared at all." Her voice was harsh. She went on, noting that she 'flew into a rage' and threw all of the soiled clothes around the laundry room. "That's when Roger came to find me. I had been supposed to start the wash and then go help him with the gutters. I hadn't shown up, and he'd come looking for me."

"Did you tell him what you'd found?"

Weeping a bit, Elizabeth nodded. "Yes." She sighed. "I'm sorry: talking about it brings it all up again," she said, wiping tears from her face.

"And when did you decide to kill your father, using the abrin from inside the jequirity bead bracelet?" Jack asked.

Elizabeth said that while Roger was calming her down that Sunday morning, she remembered the bracelet, and recalled what she'd read about jequirity, and the toxin inside the beads. "Like I told you, Detective, I think the knowledge had stayed with me, and suddenly, I just knew what I needed to do. I knew where I could find my mother's bracelet." She smirked. "It was easy to slip upstairs during all the hullabaloo that afternoon, and snap the elastic string the beads were on. I left it in mother's jewelry box, thinking that she would just assume she'd broken it taking it off, and hadn't noticed," she said.

Jack knew from talking to Maddie that that was exactly what she'd thought.

"Then I brought the bead home. The next day, I broke it with a hammer and ground up the insides using a mortar and pestle. I put the powder in a baggie, ran the mortar and pestle through the dishwasher twice, and washed my hands thoroughly."

"And how did the powdered abrin come to be in your father's vodka bottle?" Jack asked.

Again, Elizabeth smiled, but it was almost a proud smile. "I just went over to my parents' house one morning, when I knew mother would be out, and of course my father wasn't home," she said dismissively. "I went into my father's study, got the vodka bottle, put the abrin in and shook it till it dissolved. Didn't take long."

She paused. "But I'd forgotten to wear gloves, and I knew that once he died, there would be an investigation. So I wiped all the surfaces I'd touched with a wet wipe from the downstairs bath and a wad of toilet paper. Then those, and the baggie, got flushed. I washed my hands again, and I left, and waited for nature to take its course."

Chapter Fifty-one

Jack wasn't sure what would happen as far as Elizabeth's possible trial: when Popovitch returned on Monday, he might want to try for a plea. However, public outcry might prevent him from doing that. It was, after all, premeditated murder, done by a daughter to her father, and with that father a State Senator. Jesperson's warts and blemishes aside, it was still murder.

Jack also contacted the Massachusetts Attorney General's Office with regard to the late Senator's record, or lack thereof. Telephone records showed numerous calls between the Senator and the three Magistrates with whom he was suspected of having illegal arrangements: Le Bron in Boston, O'Dea in Westborough and Ragans in Belchertown. Jack told the AG everything he—and Gracie, though he didn't mention her involvement—had uncovered. He also suggested they speak with Detective Geene at the Boston PD, who could give them more information about incidents in Boston.

"What about the money we think Jesperson diverted?" Gracie asked when Jack called Friday morning to catch her up with Elizabeth's arrest and his conversation with the AG's office. She had told him about her chat with Sandy Cocker, and specifically recommended he check into the CDBG funding to see if it had been inappropriately used.

"I'm only one person, Gracie, I'm working on that now," Jack shot back, aggrieved, and gestured to the files on his desk, even though Gracie couldn't see them. "I've also discovered that there was an administrative assistant listed on the late Senator's office payroll, but that she was more of a personal assistant to him, and his speech writer."

"And?"

"Well, her salary came out of a couple of grants, and I don't think that's what they're supposed to be used for," Jack revealed. "I'll have to check with the state."

"Wow. OK, Jack: keep in touch," Gracie asked.

"I will. I should be done by this afternoon. And I'm still working on Amy Dawes, too" he reminded her.

"Have you hammered out that plea agreement?" Gracie asked.

"Yes. It's ready for Popovitch's signature and Amy is behaving under threat of the plea being revoked," Jack said. He explained that because Amy would certainly be charged with something, even if it wasn't the list of serious offenses her husband was looking at, she had been given the weekend to get her affairs in order and was to present herself Monday afternoon for a preliminary arraignment. "Once Popovitch has signed the plea," Jack finished.

"Where will the children go?" Gracie asked.

"Probably to Amy's mother's," Jack said. "And before you ask, yes, I've called the CMP and they're supposed to be taking Richard Dawes into custody today. I promise to tell you all the details of Amy's plea, and what she told me about their scheme, but I don't have time right now."

Jack had all the Jesperson financials pulled and organized by Friday afternoon. Although he wasn't an expert at forensic accounting by any means, a few things jumped out at him when he ran his eye down the various accounts from the late Senator's office. The funding of the 'administrative assistant' was a start. Her salary came partly out of a Humanities grant for the development of cultural initiatives and attractions, and partly out of an Enterprise Zone grant. From what Jack had seen of the 'administrative assistant' and her work, she was involved in neither of these two spheres.

Gracie had told Jack to check the Community Block Grant award to the state, and she'd been right: it looked to Jack as though the Senator had deliberately diverted funds from that account into other accounts over a period of years. Those other accounts were all development and building/construction type funds.

However, a quick glance into those funds showed that they hadn't been used for the construction of low to moderate income facilities of any sort, which is what CBG money was for. Rather, they'd been used for building upscale hotels, conference centers, a golf course, athletic clubs and similar types of recreational venues. The athletic club where Sandy Cocker worked was, perhaps not so coincidentally, one of the facilities constructed in part with the suspect money.

Jack saw several familiar names of developers involved in the projects, especially three of them, who had also been among Jesperson's biggest campaign contributors, and part of the group of 'movers and shakers' who had been the ones to get Fred elected Mayor and then elected to the State Senate.

Jack called the local office of the FBI and gave them a rundown of what he'd found. Because the Community Block Grant was federal money that was awarded to Massachusetts, investigating how that money had been used was a task for the FBI. They said they would send an agent to Jack's office Monday to collect his evidence.

Turning to the other big case occupying his 'in' box, the Dawes/Colletti murder, Jack had got some good information from Amy about the scheme she and her husband had concocted with regard to Ryan Colletti and the insurance money. Gracie's deduction, that Richard Dawes had planned for Colletti's body to be mistaken for his, and for Amy to collect on the life insurance, thus solving their money problems, had been spot on. Amy had also told Jack how her husband had shot Colletti at his trailer but then moved the body to the park where it would be discovered. She said that Richard had, after the fact, told her what he'd done, and that he'd planted his ID on the dead man. She said that Richard had left her one of his credit cards to use, and given her instructions concerning the withdrawal of their assets, and where to meet to hand over the cash and the extra gasoline. Amy told Jack she really hadn't heard from her husband, and had seen him for the first time in several days on the night of the meet in Bloomingdale, NY.

On Friday, Gracie wrote up a bulletin for the *Intelligencer* outlining the charges against Elizabeth, and giving a synopsis of the way the poison had been administered. She was grateful that the bulletin didn't require a lot of detail, because she hadn't had a chance to really read the Affidavit attached to the criminal charge file sheet. Those details would come the following week, in her full article.

She wanted to begin writing the article wrapping up the Dawes/Colletti murder, too, but needed more information. On an impulse, she drove down to the courthouse late Friday afternoon and just caught Jack as he'd been about to leave his office.

"I was hoping I'd catch you," she said brightly. The rest of the staff had already left, and the DA's suite was deserted. "He comes back Monday, huh?" she asked with a chin jut to Popovitch's closed office door.

"Awww…don't remind me," groaned Jack good naturally.

"You must be beat, you've been up most of the night," Gracie said sympathetically. He had told her that by the time he'd finished interviewing Elizabeth Jesperson Colcannon and she had been processed it had been nearly two in the morning.

"Yeah, but now I'm wired," Jack admitted with a rueful laugh.

"Listen, I have an ulterior motive for popping in like this: I want to hear what Amy told you about that cockamamie scheme she and Richard cooked up, and I'd really like to go over that Affidavit on Lizzie Jesperson, too, and I know you're too tired to cook anything, so why not just come to dinner? Bring Woof. I'm making stuffed peppers," she coaxed, knowing that was one of Jack's favorites.

Jack was too tired to argue, and frankly, looked forward not only to a meal cooked by Gracie, but to talking over both cases with her. It seemed that the two had concluded in a thirty-six hour whirlwind, and he thought talking through the evidence and the charges might be beneficial.

Chapter Fifty-two

Jack showed up shortly after five p.m. and although it was a bit early, Gracie already had dinner going, figuring he'd be hungry. Woof came as well, and nibbled at some food, then snuggled with Pumpkin in front of the unlit gas fireplace in a corner of the kitchen while Gracie and Jack visited.

Gracie gestured to her barn board table, which was set for two, and asked Jack if he wanted wine, coffee, water, or what.

He took a half glass of wine, noting that it might help him relax. Then, while Gracie assembled the chopped vegetable salad she had decided to serve with the stuffed peppers, Jack began.

"Let's start with the Affidavit of Probable Cause in the Jesperson case," he began. Gracie's copy of that document was at his elbow, in case he needed to reference it. "Basically, Elizabeth confessed to finally 'having had enough' of the way her father treated her mother, and her and her younger brother, too. She told me the 'last straw' was when she discovered evidence of one of her father's assignations on his clothes when she was helping with the laundry that Sunday in April." He paused. "She said that what really upset her the most and made her decide to do something, was the thought of her mother finding his stained clothing 'reeking,' as she put it, of another woman's scent."

"But she could have confronted her dad," Gracie objected. "She didn't have to kill him." She tore baby lettuces in put them in a large stainless steel bowl. In one of her ovens, the stuffed peppers were baking nicely and the aromas of their filling, made with orzo, chickpeas, olives, sun dried tomatoes, onions, garlic and cheese, was tantalizing.

"Agreed, Gracie. She told me she didn't think it would have done any good. Roger said he thought it was the pregnancy hormones that made her react so—well, over react, actually," Jack finished.

Gracie frowned. "I hadn't noticed that she's pregnant: how far along?" she asked, curious.

Jack shrugged. "A few months. I think she's just starting to show, and Roger said she had been having a difficult pregnancy," he added, remembering.

"Still, Jack, gazillions of women have babies all the time and they don't go running around killing people," Gracie noted with a shake of her head.

Again, Jack nodded. "I agree. But that's what Roger said." He took a sip of wine, and sighed. "Elizabeth told me that when she and her brother were small—her brother's five years younger than she is, so this would have been when he was a baby—things were different. She said Jesperson had been a great father, and that they'd done family things together all the time, like trips, and picnics and camping and so on," Jack recounted. "She said even after her brother was born, and I guess that's when Maddie became ill?"

Gracie nodded from across the kitchen.

"Elizabeth said that even then, her Dad was still around most of the time."

"He was Mayor then?" Gracie asked.

"Yes. But he helped out a lot at home, Elizabeth claims. Then after a year or so, that stopped. I'm not quite sure why, and maybe we'll never know, since Fred Jesperson can't tell us. But there seems to have been a perfect storm of events. As you found out from Hilda Senter, the couples in the original—what did you call them, the *Donna Reed Show* group?" he asked, smiling.

"Exactly!"

"Well, they had their children, and the wives gradually stopped going to the golfing outings, and then the makeup of the group changed and they started going away to play in tournaments. Coincidentally, Fred and probably some others were getting to be pretty good golfers." Jack sighed. "Anyway, also around that time, after Edward was born, Maddie became ill, and that put a strain on their marriage. Elizabeth said that that's when her father started staying out late, and drinking more than he used to."

"But, Jack, that happens in millions of families, and the kids don't kill their fathers!" Gracie protested again.

Jack nodded. "I know. But Fred's behavior seems to have affected Elizabeth very strongly." He paused. "She told me that Eddie was crushed when Fred failed to show up for a Cub Scout father son camping trip. It meant he couldn't go. And there was more, directly relating to Elizabeth: Fred stopped going to her dance recitals. She took tap, and she told me she was always so happy to see her Dad in the audience, so proud of her. But when she was in her early teens, that stopped. Her school held a Father Daughter dance for juniors, and Fred didn't show up for it. At the last minute, Maddie asked Tom Spears to step in and I guess he jumped into his tux and rushed over to Elizabeth's school. But her father had broken another promise to her. And I think that devastated her."

Jack continued to fill Gracie in on Elizabeth's story, employing the phrase he'd used in the Affidavit: 'a history of disinterest in his children' on Fred's part. "Even the grandchildren, Elizabeth told me, I mean, Jesperson played with them and so on, but he didn't seem to really care, if you know what I mean. Martha's taking ballet, and Fred hasn't been to any of her recitals."

"History repeating itself," Gracie murmured.

Jack nodded. "And I think that really angered Elizabeth." He shrugged. "She's been aware of her father's habits, at least when it comes to the drinking and the women, for years. Roger told me that once, fairly early on, Fred bragged to him that if Roger ever got a speeding ticket or a parking ticket, Fred could have it 'taken care of.'"

Gracie stopped what she was doing—sectioning hot house tomatoes from Whole Foods—and stared.

"Yep. And Fred, according to Roger, then went on to say that he, Fred, had had a 'little fender bender' and had that wiped from any records. It took a while for Roger to remember where Fred had said it had happened, but he finally did, and it was in that Magistrate Ragans' jurisdiction."

"You're going to call her in for questioning?" Gracie asked excitedly, and then realized that no, it was out of the county.

"No, it's Hampshire County. But I've called the AG's office. And the FBI."

"The FBI?"

"Not about the murder: that's here in our county, and we'll prosecute Elizabeth. No, the AG's office is looking into the 'favors' done by various magistrates and police personnel for the late Senator, and any payoffs he may have made to them in return. That includes trips, cash, vacations…"

"Jewelry?" Gracie asked, and reminded him of Magistrate Ragans' gold Rolex.

Jack nodded grimly. "Yes. All of that type of thing. Drinking and chasing women aren't crimes. But drinking and driving and then hushing it up with the help of officials, well, yeah, that's a crime. So there you have the magistrates and the Chief of Detectives at the Boston PD. And probably a couple of cops too," Jack assessed. "And as for the skirt chasing, well, you mentioned that Detective Geene said the late Senator had patronized known prostitutes, but had never been charged. And she suggested that the Chief of Detectives was protecting some known prostitutes as well?" he confirmed what Gracie had told him earlier.

She nodded. "Yes, and she said the Chief would sometimes hook the late Senator up with one of them."

"Mmmm..Well, the AG's office is going to speak with Geene about that, and about the late Senator's proposition to her."

"Did you tell them about Regina Vioni and Sandy Cocker?" Gracie asked, and was pleased when Jack nodded that he had. "Now the FBI," Jack went on, "I called them in because of the Community Block Grant money. That's federal funding, even though it's given to the state. So it's the FBI's bailiwick."

"Did you discover for sure any money that had been diverted when you looked at the financials?" Gracie asked, curious. The salad was done, now she had to make the dressing.

Jack explained that he wasn't a forensic accountant, but that he'd seen a few suspicious things when he'd looked over the late Senator's financial records, including the 'administrative assistant' funded with grant money intended for other projects, and had mentioned those, along with luxury construction projects funded in part by CBG monies, to the FBI.

"So Elizabeth has been charged with the murder of her father, and his indiscretions are being investigated by the proper authorities," Gracie summed up, sounding satisfied. "But why was Roger's fingerprint in the study?"

Jack shrugged again. "That was a red herring, as it were: he'd been in from time to time, usually helping Maddie clean up or something, and he must have adjusted the blinds. CSU just missed it on the first pass. The real giveaway was when only Fred's prints showed up on the fridge door, the bottle and the doorknob: Elizabeth told me she'd wiped those down after poisoning the vodka, because she'd forgotten to bring gloves, and hadn't wanted to stop to find a pair at her parents' house."

Gracie chose a bright green olive oil with a lively bite along with a fresh apricot white balsamic vinegar and a dash of cumin. She shook everything vigorously until it emulsified into a pale tan dressing: she'd drizzle this over the ready salad just before serving. "That makes sense," she told Jack, referring to the Jesperson case.

A peek in the oven told her that the peppers were done, so she topped up her wine, plated the peppers with the salad, dressed it, and plopped the plates on the table.

Chapter Fifty-three

"I hope you like the stuffing," Gracie said, adding that she had made it 'Mediterranean style.'

Jack didn't say he'd probably like anything she put in front of him, but he dug in with enthusiasm and pronounced it 'really good.'

"Now, tell me about Amy and Richard Dawes," Gracie demanded as she forked up some stuffing. "Did they really kill Ryan Colletti and put Richard's ID on him in the hopes of passing Colletti's body off as Richard's, and collecting on the life insurance?" she asked. "I can't believe they were stupid enough to think it would work!"

Jack had to give her that one. "Well, I don't know how stupid they are, Gracie, but they sure didn't think their plan through. And they were desperate, or at least Richard was. Amy said Richard was terrified of losing the house, and having their kids taken from them because of his massive debt."

Gracie nodded sympathetically. "But why Colletti?" she asked.

Jack shook his head and had another sip of wine. "Amy said she didn't know a lot of detail, because Richard had only told her what she had to know. Oh, and by the way, they didn't use cell phones, just pay phones, to contact each other, and that was very limited. And you were right about the ATM: we requested the camera feed from the bank, and sure enough, there's Amy plain as day, withdrawing money from their account."

Gracie smiled over at him, pleased.

"Amy said that Richard picked Colletti because they looked alike and were the same height and weight. He knew Colletti because the guy hung around the truck depot, selling amphetamines and other stuff to some of the drivers. Not Richard, at least, not that we know. But Richard knew Colletti was a loner, no relatives to speak of, and did just enough recycling to stay alive." He sighed. "Anyway, Richard assumed that his ID would be sufficient to identify Colletti's body as his, with no further questions asked." He paused. "Actually, he and Amy had worked out that Amy was going to request there not be an autopsy, and try to tell the coroner it was against their religion. But the law is pretty strict in these circumstances, religion aside, and in any case, because it was murder it was kinda out of their hands."

"How did he kill Colletti?" Gracie asked. "I mean, I know he shot him, but…"

"Amy said Richard went over to Colletti's trailer that Friday night, the night he was supposed to show up for work. He pretended to want to buy some drugs. He said Colletti knew him from having seen him around the truck depot, so he welcomed him in, and then Richard shot him. He left the body there, locking the trailer behind him, and figuring no one would come by looking for the guy, and he was right. Richard holed up in that no tell motel on the outskirts of town," Jack revealed. "Paid cash, kept a ball cap pulled low over his head, so the desk clerk never got a really good look at his face, used the name 'Oscar Hood' to sign the register," he elaborated.

"No significance to that, Amy says: he told her he saw the name Oscar and the name Hood on some canned food he'd bought to eat while he was in hiding out at the motel, and that's where he got his alias."

"Wow!"

"We had, in the course of searching for Richard Dawes, checked all motels and hotels in the area, including that one. But the cash meant no record other than the name he signed in the guest book…"

"And how were you to know the alias," Gracie chimed in supportively.

Jack sighed. "Dawes moved Colletti's body to the park on Sunday night, so it would be found Monday morning. He used a tarp, and his truck…"

"And then he left town?" Gracie queried.

"And then he left town."

"The CMP confirmed the information about Richard's uncle William up in Lockport, just like you said," Jack told her with a grin, and Gracie gave a little 'yay!' and a whoop.

Who didn't like to be right?

"They should be picking Richard up some time tonight or tomorrow," Jack continued. I've requested extradition, and since it's a case of murder, and the murder happening here, I think they'll ship him back pretty fast, and without too much red tape," Jack told her with more confidence than he felt. This was his first time dealing with an extradition case from Canada, and he honestly didn't know how it would turn out.

"That's great, Jack. So what are the charges against Richard?" Gracie queried. She knew that as soon as the paperwork was done, Jack would see she had a copy, so she could write it up for the newspaper.

"Murder one, abuse of a corpse, obstruction of justice, attempted insurance fraud, for starters. Oh, and fleeing and eluding, probably."

"And Amy? You gave her a pretty good deal," Gracie told him. She'd seen the draft plea agreement: all that was needed to make it official was Popovitch's signature on Monday.

"I dropped all the conspiracy to commit murder charges, that's the big thing. I kept aiding and abetting, but made it a lesser offense. I kept attempted insurance fraud, too. But Amy said that Richard had been the one to carry out the murder and plant the body in the park with his ID. According to her, she hadn't helped with that, and hadn't known specifics until after the fact," he added in a doubtful tone. "But with the children going to her mother, she will be able to serve any sentence imposed, even if it's a short one."

Gracie nodded.

"What about Maddie's grandchildren?" Gracie asked suddenly.

Jack smiled, and told her how happy Maddie had been to be given temporary custody of her grandkids. "In a way, I think, it kinda made up for what had gone down with her daughter," Jack advanced. "I think it gave her hope, and a renewed purpose in life, you know?"

Gracie cleared the dinner plates, and brought out a serving of Paolo's tiramisu that she'd brought home from Mange Tout the evening before. She put the dessert half way between her place and Jack's, and gave them each a fork. "Coffee?"

"No, thanks, Gracie, this will be fine," Jack answered. "I'm hoping I can get some sleep tonight," he added.

"I'm sure you'll crash the minute you get home," she told him with a grin.

"Anyway, I explained to Maddie that I was going to be lenient on Roger, for a lot of reasons, but that I had already contacted Child Services and they had agreed that if she were willing, she should take temporary custody of her grandchildren. Roger will have supervised visitation, at least at first. He probably won't do time, but he will have community service and other punishments, maybe house arrest for a bit, I don't know. It depends on what agreement Popovitch okays, and then, of course, what the judge sentences Roger to."

"What about Elizabeth's baby?" Gracie queried.

"The baby will come to Maddie as well, once it's born. I think she'll hire a nanny or a nurse or something, at least for a while, but really, she seemed absolutely delighted at the prospect of bringing up her grandchildren," Jack concluded.

Gracie sighed happily. She was about to suggest they move to the Oak Room until Jack wanted to go home, when his beeper and her police scanner went off simultaneously.

"Uh oh," he said, and grabbed for the small device on his belt. Seconds later, he was on his phone, and had moved into the pantry adjacent to the kitchen to make his call.

Gracie was standing in front of her refrigerator, listening intently to the dispatch from the scanner that stood atop.

'All stations be advised a 10-35, 10-50 at the location of Greylock Mountain. Report soonest, with 10-40," came the disembodied voice.

Gracie knew the 10-35 meant a major crime and the 10-50 meant a fatal accident. On Mount Greylock? She glanced out the kitchen window: the sun had set, but not long before. She supposed it was possible that someone had been climbing or hiking and had fallen…

"I've got to go," Jack told her, seconds later, coming back into the kitchen.

"Are you sure you're okay?" Gracie asked, concerned.

"Yeah, I only had a half glass of wine," he replied. "And that was an hour ago."

"No, I meant because you barely got any sleep last night," Gracie rejoined.

"I'll be all right." Jack paused. "They found a body," he said, and Gracie winced.

"I thought that must be it," she murmured.

"It looks like someone fell and smacked his head on the rocks," Jack added grimly. "I'll know more after I get there, and I'll let you know anything I find out, okay?"

"Okay."

Maybe it was the tiredness, maybe it was the relief at having solved two big cases, maybe it was just a gut response in the face of a fatal accident, but Jack drew Gracie to him, then, in a fast embrace. He kissed her on the forehead, and then looked, panicked, at Woof.

"I—"

Mount Greylock was in the opposite direction from Jack's place. If he brought Woof home, he'd lose valuable time getting to the crime scene, not to mention any lingering daylight.

"Woof can stay here tonight," Gracie put in quickly. "I have plenty of his food, and I'll be happy to have him. Go."

"Really?"

"Go. Come pick him up tomorrow," she said, "or whenever you want. I'll be home."

"Thanks, Gracie," Jack said with a sincere smile, and he hurried off.

FINIS

—33—

www.ingramcontent.com/pod-product-compliance
Lightning Source LLC
Chambersburg PA
CBHW072335020726
47506CB00004B/892